THE BRONZE SCROLL

PRAISE FOR *THE BRONZE SCROLL*

"Think *The DaVinci Code*, blended with the fast pace and ancient mystery of an Indiana Jones production. Then add a healthy dose of romantic entanglement to the action, for a sense of how compellingly rich *The Bronze Scroll* feels." –Diane Donovan, Senior Reviewer, Midwest Book Review

"A must-read mystery novel. A gripping tale of ancient power, secret societies, and inner-strength and heartfelt romance, readers will be hard-pressed to put this novel down, and will be on the edge of their seats in eager anticipation of the next installment of this brand-new series." –Tony Espinoza, Pacific Book Review

"You're saying the explanation for all these treasures of the ancient world is a poem?"

"Sam Romero is enthralled by an exhibit he recently viewed at the Getty Museum: The Copper Scroll. Discovered in the Dead Sea in the 1950s, the scroll itself is actually made of bronze and contains a treasure map that details sixty-four locations with a description of each treasure and how to access it. Sam heads to Rome on a business trip, intrigued by thoughts of deciphering the scroll and by Rebecca, an investigative journalist he has recently met. He plans on seeing both Rebecca and his mother, Dawn, on this trip. . . . Contacted by a man named Roy Griffin to help with a legal matter, he soon discovers that he is caught in the middle of a conspiracy to steal the scroll. With everyone he loves in danger, Sam must save them and the scroll.

"In this first novel of a series, the authors brilliantly set up the beginning of the adventures of the protagonist, an investigative attorney. The book is a fascinating read which will certainly entertain. It is also the story of the blossoming love between Sam and Rebecca. . . . There are plenty of thrilling plot twists as Sam fights against the evil Roy. The novel deftly sets up the second novel's plot with an ending that leaves one excited to read the next installment. This book will likely keep readers turning pages long into the night." –Kat Kennedy, US Review of Books

"Big reveals, big betrayals, and lots of thrills in a life-and-death race against time. The end is astonishing as well and segues nicely into the next leg of Sam's adventure while still wrapping up this mystery quite neatly."–Fiona Ingram, Word Magic

"A very well written adventure romance book." – Sefina Hawkes Books

"Everything feels grounded, in a hyper-stylized context a la Indiana Jones and the Raiders of the Lost Ark." – Alexander Marias, The Magic Pen

KNIGHTS OF THE LOST TEMPLE

Book 1: The Bronze Scroll

PAUL DONSBACH
AND ALIA SINA

ISBN: 978-1-7373978-1-6 (Paperback)
ISBN: 978-1-7373978-2-3 (Hardback)
ISBN: 978-1-7373978-0-9 (Ebook)

Cover Design by Berge Design

To my children,

For inspiring me to begin new adventures,
to seek answers to life's greatest mysteries, and
to always remember that love matters most.

Paul

To my family,

For your support, encouragement, and hugs.
And especially to my husband
for showing me what true love is.

Alia

CONTENTS

1	In the Beginning	1
2	The Heavens and the Earth	13
3	Let There Be Light	27
4	In Our Image	33
5	She Shall Be Called Woman	45
6	Your Eyes Shall Be Opened	57
7	To Make One Wise	73
8	Like One of Us	93
9	Knowing Good and Evil	107
10	Darkness over the Land	115
11	Parting the Waters	135
12	An Angel Before Thee	151
13	This Is the Land	163
14	Better than Wine	183
15	The Waters of Jordan	205
16	Thou Shalt Not Kill	227
17	Justice like a River	251
18	Like the Light of Dawn	283
	About the Authors	291

1

IN THE BEGINNING

Sam slept as his flight crossed the heavens. He dreamed of the void beneath him, the earth without form. Nothing but darkness on the face of the deep. He dreamed of a spirit as free as the waters below.

Then there was light. And it was so.

Sam stirred a bit, still blissfully dreaming. The waters divided, and a strip of verdant land appeared on the horizon. He dreamed of a fertile garden. A tree with soft fruit, luscious and ripe.

Stirring a bit more, Sam began to awaken. His eyes opening, he woke up hungry. The blissful spirit had left him, and his mind filled with thoughts and desires.

The flight had gone well, he thought. Thirteen hours from Los Angeles to Rome. He had finished his projects and fallen asleep. With the cabin still quiet and dark, Sam could see a faint glow through the oval window shade.

He thought of the garden in his dream and closed his eyes to relax. Serene and calm. The fragrance of lilies in bloom. The warmth of the midday sun.

The cabin began to brighten as the passengers started opening their window shades. Sam opened his eyes again and looked out the window. He blinked at the bright golden sunshine as the plane approached its destination.

Sam turned his head and noticed the old man in the seat next to him. He glanced back at the flight tracker on the screen in front of him.

An hour left to Rome. More than enough time to get ready. He was grateful the flight was so quiet, as this would help him to relax and maybe get some more sleep.

"You're awake," said the old man.

Sam closed his eyes and pretended not to hear.

"You've been sleeping a lot," the old man said.

Sam opened one eye and turned to the stranger. "Not enough, I think. These red-eyes are rough."

"It's my first trip to Rome," the old man said cheerfully.

"Mm-hmm," Sam grunted, closing his eyes again. He could almost see the garden again.

"There's so much to see that it's hard to decide," the old man continued. "Have you been there before?"

Sam knew that he wouldn't be able to sleep now. Like the old man, he was excited to see Rome. The garden would have to wait.

"I spent a year there after college," Sam said, turning toward the stranger. "I've been back a few times, but not recently. Sam Romero, by the way," he said, nodding his head as an introduction. "What's *your* name?"

"Solomon," the old man replied. "Like in the Bible," he said with a smile.

Sam looked at the old stranger and thought the name was about right. He looked wise, and the white hair and trimmed beard lent an air of distinction. He's pretty old school, Sam thought. Maybe a professor, he guessed, looking at his pressed white shirt and brown tweed jacket with dark elbow patches.

"Business or pleasure?" Sam asked the old man.

"Both, really," Solomon replied. "It's mostly for fun, but I'm also a poet. The trip is a gift from my children. They think I'll be inspired and write some poems."

"Rome's the place for that," Sam said with a smile. "Plenty of scenery and history. What kind of poems do you write?"

"Mostly about wisdom," the stranger said, smiling. "When your name's Solomon, what else can you do? Wealth, fame, success, living the good life," the old man continued. "How to satisfy a woman," he said with a wink.

"All that in poems?" Sam laughed.

"Of course!" Solomon smiled, nodding. "What else would you write poems about?"

"I don't know," Sam said, shrugging. "Aren't they all about trees and nature? Maybe a garden?"

"Not mine," Solomon replied. "No garden can match a woman's beauty. She's nature's most exquisite design," he said with a sigh.

"It sounds like your poems are kind of romantic," Sam said, impressed.

"That's what they say," Solomon said, nodding. "Romantic attraction can be so mysterious, and I do love a mystery. But my readers mostly think of me as writing about life itself," the old man continued. "What's the point of learning and striving when life is so short? How should we live our lives?"

"By visiting Rome, apparently," Sam said with a smile.

"Good point." Solomon nodded with approval. "There's good food and good wine. And maybe a beautiful woman."

"You've got that right," Sam agreed. "*La dolce vita.*"

Sam was getting hungrier. The meager airline food had left him unsatisfied. Maybe breakfast would be better. A Roman cornetto pastry glazed with orange marmalade and a doppio espresso would hit the spot.

"Are any of your poems about food?" Sam asked. "I'm really hungry. Let's hope they serve breakfast soon."

"Sure," the old man replied, "my most famous poem is about a man who enjoys his life. Eat, drink, and be merry, it says. That's the secret to a happy life."

"It sounds simple," Sam said, leaning back. "I'll look it up sometime. What's the name of your poem?"

"Kohelet," Solomon responded. "Except in English, it's Ecclesiastes."

"What?" Sam shot back. "What kind of poem title is that? How did you come up with that? Is it supposed to mean something?"

"Well, I wrote it in Hebrew, and it's been translated into Greek and then English." Solomon shrugged. "Maybe a little was lost in translation."

"It sounds like it," Sam agreed. "What does the title mean?"

"The Teacher," said the old man. "Like a professor or someone talking to an audience or a group of listeners."

"Okay, so how does it start?" Sam asked.

"The words of the Teacher, the son of David," the old man began.

"David's your father?" Sam asked. "Is he a part of the story?"

"Exactly," Solomon replied. "A big part. He fell in love with my mother while she was still married to her first husband. She was lonely at the time because her husband was in the military, serving in combat. My father saw her bathing at night from his rooftop terrace," Solomon went on. "Apparently, her beauty in the moonlight was too much. He arranged to meet her, and they fell in love. Soon, she was pregnant.

"Wanting to protect her, my father tried to get the husband back home on leave," the old stranger continued. "The plan was that she'd sleep with her husband and no one would find out about the affair. The first child would be born, and the husband would think he was the father.

"Well, the husband was so dedicated to his battalion that he refused to go on leave," Solomon went on. "The story gets complicated, and essentially my father arranged for the husband to go on a dangerous mission. The husband got killed as a result, and this treachery amounted to a curse on the pregnancy. So the baby died a few days after birth."

"Wow, is all this true?" Sam asked.

"It's all in the poems," Solomon replied. "Anyway, my mother and father were finally able to marry. I was the next child born, and the rest is history."

"A pretty good story," Sam said, nodding. "Tell me more about your father."

"Oh, he was a musician and adventurer," Solomon said with a smile. "I have so many stories about him, we wouldn't have time. A few songs too."

"I see where you inherited your artistic talent, then." Sam smiled.

"It runs in the family," Solomon agreed.

"Right," Sam said, nodding. "And you're a teacher too?"

"Yes, a teacher," the old man agreed.

"Kohelet?" Sam queried.

"Right, exactly," Solomon agreed with a nod.

"You just need to change the name," Sam insisted. "No one's going to know that Kohelet means the Teacher. It's just too obscure."

"Well, readers don't like it when you change the story," Solomon said with a sigh. "I know what you mean, but it's hard to change a story that's already been told."

"I guess so," Sam agreed. "So, could you do a better translation? You said maybe something was lost."

"Sure, I suppose," the old man replied. "Translating from Hebrew offers some choices. I'm pretty old school, and the Hebrew script that I use doesn't spell out the vowels. So doing a translation can get pretty creative."

"Interesting," Sam said, rubbing his chin. "So, Kohelet is spelled K-H-L-T?"

"You got it," Solomon replied. "When you're translating that, the first thing you have to figure out are the vowels. It could be Kahalat, Kohlit, or lots of other combinations. Kohelet is just one of those options."

"Well, I'd suggest keeping it simple," Sam said. "Maybe just go with the Teacher—something your readers can easily understand."

The conversation paused as Sam noticed the flight attendants getting started with breakfast in the galley. His stomach growled.

"How does the poem end?" Sam asked.

"Well, it says that to everything there is a season, a time to love and a time to hate," Solomon replied.

"That's pretty good," Sam said. "Really poetic."

"Thanks," Solomon said, smiling. "Then it says that a lust for gold and silver can never be satisfied. Material things bring no joy. But a man's love for a woman can be meaningful and deep. Ultimately, the simple pleasures of a life well lived are the best we can do in this world. Take time to live slowly. Enjoy the warmth of the afternoon sun. But always remember, the spirit is eternal, so don't be too attached to your life in this world. Respect the laws and traditions, which keep the physical and spiritual worlds in harmony. Live each day like it was the last. Because one day, it will be."

"Very nice," Sam said with a smile. "I'll be sure to read it. Some of my friends and family are pretty spiritual and would like your poem. I'll have to pass it on."

"You're very kind," said the old man. "I may be an old teacher, but people say my poems help them find peace. That's what my name means, you know."

"Kohelet?" Sam looked puzzled.

"No, Solomon. It means peace," said the old man.

"I see," Sam replied. "That's a nice name."

"How about you?" Solomon asked. "What does Sam mean?"

"Oh, that's not my real name," Sam responded.

"You have more than one name too?" the old man asked.

"Just the real one," Sam replied. "It's Surat…S-U-R-A-T. Vowels included," he said with a grin.

"Sounds like there's a story there," the old man said, smiling.

"Yes, exactly," Sam replied. "My parents were hippies back in the day. They backpacked through India, and I was born there. I think it means 'awakening' or something like that. I guess I've disappointed them," Sam said with a laugh. "My mom's an actress, and she's traveled all over the world. When I was young, she took me to all these spiritual places hoping I'd get interested and it would stick. I did get interested," Sam went on. "But not how she expected. Being exposed to all these different religions and philosophies somehow made me more cautious. I respect what I've learned, but I don't want to commit to believing something that might be wrong or contradicted somewhere else."

"I see," Solomon said, leaning his head back. "You think that belief in one thing means disbelief of something else? It's one or the other?"

"That's how it seems," Sam responded. "I can't have my cake and eat it too. Or a Roman pastry, if we're getting lucky," he said with a grin as he watched the flight attendant approach with her cart.

"Well, in my poem," Solomon said, "the Teacher says to eat, drink, and be merry. Enjoy your life, but also follow the eternal laws. So it's not really one or the other. You can do both."

"So I could meditate like the Buddha in the morning and pray the rosary in the evening?" Sam asked.

"Maybe," Solomon replied. "There's a time to every purpose under the heaven."

"So I hear." Sam smiled back.

"Just be careful about graven images," Solomon said with a wink. "It's okay to enjoy the scenery, but be faithful to your truth when you find it."

"I'll try to remember that," Sam said, nodding.

Sam looked up and noticed the pretty flight attendant leaning toward him.

"English muffin or toast?" she asked, smiling as she pushed back a long lock of her silky black hair. Sam noticed her name tag. Elena. Very pretty.

"No cornetto pastry today?" Sam teased, trying to flirt.

"The English muffin is pretty good," the flight attendant, Elena Bellini, said with a smile. "It's a little tough and resistant on the outside, but it's soft and warm inside," she said, flirting back.

"I'm definitely a muffin man, then," Sam said, feeling a spark of excitement as he looked up at her brown eyes. "With a double espresso. Two shots are better than one, you know."

Sam pretended not to look down her blouse as Elena pulled a tray from the cart and leaned forward toward his seat. He could sense her warmth and fragrance as she came near.

As Elena promised to return, Sam touched the warm muffin. It wasn't exactly a Roman pastry, he thought, but a warm breakfast from Elena was heaven sent.

"*L'Chaim!*" Solomon toasted with his cup of orange juice.

"To life!" Sam replied, raising his cup of orange juice as well.

Finishing his orange juice, Sam noticed that the old man was still smiling at him.

"I see you like the ladies too," Solomon said, nodding toward Elena as she moved down the aisle. "She's just gorgeous."

"Yes, I noticed," Sam said with a sigh. "I wonder what *she* would look like bathing in the moonlight."

"Yes, the world is so beautiful, isn't it?" Solomon smiled. "But tell me, have you found love that is meaningful and deep? You know, like in my poem?"

Sam looked at the old man, remembering that night in November. The instant connection he had felt the first time he heard her voice. The softly poetic way she expressed her thoughts—like a musician composing her latest melody. He had never seen a smile so pretty. He thought about that kiss.

Meaningful and deep? He wasn't sure he should admit it. Especially to a stranger.

Sam smiled at the old man. "You mean like that magical woman of your dreams who takes your breath away when you see her bathing in the moonlight? No, I really haven't met her yet," he lied.

"Well, you're a smart man," Solomon said. "I'm sure you'll know right away when you've met her. It's like nothing else under the sun, as my poem says. But when that magical moonlit night happens, don't let it slip away. Every season has its time. It's what we do with that time that matters. It's all up to you."

"Pure magic, huh?" Sam smiled. "I think I know what you mean. I'll keep an eye out for that," he promised.

Sam looked at the old man again. "But, Solomon," he asked, "how do I tell her about my feelings? You know, when I meet her. With the moonlight and all that."

"Ah, that's easy." Solomon smiled. "Write her a poem. It doesn't have to rhyme, and it could even be a story or a novel. That's much better than flowers or a card. If she's the right woman, she'll know what you're thinking."

"Thanks, Solomon. That sounds like a good plan. I'll get right on that. I mean, when I meet her, you know," Sam said with a nod.

Solomon smiled. "So, now you know about my poems. What about you? What's your story?" he asked.

"I'm an attorney," Sam replied, finishing his breakfast. "Mostly doing investigations now," he added, pushing away the plate. "My clients all have whistleblower hotlines and compliance committees. When they get a report of internal fraud or white-collar crime—something like that—they hire my firm to find out what happened and write a report. They have insurance for embezzlement and that sort of thing. So they always have to tell the insurance company about possible claims.

"I do the investigations and reports. I like to think of it as solving mysteries," Sam said, strumming his fingers on the armrest. "I was always reading stories as a kid, and it seems like they stuck. For me, there's nothing more fun than combing through clues and piecing stories together. I guess it's the same as you feel about poetry."

"Right, and a poem's a story too," Solomon agreed. "Maybe everything's a story if you think about it. Are you working on an investigation now? Maybe something in Rome?"

"Sure, there are plenty of scandals in Rome," Sam said, raising an eyebrow. "I'm not supposed to talk about my work cases, but I do have a new mystery that's caught my attention, and it's not about work."

"What is it?" Solomon asked.

"It's called the Copper Scroll," Sam replied. "Except it isn't. Well, I mean, it's really bronze. Which fits because nothing about this thing makes sense. My friends took me to the Getty Museum as a birthday present, and we toured this traveling exhibit about this Copper Scroll. I mean, bronze, you know. This ancient metal scroll was there, of course. It was found in one of those Dead Sea caves, back in the 1950s. It's made of three thin bronze sheets riveted together, about one foot wide and seven feet long. The bronze sheets are thin enough that they could be rolled up like a scroll, which was how they were found. Except the rivets holding the third sheet to the second sheet broke when they were rolled up, so the scroll was found in two pieces.

"Anyway," Sam went on, "it took three years for the scientists to agree on how to unroll it. A research team had it cut up into pieces so they could read it. The bronze itself was dated to about the first century, and it was engraved with the Hebrew script of that time. There were also etchings of seven sets of ancient Greek letters, with two or three letters in each set. Once all this was translated, the researchers realized it was an ancient treasure map. The scroll identifies sixty treasure locations—or sixty-four if you count the locations with multiple treasures separately—and the same format is used for each location.

"Without exception," Sam continued, "the treasure locations are described in seven parts, using the exact same sequence. First, the specific type of location is listed. For example, a monument, ruin, or cave—some kind of structure or natural place. Second, the geographical location of the treasure is listed. These are places in ancient Israel, like the Valley of Achor, the Eastern Gate of the Jerusalem Temple, or the village of Kohlit."

"Kohlit?" Solomon asked. "How do you know?"

"It's hard to know," Sam said with a shrug. "That's what the translators came up with."

"So, it could be something else?" the old man asked.

"Sure," Sam agreed, "it's not set in stone. So, third is an instruction on how to uncover the treasure. Like digging or going into a cave. Fourth is a distance measured in cubits. Fifth is a description of the treasure. Gold, silver, coins, or even another scroll. Some of the locations get mysterious here. Sixth is a commentary on some of the locations. The seventh and last one is the biggest mystery. There are ancient Greek letters in seven sets of two or three letters each next to some of the listed treasures.

"So this format is followed for all sixty locations," Sam went on, "in exactly this sequence. Now, some of the locations don't have all seven parts. But the scroll always follows this format, regardless of how much detail is provided for each location. Obviously a lot of thought went into this scroll. It raises a lot of questions."

"I see what you mean," the old man agreed.

"Now, here's what I think," Sam said, leaning toward Solomon. "It's a story. It always is."

"What do you mean?" asked the old man.

"It's like you said in your poem," Sam said, patting the old man's shoulder. "Gold and silver aren't really treasures. It's in the eye of the beholder. A treasure is something you'd die for. An idea, a person, a moment. The scent of a lover," he went on, noticing Elena walking back up the aisle toward the galley. "Gold and silver are like chasing the wind. Or whatever your poem said. Nice to have, but you can't take them with you. I just have to figure out the story. This scroll—copper, bronze, or whatever—has a story to tell. I just need to know how to decipher it."

"I'm sure you'll figure it out," Solomon said, clasping Sam's shoulder. "Maybe you're a poet too. Some ancient wisdom will find you," he suggested. Now maybe you should rest a bit. You've got a lot of adventure ahead of you in Rome. And wherever else you go. But remember, it's the simple things that we're here for," the old man said, leaning back in his seat. "Music, laughter, good friends and family. A time for every purpose."

His eyes closing, Sam nodded. He let his mind drift with songs, henna blossoms, and the delicate flower of a woman's beauty. Back to the garden.

Then dreams of luscious fruit and a woman's fragrance aroused him. A warm hand on his shoulder, Sam awoke.

It was Elena. He smiled and was starting to wake up.

"We're about to land," she said, leaning close. "We're starting the final approach."

Sam noticed the book in Elena's hand. "Doing some reading?" he asked.

"No, actually, this is for you. An older gentleman back in coach said it belongs to you," she said, handing him the book.

Sam looked at the cover: *The Book of Kohelet.* "Oh, this must be from Solomon," he said. "He's not in coach. He's right here," Sam said, pointing to the seat next to him. Which was now empty.

"He must have stepped away," Sam told Elena.

"You really *have* been dreaming, haven't you?" Elena laughed. "That's an empty seat, and you've been alone the whole flight."

Sam was confused. The old man was gone. Had he dreamed him? These red-eyes could get strange.

He opened the book and noticed handwriting on the first page:

In the land of Kohelet, across the sea,
a woman bathed in moonlight, a time to love.

Sam blinked and read it again. How did the old man know? Sam hadn't said anything at all.

Sam looked up and noticed that Elena was still talking. "So, what do you think?" she asked.

"I'm sorry," Sam said, "I got a little distracted by this book. What were you saying again?"

"Just about dinner," Elena said, "you know, in case you're free. I'll be in Rome for a couple of days, and we could go hang out if you don't have any plans."

"That sounds awesome," Sam said, smiling. "But it looks like I'll be changing my plans and won't be in Rome long. I think I just figured out that treasure map."

"Treasure map?" Elena looked puzzled. "Well, that sounds exciting."

"Yes, I think that old man is on to something. I really should go back and thank him," Sam said, moving to unbuckle his seat belt.

"Not right now," Elena said firmly. "The seat belt light's on, and we're about to land. Maybe you can find him later."

Sam looked out the window.

The sun was bright and warm. He saw the green hills below and the blue sea in the distance. He knew what he needed to do.

And it was good.

2

THE HEAVENS AND THE EARTH

Sam stirred when the room began to brighten at dawn. It was Saturday, and he was in Rome.

He thought about the old man's words. What was his name? Solomon? A poet, right?

He thought about Rebecca Schreiber. That reporter for the *Jerusalem Post.* They had met at the conference in New York in November. Just a few weeks ago, really. He had admired her presentation on investigative journalism.

What had she called her presentation? *Four Principles for the Fourth Estate*? Cute, he thought. But it was a serious topic. Rebecca believed in holding journalists to the highest standards in their work. After all, if we couldn't trust journalists to avoid conflicts of interest or disreputable sources, how long would we have a free press?

Sam had approached her after the presentation, and they talked about some of their common interests. They realized that they served on one of the same committees—Multinational Corporate Investigations, of course.

Sam had invited Rebecca out for cocktails at the Press Lounge rooftop bar. She had accepted his invitation, on the condition that they get separate checks. She didn't want to have his law firm picking up her tab, of course. Even if it was just a pink negroni. Or two.

They had talked for hours about secret Maltese bank accounts, holographic encryption, Mayan hieroglyphics, and molecular gastronomy. She wasn't a fan of fake caviar, it turned out. They had agreed that decoding the Mayan script was a good thing. Sure, some of the old, romanticized views of their culture might be lost. But wasn't knowing the truth about their religion, wars, and love stories more important?

They had lost track of time and decided to finish the evening at one of New York's late-night, fluorescent-lit institutions. Famous Original Ray's Pizza on Seventh Avenue in Midtown. Slices of "cheese pie" so large they had to fold them over to take a bite. A Manhattan classic with shakers of fragrant oregano, spicy chili flakes, and snowy Parmesan powder.

Rebecca had to catch a flight back to Tel Aviv the next day, so they hadn't stayed out late. They had promised to stay in touch, and Sam got her mobile number. Riding alone together in the elevator downstairs, Sam had been close enough to enjoy her gentle, rosy fragrance.

They had gotten an Uber together, and they both stepped out at her hotel. While the driver waited at the curb, Sam walked her to the hotel entrance. After they each said good night, Sam leaned down to kiss her, sliding his right arm around her waist.

It was a soft kiss. Her lips tensed and then surrendered to his warm embrace. A moment of pleasure. A sense of *being*, beyond thought. A presence serene and unseen.

Sam had been calling her quite often since then. She had grown up near Tel Aviv, and he had assumed that she was Jewish. It was more complicated than that, she explained. She was a Samaritan. But what did that even mean?

Rebecca had patiently explained the difference, but Sam still wasn't quite sure he understood. No Hanukkah or store-bought matzo. More traditional, really. Samaritans use an older Hebrew script and consider only the Torah—the first five books of the Jewish tradition—to be authoritative. Oh, and they pray facing a mountain in Samaria rather than Jerusalem, as most Jews in Israel and the diaspora do.

Rebecca was brilliant and gifted. She had followed her own compass her whole life, as if it were a canvas on which she had carefully chosen each color and texture. Sam could *feel* the power of her free spirit and intuitive sense of purpose and meaning. It was as though she had gone beyond *thinking* and was simply *being*.

Sam had never met someone so accomplished and yet so connected. He wanted to know more and was grateful that they had so much in common. They both loved stories and enjoyed talking for hours about their lives and plans and new books they had read. Mysteries, of course, were their favorites—the more ancient the better.

Then there was her beauty. Her hazel eyes and luscious auburn hair rolling down past her shoulders. The graceful elegance of her powerfully toned body, silently dancing to a ballet that only she knew. Her soft lips stained pink. Her curves like the soft, ripened fruits of a secret garden.

He was captivated.

He had called her about a week ago. She was in New York again, visiting family. They had talked about getting together. Both of their schedules were busy, and he had told her about his trip to Rome.

Rebecca wasn't sure her schedule would work to meet him in January, either in Israel or Rome. She had some family commitments and a few plans before and after Sylvester—that cute word she used for the Gregorian New Year's holiday on January 1.

They *had* agreed to meet at the conference in Geneva in February. Sam hadn't been to a human rights conference before, but now he wanted to see her presentation and to take her out for another round of pink negronis. Or maybe a tequila sunrise?

Rebecca had laughed when Sam told her he had read about the Samaritans' patrilineal tradition. Yes, her parents would be thrilled if she fell in love with a Samaritan man and kept the traditions going. But there were less than eight hundred Samaritans now, she explained, and she wasn't *that* traditional.

She was actually pretty adventurous, she had hinted when they last spoke a week ago. Sam thought she was a polymath—a woman of many interests and talents, maybe some not yet discovered. She loved to travel, of course. Strasbourg for the human rights conference. Surfing on the Mexican Riviera. Swimming in underground caves near Tulum. And, of course, trekking in Tasmania.

Sam glanced at the window in his hotel room again. It was growing brighter in the Roman sun. Today was New Year's Day—the Gregorian one—and he was supposed to meet Donovan later this morning.

Donovan was his father. Not the one in his dream, of course. The *real* one. Life was like that, Sam thought. Shadows and mist. The pure light was just in your dreams.

Sam picked up his phone from the nightstand. He found the name: Donovan Romero.

Sam had wanted to love him enough to call him Dad. But usually it just came out as Donovan. The connection just wasn't there. It sometimes felt surprising because when he dreamed about his father, there was always a strong bond that he never felt in real life.

Sam's parents had broken up before his second birthday. Still, he respected Donovan and had tried to stay close. At least, as close as two weekends per month had allowed. Sam had spent most of his youth with his mother, and he really hadn't gotten to know Donovan that well.

Sam tapped on the phone. Donovan had flown in a day earlier, and it would be good to see him.

> *Hi Donovan, I survived the flight, and I'm up and around now. Want to get together around 10 am? Maybe meet near the Colosseum and go from there? Look forward to seeing you! Sam*

Sam got out of bed and looked at his reflection in the bathroom mirror. He had lost his tan from the trip to Cabo in early December with his friends Jason Baldwin and Steve Bellamy. But he still felt a bit of a glow inside from all the outdoor activities this fall and winter.

Sam ran his right hand through his wavy, dark brown hair. He had always tried not to look like a lawyer. Maybe his longish hair was a small form of rebellion against a career that could otherwise be stifling. A corporate lawyer was the very *idea* of a conformist, right? Wasn't that part of the appeal of whistleblower investigations? Living in a world of rogue executives, offshore bankers, and money launderers breaking all the rules?

Sam showered and dressed and walked out of the apartment—really, part of an old villa—and walked down the flight of stone steps to the lively sidewalk below.

Ah, Rome, he thought. His apartment was on the Piazza Navona across from the Fountain of Neptune. The god of the waters with his trident and some pretty mermaids.

Sam enjoyed looking at the fountain scene with the splashing water as he walked down the street to a coffee bar.

Sam walked up to the bar inside. "*Un doppio, per favore,*" he said, ordering his favorite. A double espresso with as much sugar as you want.

Starting to revive with a double dose of *caffeina*, Sam stood at the bar and looked at the street scene outside. It wasn't an official holiday, but most of the locals were taking the day off anyway, walking their dogs or enjoying some rare January sunshine.

It was still early morning in Rome, so Sam decided to text his friends back in Los Angeles. Sam scanned through the holiday and birthday greetings until he found the group text with Jason and Steve.

> *Hey Sam, happy New Year! I hope your flight was good and the Italian girls aren't bothering you too much. It was great hanging out with you and Steve at the Getty the other day. Let me know how things are going there. Still hoping to make this trip work. Catch you soon! Jason*

Hi Sam, felice anno nuovo, lol! Have a great trip and send me some pics. I'm sure you're having a great time, and I'm still hoping to experience some of it with you guys! Steve

Sam smiled and still hoped that they could all do a trip together soon. They had done that for a few years in a row, and Jason and Steve had talked about joining him in Rome for this trip. It just hadn't worked out yet.

They had all met in college. Hard to believe, he thought, that it was already seventeen years ago.

They had met as freshmen at Occidental College in Los Angeles. Known to its students as "Oxy," it's a mostly liberal-arts college located in the Eagle Rock neighborhood.

No one actually lived in LA, Sam had often said when asked where he lived. Even a city resident like Sam had to explain: he had a loft in DTLA, which was really its own separate place, even though the abbreviation stood for downtown LA.

It was one of the things he loved about LA, Sam liked to tell visitors. Every neighborhood was different and had its own story.

Smiling as he read the messages, Sam really hoped a trip would work this time. Jason was a heart surgeon living in Malibu with a busy medical practice on the westside near Cedars-Sinai Medical Center. Sam knew the schedule might be tough, but Jason said he had been invited to replace another speaker at a conference in Germany this week. So it seemed like it might work out for him to add a few days to his trip and join Sam in Rome.

Steve had a technology firm in Menlo Park and lived in Half Moon Bay. His start-up focused on artificial intelligence applications in communications, with an emphasis on big data analytics. As the CEO and founder, Steve could travel when he wanted, and he had told Sam that a trip around or after the holidays seemed to work.

Sam remembered some of the trips they had taken together after college. The trip to Cabo in early December, and a trip to Bali the year before. They had even met up in India once—their greatest adventure so far. They had gone trekking near Rishikesh in the Himalayan foothills and had some narrow escapes on rope bridges and at some ancient temple ruins.

Sam smiled, recalling how things had always worked out for them. Except for that group history project in senior year. The professor had assigned each group to try to solve an ancient mystery and to write about the experience. Sam, Jason and Steve had decided to work on the mystery of Antony and Cleopatra's tomb. It was supposed to be near Alexandria in Egypt, but for some reason, the exact location had been lost to history.

Defeated by Octavian, the first emperor of Rome, and believing that Cleopatra had already taken her own life, Antony had stabbed himself with his sword. When he learned that Cleopatra was still alive, Antony had asked to be taken to her, and he died by her side. Then, given the choice of poisons by her Roman guards, Cleopatra had asked for a cobra and had it bite her, according to legend.

The three friends had enjoyed working on this mystery but were disappointed that they hadn't managed to solve it. They had each received a passing grade, but the professor was a little critical about some of the locations they considered. The professor had thought that Babylon was a creative location but ultimately was too far away to make sense. He had thought that the shrine in northern Ethiopia was also an interesting choice but that there was just no evidence for this. Finally, the professor had thought that the lost city of Tanis was a wonderfully romantic location but likewise had no evidence to support it.

While he gave all of them a passing score, the professor had suggested that the students work a little harder on understanding the underlying story. Despite their legendary status, Antony and Cleopatra were real people with more than their share of human drama. The professor had told them to focus more on those stories, and the truth would emerge.

Sam was happy that Jason and Steve had chosen the bronze scroll exhibit at the Getty for his birthday present. It was a thoughtful gesture that reflected Sam's enthusiasm for mysteries and untold stories. He just wanted to make sure that his excitement about this ancient mystery wasn't so strong that it would scare them off. He had tried to play it cool at the exhibit, but it was hard not to get excited about all those hidden treasures—100 gold bars, 900 talents (23 tons or 20,000 kilograms), 600 talents (15 tons or 13,000 kilograms), and so forth.

Plus, maybe the bronze scroll would be a good excuse for a trip to Israel. Sam respected Rebecca's busy schedule, but he really didn't want to wait until February to see her. He had never been to Israel before, and he wondered if her homeland was as beautiful and poetic as she was. He wanted to see the gorgeous Mediterranean beaches and the wind-carved deserts. But mostly he wanted to see Samaria. Maybe she would show him that sacred mountain. Laden with treasure, no doubt.

Finishing his espresso and walking out of the coffee bar and onto the sidewalk, Sam blinked at the bright January sunshine. He had decided to walk around the Piazza Navona to begin getting reacquainted with Rome.

Walking to the center of the piazza, Sam stopped in front of the spectacular Fountain of the Four Rivers, whose magnificent statues represent the four greatest rivers known when the fountain was built in the seventeenth century. Each river sacred to the peoples sustained by its waters—the Nile, Ganges, Danube, and Rio de la Plata—together they show the power of nature in service to the divine, as symbolized by the dove atop the first-century obelisk, high above the fountain's splashing waters.

Sam decided to go back upstairs and relax while waiting to hear back from Donovan. He had promised to stop working so much and to enjoy life more. It was one thing to make promises to his friends and colleagues. But another thing entirely to promise something to his mother. Dawn Hughes was a force of nature, an oracle of wisdom, and the judge and jury in Sam's life. Oh, and also an A-list film actress with two Academy Awards. Three if you count the time the presenters got the wrong envelope.

In other words, Sam didn't have a normal childhood. After the breakup, he had lived mostly with his mother. Well, if you considered following your mother around the world *living*. As a child and teenager, Sam hadn't been sure about that. His friends back in LA had thought his life was glamorous, but really her theories about tutors and firsthand learning were overrated. After all, the Taj Mahal's really just a tomb, and all those mummies in Egypt were more than scary to a six-year-old. Sam had decided that history was just about dead people, and religion was only about how to die well.

It was the books that had saved him. Real people like Tom Sawyer, Holden Caulfield, and Atticus Finch. Well, they had *seemed* real. More than the mummies and temple statues in the places they lived. Wasn't he an orphan like Tom Sawyer too? It felt that way, Sam had thought. It was these stories—getting expelled from prep school, running away from the scary neighbor Boo—that had made him feel alive.

But young Sam *did* like living in Rome, he had to admit. They had lived here for a few years, long enough for him to get hooked on strong coffee and swearing in Italian. Rome had seemed alive, even with all those monuments for dead emperors and philosophers. Not to mention the *belle donne*. Italian girls were just heavenly, Sam thought.

Walking from the plaza and up the stairs to his apartment, Sam heard a ping on his phone. As he stepped inside the apartment, he looked at the message from Donovan:

> *Hi Sam, glad you survived the flight! Yes, let's do 10 am by the Colosseum. Hopefully, the lions aren't hungry. See you then! Donovan.*

Sam sent a confirming text back, picked up a few Rome sightseeing books, and sat down next to the window overlooking the inner courtyard. He had an hour to relax and wanted to catch up with his mother too. They had talked on Christmas Day, when she called to wish him happy birthday and to finalize plans for the rest of the holidays. She was staying at her place on Capri, which was part of the reason that Sam decided to spend a month here in Rome.

She was excited about his visit and was already making plans. A tour of imperial ruins with a German archaeology professor? A private tour of the Vatican Museums? Backstage at the opera in Rome?

Sam loved all of her ideas. Well, maybe the erotica tour at Pompeii would be a little awkward. But the sunset sail from the Capri marina and around the island to see the twelve villas of the emperor Tiberius would be amazing.

He was happy to be close to his mother this trip. She had never stopped traveling the world, with homes in Laurel Canyon, Kauai, Bali, and Chamonix. But a few years ago, she'd added a villa in Capri to her collection, where she started a new hobby painting in the Italian impressionist style. She had said her balcony overlooking the marina at sunset was the perfect inspiration.

Sam always saw his mother a few times a year. But being so close for a month this time, it would be a more leisurely visit and he could hear about more of her adventures. He was close to his mom, and the four-hour drive from Rome was just perfect for a bachelor son. Not too far, not too close.

> *Hi Mom, I hope you're having a great start to the New Year! Got in yesterday and doing a little sightseeing today. Look forward to seeing your place again and catching up. If you're still good for tomorrow and Sunday, I can't wait to see your latest paintings. I'll keep you posted on Jason and Steve too. Still hoping they can make it out and that you're ok hosting all of us for a long weekend. Ciao! Sam*

Sam was pretty sure that his mom would let him and his friends stay at her Capri villa for as long as they wanted. She had always gotten along well with Jason and Steve, and putting them up in Capri was an extra incentive for them to fly out. His mother was a fun host, and you never knew when another movie star or a pop singer might stop by.

From the sound of it, his mother wasn't dating anyone right now. So he and his friends would mostly have the run of the place. She'd had some nice love affairs—at least according to the tabloids—but she had always been pretty independent. He was too young then to remember her living with his father, so he had never really seen her truly in love. She had almost the perfect life, and he figured that some people would just never find that one perfect partner. Maybe he was like that too, he wondered. Like mother, like son.

About an hour later, Sam met Donovan across from the Colosseum. They hugged warmly and walked toward the ancient amphitheater.

Donovan looked up at the enormous stone walls. "It sure is impressive," he said. "Have you done the tour?"

"I had planned to when I lived here," Sam replied. "But I was living with Mom then, and you know how she is. She has pretty strong feelings about this place."

"Really?" said Donovan. "I think I can understand that. It was pretty violent here, and a lot of gladiators and slaves got killed. Didn't the Roman emperors also have some Christians and other religious dissenters fed to the lions here too?"

"That sounds right," Sam replied. "But for Mom, it's more personal. It's about her being an actress. She found out that the ancient Romans hated actors so much they wouldn't let them into the Colosseum. For whatever reason, the Romans thought actors were the worst kind of people and treated them almost as badly as if they were women. Who had it even worse."

Donovan smiled. "Maybe she's got a point. I do love old monuments, but some of these old traditions were pretty awful. It's good to stand up for your beliefs."

"You know Mom." Sam laughed. "Fighting for her beliefs is never a problem. She's got lots of those."

As they were talking, Sam took a pamphlet for one of the Colosseum tours. "See, here's a good example," he said to Donovan. "Check out this inscription on one of the Colosseum walls."

Imperator T Caesar Vaspasianus Augustus
amphitheatrum novum
ex Manubiis fieri iussit

"Here's the translation and explanation," Sam said, reading aloud.

Emperor Titus Caesar Vespasian the Magnificent
Ordered a new amphitheater to be made
From the spoils of war

"So, basically," Sam went on, "this inscription says that the Colosseum was paid for with the spoils of war. The ancient Roman emperors were actually proud of that. And look at this. The pamphlet says the *T* for Titus was added later. It's a typical father-son rivalry. The inscription was originally written for the emperor Vespasian. When he died, his son Titus became emperor and had a *T* added to this inscription so he would get credit for the new amphitheater."

"Hmm," Donovan said, nodding. "Sounds like the son was pretty competitive. Looking to one-up his father. Funny how that works."

"Well, in this case, it's fair for Titus to get most of the credit," Sam replied. "He won the war, if you want to call it that."

"Let me guess," Donovan jumped in. "They were fighting Carthage or Gaul or something like that. Protecting the Roman homeland. I learned a little Roman history in college."

"Well, not exactly," Sam replied. "Before he was emperor, Vespasian was the general in charge of crushing the Jewish revolt in the year 66. After Nero died—well, actually, was forced to commit suicide—Vespasian became emperor, and his son Titus took over the job. Titus destroyed Jerusalem and its Temple, and his army killed or enslaved most of the people there. They found so much gold and silver at the Temple that they were able to build the Colosseum and some of the other monuments we can see here today. According to this pamphlet, if the Colosseum were built today, you would need about ten tons of gold to pay for the construction, which is about four hundred million dollars. These ancient Romans sure stole a lot."

"Do you think they had that much gold at the Jerusalem Temple?" Donovan asked. "Ten tons? That sounds pretty tempting to a ruthless emperor. Maybe the Jewish people were right to revolt."

"I've actually been reading about it," Sam replied. "The Romans did a lot of good things, and maybe they meant well in certain ways. It was a brutal time, and it's hard to say that they were more violent than the other empires. But, sure, no one would want their homeland invaded by the Romans. If you didn't surrender right away, they would destroy everything to make you an example. The Romans were very direct about that. After his son Titus destroyed Jerusalem, the emperor Vespasian had a new coin minted. Today, we call it the Judea Captive coin. It shows a Jewish man tied as a slave, next to a woman crying next to the victorious emperor by a trophy and weapons. Not subtle at all."

"Wow, pretty sad," Donovan said, exhaling. "Should we head down to the Forum? Maybe there's something more cheerful down there."

"Not exactly," Sam replied. "But it's good to walk around and great to catch up."

A few minutes later, Sam and Donovan were standing in front of the Arch of Titus, built in the year AD 80 to commemorate the future emperor Titus's destruction of Jerusalem and its Temple and his army's looting of the Temple treasury.

Donovan looked up at the carved sculpture underneath the Arch. "So the emperor Titus had this built to show some of the treasures he had stolen from the Jewish people? Spoils of war and all that?"

"That's right." Sam sighed. "The golden menorah lamp, a golden table for sacred bread, and other important artifacts of the Jerusalem Temple. For the Jewish people, it wasn't about the gold. These things were sacred to their religion. And for the Roman emperor, that was part of his message. If you didn't play ball with the Romans, they would destroy everything that you loved."

After walking through the Forum, Sam and Donovan headed out for lunch at a sidewalk café. It had stayed sunny, and it was fairly warm for January. A bit like LA, Sam thought. Except for the gorgeous architecture, blue skies, and the endless parade of beautiful people going about their day.

Donovan asked Sam about his work. They were both attorneys, which was how Sam had gotten interested in law school in the first place. Sam had always enjoyed talking to him about his work. Donovan had explained how to talk about their cases without violating privilege. You just had to be a little vague and not give names. Not exactly how the professors had explained it, but it was definitely how all the lawyers worked around it.

After all, if you could never talk about your work, some of the normal conversations with friends and family would get a little awkward.

Sam told Donovan that he had an interesting new case from one of his clients' compliance hotlines. A whistleblower had reported that the company paid a bribe for a land development permit. The land permitting official had already been arrested and was awaiting trial. On the surface, it was a simple investigation. A corporate bribe got paid, and Sam would figure out who was involved and approved the payment. Then the corporate board would decide on a scapegoat to fire, regardless of what the report said. Case closed.

Still, this one was different, Sam thought. The whistleblower didn't have a grudge or some benefit from reporting the bribe. In fact, the whistleblower had provided all sorts of irrelevant information about bribes that Wechsler had received from other businesses. Sam's client couldn't care less. But Sam found it intriguing. It was almost as though the whistleblower wanted to blow the whistle on something bigger. But what was it?

Donovan shrugged. He was a trial lawyer and had always tried to steer clear of his clients' office politics. Donovan had sometimes commented on the dangers of "knowing too much" and how cynical corporate clients could be in handling legal compliance issues. Might makes right, Donovan had told Sam more than a few times.

After more sightseeing and catching up that afternoon, Sam and Donovan called it a day. Sam was still a little groggy from the time difference with LA and wanted to relax a bit back at his apartment. They agreed to get together early next week before Donovan would fly back to LA.

Sam gave Donovan a man-hug as they left the café. It was nice seeing him, and he was glad they had gotten together. Donovan did look a little tired, though. Just something a little off. Maybe he was working too much. Or he was in over his head on some kind of project. Sam knew he didn't want to end up that way.

Back at the apartment, Sam looked through the pile of Rome travel guides he had put on the coffee table. He noticed the *Treasures of Israel* travel guide near the bottom of the pile. He had brought it along, just in case.

He picked up the book and skimmed through it. It all sounded good. The salty waters of the Dead Sea, warm enough to swim all year, even in January. The mysteries of Jericho—the world's oldest city. Jerusalem, of course, with its largely barren Temple Mount—sacred to more than half of the world's population—and its lively blend of ancient and modern neighborhoods.

Even Samaria and Galilee had undiscovered wonders, according to the book. Vineyards, orchards, rustic towns, and much more. The book said that Samaria's greatest treasure was its remarkable people, and Sam couldn't agree more.

Sam knew that Rebecca was still in New York, wrapping up a family visit. He was tempted to send an email but decided to wait another day or two. Maybe, once she was back home in Israel, the idea of him making a quick visit wouldn't sound like too much.

After all, wouldn't a quiet afternoon at a hilltop farm or organic winery be a nice break from a busy life? Some of those romantic inns sounded pretty nice too.

After reading a while longer, Sam turned in for the night. He fell asleep, still thinking about the world's prettiest smile and an irresistible accent.

And it was so.

3

LET THERE BE LIGHT

That night, Sam dreamed of his father.

"Read me another story, Dad," young Sam asked, sitting up in bed. "You haven't read to me in a while."

"All right," his father said. He had been traveling and hadn't read his eight-year-old son a bedtime story in weeks. "Which one would you like?"

"Maybe something from your travels?" Sam asked. "One of those ancient stories? Like the Buddha and the fig tree? Or Aladdin and the magic lamp?"

"Okay, how about a new story?" his father suggested. "I mean, it's ancient, but I haven't told it to you yet."

"How does it start?" Sam asked.

"Once upon a time, of course," his father said, smiling.

"That's a good start," Sam agreed.

"So, a long time ago in a land far, far away, a child was born to a priest named Nedebeus," Sam's father began. "He had wanted very much to have a son. So, when he and his wife had their first boy, they named him Ananias, which means 'God has given.'"

"Nedebeus and his wife loved their new son very much. They taught him everything about the culture, traditions, and beliefs of their home in Jerusalem. As Ananias grew older, his parents had scribes and sages visit their home to teach him more about the law and the wisdom of the books.

"Ananias lived in a small, fertile land known as Judea," Sam's father continued. "For centuries, this land had been a crossroads between empires. Mighty Egypt to the west, ferocious Babylonia to the east, and heroic Greece to the north. It was important for Judean families to teach their children the ancient stories of invasion, exile, and return so that each new generation would know how to live in this small land between the empires.

"Young Ananias excelled at his studies and showed great talent for the law and the customs of his people. He mastered the Aramaic language used for daily life and the Hebrew language used in the books and at the

Temple, and he learned enough Greek to speak with merchants and travelers. He soon caught the attention of his elders and extended family, who predicted he would go far and that his name would be remembered.

"Ananias enjoyed his work and studies," Sam's father went on, "but he especially enjoyed the festivals and holidays. Ananias went to the Temple to pray and chant with his father regularly. But the festivals were special times when the family would bring an animal to the Temple to be sacrificed and prepared by the priests for a festive meal, along with the throngs of pilgrims celebrating the festivals."

Young Sam looked up at his father. "It must have been a big Temple," he said.

"It was enormous and built of magnificent stonework, decorated with shining gold and bronze," Sam's father replied. "It was one of the largest temples ever built in the world. Majestic like the Karnak temples in Egypt and glorious like the Roman temples at Heliopolis in ancient Syria. The Temple in Jerusalem attracted hundreds of thousands of pilgrims from across the Roman world for each of the festivals."

"What was his favorite festival?" Sam asked.

"Young children really enjoy Passover," his father replied.

"What's that?" Sam asked.

"It's a weeklong celebration of Ananias's people escaping from slavery in Egypt," his father responded. "A great man named Moses was called to lead the people known as Israelites out of Egypt to freedom. He told the people that a plague would take the firstborn sons of all Egypt and for the Israelites to mark their doors with lamb's blood so that the plague would pass over their families.

"After Moses had led his people out of Egypt, they began a tradition of sacrificing lambs at the Temple on the day before Passover began," his father continued. "The lambs were roasted and eaten that night, along with a special type of flatbread and bitter herbs to remind them of the sacrifices that had been needed to win their freedom. Each year, hundreds of thousands of pilgrims gathered at the Temple for this festival, and it was viewed as a joyful celebration with candies for the children and songs for everyone."

"Tell me the rest of the story," Sam said. "Did Ananias become a priest like his father?"

"Well, it's a long story, and we won't finish it tonight," his father replied. "But I can tell you the next part. At the age of thirteen, Ananias took on the responsibilities of a young man. He began leading prayers and became more active at the Temple and in his daily work at home. He had learned that, under the law, he was now responsible for his own actions and would be judged accordingly. Not long after came an event that made an impression on him and that he would remember his whole life.

"It was a week before Passover, and everyone was getting ready. Families were cleaning and purifying their homes, and pilgrims were traveling to Jerusalem for the festival. But one week before Passover, a teacher from Galilee in the north traveled along the pilgrimage route to Jerusalem. The Teacher, known as Yeshua of Nazareth, was believed to work miracles, and his presence excited the crowds of pilgrims on the road to Jerusalem. They began waving palm branches in his honor.

"Several days after he arrived in Jerusalem," Sam's father continued, "the council of elders had Yeshua arrested. They were worried that he was causing civil disturbances that might provoke the Romans. Among other things, he had overturned the tables of the money changers, accusing them of cheating the pilgrims when they exchanged their Roman coins for the local coins that were viewed as being spiritually pure enough to be used at the Temple. He went so far as to tell the crowd of pilgrims that no commerce at all should be conducted at the Temple and that it should be only a house of prayer. The Judean leaders saw this as extreme and dangerous. After all, the Temple was the center of virtually everything in Jerusalem, and many thousands of jobs in the city depended on these activities. Their greatest fear was that disturbances like these would disrupt the economy and lead to a militant faction seizing power and starting a ruinous war against the Romans.

"For centuries, the Romans had conquered nation after nation and had never lost a war," he went on. "Having maintained a degree of independence from empires for most of the last five hundred years, the Judean leaders wanted to make sure that their careful diplomacy and statecraft would not be disrupted by militants or new spiritual movements.

"Ananias's father, Nedebeus, was worried. He told the family that the high priest, Joseph ben Caiaphas, had made clear that it was better for one man to die than for the whole nation to be destroyed. Now a teenager who was himself responsible for his own actions, Ananias carefully considered these words. He believed in the golden rule to love your neighbor as yourself, and he wished no harm to anyone. But, at the same time, didn't the leaders have an obligation to protect the nation at all costs?

"Like most of Jerusalem, Ananias followed the news of the teacher's arrest and trial closely," Sam's father continued. "On the morning of Passover Eve came the news that the Teacher Yeshua had been convicted the night before and would be executed that day. As Ananias and his family brought their lamb to the Temple for slaughter, the Teacher was nailed to a cross on a hill outside the city, where he died three hours later.

"As Ananias and his family celebrated the traditional Passover dinner that evening, this violent episode was naturally on their minds. Peace with the Romans seemed secure for now, but at what cost? By now, Ananias had ambitions of being a leader at the Temple one day. How would he balance the safety of the nation against justice for one man? Or was this Galilean Teacher simply guilty of being in the wrong place at the wrong time?"

Sam was quiet as he reflected. "I think his name was Jesus," he said finally.

"Jesus?" his father asked. "You've heard this story already, huh?"

"Of course," Sam replied. "Not the Ananias part. But the Jesus part. Except you're calling him Yeshua."

"Right," his father responded. "That was his name, actually. His followers wrote his story in Greek to reach a broader audience. They translated his name into Greek so that it would be easier to understand. Sometimes the translations make a difference, and sometimes they don't. Everyone has to decide for themselves."

"Well, that's complicated," Sam said. "Don't you have any easier bedtime stories?"

"I think you like the tough ones," his father said, laughing. "Like the Buddha and Aladdin stories, right?"

"Is there more to the Ananias story?" Sam asked.

"Oh, yes," his father replied. "It gets really interesting."

"Can you tell me the rest?" Sam asked.

"Not tonight," his father responded. "You need your rest. One day, you'll learn your own stories. But to grow up right, you need to get lots of rest."

"So, where are you going?" Sam asked. "Back to India, Fiji, Peru, or someplace like that?"

"Something like that," his father said, patting Sam's shoulder. "I'll bring back more stories." He turned off the light.

"I love you," Sam told his father.

"I love you back," his father said. "I'm always there."

His father gone, Sam lay still in the quiet darkness as he drifted off to sleep. The moon cast a soft glow through the curtained window.

The lesser light ruled the night.

4

IN OUR IMAGE

The room brightened in the morning sun. Sam rolled over in bed and began to wake up.

It was Sunday, and Sam had another day off. He was meeting Donovan for breakfast and then heading out to his mother's place on Capri for the rest of the day.

No sightseeing or symphonies. Just resting and relaxing.

Sam thought about Rebecca. He knew she was flying back home from New York today. At least she would be closer. He would send her a message tomorrow to check in.

Sam picked up his phone from the nightstand to check his messages before getting started with the day. Just some nice New Year's greetings from friends and family.

Nothing much in his work email. Just a few Google alerts. He had been getting them every day since he had set up the news alert on Daniel Wechsler, the official with the Israel Land Authority who had been indicted on bribery charges a few weeks ago.

The Wechsler bribery scandal was the reason that Sam had been able to take this trip to Rome and get some downtime while working part time. Sam's client Bacchus Wines & Spirits had gotten a whistleblower report on its internal hotline that Wechsler had been bribed to issue a permit for its new warehouse near Tel Aviv. Bacchus had hired Sam and his firm to investigate and issue a report for its board of directors.

As usual, Sam was grateful for the human weaknesses and moral contradictions that led to these scandals. Sam loved the work and the process of uncovering the facts. Wechsler seemed like a good person who just had some debts to pay off and had gotten in over his head. It wasn't a big scandal, just another ordinary temptation gone wrong.

Sam opened the first alert and looked at the headline:

The Jerusalem Post

> *Sunday, January 2*
>
> *LAND OFFICIAL IS FOUND DEAD IN APPARENT SUICIDE*
>
> *A senior official with the Israel Land Authority who was indicted last month on bribery charges apparently shot himself in his office. According to a police report, Daniel Wechsler, age fifty-six, had arrived at work that morning and was found dead at his desk around 4:00 p.m. on Friday, with a gunshot wound to the head. The police recovered a pistol at the scene. The police believe that Wechsler took his own life, based on documents and personal items left at the scene. According to Amon Ehrlich, a senior detective working on the case, the investigation is continuing, but there is no evidence to contradict a suicide.*
>
> *Wechsler was arrested on December 13 on bribery charges related to Cobra Construction's planned thirty-story residential tower in the Jerusalem City Center. The investigation is being carried out by the Lahav 433 unit, which has investigated numerous senior officials and political leaders since its creation in 2008. Investigators suspect that Wechsler accepted bribes in return for approving permits related to the acquisition of the tower property. If convicted, he faced up to ten years in prison.*
>
> *Wechsler is survived by his wife and three children. The family has not provided any information about a memorial service at this time.*

Wow, Sam thought. A suicide on New Year's Eve? It didn't fit the profile. Not exactly a day of hopeless desperation. Most suicides occur on Mondays or late at night when problems can seem unsolvable. Sam wondered what had really happened. Taking your own life on New Year's Eve at 4:00 p.m. didn't sound right.

Sam checked the rest of the alerts. It was the same news. A tragedy and a heartbroken family. He felt tempted to send flowers. He had learned quite a bit about Wechsler's work and personal life from the investigation. Now he needed to know more.

But now wasn't the time, Sam thought. It was the day after New Year's and a Sunday as well. He shouldn't be working and certainly not on a sad story like this.

Sam sent a confirming text to Donovan and got up, showered, and dressed.

Sam met Donovan for breakfast at the coffee bar near Sam's apartment on the Piazza Navona. He ordered his usual doppio espresso with a marmalade-glazed cornetto pastry, and Donovan ordered a *caffè* macchiato with a *maritozzi* pastry filled with whipped cream.

"How's your working vacation going?" Donovan smiled.

"It's working well," Sam replied. "I mean, mostly I'm not working. So the plan is going well. I'll keep working half time for the next month or until the next big case comes along."

"Anything new on your whistleblower?" Donovan asked.

"Well, I got some news today, but it's pretty sensitive. I'll tell you later, if I can," Sam replied.

Sam paused. His conversations with Donovan were usually about work, travel, or sports. It had been a while since they talked about their personal lives.

"The dreams are back," Sam said finally.

"Hmm." Donovan looked down at his coffee. "Because you're back in Rome?"

"Maybe," Sam replied. "LA can be pretty sterile. Maybe there's something about these ancient places that triggers the dreams."

"Or just travel." Donovan shrugged. "Didn't you say that your visitor is always traveling around the world?"

"That's right." Sam looked up from his coffee. "India, Fiji, Peru. All those places a spiritual person goes to."

"Rome?" Donovan queried.

"Sure," Sam responded. "There's spirit here. Some darkness too. But definitely both."

"So, your visitor is some kind of spiritual avatar?" Donovan asked. "With something to teach you?"

"It might be easier if he just sent a book," Sam joked. "Of course, maybe he did. There *was* that poetry book from Solomon the other day."

"Huh?" Donovan tilted his head.

"Oh, nothing," Sam said. "Just sort of a gardening book. The four seasons and all that."

"Well," Donovan said, "if you need any help interpreting dreams, just let me know. Remember, I helped you figure some of them out when you were a teenager."

"Oh, sure," Sam said with a mock grin. "You told me to be cold and hostile to the visitor. That was a little traumatic, don't you think?"

"Just helping," Donovan said, shrugging. "You don't want to let just *anyone* into your dreams, do you? Sometimes what you *don't* know is what buys you peace."

"Not for me," Sam said, stirring another espresso. "I'd rather know."

"I know what you mean," Donovan said, putting his hand on Sam's shoulder. "But be careful with that. Some things are much bigger than you think. It can be overwhelming if you learn too much too fast."

Sam nodded but dismissed this as another one of Donovan's mysterious comments that never made sense. He really must be working too hard, Sam thought.

They finished their breakfast and agreed to catch up early the next week, before Donovan would go back to LA. Sam gave him a man-hug and headed back to his apartment to start packing for Capri.

Back at the apartment, Sam gathered two days' worth of weekend clothes, plus a few dressy things just in case. He had learned to prepare for the unexpected around his mother. People had a habit of stopping by. Beautiful singers, actresses, and writers, he recalled, adding a nice linen jacket to his pile. Of course, according to his mom, they mostly weren't good enough for him. She had told him all the insider gossip, but this usually just made them seem even *more* interesting.

Sam took an Uber to the train station and boarded the train to Naples. It was about a three-hour ride to Naples and then a short trip to the ferry terminal. Then about an hour by ferry to Capri. He would be there by late afternoon.

Sam spent the train ride having some fun with the bronze scroll clues. He opened up his laptop and added more clues to the sixty-site spreadsheet that he had created on the flight to Rome. Nothing was making sense. The locations seemed to be mostly vaguely described caves or biblical locations where this or that event had occurred. Why would anyone hide tons of gold and silver at someplace that you had to read the Bible to find?

After leaving the train station in Naples, Sam walked to the ferry landing, enjoying the sunshine and cool, crisp air. He was looking forward to seeing his mother.

"Hi, Sam dear!" his mother called out, as Sam's ferry arrived on Capri and he disembarked.

Sam squinted in the golden late-afternoon sun as he walked down the ferry ramp toward his mother.

He held out his arms to greet her, and she gave him a big hug. Dawn Hughes was even more lovely in person than in the magazines and films. Emerald eyes and soft strawberry-blond hair. She had a talent for everything artistic, and she had decided that living well was a form of art too. Living on Capri in the winters was part of that. Like another canvas or roll of film to make beautiful.

"Great to see you, Mom!" Sam beamed, hugging her back.

"Oh, wonderful to see you, dear!" she said with a glow. "I've rented you a scooter for the weekend so we can get around together," she said as they began walking down the waterfront.

"Still not driving here, huh?" Sam grinned. "This is so *not* LA."

"I have a car, but I rarely use it," Dawn replied. "This is so much nicer," she said as they walked up to the parked scooters.

"So, you were talking about some plans," Sam said. "Maybe something about a dinner?"

"Yes, of course," she replied. "You know how I like to show you off. I'll tell you about it when we get to the villa."

Sam and his mom got on their scooters and headed up the hill, away from the Marina Grande. They sped through the town at the top of the hill and cruised down toward Dawn's villa on the hillside overlooking the Marina Piccola.

As they walked into Dawn's villa, Sam remembered why he loved this place. An elegant, traditional villa with a red-tiled roof over whitewashed stucco, with white textured walls and green-and-gold tile floors inside and a string of terraces outside overlooking the marina, with a full bar and an outdoor pizza oven.

Dawn showed Sam to his favorite bedroom with an endless view of the blue Mediterranean. "The dinner guests start arriving around 8:00 p.m.," she said. "You remember things run late here."

"Sounds like fun," Sam said. "Is this one of your famous dinner parties?" he asked. "With you, it's either big or bigger."

"Oh, it's not like that," his mother replied. "A small gathering. Just twenty people, I think. You'll have fun."

"Sounds great," he replied. "Anyone I know?"

"I don't think so," said his mom. "Just some people I've met here. There's a priest, a rabbi, a yogi, and—"

"Oh, now I get it," Sam said, laughing. "Another one of your spiritual-themed events. Good thing I've been reading about ancient religion lately. I'll be able to follow some of the conversation."

"But you've always been good at world religions," Dawn jumped in. "This will be a perfect group for you. Maybe one day you'll even choose something you believe in and stick with it," she said with a smile. "You know, instead of looking around and avoiding commitment. Maybe find a real woman too," she said as Sam groaned.

"Well, somehow I think with the priest, the rabbi, and the yogi, this won't be the night for that," Sam said. "There's plenty of time to settle down, right? I mean, you still haven't found your true love yet. At least, that's what the tabloids say."

"Hmm, don't believe that nonsense. There's a true love for everyone, even me. When you're old enough, I'll tell you about it," she said with a wink.

"Old enough?" Sam laughed. "I'm thirty-five now. If there's something you want to tell me, I think I can handle it."

"We'll see about that," Dawn replied, leaving Sam to change for the evening. "There's a time for every season."

Sam laughed. "You read that book too, huh? It must be on the best-seller list or something."

"I don't know what you mean," Dawn said, looking a bit confused. "Oh, by the way," she said as she stood in the doorway, "I'm working on a small trip to Israel in about a week. One of those photo shoots with a few other cast members. I spoke with your friends, and it sounds like they're ready to commit to a visit. One week in the Holy Land, and one week on Capri or wherever they want to go in Italy."

Sam couldn't believe what he was hearing. "Israel?" he said. "Oh, yes, that sounds wonderful. You talked to Jason and Steve? And they're good with this? I've been hoping they'd fly out here, but it's been tough to plan around everyone's schedules."

Dawn smiled. "Maybe the after-party with Ava Stern helped persuade them. She's pretty hot in that new Mata Hari film, and I promised them a personal introduction."

"Well, count me in, then," Sam said, his eyes lighting up. "Can I go to the party too? You know how I like historical films."

"Mm-hmm, that's what I thought," she replied. "She won't be dancing at the after-party, you know."

"That's a shame," Sam said, disappointed. "But at least I could meet her. We probably have a lot in common."

"Right," Dawn said with a smile. "You could both use acting lessons. You're pretty transparent. Now, go ahead and unpack and change. I want to show you my latest painting," she said, exiting the room.

Sam started unpacking, imagining hanging out with Ava Stern. He reflected on what his mother had said earlier too. A *real* woman? What does that even mean? Ava Stern's pretty real, he thought.

But his mother had talked about beliefs. Maybe that's what's supposed to be real. Believing in something?

Like in Sam's dreams? Right, because *those* are real, he thought. Well, maybe if you believe in them. So, *belief* is what makes things real? Even dreams?

Sam smiled. This was good practice for the dinner party with the priest, the rabbi, and the yogi, he thought.

He finished unpacking, got changed, and headed down the hall to see his mother's latest artwork.

Sam liked his mom's new painting. "The red bougainvillea over the marina is really powerful with the glow of the sunset behind it. I guess living here is really inspiring."

"You know all those myths about the sun and the moon? You really feel them here. It's an ancient place, but it feels new every day. So, how's your work-life balance going?" Dawn asked. "Are you staying away from the office?"

"So far so good," Sam said with a nod. "I haven't even been there yet, and I haven't done any work. Well, except for checking emails and maybe calling a reporter today."

"Good, that's progress," said Dawn, patting his shoulder. "You're starting to figure this out. Working all the time is like chasing the wind."

"There you go again," Sam said. "Another poetry lesson. I'm not sure it will help with your guests, though. I don't think I've ever talked to a priest, a rabbi, and a yogi all in one evening. Are you sure we won't start a religious war or something?"

"You don't have to close your mind to believe in something, you know," his mother replied. "Belief doesn't really have anything to do with the mind anyway. It's in your heart. Your mind still gets to question anything and everything. You just don't want to be trapped by that."

"Hmm, sounds like you're still studying Dharma and all that," Sam said as they walked outside to a terrace to enjoy the sunset. "So, what's with the priest and the rabbi? Aren't you supposed to stick with yogis and gurus?"

"Well, I think every tradition really gets you to the same place," Dawn replied. "The unseen light," she said, gazing at the sunset. "Belief is like a doorway. You can choose whichever door you want. Each one is just a different path to the same destination. The point is to choose, and it's nice to share that with others along the way."

"I get it," Sam said, watching the sun disappear into the darkening blue sea. "The light's always there, no matter what. Believing just helps us to see it, right?"

"Something like that," Dawn replied, patting his arm. "I'll go check in the kitchen. People will start arriving soon, and I should see how the chefs are doing," she said, heading back into the house.

Several hours later, after an evening catching up on his mother's latest film shoots and openings and other adventures, the dinner guests started to arrive.

"*Saluti!*" Father Luigi toasted the group. "Happy New Year! Eat, drink, and be merry."

Everyone raised their glasses and joined in the toast. "*L'chaim!*" "*Fe Sahetek*!" "*Cheers!*" "*Sante!*"

"Dawn, tell us about your new movie!" Rabbi Cohen shouted out as others joined in. "What are you filming?"

"I thought you'd never ask," Dawn said, laughing. "It's about Cleopatra."

"You mean *Antony* and Cleopatra?" Yogi Sharma joined in.

Dawn smiled. "You know I don't do second billing. We brought in that director who does alternative endings. I hate snakes, so we had to fix that too."

"It sounds like Cleopatra conquers Rome this time around," Sheikh al-Rashid jumped in.

"How did you know?" Dawn laughed. "This time, that obnoxious Octavian won't get his way. He was a small man, after all. Not at all like my beautiful Mark Antony."

The dinner guests enjoyed the bruschetta, carpaccio, and braciole al ragù, with salads served afterward, of course. But they enjoyed Dawn's larger-than-life stories even more. After a round of grappa was served, the lights went out.

One of the chefs emerged from the kitchen holding a large chocolate cake with candles ablaze, heading toward Sam. "Happy birthday to you," they began singing as Sam felt himself turning bright red.

The lights came back on, and Dawn stood up to make a toast. "You remember my Christmas baby," she began. "Well, he's all grown up now," she said, raising her glass proudly.

"Congratulations!" Father Luigi stood and raised his glass. "You know, Christmas mothers and babies sometimes get forgotten in the holiday rush. But never in our hearts. *Saluti alla madre e al figlio*," he said, nodding his head to both Dawn and Sam. "Now for the gifts!" said the priest, gesturing toward Rabbi Cohen. "You had everyone bring gold, frankincense and myrrh, right?" he said, to laughter.

"No, I didn't get the memo," the rabbi said, laughing. "I was too busy with Hanukkah and somehow missed that star over Bethlehem."

Dawn laughed, taking a sip of grappa. "You're just a bunch of wise guys. Just remember that I'm playing Cleopatra again this year. Gold's good for a start, but diamonds are even better."

"Count me in for the frankincense," Sam said with a smirk. "Burning it will keep me warm while I'm sleeping outdoors in the manger tonight. With the shepherds and all that."

"Spoken like a true Christmas baby," Dawn said, smiling. "But you know, I've never understood the part about the frankincense. What does that have to do with Christmas?"

"Sort of like birthday incense, I guess," Sheikh al-Rashid jumped in. "I'll call Melchior and ask him about it. He was there, you know—"

"Okay, that's enough," Dawn interrupted. "Some mysteries can wait for the next birthday. Now, where's my slice of birthday cake?" she asked, picking up her fork.

Sam took another sip of grappa, enjoying the scene. His mother's dinner parties were always like this. When it wasn't the Hollywood crowd or a gathering of avant-garde painters or musicians, it was a group of diverse free spirits just like this. Sort of a gathering of wise men, you might even say.

As he finished his birthday cake, Sam remembered that it was about time to send a message to Rebecca. She should have landed and gotten home by now.

Rebecca would know more about Wechsler too, he thought. She hadn't told Sam much about her current assignments, but he followed her reporting closely online. She had broken the story about Wechsler and had been digging into it further.

Sam looked down at his empty grappa glass. All this spiritual talk must be getting to him, he thought. A pretty sure thing when you have a dinner party with a priest, a rabbi, and a yogi. Not to mention an imam from Arabia. What was that sheikh's name?

Sam excused himself from the dinner table and went to give his mom a big hug. "Thank you so much," he said as he leaned over to hug her, "for the wonderful dinner party and the birthday surprise."

"Oh, happy birthday, honey," Dawn said, hugging him back. "I'm so glad you're here. You're going to bed now?"

"Pretty soon," Sam responded. "I need to send something out to a reporter, and then I'll get to bed after that."

"Wonderful," his mom replied, "and we'll have a nice day tomorrow. I want to show you a few things around the island. And maybe we can talk about some other travel ideas I have too?"

"Yes, of course," Sam said. "That all sounds fun."

"Just one last thing." Dawn looked up at Sam. "That reporter—is she pretty?"

"What? Who?" Sam asked, surprised.

"You know, the reporter," his mom repeated.

"*Pretty*?" Sam shook his head. "How did you even know it's a woman reporter?"

"Please," his mother said, rolling her eyes. "It's after eleven. I don't think you'd be sending messages to some old journalist with a beard."

"Well, sure, then," Sam relented. "She's pretty. *Beyond* that, really. I mean, we really connected for an evening. You know, your doorways and all that. It's hard to explain."

"Hmm, I know the feeling. It can't really be explained," she said.

"Donovan?" Sam asked.

"Oh, it's a long story," his mom replied. "But, sure, it's about your father," she said, looking at Sam. "I'll tell you another time."

"All right, but what's up with all this mystery?" Sam asked. "Donovan was acting this way too this morning. He was hinting about some mysteries he thinks I'm supposed to learn. Except not just yet, apparently."

"He might be right about that, but you're supposed to be relaxing this weekend. It's your birthday celebration," Dawn reminded him. "Besides, weren't you going to send a message to that reporter?"

Sam looked at his mother, wondering what she wasn't telling him. But he knew better than to keep pushing. He wished her good night and walked around the room, giving his regards to the dinner guests.

Back in his bedroom, Sam sat up in bed with his phone. He started a text message to Rebecca.

> *Hi Rebecca, just a heads up that I may be doing a trip to Israel this month after all. I know your schedule may be too busy to get together, but everything else is falling into place. First I got a work project out there, on that Israeli land permitting scandal you've been reporting on. Then my mom invited me and my friends Jason and Steve to a photo shoot that she's doing there on the tenth. My starstruck friends accepted right away, once they found out that the "hot" (their word) actress Ava Stern will be there too. I'm not so crazy about these Hollywood-style events, but it will be nice to see my mom and my friends. Any chance we could meet up while I'm there? I'll probably fly out on Saturday and stay about a week. Maybe another round of cocktails? I hear there are interesting martinis over your way. Sam*

Sam reread his message before sending it. He didn't want to sound too aggressive or pushy. He hadn't told her about his feelings. He exhaled slowly and hit send.

Sam turned out the light and got back into bed. He fell asleep with the thought of hazel eyes. A blazing smile and an alluring accent. A hint of soft fragrance. And the unseen light.

5

SHE SHALL BE CALLED WOMAN

Sam awoke to the thought of a woman with wavy auburn hair and an irresistible accent. It was Monday. Another day off, Sam thought, pleased.

Sam picked up his phone and checked for messages. No reply from Rebecca yet.

It was barely after 7:00 a.m., and he hadn't really expected a response this early.

He thought about the kiss again. He wondered if he would see her next week. He looked out the bedroom window at the blue Mediterranean and remembered the slightly salty taste of her lips.

He decided it might be a while before she texted back. She wasn't exactly tethered to her phone, he remembered. Something about technology being a tool and not an addiction. He thought she would smile when she got his message, and he wished he could be with her, wherever she was.

But first, Capri. Sam really enjoyed his mother's grand tours. The island was just a few miles across, but his mom knew every inch. Sam was sure to get another lesson in the history of Roman emperors, secret lovers, and ancient curses.

He got out of bed, took a shower, and dressed. Then he found his mother on the terrace with a large charcoal sketchbook. She had begun tracing a sketch for her next painting.

"*Buongiorno!*" Sam greeted her.

"Good morning! Did you sleep well?" she asked.

"Sure did," he replied. "I haven't heard back from my reporter friend yet," he added. "You know, the *pretty* one," he said with a wink.

"Pretty girls sleep in on Sunday mornings," his mother said, looking at her sketchbook. "Unless they're starting a new painting. Dawn can be inspiring, you know."

"So I hear," Sam said, grinning. "What's for breakfast?"

"The chefs made some pastries last night," Dawn replied. "They're in the kitchen. Can you bring them out with some coffee? I'd get up, but I want to sketch those boats before they sail off."

"*Sì, naturalmente*," Sam said, walking back inside. "Be right back."

Sam returned a few minutes later with a tray of coffee and pastries. "Ah, my favorites," he said, inhaling the aromas. "*Cornetti* with orange marmalade. They look delicious."

"An extra birthday treat," Dawn said with a grin. "You can't see the island on an empty stomach, right?"

"So, what's the plan?" Sam asked, sitting down.

"Oh, you're going to love this," Dawn promised. "Even better than your last visit."

Sam remembered the sailing cruise in the local Mediterranean waters and the excursions to the Blue Grotto and the Villa San Michele with the Roman and Egyptian antiquities. Hard to beat, he thought.

"Professor Lehrer will meet us the Villa Jovis at 11:00 a.m., if that works for you," his mother went on. "He teaches Archaeology at the Free University in Berlin and has a senior position at the National Archaeology Museum in Naples. Oh, and of course, he has a place on Capri. He's a good friend and offered us a private tour at the emperor Tiberius's villa here."

"Nice," Sam said. "Too bad Jason and Steve will miss this. Especially Steve—he really likes history."

"Well, maybe he can do another tour if Jason and Steve decide to visit here after the Israel trip," Dawn suggested. "His private 'Capri after dark' tour is really amazing. Lots of scandals on the island in the old days. Those old Romans and Swedish industrialists would have kept your law firm busy."

"I do love a scandal," Sam agreed. "Is there any more news from Jason and Steve about the Israel trip? I didn't hear from them yesterday, and it sounds like you're taking the lead on this."

"Yes," Dawn said, looking down at her tablet. "I got confirmations overnight. My assistant, Mirabella, will book the flights and hotels today. We'll be at the American Colony Hotel in Jerusalem. It's classy and old school. Just your kind of thing."

"Awesome," he said, impressed. "That was fast. Wait, actually, let me just book my flight through the firm," he added. "I can charge it to the case I'm working on."

"Hold on," Dawn said, looking up from her tablet. "You're making this a work trip? Your friends are flying out, and I'll be there too. You really should be taking a break from work."

"For sure," Sam agreed. "I'm not planning to do much work on this trip. This is just an accounting thing so the firm knows where I am and what I'm doing. I was thinking about meeting that reporter, and the firm's supposed to know about all my meetings."

Dawn smiled, shaking her head. "The reporter? You mean the pretty one?"

"Yes, Mom." Sam agreed. "The pretty one who's not an old journalist with a beard."

"Well," Dawn said with approval. "Now that we know your priorities, I'm sure we can make this work. We'll just schedule the sightseeing and trip events around the meetings with your pretty reporter friend. You might end up missing the after-party with my movie star friend Ava Stern. I hear she may be doing one of those Mata Hari dances after all."

"What?" Sam replied. "I wouldn't want to miss that. I mean, culturally, you know. Maybe we could invite Rebecca too? You know, the reporter."

"On a first date?" his mother said, rolling her eyes. "Have I taught you nothing?" she said, smiling back at him.

Sam looked back at his mother, taking another bite of his cornetto pastry.

Dawn turned back to her sketchbook. "If that's your idea of a first date, it's no wonder I don't have any grandchildren yet."

Sam almost choked on his coffee. "Grandchildren? Who said anything about that?"

"Not me," his mother said with a shrug. "I've got plenty to do here already. Not even thinking about the cute, little ones I could be spoiling if you got your act together."

"Well," Sam offered, "maybe your professor could give me some dating tips. Didn't you say he does an 'after dark' tour?"

Dawn nodded. "We should get going. It takes a while to get there, and the scenic route is the best way to go."

About an hour later, Sam and his mother got out their scooters and rode across the island to the Villa Jovis on the northeast point, facing Naples and Mount Vesuvius. They locked up their scooters in the park near the villa and walked the rest of the route until they arrived at the entrance.

"*Ciao*, Ernst!" Dawn shouted out, reaching out to hug the professor. "You look so good! *Wie geht es dir?*" she asked in German. How are you doing?

"*Ciao, bella!*" Professor Lehrer replied. "*Sto bene. E tu?*" I'm well, and you?

"*Molto buona*," Dawn replied. "You remember my son, Sam?" she said, bringing him by the arm to greet the professor.

"*Schön, Sie zu treffen*," Sam said with a handshake and a slight bow. Nice to meet you, sir.

"You speak some German?" the professor said, returning the handshake warmly. "Not what I expected on Capri."

"*Ja, natürlich. Danke für die Tour*," Sam replied. Yes, of course. Thank you for the tour.

Sam looked at the professor, not sure whether he was just a friend of his mother's or if there was something more. Either way, he thought, the professor seemed impressive and trustworthy. He had a German's usual lean and tall physique, with longish salt-and-pepper hair and a neatly trimmed beard. He had a crisp blue linen jacket over a white linen shirt and khaki pants that seemed to suit him.

"Let's get started," the professor said, leading Dawn and Sam toward the ruins of the emperor Tiberius's main villa. "This was the island home of Tiberius, the second emperor of Rome," he said, sweeping his arm across the landscape in front of them. "The most miserable emperor of all, probably. And that's saying a lot. Many of them were deeply unhappy. When he was two years old, Tiberius's father, a great Roman general, allied himself with the rebels Antony and Cleopatra against their rival Octavian, who would become the first Roman emperor, Caesar Augustus. Octavian soon gained the upper hand, and Tiberius's father had to appease him. By then, Octavian had fallen in love with Tiberius's mother, Livia, and had demanded her hand in marriage. Tiberius's father was forced to walk her down the aisle and give away her hand in marriage to Octavian."

"That *Octavian*," Dawn said with disgust. "Always causing problems. No wonder Tiberius was miserable. He got stuck with him as a stepfather?" she asked.

"Yes, exactly," the professor replied. "But later on, there were rumors that Livia had eventually murdered Octavian with poisoned figs."

"I like her already," Dawn said with approval. "Poisoned figs? That's kind of a classy touch. I would have used poisoned dates. But you know I can't stand Octavian. You remember my Broadway show a few years back? *Kiss My Asp*? We won a few Tonys."

"Yes, that was great," Sam said, grinning. "Somehow I always knew you'd make a great Egyptian pharaoh."

"Greek," his mother corrected. "She was Greek. You're right that she was an Egyptian pharaoh, but she was actually Greek."

"Yes, that's right," the professor jumped in. "Cleopatra was a Greek ruler of Egypt. Things weren't so different in those days. Really, a lot like us. Here we have a German professor who teaches in Berlin and works in Naples, with a home on Capri. With beautiful American friends, whose work takes them all over the world. An exquisite Academy Award winner, with a beauty like Cleopatra herself—"

"Oh, Ernst," Dawn interrupted. "You're such a charmer," she said, putting her hand on his forearm as Sam silently groaned.

Ernst gazed at Dawn's emerald eyes. "They lived in a cosmopolitan world like ours," he continued. "There were Greeks, Jews, Nubians, and many other nationalities living in Egypt. It was the same all over the Mediterranean. Different communities sharing the same space. Now, let's go see the ruins," the professor said, holding out his elbow for Dawn to take hold. "You won't believe the stories about Tiberius and his adopted son, Caligula. True Capri legends," he promised.

As they walked up to the ruins, the professor showed Dawn and Sam a color drawing of the villa as it originally stood. Four stories of gleaming white marble perched on a cliff overlooking the blue sea. The ruins only hinted at the villa's former grandeur, but the views across the water to the mainland were certainly spectacular.

"After his mother's marriage to Octavian, young Tiberius was taken from his mother and sent to live with his father," the professor began telling the story again. "He had been adopted by Octavian as part of the arranged marriage, but his stepfather had no use for him. Tiberius was only happy for a while in his younger years. At the age of eighteen, he fell in love with a beautiful fifteen-year-old girl named Vipsania. They married a year later, and Tiberius began a successful career as a lawyer."

"He sounds pretty happy and successful to me," Sam jumped in. "A top lawyer in Rome with his emperor stepfather couldn't have been all bad."

"It only lasted for a while," the professor said with a sigh. "Soon, Octavian decided to marry his spoiled daughter Julia to Tiberius for political reasons, so he ordered him to divorce his beloved Vipsania. His life entirely controlled by his adopted father Octavian since the age of two, Tiberius felt he had no choice but to follow this order, and he left his brokenhearted Vipsania and married his bitter, resentful stepsister Julia.

"Of course, Tiberius's sacrifice brought him no happiness," the professor went on. "In due course, he became the second emperor of Rome after Octavian died, but his heart was not in it, and he accomplished nothing important during his twenty-two-year reign. He was so despondent that after twelve rudderless years as emperor, he retired to Capri at this Villa Jovis—named for the god Jupiter—and left the administrators in Rome to rule in his place. Unfortunately for Rome, Tiberius brought with him his fourteen-year-old nephew and adopted son, who would later be known as the emperor Caligula. According to the rumors of the day, Tiberius exposed the young Caligula to sadistic and bloodthirsty orgies with a mix of willing and unwilling participants, along with displays of disrespect and contempt toward the gods.

"A decade later, when Tiberius died and Caligula became emperor," the professor continued, "Caligula nearly destroyed the empire with his scandalous behavior and delusions of being a god. He called himself the 'New Jupiter,' perhaps remembering the perverse and hubristic excesses at this Villa Jovis. He had the heads of statutes of gods in Rome removed and replaced with his own likeness. Caligula's obsession with being a god led even to a revolt in the east. He ordered the Temple in Jerusalem to be renamed the Temple of the New Jupiter in his own honor, with an enormous bronze statue of himself to be installed in the Temple. As even Caligula was aware, this was the worst possible offense against the Jewish religion and its rule against graven idols.

"The Roman administrators in Judea delayed implementation of this scandalous order but were unable to persuade Caligula to back down," said the professor. "In the year AD 41, a full-scale Roman-Jewish war was avoided only because Caligula was finally murdered in Rome by a group of prominent senators and other opposition leaders. This episode, however, might have contributed to poisoning the relationship between the Roman rulers and the Jewish leadership in Judea," the professor suggested. "At the very least, it undermined the legitimacy of Roman rule in the east, where a highly educated priesthood took matters of religion much more seriously than this new style of self-aggrandizing Roman emperor."

The group stood near the highest point of the ruins, looking across the sea at the volcano Vesuvius to the east. "Such a peaceful place," Sam said after a while. "Maybe these emperors needed to find peace inside themselves too. Otherwise, it all just went to waste."

"*Ja, den Wind jagen*," the professor said, wistfully. He looked at Sam. "Life without love is like chasing the wind."

Sam looked at the professor. "That poem got translated into German too, huh?"

Dawn smiled at Sam. "It sounds like you're interested in poetry these days. Maybe you'll be ready soon to find true love and settle down."

"You never know," Sam said, smiling back. "I think we should be heading back now. I should catch the afternoon ferry and get back to Rome. Maybe catch up with that reporter."

"Sounds good to me," Dawn replied. "Ernst, can you join us for lunch? Maybe you could tell us stories about Tiberius's other eleven villas on Capri."

"*Natürlich*," the professor responded. "Yes, I would be delighted. Sam," the professor said, resting his hand on Sam's shoulder, "I think you'll be interested in the Palazzo a Mare. It was Tiberius's summertime residence on the north shore of Capri. According to Roman tradition, these natural grottoes were the homes of nymphs, who were beautiful young goddesses of the sea. The palazzo was built near one of these grottoes, and according to legend, the most beautiful nymph still swims in the waters on moonlit nights looking for a heroic young man who will conquer her heart."

After their tour of the Villa Jovis, Sam, Dawn, and Ernst had lunch at the Villa Verde off the piazzetta in the historic center of the island. Ernst told them more ancient stories about Capri, and Dawn shared some gossip about more recent scandals involving American actors and artists living on the island.

After lunch, Sam and Dawn thanked Ernst for the tour, and they headed back to Dawn's villa. Sam packed for the trip back to Rome, and he and his mother rode back on their scooters to the ferry landing at the Marina Grande on the north shore.

At the ferry landing, Sam hugged his mother and thanked her for the wonderful stay on her island. They planned to do a call later in the week to finalize the details of their trip but had already decided that they would spend Sunday together sightseeing in Jerusalem. Jason and Steve would be arriving the next day, and Dawn promised that they would all have a good time together.

On the way back to Rome, Sam felt happy with the visit to his mother's place. She could be larger than life, but her heart was always in everything she did. A pretty good way to live, he thought. Pretty amazing that all of those emperors hadn't figured that out. It was like the old man Solomon had said. The simple pleasures of a life well lived are the best we can do. Constantly grasping after more would just bring emptiness.

As the ferry landed in Naples, Sam heard a ping on his phone. He looked down and saw a message back from Rebecca.

> *Hi Sam, so great to hear from you! I'm out and about today and will text you back tonight, if that works. Maybe a call, if you're around. Talk to you soon! Rebecca*

That's *so* Rebecca, Sam smiled. Definitely not tied to her phone. It would be fun to catch up, and it would be wonderful to hear her voice again.

Back at his apartment in Rome, Sam unpacked and began to get ready for bed.

Around 10:00 p.m., Sam heard a ping on his phone. It was a message back from Rebecca.

> *Hi Sam, I wanted to reply earlier, but it's been a busy day. Did you see the news about Wechsler? It seems quite strange and surprising. I'd love to get your thoughts on this. And to hear more about your travel plans. Are you free for a quick call tonight? Interesting to hear we'll be bumping into each other. Cocktails could be fun. I do like martinis. Do you like them dirty too? Rebecca*

Sam gulped. Now he was really distracted. He could imagine Rebecca swimming around in the waters of one of those grottoes.

He tapped Rebecca's number on the phone.

"*Halo?*" Rebecca answered softly.

"Hi, Rebecca, it's Sam," he said. "Just got your message."

"What a nice surprise," Rebecca said warmly. "You're in Rome?"

"Well, I was," Sam replied. "I mean, I am. But now I'm thinking I'd rather be in Tel Aviv. Ordering us a round of martinis. Just the way you like them."

"I don't know what you mean," Rebecca said, laughing. "You seem to have all these ideas about me. I have no idea where you get them."

"Just my imagination running away, probably," Sam said. "Thinking about all sorts of things."

"Well, don't stop thinking," Rebecca said. "It sounds like we may be seeing each other again soon. Maybe you can tell me about some of your ideas in person."

"Count on it," Sam promised. "It would be awesome to see you."

"So, did you see the news about Wechsler?" Rebecca asked. "I think you know that I've been reporting about his story. A good man, really, and he just got caught up in a scandal. I don't quite understand why he would have killed himself, though."

"It doesn't make sense at all," Sam replied. "I'm really just getting started on my piece of the investigation, which so far is pretty small. But none of this rings true to me."

"It's a pretty big scandal," Rebecca said, "and I'm glad you're involved in a piece of it. We can compare notes to some degree. We both have our confidentiality rules, of course, but you know how this works. We can share some general ideas on what's going on, so long as we don't reveal the specifics or our sources. Right?"

"Exactly," Sam agreed. "I work with reporters on my investigations all the time, and the rules make sense. We can exchange some of the basic facts for purposes of my investigation and your reporting. We'll just leave out the who, what, where, and when so we don't violate any confidentiality rules. This makes perfect sense to me."

"That sounds good," Rebecca said. "There's another important thing that we have to talk about too."

Sam wasn't sure what this could be. Rebecca had an impeccable reputation for journalism ethics, and he was a little nervous that she might want to hold off on dating while they both had a project on the same investigation.

"When are you getting here?" Rebecca asked.

Sam exhaled. This was a good sign. "I'll be there on Saturday," he said, relieved. "Do you have any plans?"

"Maybe," Rebecca said softly. "I'm open to changing them for you. Can I let you know tomorrow?"

"Of course," Sam said. "I'll keep Saturday wide open. And, really, pretty much the whole week too. Who needs work when you have beautiful beaches and a gorgeous girl who could lay in the sand next to you?"

"It's January, Sam," Rebecca replied. "I think we'd be pretty chilly at the beach."

"Good point," Sam said, "I did see that in my travel guide. So we'd probably go to the Dead Sea, then, and float around in the salty waters after a mud bath."

"Mmm, you're getting warmer," Rebecca teased. "I like salty water and mud baths."

"Then maybe an evening by the campfire under the desert stars," Sam continued, "with a night or three in one of those Bedouin tents."

"I don't know," Rebecca replied. "It gets cold in the desert at night. I'm not sure how we'd keep warm."

"Well, I'll keep you warm with body heat, of course," Sam replied. "Plus the campfire and maybe some s'mores."

"The body heat and the campfire sound interesting," Rebecca said, "but I don't really know about those s'mores. How about some Krembos and Lieber's Honey Grahams instead? Melted over the campfire?"

"Yes, definitely Krembos," Sam replied, a little bewildered. "That sounds really romantic."

Sam quickly looked up Krembos on his tablet. "Right," he said, "chocolate-coated marshmallow treats definitely go well with a campfire and a sky full of stars."

"Well, now I can't say no," Rebecca teased. "I can't resist a campfire and Krembos. I'll let you know tomorrow about Saturday. And maybe a weekday too? You know, since you'll be here all week?"

"Awesome," Sam said. "I'll keep my schedule flexible, and I can even skip that Mata Hari dance too. I heard she left her seven veils back at the studio, so there might not be much of a show."

"Well, I can lend her my seven-veils costume if that helps," Rebecca offered. "I got a little tired of Zumba and started going to an exotic dance class a while back. It's a really great workout."

Sam stared at the wall blankly. "I'm sure there's a poem for that," he said finally. "I'll have to ask Solomon."

"Solomon?" Rebecca seemed puzzled. "You mean my uncle Solomon in Long Island City?" she joked.

"No, not that one," Sam said with a laugh. "Just a poet I met on my flight. I've got his book and was thinking about getting in touch. He's pretty smart and may have some insights about your dancing lessons. He might be tough to reach, though. He seems to show up only when you're asleep."

"Well, that sounds nice," Rebecca said, a bit puzzled again. "You know, I'm pretty jet lagged and should get to bed."

Sam didn't really want the call to end but understood that Rebecca needed her rest. An award-winning reporter with an exotic-dancing hobby would need plenty of sleep.

"Yes, of course," he said. "Can I call you tomorrow night?"

"That sounds nice," she responded. "Maybe you should call around ten. Nine o'clock your time, right?"

"Nine o'clock it is," Sam agreed. "I'll call you then."

"Perfect, I'll look forward to that," she replied. "Maybe we should actually talk about our investigation then too. I think we forgot about that tonight."

"What investigation?" Sam teased. "Oh, you mean, like our work? Yes, for sure, we should talk about that too."

Sam was quiet for a moment.

"So, good night, then," Rebecca said softly.

"Good night, Rebecca," Sam said, closing his eyes to picture her beauty. "Sweet dreams."

"You too," she said as they both hung up.

Sam looked at the phone and sighed. He glanced at his empty bed and imagined what it would be like to be with her.

There's just something about her, he thought. Some mystery that he wanted to learn. He glanced at his phone again and tapped out a search: What does the name Rebecca mean?

> *Rebecca or Rebekah is a feminine given name originating from the Hebrew language. The name comes from the verb rbq, meaning to "tie firmly." Some sources suggest the name means captivating beauty, or "to tie," to "bind."*

That sounds right, Sam thought. She's captivating.

He thought of the poem. A man's love for a woman. A time for every season.

Just then another ping, though. Sam looked at his phone.

> *Nice chatting with you, Sam. I'll be dreaming about a campfire and a warm tent. And whatever happens next. Sweet dreams!* Rebecca

Sam texted back three red hearts and smiled. Maybe she *was* one of those nymphs.

He closed his eyes and went to sleep. Dreaming of a grotto on Capri. On a moonlit night. He saw her bathing.

6

YOUR EYES SHALL BE OPENED

Sam's alarm rang. He picked up his phone and turned it off. It was Tuesday, and he had set his alarm for 7:00 a.m. He wanted to talk to his friends Jason and Steve before it was too late in their California time zone.

Sam had dreamed all night about that veil dance. Underneath the desert stars and moonlight. With the most beautiful nymph in the grotto. Do deserts have grottos? Probably in Samaria, he thought. It's obviously a magical place where anything is possible.

Sam brewed some coffee and took a quick shower. He was ready to go by the 7:30 a.m. call time.

"Hey, Jason! Hey, Steve!" Sam was happy to talk to them.

"Hey, there!" Jason greeted him back.

"Hi, Sam! How's it going?" Steve joined in.

"Great to talk to you guys," Sam started.

"You bet!" Steve replied.

"Likewise," said Jason, "how's Rome?"

"Still standing," Sam responded. "But I've only been here a few days. Give me a chance," he said, laughing. "So, anyway, I hear you guys are flying out here. Or somewhere around here."

"You got it," said Jason. "Your mom wouldn't take no for an answer. She said something about an exotic dancer and Cleopatra's curse, and I just figured it was easier to say yes."

"Same here, man," Steve jumped in. "Apparently, we're all getting free flights to Israel now and VIP tickets to the Cannes Film Festival this summer. She pulled out all the stops."

"Cool," Sam said. "So we're meeting in Israel? You're getting in Monday afternoon?"

"That's what the tickets say," Steve replied. "We're all staying at some classic hotel in Jerusalem—the American Colony, I think. We're breaking up the schedule a bit. We'll have plenty of time to hang out together, and then Jason and I will go enjoy the beach or someplace fun while you and your mom visit her usual temples and shrines."

"Sounds like old times," Sam said. "You guys have all the fun while I'm getting all enlightened. But there is a twist this time. You remember that reporter I told you about? You know, from the conference in New York?"

"You mean the gorgeous one that you couldn't stop talking about for weeks after you met her?" Jason said, laughing. "How could I forget? I mean, I could have tried, but you kept talking about how she's so smart and talented and all that."

"Yes, she's really kind of perfect," Sam reminded him. "Besides, it's partially just a work thing. I'll need to peel off and meet her to cover some things on an investigation I'm doing here."

"Well," Steve joined in, "it sounds like you might miss that DJ event we were going to do for your birthday. You know what happens when you get distracted by a new girl."

"Sounds like fun," Sam replied. "But you guys already did something for my birthday. Remember that bronze scroll exhibit at the Getty a few weeks ago? Which, by the way, I wanted to mention."

"I think I know where this is headed," Steve said with a sigh. "Sam. Girl. Investigation."

"I know, we've lost him, haven't we?" Jason joined in. "He can't resist a good mystery. Especially if there's a woman involved."

"So, what does she look like?" Steve asked.

"Beautiful," Sam replied. "Tall, athletic, reddish-brown hair, the nicest curves I've ever seen. Or not seen, really," he said longingly. "Just thinking about them."

"Apparently," Jason said. "Steve, it sounds like a good thing we're flying out there. We can meet this new girl before Sam runs off and marries her. We'll want to make sure she's right for our Sam."

"You mean like that actress that Steve met last year?" Sam smiled. "What was her name, Irina?"

"Right," Jason jumped in. "Not a great match. She played a psychic in some movie sequel. *The Curse of the Empty Skull* or something like that. The skull was supposed to make her magically smart. But somehow it backfired."

"Yes," Steve joined in. "I thought she was really smart and creative at first. But then I realized that all that talk about alien beings, telepathy, and Mayan code words was just from the movie."

"I know," Sam agreed, "none of that ever made sense to me. But I hear the next one in the series is supposed to be really good."

"I've heard that too," Jason replied. "I just hope they get that part about the lost city of Tanis figured out. That didn't work for us at all in our Cleopatra project back in school."

"Don't remind me," Steve groaned. "You won't find any treasures there. Nothing but sand and snakes. So, anyway, back to the bronze scroll. You remember? The eighteen tons of *real* treasures? I've been figuring it out, and I really think we can do something with this."

"It depends," Steve shot back. "Does it come with a curse? Gold and silver won't do much good if you're eaten by mummies or snakes."

Jason laughed. "I don't think mummies eat people. They actually don't really do much. I'd be more worried about some sort of demon haunting us for stealing buried treasure. There are some pretty scary demons in the Bible and the Quran, and I wouldn't want them showing up in *my* dreams."

"Tell me about it," Sam agreed. "*Anything* can happen in a dream. There's nothing more frightening than that. So, since it sounds like you've agreed to help me, I have some assignments. You know that's how investigations work. Divide and conquer, just like the Romans did. Jason, you're in charge of the religion side, since you studied that in college and know all about the Bible and the Quran. Steve, you'll do the history parts, since that was your major and you can figure out all the Roman-Jewish stories that we'll need to know to figure this out. I'll send a list of the research that I think we'll need to do, along with some timetables for putting this all together during our trip. Remember, there are eighteen tons of gold and silver waiting for us—along with some mummies, snakes, and demons, apparently. We'll want to do this right. Any questions?"

"Yes," Steve replied. "What are *you* doing? I mean, aside from chasing some gorgeous reporter girl with green eyes who looks great in a bikini? I didn't hear anything about *your* role."

"Well, I'm the classics major, remember?" Sam responded. "So I'll work on figuring out the ancient stories and legends that might solve these mysteries. We've got sixty treasure locations to figure out. In the end, everything's a story, and we may have sixty different ones to piece together."

"That sounds fair," Steve responded. "But how do we divide up the treasures?" he said, jokingly.

"Obviously," Jason said, "I'll take the gold. Steve, you take the silver. And, Sam, you get whatever else is there. A few scrolls and a dusty old box, from the sound of it."

Sam was impressed. "Jason, you've been reading about the bronze scroll, huh?"

"Me too," Steve jumped in, "it gets pretty interesting once you get past the indecipherable Hebrew script, the random Greek letters and all the treasures hidden at this place Kohlit that doesn't seem to exist. I don't think that me getting just the silver is all that fair, though. Didn't you notice that the treasure locations with silver are mostly just small amounts? I think whoever had that silver wasn't really wealthy enough to be hiding treasure. Besides, it wouldn't be fair to leave Sam with just a dusty old box. Unless there's something valuable in it, of course. What would you find hidden in a box from two thousand years ago?"

"Well, I'm guessing that whatever's in an ancient box like that would be at least that old too," Sam said, laughing. "Maybe just dust at this point. Anyway, we're really just doing this for fun. I can look into the law over there. But generally buried treasures belong to the government."

"Oh, no wonder no one's found any treasures," Jason said, laughing back. "Whoever finds them can get cursed, while everything valuable ends up in a museum?"

"That sounds about right," Sam replied. "But we would at least have the satisfaction of knowing that something lost was returned to its rightful owner."

"Sounds fair," Steve said. "I wouldn't even dream about keeping any of those gold bars. I really don't have room in my place for eighteen tons of gold."

"All right, then," Sam said as everyone was ready to go. "See you guys in Jerusalem on Monday."

"Great, next Monday in Jerusalem, then," Steve said, thinking his paraphrasing of an old prayer was clever.

"Um, no," Sam jumped in. "That really doesn't sound good. Let's be careful about how we use old prayers. You guys are going to be on your best behavior, right?" Sam asked, a little worried.

"What?" Steve asked. "We're just some friendly Americans traveling abroad. The rest of the world already understands that we're clueless about their local customs and traditions. They really don't expect much."

"That may be true," Sam said, "but we could still aim a little higher. Some people think that America's been a little embarrassing lately, and maybe it's time to start repairing the damage."

"You got it," Steve promised.

"Good," Sam replied. "Now, just remember you'll be meeting a girl who's really special to me. No tasteless humor or really anything else that clueless American travelers would do. Definitely no Aloha shirts or plaid or anything else you might see on a golf course."

"You bet," Jason promised. "See you guys on Monday!"

"*Hasta la* Monday," Steve said, signing off.

"Catch you then," Sam said, hanging up.

Sam exhaled. He loved his friends but was still a little nervous. At least they'd be busy with their treasure assignments, he thought. Better keep it that way so they'll stay out of trouble.

What did Mark Twain say about Americans traveling abroad? Sam was getting late for work, but he looked it up on his phone anyway. Maybe it would help keep Jason and Steve in line.

> *The gentle reader will never, never know what a consummate ass he can become until he goes abroad. —Mark Twain, The Innocents Abroad*

Well put, Sam thought as he headed out the door. Perhaps this time would be different.

Steve was right about most of the treasure locations with silver, Sam thought. Almost half of the sixty treasure sites—twenty-seven to be exact—had only small amounts of silver. Why would a treasure map have so much effort spent on such small treasures? Must be part of the story, Sam assumed. He just hadn't figured it out yet.

Sam checked his phone for messages before heading over to the Borghese Gardens to go running. He hadn't gotten any outdoor exercise on the trip yet, and he was looking forward to clearing his head. He noticed a new message from his mom.

> *Hi Sam, so lovely to see you over the weekend! Just a reminder that your private tour of the Vatican Museums is set for 1 pm today. My friend Dr. Pomeroy will meet you at the visitor entrance. Don't forget to dress nice! They're pretty old school there. Have fun! Love, Mom*

Sam laughed. He couldn't remember a time when his mom *wasn't* setting him up with these little projects. The summer solstice at Stonehenge. Yoga classes in Rishikesh. A private audience with the Dalai Lama. She never seemed to run out of ideas for his spiritual improvement.

He couldn't wait to meet this Dr. Pomeroy. If she works at the Vatican, she's probably a cross between a cloistered nun and an ancient librarian. He texted back:

> *Hi Mom, thanks for setting that up. I'll be there on time, with a nice shirt and nonripped pants. Thanks again for the wonderful weekend! Looking forward to our trip to Israel next week! Love, Sam*

After running in the gardens, Sam went back to his apartment and got ready for his afternoon at the Vatican Museums. He stopped for a *porchetta* panino with a *limonata* for lunch near the Trevi Fountain and checked his messages again.

Sam read through some of the New Year's messages from friends and colleagues. A friendly greeting from Richard Delacourt, the law firm's managing partner. An even nicer one from Mackenzie Walker, that new attorney in the Texas office whom he'd been working with on the offshore lease corruption scandal. He had been dazzled by the work she was doing, and some of the partners said she was the brightest attorney they had ever met. It was only later that he found out she was beautiful too, after being teased for sending her so much work.

He really didn't mind the teasing. The legal work needed to get done, after all, and she was the best junior attorney in the firm. Maybe they would meet one day, and he could see for himself if the rumors about her tanned, athletic beauty were true. It wasn't really a distraction, he thought, and somehow he sensed that they would be teaming up on something even bigger soon.

After checking the rest of his messages, Sam headed out for the Vatican Museums. Taking the scenic route through some side streets, he arrived at the visitor entrance promptly at 1:00 p.m.

"Sam?" he heard his name. He saw a young woman approach. Must be Dr. Pomeroy's assistant, he thought. Long blond hair, sky-blue eyes, and a dazzling smile—what was *she* doing here?

"You must be Sam," she said, taking his hand. "I'm Juliette Pomeroy. A friend of your mother."

"Right," Sam said, still a bit confused. "I'm Sam Romero. But I guess you already knew that," he said, raising his eyebrow. "You're Dr. Pomeroy?"

"I sure am. Just call me Juliette, though," she flirted.

"Nice to meet you. I was expecting someone more Vatican-ish," he flirted back.

"I know what you mean," she said with a laugh. "I'm on staff here. More on the academic side, really. It does confuse people sometimes. Do you want to see the museums?" she asked, waving at the hall behind her.

"Yes, of course, thank you," Sam said, walking beside her. "It sounds a little intimidating. How many museums does the Vatican have?"

"There were fifty-four galleries here at last count," she replied. "But sometimes we lose track of them. I still get lost sometimes. Let's head over this way," Juliette said, waving Sam toward the first gallery. "The Egyptian galleries are spectacular!"

Sam followed her through the magnificent halls toward the first set of galleries. She looked enticing in her lipstick-red dress. "How do you know my mom?" he asked.

"She was one of my professors at knight school," Juliette replied. "My favorite, really. She knows history and religion like the back of her hand."

"Tell me about it," Sam said, shaking his head. "I don't remember her teaching night school, though. The only class I remember her teaching was that film class at USC."

"Just knight school in Athens," she said with a smile. "Not really accredited. More for personal use."

"I'll have to ask her about it," Sam said as they walked into the first Egyptian gallery.

"Just look at this exquisite artistry," Juliette said, pointing to one of the stone tablets with carved Egyptian figures and hieroglyphics. "Much of our collection came from the ancient Romans. They loved Egyptian artworks and brought them over by the ton. So expressive and mysterious. Roman art was often beautiful, but there's nothing like the mystical style of the east."

They walked through most of the other eight Egyptian galleries, heading toward the ancient Roman halls. When they arrived, Juliette showed Sam the noble face of Julius Caesar in white marble.

"This was made not long after his murder in the senate," she said. "The end of the Republic. His last name—pronounced 'kai-zer,' by the way, and not 'see-zer'—became synonymous with the title of emperor after his death. According to legend, Julius was part god, an heir to the goddess Venus. Julius held virtually every position of honor imaginable in ancient Rome. He served as high priest of the Roman religion, commander of the army, head of the courts, chairman of the senate, and, finally, dictator—the absolute ruler of Rome.

"He was the bravest Roman ruler of all," Juliette said as they stood before Caesar's marble face. "When he was captured by pirates as a young man, the pirates demanded a ransom of twenty talents of silver from the Roman army. Julius scoffed and insisted that they demand *fifty* talents. He was worth no less, he assured them. Julius promised the pirates that he would return after being ransomed and personally have each of them killed. Sure enough, after his release, Julius gathered a fleet and chased the pirates across the sea. He captured them, and they were all promptly executed under his order."

"*Et tu*, Julius?" Sam joked, looking at Caesar's white marble face. "That's what he said when he was murdered, right?"

"That's the Shakespeare version," Juliette said, smiling. "Most historians say that Julius died silently. But it's generally agreed that he was courageous to the end. He was a magnificent man—a lover of Cleopatra, a ferocious fighter, and a visionary leader. He organized a professional police force, built canals and libraries, reformed the tax laws, and even modernized the calendar."

"Juliette," Sam said, looking puzzled. "From what I understand, most of the early Roman emperors were truly awful people. Murderers, sadists, fearful and cruel tyrants. What happened?"

"It's Lord Acton's rule," Juliette replied. "You know, 'power tends to corrupt, and absolute power corrupts absolutely.' It just takes a generation or two for power to ruin a family. The first generation can be noble and selfless. By the second or third generation, the heirs are thieving, scheming cowards. They didn't earn their position and have no idea how to live without it. Pretty precarious and scary, really. Let's head over here," Juliette said, motioning Sam toward the New Wing with a long gallery filled with statues. "You're right that so many of these emperors were absolutely despicable."

They stopped in front of the famous statue of Caesar Augustus with his right arm raised in a salute. "That's *him*, Octavian," Sam said, shaking his head. "My mom can't stand him. She played Cleopatra in one of her movies, and she really grew to dislike him."

"Definitely not a Julius Caesar," Juliette said, nodding her head. "Not a Caligula or Nero either, but certainly not a hero. Born Gaius Octavius, he changed his name to *Imperator Caesar Divi Filius Augustus*. Which means 'Emperor Caesar Son of God the Magnificent.' No issues there," she said sarcastically.

"Did he build any libraries or canals?" Sam asked with a smile.

"Well, he built a lot of roads, some fire departments, and an early version of the postal service," Juliette replied. "All of which he proclaimed 'magnificent,' of course. But basically he finished off what was left of the Republic and created a dynastic empire, for better or worse. Mostly worse."

"No wonder most of his successors were so awful," Sam said, shaking his head. "Greatness inspires envy, right?"

"You read Harry Potter as a child too, huh?" Juliette smiled.

"Just that *Half-Blood* one," Sam replied. "I thought the idea of inherited supernatural powers was kind of interesting. But I got a little lost after reading about the flying broomsticks."

"Yes, Roman emperors who became gods after they died was much more realistic," Juliette agreed.

As they walked through the statues, Sam thought of the Arch of Titus and the stories he had heard about the stolen treasures of the Jerusalem Temple. "Is it true that some of the Jewish treasures stolen by the ancient Romans ended up here?" he asked. "You know, the golden menorah lamp that's shown on the Arch of Titus? I read that it's rumored to have ended up here at the Vatican."

"Well, I haven't bumped into it yet," Juliette said as she twisted a lock of her blond hair. "I'll let you know if I see it. There are lots of controversies in the antiquities world about what might have been stolen. It's not just the Jewish treasures."

"Makes sense," Sam agreed. "It just seems a little unusual for the thieves to build a triumphal arch as a monument to their thieving. I guess you could call it chutzpah. Pretty obnoxious."

Juliette continued with her private tour. She showed Sam the most interesting galleries and told him many of the stories about the artists and their ideas and the thousands of years of history present here.

As they got to the end of the tour—the magnificent Sistine Chapel—Sam looked up at the ceiling. It was breathtaking.

Juliette sighed. "Four years of painting, and he was really more of a sculptor than a painter. He thought that it was too big of a project, but somehow he couldn't resist it. Michelangelo was supposed to paint the twelve disciples. But he insisted on his artistic freedom. Instead, he painted the seven days of the world's creation—with the hands of the divine and man almost touching. He surrounded this central masterpiece of creation with images of sensuous male and female bodies as powerful expressions of the human soul. The divine and man, joined together, yet somehow separated. The feeling of presence and peace. But also a sense of loss and yearning. What it means to be human, I think."

"Pure magic," Sam agreed. "The whole universe in one ceiling. Every thought and feeling. He captured it all."

She smiled. "He was a great artist and also a very educated and spiritual man. His works are not only beautiful but full of details that have meaning and insights."

"Like what?" he asked.

"Do you see the tree in the Garden of Eden?" she asked, pointing at that part of the ceiling.

"Yes, is that Adam and Eve with the serpent?" he asked, looking up.

"Exactly," she said, leaning closer. "And you can see that it's a fig tree, not an apple tree."

"I do see that," Sam said, noticing her sweet perfume. "Figs are really more delicious. Is that why he painted it this way?"

"Actually, we think he researched what kind of tree it was," Juliette explained. "In the biblical text, it's just described as a fruit tree. But there's a tradition in Judaism that it was a fig tree. It was only later in medieval times that the tradition developed about it being an apple tree. Michelangelo was a very spiritual man and must have learned this in his studies."

"Very interesting," Sam said, "and I like how you described that. At first, I was a little worried about coming here. The Vatican has a reputation as being a little preachy, you know. God this and God that."

"I know what you mean," Juliette said. "If you didn't grow up Catholic, all that *Dominus Christi* and *Ave Maria* business can feel a little heavy."

"Right, and I'm sure this is true in all religions, but sometimes you hear the dogma louder than the spirit," he said. "Even the word *God* can seem so loaded and heavy. Maybe that's why his name is used so sparingly in the Jewish tradition. I read that it was supposed to be used only in the Temple back in the day, and for the most part, it wasn't used at all after the Temple was destroyed."

"Maybe there's something to that tradition," she said, nodding. "His name gets used a lot in our world. Pretty often as a curse or obscenity, right?"

"Exactly, and the language we use is probably more important than we think," he agreed. "I sometimes wonder if we'd be better off if we stopped using the G-word for a while. I've started saying *the divine* or *spirit* or even *universe* instead. Somehow it feels a little more relatable and approachable."

"That makes sense to me," Juliette said. "I'm sure there are people who will get offended, but that's always the case with religion, right? You could say 'source energy,' for all I care, although I've never understood what that means. I don't really feel like the Creator is something you plug a toaster into. But I do think it's good to think about our language, especially when we're talking about the divine."

"Not to mention the translation issues," Sam agreed. "I read that people today aren't even sure how the name should be translated. The ancient Hebrew script didn't have vowels, so the name was spelled Y-H-W-H with just the consonants. Depending on which vowels you add and where, you can end up with lots of different translations."

"That almost sounds dangerous," Juliette said with a smile. "If you get the name wrong, you might get hit with a thunderbolt or something, right?"

"Yes, maybe if Yahoo! had chosen a better name, they'd be bigger than Google now," he said. "You just never know."

At the exit, Sam thanked Juliette for the wonderful tour. It was so inspiring, and he would remember everything.

"Any plans for dinner?" Juliette asked Sam. "I'm supposed to be somewhere, but I could move things around. You're only in Rome for a short while?"

Sam blushed and felt hot. So tempting, and he had been noticing her slender figure and seductive glances. But he would be calling Rebecca later.

"I'd love to," Sam replied, "but I actually have to work tonight. A few projects, and I have to call a reporter."

"Is she pretty?" Juliette smiled.

"What?" Sam replied, confused for a moment. "Oh, the reporter. Yes, actually, beyond pretty. I mean, every woman's a work of art," he said, noticing Juliette's alluring blond hair and enticing red lips. "But some have that extra spark of the divine. You know, the way it feels in that chapel in there," he said, pointing back at Michelangelo's masterpiece.

"Your mom told me you'd be busy." Juliette shrugged with a smile. "She said something about grandchildren, but I really didn't follow it. Anyway, it was really nice to meet you. If you want to meet up sometime, you know how to find me. The quiet gallery in the back. You know, with Aphrodite and Venus," she said, biting her lip softly.

"I won't forget," Sam promised, leaning in for a hug. "Just divine."

Sam turned and began walking toward the plaza, waving back at Juliette as she went back inside.

He walked through Vatican Square, looking back at the Basilica bathed in the golden light of sunset. It's so inspiring here, he thought, that you could even get lost. So much beauty.

But, more than that, a feeling. The hands of the divine and man almost touching. He focused on that, walking back toward his apartment in the soft evening light.

Back at his apartment, Sam checked his messages and did a little work on his bronze scroll assignment. Then he went out for dinner near the piazza. Roman-style pizza, an *insalata mista*, and a glass of Barbera.

After dinner, Sam arrived back at the apartment. He checked the time again. It was 8:45 p.m. Fifteen minutes until the time for Rebecca's call. Not that he was counting. Sam knew he was too cool for that. He obviously wasn't going to call her right at 9:00 p.m. either. He might come across as too interested. No, he would wait until at least 9:02 p.m.

He started looking at some of the online travel guides for Israel. Tel Aviv was about an hour from Jerusalem, he noticed. How convenient, he thought. Driving an hour for a date in LA was pretty normal. Not even close to the limit, really. Most Angelenos wouldn't cross the line to Orange County, of course, and the Inland Empire was unthinkable. But Tel Aviv? It sounded just perfect.

Sam heard a ping. It was 9:05 p.m. He looked at his text messages. It was Rebecca.

Hi Sam, just running a few minutes behind. Getting out of the bath now. Rebecca

Well, *that's* distracting, Sam thought. Pleasantly distracting, for sure. He pictured her with a big, fluffy white towel. Wrapped around her curvy, toned body. Probably less tanned than in November Unless that's her natural tone. Hard to know at this point. You'd have to see the tan lines, really.

Sam's phone rang at 9:25 p.m. It was Rebecca.

"Hi, Rebecca," Sam answered.

"Hey, there, how's it going?" she asked brightly. She seemed pretty cheerful and must have had a good day.

"Really good," Sam said. "It was my last day of Christmas break, really. I'll go back into the office for a half day tomorrow."

"Nice," Rebecca said. "Then I think another holiday starts tomorrow night, right? They have a lot of those in Rome," she said, laughing. "Not like in Israel, where we work six days a week. Will you get out and do anything special for the holiday?"

"I was thinking about seeing some of the parades and parties for the witch and the Wise Men," Sam replied.

"I must have missed that story," Rebecca said, laughing again. "The witch and the Wise Men? Something from the Bible, maybe?"

"Partially, I think," Sam replied. "Not the witch part, though. She came along later, on a broomstick with some magic cookies and holiday presents. Maybe some gold bars."

"Sounds pretty Roman to me," Rebecca said. "So, do you want to hear some news about Wechsler?"

"Of course," Sam responded. "What did you find out?"

"This won't be in the newspaper for another day or two," she said. "But apparently Wechsler had been issuing land development permits all over the country, well outside his assigned areas in Jerusalem and Tel Aviv. This was really risky for him, as there's an annual audit done each summer that would catch something like that. He had worked there for twenty-six years and was risking his whole career—retirement and everything. You just don't usually see government workers taking such big chances," Rebecca said. "What would make him do that?"

"Well, I may be making some progress on that," Sam replied. "I can't say anything right now, but once I confirm it's not directly related to my client, I think I can share some of this information. Keep in mind that it's background only. Not quite kosher, so nothing that could be used in the paper."

"Sam?" Rebecca pushed back a bit. "You know what the rules are. I hope you're not taking chances with this investigation. You know me, I like to do things the kosher way," she said, smiling.

"I hear you," Sam said, "and I'm being careful. Law firms have all sorts of rules too, and it's all about who, what, when, and where you do things. Can you tell me some of the locations where Wechsler issued permits?"

"To some degree, yes," Rebecca replied. "Under journalism rules, you could be considered a source, and I'm allowed to share certain things with you if they'll help move the story forward. I don't have all the details yet, but apparently Wechsler issued several land permits in the Jerusalem area and then a few more in the West Bank and northern Israel. Something like this would definitely have been detected in the annual audit, and he would have been fired."

"Poor guy," Sam said. "Looks like he was really in over his head. I'm working on tracking down the money trail. That's usually the best way to figure these things out."

"Tell me about it," Rebecca agreed. "Follow the money. That's often where you'll find the story. So, you're still arriving here on Saturday?"

"Yes, I have a morning flight and should be at the hotel by midafternoon," Sam replied. "How about dinner or a campfire on Saturday night?"

"Hmm, tempting," Rebecca said with a sigh. "Maybe with some Krembos?"

"Yes, of course," Sam replied, quickly looking up this mysterious Israeli tradition on his tablet. "Right, that actually looks pretty delicious. Do you prefer the dark or milk chocolate flavor?"

"Dark chocolate, of course," Rebecca replied. "Intense is always better, don't you think?"

"That's what I always say," Sam agreed. "So, it's a date? Saturday night at seven?"

"A *date*?" Rebecca teased. "Were we talking about a date? You mean, like, with flirting and maybe a risqué text message or two? I thought we were just talking about meeting for the investigation."

"I haven't seen any risqué text messages," Sam teased, "so I don't know what you mean. Just something about cocktail recipes. If we were sending risqué messages, it would be more about what color lingerie you have or where your favorite nude beach is."

"Exactly," she replied. "Nothing like that going on here."

"So, you're getting ready for bed?" Sam asked.

"Yes, I'm pretty tired," she said, "and there's no holiday here tomorrow. I should ring off now."

"Right," Sam said, "get lots of rest, and I'll be working on those plans for the investigative meeting on Saturday. You like pasta?"

"Only a lot," she replied. "That could be a good choice."

"Great. Well, good night," Sam said.

"Good night, Sam," Rebecca said as they hung up.

Yes, Saturday night! This will be wonderful, Sam thought, starting to browse through the restaurant listings in Jerusalem and Tel Aviv. Plenty of pasta options.

Sam heard his phone ping. He picked it up to read the message.

> *Hey, Sam, just climbing into bed now. Wearing some black and skimpy things. And remembering that beach on Ibiza. Tan lines can be such a distraction. Nite! Rebecca*

Yes, definitely a distraction, he thought. She was in his head now, for sure. He texted back.

> *My favorite beach too. I think I saw you there, with one of those fruit cups the vendors sell. Really nice cantaloupes and cherries. And black is my favorite. It's easier to find the little silver hooks that way. Sweet dreams! Sam*

Sam put his phone away and turned in for the night. His bed seemed really empty. But somehow he didn't feel alone. He closed his eyes and pictured her swimming on Ibiza.

7

TO MAKE ONE WISE

Sam woke up with the sound of gentle surf on a small island in his head. And a tanned, slender woman in a black bikini. Or was that lingerie?

Sam shook off the night's sleep and began to focus. It was Wednesday. Three more days in Rome before the flight to Israel. Where Rebecca lived.

Another holiday starting today. Epiphany Eve in Rome. He was glad he had committed to a half-day work schedule for January. Some more time off after last year's marathon is just the right thing, he thought.

Sam got up and showered and dressed. He was interested to see his firm's Rome office. He had talked to the secretary he would be working with, Carmella Santos. She was very nice, and it sounded like the office would be a pretty relaxing place to stay caught up on work while he caught his breath from last year.

Sam's phone rang as he walked through the Piazza Navona on the way to his firm's office in Monti, a fifteen-minute walk away. He was enjoying the fresh, cool January air.

"Hey, Donovan!" Sam answered the phone.

"Hi, Sam, how's it going?" Donovan asked.

"Really good," Sam replied. "I'm just headed to work now. Going in a little late and leaving early. Sticking to the plans. Are you back in LA now?"

"I flew back yesterday," Donovan told him. "It feels good to see the air again."

Sam laughed. "When you put it that way, maybe I'll add another month to my stay here."

"So, I'm calling to ask you a favor," Donovan said.

"Yes, what's up?" Sam asked.

"I have a client who's in Rome with a small legal issue that my firm doesn't handle," Donovan explained. "You know we're trial lawyers here, and we don't do investigations or insurance things."

"No problem," Sam said. "I don't do the insurance side, but we'll see if we can help your client. Are they having a problem or just want to avoid one?"

"Both, I think," Donovan replied. "It's actually about that bronze scroll you told me about."

"What, really?" Sam was surprised. "That's a pretty huge coincidence. How did *that* come up?"

"Right, it was really unplanned and just came up in our conversation," Donovan said. "It's an international conglomerate with a subsidiary building commercial properties and housing developments in Israel. I had mentioned your bronze scroll to the CEO, and he really jumped on it. The CEO—his name is Roy Griffin—said that he knew all about the scroll, except that he referred to it as copper. He said they were looking to expand their marketing, and he thought that a sponsorship of the traveling scroll exhibit would be ideal. He just needed a legal team to review the contract, the transportation and security deals, and the insurance coverage to make sure they didn't do anything wrong. I told him I thought that an investigations attorney could help him spot all the risk and issues and that you're the best in the business. I figured your firm's transactional attorneys could handle all the contract terms but that the most important piece would be figuring out what could go wrong so those things could be prevented."

"Sounds great," Sam responded. "I'll be at the office soon. Just send me his information, and we'll get right on it."

"Thanks, Sam. He's a good client, and I know you'll take care of him," Donovan said.

"Got it," Sam replied. "I'll call him myself today. How's that?"

"Awesome, and I think you guys will hit it off," Donovan said. "He collects antiquities as a hobby, and he's supposed to have a pretty good collection. Maybe you guys can catch up on Cleopatra or something."

"I'll let you know," Sam said. "Catch you later."

"Bye, Sam," Donovan said as he hung up.

Sam put his phone in his pocket, thinking the call was a little strange. But it was sometimes like that with Donovan. Just a little off sometimes. Sam was fine doing him a favor, and it would be interesting to see what that CEO had to say about the scroll.

Sam arrived at his office. "Arrivederci!" he greeted the pretty brunette receptionist.

"Signor Romero?" she inquired.

"Yes, hi, I'm Sam from the LA office," he confirmed. "I just got in the other day, and I'll be working from here off and on for a few weeks. I think you've got a guest office or a spare one I can use. Can you show me where to go?"

"Of course," the receptionist Flora d'Angelo replied. "We've been waiting for you. I'll show you right there."

Flora brought Sam to the large corner office of the local managing partner, Aldo Armani. Nice, Sam thought, taking in the view of St. Peter's and the city of seven hills around it.

"*Buongiorno,* Signor Romero." The secretary Carmella walked into the office. "*Felice anno nuovo*! Did you have a nice holiday weekend?"

"Yes, it was a great weekend. Happy New Year to you too! I got to spend some time with my mom and do some sightseeing too. It was very nice. How about you?"

"Very nice," Carmella replied. "It's one of my favorite holidays. My husband and I went to a concert on Saturday, and we saw the fireworks in the city on Friday night. Just magic."

"Thank you for the nice office," Sam said, waving his arm at the nice view.

"Yes, of course," Carmella said. "Signor Armani is vacationing in the Alps and won't be back until next week. It's all yours until then."

"Perfect," Sam said, "I've had a change of plans and will actually be in Israel next week. So this works out well. I've got a new client to send you this morning too. I'll call the CEO this morning, and we'll just need to do the conflicts check and set up the file."

"Yes, of course," she replied. "Anything else?"

"I can't think of anything," he said. "Just a reminder that I'll probably just be working here in the mornings. Last year was really busy, and I made some promises to slow down before the next big case comes in."

"*Sì, la dolce vita*," Carmella said with a smile. "You're in Rome now. You should be out enjoying yourself. Have you made plans for the holiday that starts tonight?"

"Another holiday?" Sam laughed. "This definitely is not LA. Yes, of course, Epiphany, right?"

"Yes, Sam," she said. "The office is actually closed tomorrow, but we can get you an after-hours pass if you'll be working. But I suggest going out and having a good time. You might pick up the habit."

Carmella walked to the door and looked back at Sam. "Flora can help you with any reservations or sightseeing information. It'll be quite a party out there tonight and tomorrow. Go enjoy."

Good idea, Sam thought. He remembered spending this holiday here in Rome a few times as a child, when his mother had a home near the Villa Borghese here. It was a celebration of the Wise Men from the east. For whatever reason, it was one of his mother's favorite holidays. He put out his shoes at night, and the next day they were filled with special cookies and "sweet coal" candy left by the Epiphany witch known as *la Befana.*

Sam remembered that the Christmas when he turned six years old, his mother had insisted on an "authentic" Roman Christmas and actually refused to let him open his presents until this holiday on the sixth of January. He had really missed LA that year, and it was a good thing that she at least let him open his Christmas birthday presents. Apparently, the Epiphany witch didn't have jurisdiction over a Christmas child's birthday presents.

Shifting to a work focus—if that was at all possible in festive Rome—Sam logged into his remote access at Signor Armani's desk computer and began checking his emails. He spotted Donovan's email and forwarded it to Carmella.

Hi Sam, here's Roy's information. I really appreciate your helping out on this. Ciao! Donovan

From: donovan@hunterlockhart.com
Sent: Wednesday, January 5, 2022 9:47 a.m.
To: sromero@faustprice.com
Subject: FW: Contract review

Hi Donovan, thanks again for the referral on the Copper Scroll project. As discussed, this opportunity came up on short notice, and we'd like to move quickly. Please ask your son to feel free and call me without going through my staff or putting it on the calendar. I'm handling this personally. Happy New Year, and talk to you soon! Roy

Sincerely,

Roy Griffin III
Chief Executive Officer
Eden Holdings, Ltd.
25 Old Broad St.

London, EC2N 1HN
+44 020 7000 1000
roy.griffin@edenholdings.com

Sam picked up the phone and dialed the CEO's number. A British receptionist answered and said that Mr. Griffin was expecting his call and that she would transfer it right away.

"Sam?" answered the voice of an older man with a faded New Jersey accent. "Nice to meet you. How are you doing?" he asked with the slight lilt of the Turnpike State.

"Pleased to meet you too, Mr. Griffin," Sam answered. "I'm doing good. I hear you need some contract review and troubleshooting. We just cleared the conflicts, so let's see if we can help you."

"All right, but call me Roy," he replied. "Donovan and I go way back. He's told me a lot about you, and I'm so glad that we'll get your personal touch on this. This is pretty important for us. We've got to do it right."

"You got it," Sam responded. "So, you're sponsoring part of the Copper Scroll tour? The traveling exhibit of this ancient treasure map? Which is actually bronze, you know."

"Donovan told me you'd say that," Roy responded.

"Just reading you the fine print," Sam said. "This thing is one percent tin, so that makes it bronze. Usually, bronze is at least ten percent tin. It has to do with the alloy performance. So someone back in the day may have thought it important for the treasure map to be bronze instead of copper, for purely symbolic reasons. Adding one percent tin wouldn't do anything for how the alloy would perform. I think they just wanted to call it bronze and were just a little short on tin. At least that's my guess."

"Interesting theory," Roy replied. "If that's true, it's a little ironic that everyone calls it the Copper Scroll today. The idea that it was bronze seems to have just gotten lost. But what's the difference as a symbol anyway?"

"That's what I'm trying to figure out," Sam responded. "Everything about this treasure map is a mystery. Kind of like some of my cases. Nothing makes sense until it all does. Do you remember the Indian Goddess Stones pyramid scheme a few years ago? I can't tell you anything confidential. But we all thought that a forty percent annual return on Indian Goddess Stones was suspicious. We just couldn't prove it until we learned that the stones had been stolen from a shrine, with the same stones sold over and over to different investors. That's how it goes. You just have to figure out the story. That's the key to piecing the puzzle together."

"That makes sense," Roy responded. "Do you think you can really figure this out? Are you making progress?"

"Yes and no," Sam said. "You don't really know until you reach the end. Knowing ninety percent of the story won't get you there. The ten percent you don't know will kill you. I've learned to be thorough and complete in my investigations. I just don't prejudge things until we get there. But, really, it's a little hard to decipher this thing without being able to see it close up and in person."

"What do you mean?" Roy asked.

"The linguists and other scholars who've studied the bronze scroll have gotten stuck on some of the nuances in the script and whether certain marks were intended or just accidental," Sam explained. "If I could see the scroll in person and look at it more closely, I think I could figure more of it out."

"Interesting," Roy noted. "Maybe we can set something up."

"Well, I'm a little busy for that right now," Sam replied. "But, sure, at some point, I'd love to look at it more closely."

"Everything's all about the timing," Roy said. "Life often makes these choices for us. Not the other way around. So no hints on what you've found so far? Have you struck any gold?"

"No hints," Sam said. "It just wouldn't be responsible. People can get injured or worse going out and looking for things they don't understand. Some of these places could be sensitive too. There are quite a few political actors there that would get involved."

"I see," Roy said, trying to keep the conversation going. "So you think that a round of conspicuous activity around these sites might cause some rioting? Disturbances and a pretty big mess?"

"I really don't know about that," Sam said. "I've been working on this for fun and not as a work project. At least until now, and I don't think you're hiring my firm to start looking for treasures. That's not really in our portfolio. But we can help you make sure the contracts look good for the exhibit sponsorship and for transporting the scroll around and insuring it. We wouldn't want it to get stolen or misplaced. You're right to be careful about that."

"Well, sir, I'm really impressed," Roy complimented Sam. "How about you stop by my villa here on Friday, and we can spend some more time going over this."

"Your villa?" Sam asked. "Where's that?"

"Right here in Rome," Roy replied. "You see, it's my company, and I can live anywhere. Eden was founded by my grandfather, the first Roy Griffin, right after the war. It's been so successful that I'm partially retired now and spend most of my free time on antiquities collecting. It's my passion, inherited from my grandfather. People say I've got the best antiquities collection in Rome. Better than the Vatican, even. And they don't know the half of it," Roy said in a low voice. "No one's seen my basement yet. Want to check it out?"

Sam was annoyed but a little intrigued. Another pushy client wanting his project done yesterday. "I do have some plans for Friday. I'll need to catch up on some work after the holiday tomorrow," he said. "It's a family tradition—or, really, just my mother's rule—to make a big deal out of the twelfth day of Christmas. So I really wasn't planning on coming into the office tomorrow, and I'll need Friday to catch up."

"Perfect," Roy said. "Then I'll see you around 2:00 p.m. on Friday. You can tell all your partners that you've got an important new client to visit here in Rome. You know, Eden owns dozens of corporations all over the world. Our construction division has really been growing. We're known as Eden Builders, and our slogan is 'A Taste of the Garden.' Pretty classy, right?"

"It sounds like paradise to me," Sam replied, getting a little impatient to end the call. "Let me get back to you on that 2:00 p.m. meeting on Friday. I'll have to check my calendar."

"Great, I'll send you the calendaring email," Roy said, not backing down.

"I'll look for that and let you know if it works," Sam said. "Talk to you soon."

"Thanks, Sam. I really appreciate it," Roy replied. "I'll call Donovan now to thank him for how helpful you're being. Like I said, we go way back, and Eden's one of his biggest clients. He often says he'd retire early if we went away. I guess you'd enjoy playing golf every day with your dad, right?"

"Uh-huh, that would be awesome," Sam said, anxious to get off the call. "Let's catch up on Friday."

"See you then," Roy said, ending the call.

"*Che palle!*" Sam swore under his breath. What a jerk! If Roy wasn't big in the antiquities world, he would have hung up on him, Sam thought. Really pushy and arrogant. Right, a typical CEO. Just part of a lawyer's work life, and Sam had gotten used to it.

Sam would decide later whether to do the meeting at Roy's house. Or villa, or whatever it was. He certainly wouldn't let Roy decide that for him.

Sam looked at the time on his phone. It was 11:00 a.m. already. This new project with Roy had eaten up part of his morning. He checked his email to see if the offshore investigator on Cyprus had replied yet. Sam had phoned him on Monday and sent a follow-up email so he could get a banking search run on Wechsler for the Bacchus case.

No reply yet. Sam decided to phone him again.

"Hi, Sam," Alexander Lambros answered.

"Hi, Alexander." Sam had finally reached the Cyprus investigator. "Sorry to chase you down right after the holidays like this. I know you're on holiday tomorrow for Epiphany, and I wouldn't ask unless it was pretty urgent."

"No problem, Sam," Alexander replied. "You're a great client, and it's always a pleasure working with you. How long has it been, five years? Time sure flies," he said. "I've got some time today, if that helps. The holiday here doesn't really start until tonight. My wife, Amara, and I will take the kids out singing Christmas carols. It's the last night of Christmas, and Peter and Helena have been practicing carols all week. I have all the lyrics in my head now," he said, laughing.

"I know what you mean," Sam said with a slight cringe. "I lived in Rome with my mom for a few years as a kid. We did the caroling too, and I had to practice for weeks. After that, she wouldn't let me sing carols for months. She said they were just for the twelve days of Christmas. I thought it was a shame, really, to have those nice songs only once a year, but now I understand. So, I'll send you a message on an encrypted app with the details. It's really just running down some banking information on a subject of one of our investigations."

"All right, that's pretty easy from here," the investigator replied. "I'll send you an encrypted summary back later today. Then I'll overnight you the hard backup, in case you need it. All strictly confidential, of course. For attorneys' eyes only, and we'll keep this locked up."

"You're the best, Alexander," Sam said. "Sorry again about the short notice, and enjoy the caroling tonight and the holiday tomorrow. I hope you've gotten some Christmas presents by now. I know these Christmas traditions can be a little tough in this part of the world."

"Oh, yes," Alexander said. "We opened all of our Christmas presents on New Year's. Saint Basil was good to our family this year."

Sam looked at his phone. The audio seemed to be working fine. "What?" he said. "I thought I heard you say Saint Basil brought the Christmas presents on New Year's. Like, down the chimney?"

"No, he would get all dirty," Alexander replied. "That just doesn't sound right. Besides, Amara and I keep the fireplace burning for the whole twelve-day period to keep out the Christmas goblins—you know, the *killantzeroi*."

"Yes, those," Sam said, a bit confused. He wondered, does every place in the world really have its own holiday traditions? It seems easier in LA. The shopping malls make these decisions for everyone. Halloween starts in July, around the time that pumpkin spice lattes return to the drive-thru menus. Christmas starts with the ice skating in September, of course. And there certainly aren't any Christmas goblins to keep out of the chimney. Not that anyone has a chimney in LA.

"Anyway," Sam said, "merry Epiphany to you and your family. Watch out for those Christmas goblins, and say hello to Saint Basil. I'll look for your report."

"*Adio*, Sam," Alexander said, hanging up.

"Right, goodbye," Sam said, hanging up too.

Sam checked the Bacchus investigation off his list for the morning. He could rely on Alexander to deliver. He sent a few emails and was almost done for the morning, well before noon.

Sam heard a knock on the door, and then Flora stepped into the office. "Signor Romero, I have your building pass. Is this a good time?" she asked.

"Yes, of course." Sam waved her into the office. "Thank you, that's very kind. Please sit down," he said, motioning to one of the chairs in front of his desk.

"So, here's the building pass," Flora said, holding a white envelope with a few items inside. "You use it to get in the lobby downstairs and then again at the front doors on this floor. There's also your private mailbox key and a key to the men's room."

"Great," Sam said. "This will really help."

As Flora leaned forward over the desk to hand the envelope to him, Sam noticed the silver coin on her necklace. It looked like an ancient Roman coin. Maybe first century. Rough hewn and asymmetrical. The bust of an emperor's face.

As she handed him the envelope, Flora looked at Sam. "There's a story there, you know," she said, smiling.

"Interesting," Sam said, still looking at the coin. Suspended on a silver necklace, the coin lay against Flora's chest, just above her low-cut pink blouse. "A family legacy, maybe?"

"Something like that." Flora smiled. "My father's a lawyer, and one day he visited my mother's village on the Amalfi Coast. My mother had been arrested, and my father's job was to defend her. He impressed the judge with clever arguments and persuaded him that the law was unconstitutional."

"So they fell in love?" Sam asked.

"Yes, of course," Flora replied. "He was her knight in shining armor."

"What was the charge?" Sam asked. "A stolen coin?"

Flora looked puzzled. "Oh, the coin? No, not at all. The charge was topless sunbathing. Not allowed at our beach in those days."

"Um, okay," Sam mumbled, unsure what this had to do with the coin.

"You see," Flora went on, "the women in my village are known for their beautiful large breasts. It runs in my family too. Men look at me all the time the way you did," she flirted.

Sam felt flushed as he held the envelope. "Oh, I wasn't looking *there*." Sam blushed. "It was your coin. You know, the beautiful round one? Oh, never mind."

"Well, that's another story, then," Flora said, smiling. "I never take off my coin necklace. I'd feel naked without it."

"Right, well, it's a really nice necklace," Sam said, feeling awkward. "I mean, and it's true what they say about your village. You know, it's a very picturesque and scenic place. Something you don't forget."

"Thank you," she said, smiling again. "I get lots of compliments. You know how Italian men are. I get lots of attention at the beach."

"I'm sure," Sam said. "I know the beaches here are nice. Not like LA. The water's actually warm."

"Well, just let me know if you want an invitation," Flora said with a wink as she gave him a show leaning forward again while getting up from her chair to go. "We Italians like to enjoy ourselves," she said. "I know a really nice beach not far away. A small, quiet cove with warm water and gentle waves. Something you'd never forget," she promised.

"Amazing," Sam said, still a bit nervous. "That sounds wonderful. I'm sure the views are heavenly." He stood up and bowed slightly as she walked toward the door.

Flora got to the door, turned, and gave him a flirty wave. "Ciao," she said softly, opening the door to leave.

"Ciao," he replied, still noticing her silver coin and more.

Focus, Sam thought as he sat back down in his chair. Italy's beyond wonderful, but he would be in Israel in three days. He was excited about talking to Rebecca again tonight. Maybe she has a silver coin too, he smiled to himself.

After a few more emails, Sam grabbed his jacket and walked down the hall. He stopped by Carmella's workstation and let her know he was done for the morning. She told him everything was set up for the meeting with Roy on Friday. He had gotten her information and called her.

"We'll see about that," Sam told her. "Definitely a pushy CEO. If I do the meeting, it will be for my own reasons. I'll let him know to back off and not be so demanding if he wants to work with me."

Sam headed out, grabbed lunch near the Spanish Steps, and then climbed the steps to the Villa Borghese gardens for a relaxing afternoon.

After climbing the Spanish Steps, Sam crossed the street and entered the gardens of the Village Borghese, at the entrance near the Villa Medici. Sam had spent many hours walking the gardens when he lived in Rome before, and he had learned some of the stories about this place.

From the early days of the Roman Republic, this site had always been a garden or vineyard of sorts. During the time of Julius Caesar's first regime, known as the First Triumvirate, these gardens were laid out by a successful general known as Lucullus. He had waged war as far east as Persia and had become familiar with the Persian style of "paradise garden"—a walled, fragrant haven of perfected, symmetrical nature.

Lucullus had planted the first Persian garden in Rome here, and it became known for its lavish serenity. Lucullus's garden had become a popular retreat for the imperial family during the reign of the emperor Claudius, in 41 to 54 CE.

Claudius had become emperor after the insane Caligula was murdered by a group of senators and others who wished to overthrow the entire imperial dynasty and to reinstate the senate's previous stature in the regime. Claudius had been a skilled lawyer and politician who had personal connections throughout the imperial family's branches—his grandparents included Mark Antony, Octavian's sister Octavia, and the emperor Tiberius's mother, Livia.

Claudius had quickly outmaneuvered the senators and was recognized as the next emperor. He had moved to restore the imperial family's legitimacy in part by deifying some of his ancestors, including his grandmother Livia, whom he recognized as an official Roman goddess.

Claudius had embarked on several military campaigns to expand the empire, most notably conquering most of Britain. He had brought the restless Judea under his own direct rule, and he personally served as a judge over many of the most important trials during his reign.

Claudius's marriage to his third wife, Messalina, had not ended well. She had been unhappy in the marriage and was reported to have many affairs. In the eighth year of his reign, she had married a prominent Roman senator in a public ceremony while Claudius was away on official business without even waiting to formally divorce him. Evidently, the marriage had happened during one of the wilder Bacchanalian holidays of the year, when many Romans got a little carried away with wine, women, and song. Displeased, Claudius had sent assassins after Messalina, who sought refuge with her mother in Lucullus's garden.

As usual, the assassins had given Messalina the option of cutting her own throat, which she apparently lacked the courage to do. So, instead, one of the assassins ran her through with a sword. According to legend, when Claudius was informed of her death, he showed no emotion whatsoever and simply asked for more wine.

As Sam walked past the art museum known as the Galleria Borghese, he reflected on all this tragic history. It seemed the emperors and their dynasties were never done with their conspiracies and feuds. He wondered, was it something about their politics, religion, or culture? Are we really so different today? He thought about the next emperor after Claudius, the demagogue Nero, and some of the comparisons being made today between him and some modern politicians who seemed to do anything to please a crowd.

Maybe it's just the nature of politics, Sam thought. Everyone trying to win at someone else's expense. But could what you *believe* make a difference? Maybe the ancient Romans just didn't believe in justice or peace. Their monuments certainly didn't make the case for that, he thought, recalling the boastful plunder of the Jerusalem Temple depicted on the Arch of Titus.

It was sad, Sam thought, that such a wonderful garden of paradise had become known for a brutal, unjust murder of a woman who seemed to have married for love. Some Garden of Eden, he thought as he began walking back to the city and started checking emails on his phone.

> *Hi Sam, Roy of Eden here. Just a reminder we're all set for 2 pm on Friday. I just got a new shipment of some treasures for my collection, and I noticed something that would make a perfect gift for everything you're doing for us. Just a small thing, but I think you'll like it. See you on Friday. Roy*

That Roy would fit in with old Claudius, Sam sighed, shaking his head. Does he ever stop scheming? He would let him know to back off, Sam decided, but at the same time, he was a little intrigued by what Roy was up to. Maybe he'd show up on Friday and see what he had to say. But he would certainly not get drawn into whatever schemes Roy was cooking up. He had a bad feeling about where Roy was going.

Looking down at his phone again, Sam noticed an encrypted message from Alexander.

> *Hi Sam, I've overnighted you a set of the records you asked for this morning. As a quick summary, your subject received a €10,000 payment from a Bacchus Wines account on 14 October of last year. Of interest, he also received a €1,000,000 payment from a charity under the name Fondazione Genesis on 1 November of last year. Would you like more background on this Genesis Foundation? If so, I can update you late tomorrow, after we chase those Christmas goblins away and the children get their sweets. Cheers! Alexander*

Wow, a million euros. Sam wondered what *that* was about. Some weird money-laundering arrangement? A business investment? A bribe?

Government officials in wealthy countries could generally be bribed for a few thousand dollars or maybe a few tens of thousands. In poor countries, for a lot less. In Sam's experience, public sector bribes only got this large when something extraordinary was going on. Public workers have modest incomes and, if they're so inclined, don't need a big financial reward to do something they shouldn't.

Yes, Sam was definitely interested in learning about the Genesis Foundation. He sent a message back.

> *Hi Alexander, thanks so much for the quick report. Yes, please see what you can find on this Fondazione Genesis. Who, what, where, when. Anything you can do would be great. Thanks! Sam*

If this were a bribe to Wechsler, Sam couldn't imagine what a land permitting official like him could have done to earn it. The land development permits that someone like Wechsler issued would number in the hundreds each year, and even adding them together, they just wouldn't be worth a bribe that large. Unless something really unusual was going on, Sam thought.

As Sam crossed the street to walk back down the Spanish Steps, he heard his phone ping. He looked down and saw a text from Rebecca.

> *Hi Sam, I hope you're having a nice day! Looking forward to talking to you tonight. Also, I got some news today about our deceased official. Can't talk here, but let's catch up on that tonight too. Maybe you can share your dirty cocktail recipe too! Rebecca*

Sam smiled, thinking about Rebecca. He imagined her at her office, effortlessly choreographing hundreds of sources and colleagues, exquisitely perfect at everything she did. With a tight white sweater and a black pencil skirt split at the thigh, maybe, like she wore after the conference? With that soft rose-ginger perfume that smelled like heaven?

Focus, Sam thought as he walked down the steps. After a *caffè normale* at his usual coffee bar near the Piazza Navona, Sam went back to his apartment to change into more casual attire for checking out the Epiphany events in Rome. He sent a message back to Rebecca.

> *Hi Rebecca, having a great day, and I hope you are too! Can't wait to talk to you tonight, and also to hear about your news. I've been working on some new cocktail recipes too. How about a French kiss? Sam*

Sam left his apartment again, ready for some Epiphany Eve sightseeing. He walked through the vendor stalls in the piazza, which were full of large witch cakes, little witch cookies, and sweet black lumps of candy coal. Some of the vendors had Nativity scenes, *La Befana* witch dolls riding on broomsticks, or porcelain Wise Men on display. Sam looked at one of the Wise Men sets. Sam wondered which one was which.

"*Chi è chi?*" Sam asked the vendor, pointing at the Wise Men figurines. Who's who?

"*I tre magi?*" the vendor responded. The three Wise Men? "*Questo è Melchior dalla Persia,*" he said, pointing at the figurine of Melchior from Persia, with a white beard and holding a gift of frankincense. "*Lui è quello vecchio.*" He's the old one.

"*Questo è Caspar dall'India,*" the vendor said, picking up the figure of Gaspar from India, with a red beard and holding a golden incense burner. "*Non così vecchio.*" Not so old.

"*E questo è Balthasar da Babilonia,*" said the vendor, showing Sam the statuette of Balthasar from Babylon, dark skinned with a dark beard and carrying a gift myrrh. "*Il più giovane.*" The youngest one.

"*Prendo tutti e tre,*" Sam said, pulling out his wallet. I'll take all three. Just what an investigator needs, Sam smiled. A few Wise Men to consult when things get confusing. Who knows? Maybe Gaspar could help him find some of the gold in those Dead Sea caves. The nine hundred talents hidden in that "great cistern" would come in handy.

Sam did the calculation on his phone again. Right, twenty-three tons of gold. More than a billion dollars at today's prices. Unless some of it was silver. The bronze scroll didn't really say. But either way, Sam thought, picking up the package of carefully wrapped Wise Men, these treasures were worth at least a little effort to try to figure out.

It was getting late and was almost time for an early dinner. Not very Roman, Sam thought, but he wanted to get back to the apartment early to work on his bronze scroll project. He hoped that his friends Jason and Steve were making progress, and he didn't want to let them down by falling behind on his assignment. The story behind the scroll? He wondered if it was possible to find it after almost two thousand years. Almost impossible, right? All the more reason to try. Impossible is always more fun.

As the evening sun set over St. Peter's Basilica to the west, Sam walked up the stone steps to his apartment, still holding the package of the three Wise Men. Once inside the apartment, he carefully unwrapped and inspected them.

Each figurine had the Wise Man's name etched underneath the base. Melchior, Balthasar, and Caspar. Frankincense, myrrh, and gold—each one a symbol of something, no doubt. Sam went and got his laptop and sat back down in front of the Wise Men.

Right, Sam confirmed, frankincense was a type of incense that symbolized man's reverence for the divine. Tapped as a resin from trees grown around the Horn of Africa and in southern Arabia, frankincense signified man's worship and awe of the eternal power of the spirit. One of the main ingredients of the incense burned at the Temple of Jerusalem for centuries, frankincense was considered the purest of the dried resins used in worship at the Jerusalem Temple.

Myrrh was an essential oil that was a symbol of the presence and powers of the divine. A resin that came from the same regions as frankincense, myrrh was used in its liquid form as an essential oil for anointing the sacred. At the Jerusalem Temple—and in the Tabernacle used in the desert before the Temple was built—myrrh was one of the essential oils used to anoint the Ark of the Covenant and the sacred instruments of worship, to remind mankind of the divine's presence and powers.

Gold was a symbol of the divine itself. Eternal and constant. Gold did not rust like other metals and had a unique beauty. Soft and lustrous, it could be molded into virtually any form. Having the color and glow of the rising and setting sun, gold represented the power of the spirit as the land and waters seem to appear and disappear each day.

Ready for dinner, Sam put the Wise Men figurines in the window overlooking the Piazza Navona. It was somehow reassuring to have these symbols of the divine and its powers guarding this little piece of Rome. So much history had happened here—murders, theft, and great art and music—that maybe a little serenity would be calming.

Sam went out for dinner—*cacio e pepe*, *insalata* caprese, and a glass of Brunello. Pasta with cheese and pepper. After all, Italians knew nothing of tomatoes until the voyages of discovery to the Americas in the fifteenth century, and even pasta wasn't popular until the Middle Ages. The ancient Romans enjoyed a diet much like traditional Greek cuisine—meats, seafood, cheese, simple breads, and olive oil.

Back at the apartment, Sam finished up a few of his bronze scroll projects and started planning for the Israel trip. Pasta in Jerusalem, right? Maybe with a pink negroni? Or a french kiss?

Several hours later, Sam's phone rang. It was a little after 9:00 p.m. It was Rebecca! Sam felt a little embarrassed to be so excited.

"Hi, Sam," he heard her soft, beautiful voice.

"Hi, Rebecca," Sam replied. "So great to hear from you! How was your day?"

"Really nice," she said. "I made a lot of progress, and it feels good. How about you?"

"Busy morning at the office," Sam said, "and then I got back into holiday mode this afternoon. You know Rome," he said with a laugh.

"That's awesome," Rebecca replied. "So, do you want to hear what I found out?"

"I'd love to," Sam said. "What did you learn?"

"It turns out that Wechsler approved construction permits for work on underground aqueduct projects that don't exist," Rebecca said. "And even if they did exist, there haven't been any contracts signed to do work like this. Not anywhere in Israel, and certainly not in the Old City of Jerusalem, where the supposed aqueduct work was permitted."

"Underground aqueducts?" Sam wondered. "For moving water around the city? But if there are no contracts, then there's no water. So these are aqueducts to nowhere?"

"Not likely," Rebecca said, a little excited. "There's a long history of aqueducts and tunnels underneath the Old City," she explained. "It's pretty contentious because some of them go right under the Temple Mount."

"The Temple Mount?" Sam asked. "So what would a real estate developer want under the Temple Mount? Archaeology?"

"I'm not sure," Rebecca replied. "There may be a connection to a CEO who's as rich as King Midas. Everything he touches turns to gold, they say. I can't tell you who he is for now, under those ethics rules for reporters, but it seems like a pretty big deal."

"Funny how that King Midas story didn't turn out well," Sam joked. "Hard to enjoy your pasta when it's turning into a hard metallic substance."

"Good point," Rebecca said. "But even King Midas wouldn't waste his golden touch on underground tunnels to nowhere."

"So, do you think this is about archaeology?" Sam asked.

"Probably something like that," Rebecca responded. "But, if so, why be so secretive about it? Why pay some sort of bribe for an archaeology permit when you could probably get one going through proper channels?"

"Well, I might have some insights into that," Sam said.

"Really, like what?" Rebecca asked.

"So, here's my news," Sam began. "It's confidential, of course, and is really just for background. It comes from an insider who doesn't want to be involved in this."

"Right, this is just for background," Rebecca agreed. "Off the record, of course."

"Wechsler got a payment of a million euros on the first of November last year," Sam told her. "From a mysterious charity called the Genesis Foundation. We haven't been able to find out who's behind the charity, which is pretty unusual. Whoever it is went to a lot of trouble to keep it secret."

"Sam," Rebecca said, sounding surprised. "How would you know about this payment? Have you checked out your sources?"

"Yes, of course," Sam assured her. "It comes from someone legitimate with legal access to Wechsler's files and authority to disclose this. But, as I said, they want to stay off the record and only reported this because it seemed so unusual."

"Makes sense," Rebecca responded, "and I trust you. I just wanted to make sure you weren't putting yourself at risk or something like that."

"I know what you mean, and I'm glad you feel that way," Sam replied. "So, since this case is pretty sensitive and might even be a little dangerous, how about I make a little promise? I won't take any chances," Sam went on, "and I'll do this project strictly by the book. No matter what happens. No matter the consequences. I'll play by the rules. Fair?"

"I like it," Rebecca said. "That sounds like the Sam I know. You know, the guy who knows how to charm a girl with fancy cocktails at a rooftop bar. And a surprise good night kiss."

"You know, it almost sounds like that was a real date," Sam said. "Cocktails? A good night kiss? Was there something missing that would make it a date?"

"I'll have to think about that," Rebecca replied. "But maybe we could make this Saturday an actual date. I was thinking about wearing a slinky, black dress. That would make it official, I think."

"Yes, black makes everything better," Sam said. "And not just on the surface. A real date means getting beyond the surface and starting to uncover your feelings."

"I think it all depends," Rebecca teased. "I want to know what a man is about. You know, all the seasons of life and what he believes."

"You read that poem too, huh?" Sam asked.

"Of course, I told you poetry's my weakness, remember?" she replied. "You said you like poetry too, right?"

"Definitely," Sam agreed, "my favorite poems are about beaches. Maybe you know one where you can get a nice, even tan."

"I know what you mean," Rebecca said with a sigh. "But I try to play by the rules. Even if it means tan lines. That is, unless I make an exception. It just has to *feel* right somehow. Then *anything* goes."

"That sounds wise," Sam said. "It's good to follow your feelings."

"Yes," Rebecca replied, "and right now I'm feeling sleepy. It was a long day."

"Same here," Sam said. "So get lots of rest. Sweet dreams."

"You too," she said. "Sweet dreams."

Sam closed his eyes and pictured her beautiful face. He remembered how gorgeous she looked in that white sweater and black skirt when they had gone out in New York. He imagined her in a slinky, black dress on their date this Saturday. Her long auburn hair flowing over her shoulders.

He heard a ping and looked at his phone.

> *Just tried on my black dress. It might be too sexy for Saturday, though. It's pretty revealing, and you might notice I don't have any tan lines. I'll have to see how I feel about it. Nite! Rebecca*

Sam closed his eyes again. This time, the images were more vivid. He texted her back.

> *We're all reserved for Saturday night. Soft music and low lighting. Your nice, even tan will be our secret. Like that kiss in New York. And whatever happens next. Sleep tight! Sam*

Sam's bed was still empty. But her warmth lingered in the room. He closed his eyes, remembering the rosy scent of her fragrance. And the salty taste of her lips.

The moon shone brightly over them as they slept. The lesser light guiding them closer.

8

LIKE ONE OF US

It was Thursday. The Day of the Wise Men. *La Festa dell'Epifania* in Italy. Sam's office was closed, and he hadn't set an alarm.

Sam opened his eyes. He looked out the window. The bright Roman sun was hidden behind a gray blur of clouds. January weather had returned.

Sam thought of Rebecca. Her rose-ginger fragrance. Just two more days until he would get to see her again.

Energized, Sam got out of bed and started getting ready for the day. It was cooler, so after showering, he put on a thick sweater and casual pants. He would wear jeans on a day like this in LA. But he wanted to be a little more formal for Rome. With an umbrella, of course. That was not a habit in LA.

Sam would have gone into the office if it wasn't a holiday. He had kept his promise not to work more than half days, at least so far this trip. It seemed to be going well, and he was starting to feel more relaxed about his work as the new year began to unfold.

Except for that Eden CEO Roy Griffin, he thought. Sam wouldn't be surprised if he got a few emails from that jerk today, ignoring the holiday. Roy's insistence on meeting on Friday afternoon was completely obnoxious. Sam would tell him off. Still, he was curious enough to show up for the meeting.

Anyway, it was a holiday—at least here in Rome—and Sam had no intention of letting a spoiled old man invade it. He would mostly ignore any emails today and would only glance at his phone to check text messages. Especially for any from Rebecca. Maybe with a photo of her in that slinky black dress?

Epiphany—the perfect bonus holiday, Sam thought. No preparation needed, like with some other holidays. Nowhere you had to go or anything you had to do. Just a free day to let your mind and feet roam. He was really looking forward to seeing Rebecca on Saturday and, of course, to seeing his friends Jason and Steve. Not to mention some sightseeing with his mom too. But today, a free day with no plans at all, was really special.

Sam headed out into the city with his umbrella in tow, stopping at his favorite coffee bar for a double espresso. For a change of pace, he ordered a cream-filled *pasticciotti* pastry to pair with his coffee. It was delicious, even though he missed the slight sourness of the marmalade-glazed cornetto pastry that he usually ordered.

As Sam left the coffee bar, he noticed that a light rain had started. He walked a few blocks to the Pantheon. He felt the chill of the light rain on his face as he walked. He remembered that this was an interesting place in Rome, so he took a seat under the canopy at a sidewalk café to do some reading about it.

Built in the second century, the Pantheon was originally an assembly hall that was dedicated to the Roman gods. With the Pantheon completed during his reign, the emperor Hadrian had a throne where he would sit while presiding over public gatherings. The large assembly area under the rotunda was surrounded by statues of gods and deified emperors guarding the walls. The Pantheon was even more impressive when it was originally built, as the rotunda was covered in bronze, which glowed on sunny days.

After finishing his coffee, Sam walked over to the Pantheon and went through it, enjoying the unique architecture. It was still raining, and he could see the rain streaming through the open-air oculus at the top of the dome. Despite the clouds hanging overhead, the opening seemed to glow as the light poured in along with the rain.

Sam walked outside and thought about where to go next. It was relaxing to spend the morning without plans. As he walked through the Piazza della Rotonda, Sam noticed a costumed Roman soldier standing guard, wearing a bright red tunic, which was covered in iron and bronze armor plates. The soldier looked a little fierce in his red-crested bronze helmet, holding a large iron sword.

As Sam approached, the soldier smiled and held up a neatly typed sign advertising his private tour services in English with several translations below that.

> *Tour Rome with a First-Century Legionary. Rates Starting at 10 Denarii Per Hour. No Extra Charge for Protection from Assassins and Emperors.*

Sam couldn't resist. He walked up to the soldier.

"*Buongiorno*," Sam said, instinctively raising his right arm a bit as an informal salute.

The soldier nodded his head and bowed slightly, in the formal style of a soldier. "Sorry, I don't speak Italian," he joked. "Just Latin and English."

"Great," Sam said. "Can you do a tour now? I've got a couple of hours and would love to see more of the city from a different perspective."

"Yes, sir." The soldier nodded again. "We take Visa, Mastercard, and silver coins. Your choice."

As Sam paid for a two-hour private tour, the soldier asked what he was most interested in.

"Really, the life of the average person," Sam said. "Learning about the emperors and their families can be interesting, but I don't think I know much about what ordinary life was like then. I know they didn't have tomato sauce on their pizza, but that's about it."

"You came to the right place," the soldier said. "My name's Marcus Claudius Maximus," he said, still in character. "You'll know enough to be a real *civis romanus* by the time we're done. A true Roman citizen. Do you want to add an authentic ancient lunch to that? My aunt runs one of the best restaurants near here, and she opens for lunch once a month with a special ancient menu. Today happens to be the day. You're really in luck."

"Nice," Sam said. "That's just perfect, really. Count me in."

"*Bonum*," the soldier said. Good, he said, motioning Sam toward the street. "Shall we begin?"

As Sam walked a few steps behind, Marcus began explaining what the city looked like to the average person in the first century. The stone-paved streets were crowded with pedestrians and carrying chairs known as litters or sedan chairs during the day, with chariots and wagons only allowed at night.

"You mean like the rickshaws in old China?" Sam asked. "Sort of a passenger cart?"

"A bit like that," Marcus replied, "except vehicles with wheels weren't allowed on city streets in the daytime. These so-called 'sedan chairs' were used instead. Because horses, mules and oxen were allowed at night, the city streets were pretty messy at all hours of the day. The wealthy and important citizens didn't want to ruin their shoes, boots, or sandals, so they often traveled around in these little sedan chairs. The chair part was attached to poles that rested on the shoulders of the men who carried them around."

"I've been reading about those times," Sam said, "and it sounds like those sedan chairs were a little like the Ark of the Covenant in ancient Israel."

"Really, what do you mean?" Marcus asked.

"In those days, something important or sacred was not supposed to touch the ground," Sam replied. "Like you said, especially in cities and towns, the ground was considered dirty and impure. So an important citizen, or especially someone or something considered divine or sacred, should be carried on poles resting on people's shoulders so that he or she wouldn't touch the ground. This tradition started in ancient Egypt so that when statues of gods were moved for religious reasons, they were carried in something like an ark, fastened to poles so they could be carried without touching the ground. The imperial Roman families, who often claimed divine birth, traveled in these sedan chairs too, which were often enclosed for privacy. It was a tradition in those days to honor the sacred by respecting its purity and separation from the human world."

"That sounds about right." Marcus nodded as he continued describing the street scenes in the ancient days. Many of the streets were lined with shops displaying their wares or offering a place to eat or drink.

The cafés then were called *thermopolia*, which translates as cook-shops. Mostly simple foods were served, to be enjoyed at a common table or taken home or to a workplace.

"My aunt Mariana will tell you more about these places and the foods they served when we get to her place later," Marcus said. "For now, just imagine walking through the city streets with all the aromas of seasoned stews, grilled meats, and freshly baked breads."

As he continued the tour, Marcus showed Sam many of the sights of the city and explained what life was like in the first century. He showed Sam some of the locations of schools, where students were educated in math, science, literature, music, the arts, and, of course, Latin and Greek. The male children of wealthy families typically became lawyers, physicians, politicians, or soldiers after completing their educations.

The public baths were one of the most popular places in ancient Rome. The baths themselves were just part of the experience. The larger ones were equipped with gymnasiums, libraries, assembly halls, and small shops. In addition to cleansing and warming in the baths, the patrons could exercise, read, or attend lectures on a broad range of topics, from politics to philosophy.

Around 1:00 p.m., Marcus and Sam arrived at Mariana's restaurant. Mariana greeted her nephew Marcus warmly and teased him about his soldier costume for the hundredth time. She said he scared away all of her customers from Gaul, Illyricum, and Britannia.

As Marcus disappeared to change out of his costume and to help his aunt in the kitchen, Sam took a seat at one of the indoor tables. A waiter arrived to explain the menu. Mariana had carefully researched ancient recipes, cooking styles, and ingredients. The waiter explained that most ancient Romans had three meals a day—a light breakfast at dawn, a light snack around midday, and then a dinner starting in the late afternoon or evening.

Among the wealthy, dinners could last many hours and be accompanied by music or entertainment, along with plenty of wine. Formal dinners usually had three courses—an appetizer, a main course, and a dessert. Fish and seafood were the most popular meat courses, followed by pork sausages and poultry. Rome had a dazzling array of vegetables and fruits imported from the provinces—pears and figs from Africa, olives from Greece and Hispania, lettuce from Cappadocia, and endless other choices.

Some of the dishes would be considered unusual today. Mice roasted in honey, parrots stuffed with dates and snails simmered in milk. Bread was often dipped in wine, or sometimes baked into sweet wine cakes to make it even more delicious. The fermented sauce made from fish guts, known as *garum*, was served at virtually every table. With a salty, briny taste, garum was used to season a wide range of dishes, not unlike salsa in Mexico.

So would he like to start with mice in honey or a stuffed parrot? The waiter looked at Sam. Scanning the menu, Sam chose the spinach salad instead. Just then he heard his phone ping. It was a text message from Rebecca.

> *Hope you're having a great day! Just got some aqueduct blueprints that may interest you. I don't have clearance yet to send them, but it's no problem to show them to you. Can we do our call tonight on Zoom or whatever works for you? I can share my screen, and I think you'll find this interesting. Thinking of you! Rebecca*

Well, that's intriguing, Sam thought. He had already decided to go back to the apartment early in the afternoon to catch up on Bacchus and maybe some projects on the bronze scroll too. He wondered what the blueprints would show. What could a rich CEO possibly be doing under the Temple Mount?

Sam texted her back.

> *Great to hear from you! It's a bit rainy today, but still enjoying everything here. Hoping to meet a few Wise Men and maybe get some of those cookies. I didn't get any of that black coal candy in my stocking this morning, so apparently I haven't been naughty enough. See you tonight, and yes, Zoom works great. I'll send you a link. Thinking of you back! Sam*

Returning to the menu, Sam decided on the stew for the main course, an ancient cheese made from sheep's milk as an extra course, and seasonal fruits for dessert. The stew was cooked in red wine with apple, honey, vinegar, and spices, based on a recipe used by one of Julius Caesar's cooks.

Sam enjoyed an exquisite lunch, with the aromas and flavors of two thousand years ago. He was even given a tour of the first-century wine cellar below the dining room, complete with a preserved stone arch.

After finishing lunch, Sam thanked Marcus and his aunt Mariana and promised to return soon. Especially if they would have more of those strawberries from Gaul.

Sam left the restaurant around 3:00 p.m. He wanted to see some of the *Epifania* events in the city. He started walking toward St. Peter's Square.

Approaching St. Peter's Square, Sam walked down the Via della Conciliazione, where the sidewalks were still busy with festivities from the parade that morning. There were some Wise Men in costume that people were talking to, and Sam even thought he saw a camel in the distance.

The square itself was still very busy. The Pope has a morning mass here each Epiphany to remember the visit of the Wise Men bearing gifts for the infant Jesus. Or Yeshua, Sam thought, remembering what he had learned about the name.

After a while, Sam walked back to the Piazza Navona. It was even more crowded than St. Peter's Square. There was music and dancing and even a carousel for the children. Sam saw a few Epiphany witches in costume. The witches were a little bit scary, and maybe it was the old-style broomstick that made them seem authentic. Not like a Halloween witch, really, but she was two thousand years old, right? Still trying to get a visit with that divine infant.

Eventually, Sam headed back to his apartment. He did some work on the Bacchus investigation. He ran a few more searches on the Genesis Foundation and was still unable to find out who was behind it. Really strange, he thought. Wealthy people often used foundations and family trusts to keep some of their interests and holdings private. But whoever had set up Genesis really pulled out all the stops.

Sam spent the rest of the afternoon working on his bronze scroll assignments. These were projects he had given himself, but he wanted to take this seriously. It was just for his personal interest, but approaching it like an investigation at work was helping him to focus. Already some of the stories were beginning to make sense.

The story of the high priest Ananias and his son Eleazar was really quite powerful. Sam knew from his college studies that the historical records from the Classical period could be pretty unreliable. How extraordinary that the historian Josephus had recorded some of these events so carefully. It was starting to seem possible to figure out what the bronze scroll was really about, Sam thought.

A few hours later, Sam picked up a light dinner and brought it back to the apartment so he could keep reading more of the first-century history that would help the bronze scroll make sense. Then he spent some time on those Greek letters. That was really hard, but the online translator was starting to get some results. Sam typed in different combinations of the Greek letters as abbreviations or acronyms, and these were finally starting to make sense now.

Around 8:00 p.m., Sam sent Rebecca the Zoom link for their call at 9:00 p.m. Then he tested the video image. He knew how the camera angle and lighting could distort people's appearance, and he didn't want to look like *la Befana* with pasty white skin. He adjusted the camera angle and repositioned some of the lamps in the apartment. Not bad, he thought. It was exciting to be seeing Rebecca again. It was just video, of course, but he hadn't seen her at all in months.

Sam spent the next hour reading some of the history books he had put on his e-reader. There was an impressive amount of gold and silver in Palestine in those days. It was often surprising how much those ancient societies could accomplish without modern technology. Roads, ports, libraries, massive temples, and even a sort of postal system. Maybe they weren't so different from us after all.

At 9:00 p.m., Sam opened the link on his computer. The little wheel spun for a bit, and then Rebecca appeared on his screen with a big smile. No slinky black dress, but she sure looked nice! A soft beige sweater, hazel eyes, and that wonderful, expressive smile.

"Hi, Sam," she said with a wave of her hand.

"Hi, Rebecca," Sam replied, still captivated by her image. So alluring with her long reddish-brown hair flowing over the top of her beige sweater. He felt like touching the screen.

"So glad you set up the video," she said. "I really wanted to show you what I found. But first, cheers and happy holiday," she said, raising a glass of red wine. "It was a long day, so I thought a little treat was in order."

Sam smiled. What a great idea. He asked her to hold on while he went to his kitchen to get a glass of chilled white wine.

They toasted each other when he got back. "So, how was your holiday in Rome?" Rebecca asked. "Did you meet the witch?"

"We're old friends already." Sam laughed. "She baked me some cookies and told me some stories about the Wise Men. She just left here a few minutes ago on her broomstick. She said to say hello."

"How nice," she said with a smile. "Maybe she'll visit me here too. When people celebrate Epiphany here, it's done a couple of weeks later."

"Really?" Sam said, surprised. "The Epiphany witch shows up late in Israel?"

"Not exactly," Rebecca said, laughing. "Religion can be kind of intense here, and the rules are often different. Some people swim in the river and get baptized again. That sort of thing."

"Why is it later?" Sam asked. "Sort of a calendar thing?"

"Exactly," she replied. "The eastern church still uses the calendar of Julius Caesar. They're a little more traditional about these things. Like, by a couple of thousand years."

"Well, I can understand wanting to keep some traditions from Julius Caesar," Sam joked. "His chef made a wonderful stew."

Rebecca laughed. "It sounds like you went to one of those ancient food restaurants. Did you try the mice?"

"No," Sam replied, "the witch got there first and ate all the mice. I just had Caesar's stew. So, anyway, you said you got some blueprints or something?"

"I sure did," she replied, clicking to share her screen. "Can you see this?"

Sam looked closely as Rebecca's beautiful face collapsed down to a small rectangle and an image of a blueprint appeared on the screen.

"Look at this," Rebecca said. "It's a blueprint showing some of the tunnels under the Temple Mount. This one's the most interesting," she said, drawing a yellow circle around part of the diagram with the highlighter function.

"Do you know if this is real?" Sam asked.

"I think so," she replied. "I've been comparing this blueprint to some old newspaper articles and other records, and it seems to match up. Back in 1981, a rabbi assigned to the Western Wall had ordered a tunnel entrance to be opened, and his team supposedly found a huge tunnel almost one hundred feet long and twenty feet wide leading deep under the Temple Mount. This tunnel may have led to a location that some scholars and others have believed was a hiding place during the time of Solomon's Temple. That was the First Temple of Jerusalem, and it was destroyed during a war with the Babylonians in the sixth century BC. Some of the early treasures of the Temple were never seen after that. According to legend, they were hidden in a cave or underground somewhere.

"Apparently," Rebecca went on, "this rabbi believed that these religious treasures had been hidden under the Temple more than 2,500 years ago and that they're still there today. So he had this tunnel opened up, and he had a crew starting to drain some muddy water out of it so his team could get inside. I think this blueprint shows that same tunnel. Everything matches up."

"What was the rabbi looking for?" Sam asked. "You said treasures, but they had a lot of them in those days."

"The Ark of the Covenant, of course," Rebecca replied. "You know, like in those movies. Except the real thing. In the old stories, it's the literal presence of the divine and has supernatural powers. After the First Temple was built, only the chief high priest was allowed to see it and even then only on the annual Day of Atonement. Some religious fundamentalists—both Jewish and Christian—believe that the Ark will be discovered a short time before the coming of the messiah. Depending on your views, the Ark is either a powerful symbol of the divine or it's literally the divine's presence on earth itself. For people who take the literal approach, it's a pretty big deal. The end of the world and all that."

"So, if it's possible that the Ark is down there, why haven't teams of archaeologists tried to find it?" Sam asked.

"The Temple Mount is the most disputed religious site in the world," Rebecca replied. "It's sacred to Christians, Jews, and Muslims. That's basically four billion people. No one can do anything there without causing great offense and risking a civil disturbance. In 1981, this rabbi had to call off the tunnel work when it was discovered by the press. The prime minister got involved that same day and ordered the tunnel opening to be resealed. It hasn't been touched since then."

"So, what do you think your CEO is doing with this blueprint?" Sam asked. "You said the other day that his company doesn't have a contract to do any work there. What are they up to?"

"It's hard to say," Rebecca said. "They got a permit from Wechsler to do some work near the tunnel entrance, so maybe they think they can re-open the tunnel without being noticed somehow. But if that's what they're doing and the public finds out, it's going to be a pretty tense situation. Everyone wants the city to be peaceful. Well, I guess most people do. I'm not sure about that CEO."

"Yes, he's pretty over the top," Sam replied. "It's his way or the highway, I think. Or worse, maybe he wants to redesign things a bit. You know, making things in his own image and that sort of thing."

"He seems pretty dark," Rebecca agreed. "Did you learn anything about that foundation? You know, in a correct way? You remember your promise, right?"

"Not yet," Sam replied. "This Genesis Foundation is really mysterious. I've never run into something like this before, where it's so hard to find out who's behind it. And, yes, I'm doing all this the kosher way. I do keep my promises."

"Good." Rebecca nodded. "Then we can keep our date on Saturday. I mean, assuming it's a real date. I haven't figured out what to wear yet."

"I can help," Sam offered. "I'm pretty good with fashion. Can you show me your black dress?"

"Um, I don't know." Rebecca hesitated. "Then you would have seen the dress already. Assuming I wear it, that is."

"I don't think it's wrong if I see the dress before Saturday," Sam said. "There really aren't any rules for black dresses. Or even about dating, for that matter."

"Oh, *yes* there are," Rebecca shot back. "There's probably a wall of books with rules for dating. You have a lot to learn," she teased. "Like showing up on time, opening doors, and bringing flowers. Always being honest, unless it's about those lines I don't have under my eyes."

"Anything else?" Sam laughed.

"Oh, I could go on for hours," Rebecca replied. "But mostly it's about being truthful, open, genuine, and sharing what's in your heart. You know, the things that sound easy but can actually feel a little risky at times. Basically, the things in this blog I've gotten interested in," she said, a bit shyly.

Intrigued by her sudden shyness, Sam asked about the blog. "Really? What's the blog about?"

"Oh, anything and everything," Rebecca said. "Thoughts, feelings, ideas, dreams."

"Being open and genuine?" Sam asked.

"Exactly, and that's not always easy," she replied. "Sometimes you get these feelings or desires. Maybe just something to talk about as an idea. Other times, maybe something you'd want to feel and experience."

"Sounds like great writing," Sam said. "I'd be interested in checking it out."

"Well, it's called Veils of Desire dot-com," she said. "The writer's name is Sarah Wilde. That's probably someone's pen name. Some of the posts are pretty risqué and romantic, and she probably wants to protect her privacy. You know, so she doesn't get bothered at work about it."

"That does sound romantic," Sam agreed. "Sharing your deepest thoughts can be scary, but it seems like it's worth it."

"It's really what her blog is about," Rebecca agreed. "How good it feels to express your thoughts and feelings. Even your most secret desires and fantasies. The forbidden things that you dream about too. Hold on, I just spilled some red wine on my favorite sweater. I get a little clumsy when I think about these things."

As he turned off the screen-share feature, Sam watched her get up from her chair and walk away from her computer. Wearing that nice beige sweater that now had a splotch of red wine. And wearing not much else.

Soft red panties and fuzzy white slippers. Sam felt his pulse race. She must have forgotten about the camera angle as she walked away.

Apparently, she forgot about the mirror on the wall too. The one showing her image as she walked into the bathroom and stood at the basin. Still wearing that beige sweater, red panties, and white slippers.

Sam decided he should tell her. "Hey, Rebecca," he said.

"Hang on, I'll be right back," she called out from the bathroom.

Sam watched as she pulled the stained sweater up over her head. Her long auburn hair bounced free as it came off.

Delicious curves held firmly in a delicate red bra matching her panties. Those beautiful lips slightly parted and red like the wine. That cute gesture she did when she pulled her hair back behind her ear.

Sam was enjoying Rebecca's meticulous approach to cleaning her sweater. She put a bit more soap on the sweater and splashed more water. Her chest visible in the mirror reflection, she rubbed the sweater vigorously, her curves shaking slightly but firmly as she removed the stain.

Maybe it's best not to tell her, he thought. He watched as she blotted the sweater with a towel and pulled the sweater back over her head and her tightly filled bra disappeared.

Sam turned his attention to the view of her bedroom as she walked back from the bathroom. A big luscious bed with a thick white comforter hiding sexy pink sheets.

A vanity table and chair in the corner. One wall painted pale blue. Some interesting wall art. Monet, Kahlo, and Gauguin.

Flushed and hot, Sam looked away from his screen as she approached. Yes, he liked Gauguin too. This one made his heart pound.

Moments later, Rebecca returned to the screen. Just her face and the beige sweater in view now.

"Sorry to make you wait." Rebecca sighed as she sat back down in front of her computer. "You've got to catch those stains fast."

"Oh, no problem at all," Sam said, nodding. "I was just admiring your nude."

Rebecca looked surprised. "Oh, you mean the Gauguin?" she said, turning her head to look at the wall. "I didn't know you could see that. I really need to figure out that screen-blur feature. You just never know what someone's looking at on these video calls."

"A masterpiece, really," Sam replied. "You can't put it into words. So, best to skip that screen-blur. I really like your Gauguin. So luscious and warm. It's almost like I can feel it."

"Well, you're quite the artist." Rebecca smiled. "See, being genuine and open has its rewards."

"I'm really learning about that," Sam agreed. "Especially the open part. When you're open to new thoughts and feelings, that's when the magic happens."

"That's a good thought for the night," Rebecca agreed. "I'll be dreaming about some of that magic tonight."

"Me too," Sam said with a sigh, glancing at his empty bed. "You're off to bed now?"

"Yes, I guess you can see my bed," she said, laughing. "Right next to the Gauguin. You can see my whole bedroom."

"Right, and those pink sheets are pretty sexy," Sam added. "Kind of a warm, sensitive color."

"I don't know what you mean," Rebecca flirted. "But I need to turn in now. So I'll be signing off."

"That's a shame," Sam said. "But I get it. Time for bed."

"Well, night, Sam," Rebecca said softly.

"Good night," Sam said as the call ended.

Sam looked at the empty Zoom screen. Rebecca was gone. The Gauguin and the mirror were gone too.

Sam remembered everything, though. Her figure. Pink sheets. He started thinking about Saturday.

Then his phone pinged, as he had hoped.

> *I feel a little naked that you saw my Gauguin. It's so sensuous and really expresses my wilder side. Some secret desires and passions that I've been holding back. Can I trust you to keep my secrets? Nite! Rebecca*

Sam looked at his bed. No pink sheets here.

> *Your secret desires are safe with me. I feel like I've seen your wilder side already, and I want it all. You know, flowers and opening doors and all that. Until Saturday! Sam*

Sam exhaled. He really liked her Gauguin. Her taste in art was just exquisite. Poetry in motion.

Sam went to bed and closed his eyes. Just two more days, and he'd be there with her. Maybe in Gauguin's garden.

9

KNOWING GOOD AND EVIL

Sam fell into a deep sleep. He was no longer alone.

"Dad, you're back!" Young Sam sat up in bed. "Can you finish that story you started the other night?"

"Yes, of course," his father said, happy to see him. "I promised, right?"

"Have you been traveling again?" Sam asked his dad. "India? Peru?"

"Yes, but it's really nice to be home," his father answered. "So, do you remember where we stopped?"

"Uh, they were having a holiday dinner," Sam said. "I think you called it Passover. The main character—Ananias, I think—was a teenager. He was studying and learning about the world."

"Good place to start." His dad nodded.

He started the story where he had left off. "The seasons passed, and young Ananias grew into a man. He finished his studies and took on more responsibilities at the Jerusalem Temple in the land of Judea. People said he would be the chief high priest one day—more important to his people than even the Judean king or the emperor in Rome—and he didn't disagree.

"One day, his father, Nedebeus, took young Ananias to a large gathering at a home in the Upper City where they lived," Sam's father went on. "While he was there, a beautiful young girl caught Ananias's attention. Her name was Hannah, and she was the prettiest girl he had ever seen. When Ananias mentioned this afterward, his father said that the time had come for him to begin thinking about his own family. Ananias was quite embarrassed but said he wanted to get to know Hannah and to start thinking about making his own home and his own life."

The story continued. "Months went by, and Ananias and Hannah got to know each other quite well. Finally, Ananias asked her if she would consider marriage and starting their own family. She said that she was not in a hurry but that definitely yes, she would choose to be with him.

"A few months after that, Ananias and Hannah met with their families under a wedding canopy, with gifts for Hannah, a symbolic coin for Hannah's family, and a cup of wine for Ananias and Hannah to share. As was the custom then, the bride and groom recited their vows and then returned to their family homes that night. They would not live together until Ananias had moved out of his parents' home and had made his own home for them to live in.

"Hannah and her family began sewing a beautiful veiled wedding gown for the special night when their marriage would finally begin. As was also the custom, she put an oil lamp in her bedroom to light at midnight on the night when Ananias would come for her, after the new home was ready. Hannah knew that most brides could wait up to a year for their groom to make their new home. This was also around the time of a brewing revolt against the Roman emperor Caligula's orders to make the Jerusalem Temple a shrine to himself, created in his own image as the New Jupiter. It was a difficult time, and Hannah thought it might be many months before she and Ananias could start their new lives together.

"One evening, though, Hannah got word from Ananias that he would come for her at midnight. He had put great work into making their new home, and his father had finally agreed that he was ready and that the time had come. So, at midnight, Ananias arrived at her door, along with a torch-lit procession of his friends and family and several wedding musicians.

"As the traditional wedding horn sounded, Hannah rushed to light the oil lamp and put on the gown that had been sewn for her wedding night. When she was dressed and veiled, she went outside and climbed into a covered wedding carriage that was carried through the streets to their new home, where the families gathered for the final wedding vows to be recited and another cup of wine to be shared."

The story went on. "Finally, late that night, Hannah and Ananias went to bed and started living as a married couple. About a year later, Hannah gave birth to a son, whom they named Eleazar ben Ananias. Not long after that, another son, named Simon ben Ananias, was born."

"Dad?" Sam interrupted, "this seems pretty happy for a bedtime story. No one's been killed yet or been eaten by a witch. But this marriage stuff is a little over my head, don't you think?"

"Your time will come, trust me," his father replied. "But okay, I'm ready to move on anyway."

"Not long after Ananias had started a family, he was appointed as the chief high priest of the Temple. This was a great honor, and Ananias was happy to be serving at a time when peace had returned to Judea. The emperor Caligula had been murdered by a group of senators, and—"

"*There* you go." Sam nodded. "That's more like it. Bedtime stories *always* have death and destruction, right? Otherwise you might just fall asleep."

"Um, I suppose," his father said with a laugh. "Of course, the whole purpose of the bedtime story is to put you to sleep. But, anyway, Ananias served as the chief high priest for twelve years—an unusually long time for this top position. Even after his last appointed term had ended, Ananias continued to serve as a senior high priest in the Temple for the rest of his life. Ananias became well known for his strong beliefs in unity, diplomacy, and compromise. He often said his larger goal was to guard the peace of the nation, and he strongly opposed leaders and movements that he saw as threatening the security and stability of the people."

The story continued. "There were two great events in Ananias's life that tested these beliefs and for which we remember him today. The first great event was the trial of a man named Paul of Tarsus, who was part of a new group known as the 'Way.' This group followed the ideas of that teacher I told you about—the one named Yeshua. This group had attracted quite a few followers, and many people saw it as a threat to the peace that had been so hard to achieve.

"At the trial, this man Paul was accused of breaking a rule against bringing nonbelievers into the sacred areas of the Temple. By tradition, beliefs had always been viewed as belonging to a people. In the Roman world, each nation was free to follow its own beliefs and to worship the divine under its own traditions. Conservative leaders like Ananias believed that this was essential to peace; otherwise, there would constantly be conflicts and wars over what beliefs to follow.

"The teacher named Paul had broken this tradition. He was teaching that beliefs were *universal* and that there was only one truth that applied to everyone in the world. During the trial, as Paul denied any contradiction between the beliefs of the Way and the traditional beliefs of Judea, Ananias became angry and told one of the guards to strike Paul. This led to an uproar and accusations that Ananias had violated Roman law by threatening violence against a Roman citizen. Ananias was sent to Rome for trial before the emperor Claudius, who acquitted him.

"The second great event in Ananias's life began to unfold a few years later. The emperor Claudius had died and was replaced by a new emperor—a murderous monster named Nero. The educated classes in the Roman empire saw Nero as an unprincipled clown who knew how to play to the crowd. He became popular with the uneducated masses, whom he entertained with scandalous public appearances dressed up as an actor, poet, or soldier. His outrageous mockery of the educated Romans' pretensions won him the admiration of those who had felt forgotten by the empire. The resentful classes seemed not to care as news of the latest scandals spread—the murder of his own mother and marriages to his slaves Pythagoras and Sporus, the latter only a child. The educated and wealthy classes loathed him and conspired to assassinate him.

"Sadly, this insane, murderous emperor ruled until he was hunted down by assassins in AD 68—long enough to plunge the empire into mad carnage and open revolt. For Ananias, the year AD 64 must have been especially painful. Not long after the news had arrived that Nero had watched most of Rome burn, singing songs while dressed up as an actor, a new Roman governor arrived in Judea. The new governor, Gessius Florus, was close to Nero's inner circle and seemed not to care about the latest scandals—palace murders and new forms of torture used on the victims—this same Paul of Tarsus and the followers of Yeshua—whom Nero falsely blamed for starting the fire."

"Okay, Dad," Sam interrupted again. "Are we done with all the torture and slavery now? A bedtime story's supposed to have some death and destruction. But this Nero is a little over the top."

"Yes, we're pretty much done with Nero," his father replied. "Now, by this time, Ananias and Hannah's sons had grown up and become men themselves. Ananias and Hannah were proud that their oldest son, Eleazar, had been appointed as the chief administrator at the Temple and that Simon had also made a name for himself in Jerusalem.

"What happened next surprised everyone. In May of 66, the governor Florus took advantage of the chaos in Rome by stealing nine hundred pounds of gold and silver coins from the Temple in Jerusalem. He claimed this was owed as taxes to Rome, but everyone knew that the stolen coins donated by the faithful at the last festival would go into Florus's pockets.

"Suddenly, everyone felt like they had to take sides. One night, after dinner at Ananias's large, comfortable home in the Upper City, Ananias and his son Simon spoke about what to do next. Simon said that Eleazar was now leading in the militant uprising from the Temple. He said that Eleazar had told everyone that the time had come to stand up for what was right. He believed that new leadership was needed to prevent Judea from descending into the lawlessness and carnage that Nero had set loose in Rome. Eleazar was ready to lead Judea in this direction, even if it meant challenging his own father, Ananias.

"Ananias told Simon that he strongly disagreed. A leader must not only follow his conscience; he must also be wise. Leadership was not about having the right beliefs, he said. Rather, it was about knowing how to understand and respect *others'* beliefs and how to negotiate and compromise. Otherwise, the nation would be doomed to constant disagreements and warfare over which beliefs were right. This would pit brother against brother and father against son, he warned.

"Simon asked his father whether there might be common ground. Surely a nation of believers could defeat a mad emperor's armies. Wasn't the new governor's corruption a weakness? An empire that believed in nothing beyond the personal enrichment of its rulers would eventually collapse, he argued."

The story continued. "Ananias told Simon that there would be public meetings so that these issues could be debated and an agreement could be reached on how to respond to the governor's thievery. The king would speak in the Upper City, and Ananias and other leaders would speak at the Temple. Ananias's speech would be in front of the Bronze Gate leading to the inner courtyard and sanctuary of the Temple.

"Ananias would remind the audience of the meaning of the gold and bronze used to build the Temple. The sanctuary, he said, was decorated with gold as a symbol of the divine—the menorah lamp, the incense altar, the tables for sacred bread, and the gilded walls and doors. These golden instruments showed the presence of the divine at the center of the Temple. The Ark of the Covenant that had led the people out of the desert was decorated with gold for the same reason.

"Ananias would remind the audience that the bronze used to decorate the courtyard area leading to the sanctuary was a symbol of the sacrifices necessary to gain access to the divine. An alloy, bronze was man made, he would say. Mostly copper, but with tin or another metal added for strength and resilience. The wash basins for purification and the altar where sacrifices were burned were made of bronze, representing mankind's cleansing, atonement, and offerings to the divine.

"Ananias would announce to the audience that a *new* instrument of bronze had been made in an effort to bring peace to the nation. This new symbol of the people's sacrifices—a seven-foot-long scroll of bronze—was an official inventory of the Temple's treasures. It listed the gold and silver of the nation's treasury and where these items had been hidden for protection during the crisis.

"More importantly, the bronze scroll described the even greater treasures of the nation—a heritage of justice, mercy, compassion and peace. The scroll not only listed the locations of hidden gold and silver but included the names of the great stories of the people. A story of justice—a guilty thief's sentence for stealing gold and silver from the Temple. A story of betrayal and mercy—a son who led a revolt against his own father but who was forgiven and still loved. A story of a king who searched for wisdom and found meaning in the seasons of his life—a time to love and a time for peace."

The story continued. "Ananias would tell the audience that the Roman governor can steal our gold and silver. The emperor's armies can burn our cities and destroy our Temple. But they cannot take our real treasures—our beliefs in justice, forgiveness, love, and peace. But, like gold and silver, these treasures must be earned. Each new generation must renew and protect this heritage—through the spiritual cleansing and redemption symbolized by bronze.

"Ananias would close his speech by reminding the audience of the golden rule of the teacher Hillel. All men are made in the image of the divine. Even the Roman governor. Love thy neighbor as thyself. Especially when it's hard. This would not be an easy time, Ananias promised the audience, but with unity and purpose, we could honor our values and restore peace.

"Ananias hoped that his speech would make a difference. Only time would tell. Of course, it didn't help that his own eldest son, Eleazar, was leading the militants and was attacking Ananias and the other conservative leaders as corrupt, elitist, and weak against the Romans.

"This betrayal stung, but Ananias still loved his son. He hoped that Eleazar and the other militants would find the wisdom to do the hard work for peace. Starting a revolt was easy, he thought. As Solomon taught, learning to live a peaceful life under the sun and in harmony with the seasons could be harder. Ananias would trust in the divine and accept that there was a time for every purpose under the heaven. He could rest now."

Sam's father paused.

"Dad? What's the rest of the story?" Sam asked.

"Well, this story never ends," his dad replied. "This is where Ananias's story stops, but really it goes on."

"That's *really* confusing," Sam said.

"It can be," his father said. "The meaning of the story is that we all get to decide how we live. Do we choose gold and silver or love and peace? Maybe all of these?"

"That sounds good to me," Sam responded.

"But sometimes we *can't* have it all and have to choose," his father said. "That's what Ananias meant with his bronze scroll."

"He chose bronze instead of gold?" Sam asked.

"Well, yes, in a way," his dad replied. "He could have made a scroll out of gold, silver, papyrus, leather, or anything else that rolls up. He chose bronze to remind the people of the meaning of sacrifice. Sometimes a sacrifice is just taking something that you've worked for and sharing it with others. Other times a sacrifice means choosing the harder path because of something you believe in."

"So the story ends with the bronze scroll?" Sam asked.

"Not really." His father shook his head. "The story *never* ends because, as Ananias said, each generation has to choose the values they will live by. They can choose to believe what their parents believed, or they can decide on something new. Ananias knew what was right for him, and he lived his life that way. Not a bad example for the rest of us."

"So, he's a hero?" Sam asked.

"To some people. To others, he's a villain," his dad replied.

"What do *you* think?" Sam asked.

"I think it's time for you to sleep," his father responded, laughing and patting Sam on the arm. "A time for every season, right?" His father smiled. "Right now, it's bedtime."

Sam closed his eyes as his father turned out the light.

Sam dreamed of a beautiful Temple that night. Adorned with shining gold and polished stone and surrounded by a vast tiled plaza.

But the most beautiful sight in Sam's dream was the gate made of bronze. The path to understanding, acceptance, and love.

10

DARKNESS OVER THE LAND

It was Friday. The Wise Men and *la Befana* had gone. The clouds had grown darker overnight. It had rained off and on, sometimes falling in torrents. Unusual for Rome in winter.

Sam rolled over in bed. He thought of the ancient times. There were dark days back then too.

Sam thought of Rebecca. The Gauguin in her bedroom. A woman in a garden. Seductive and tempting.

Sam got out of bed. He was excited to see Rebecca tomorrow night. He hadn't seen her since the conference in November. Well, unless you counted *seeing* her last night. Or was that just a dream?

Sam showered and picked out a suit that would be warm and suitable for the rain. A nice dark blue, and it would go well with a green tie. He planned to work in the office all morning and leave on time to be at Roy's villa at 2:00 p.m. He wasn't planning on staying long, given how obnoxious Roy had been about the meeting. Also, Sam needed to pack and get ready for the flight to Tel Aviv on Saturday. He wanted to make sure he looked good for meeting Rebecca on Saturday night.

As he was about to head out the door, Sam got a text from Rebecca.

> *Happy Friday! I hope you're having a good morning. Just a heads up that I'll be staying at my parents' place tonight. They're pretty old school and follow the sabbath traditions here. You know, sundown Friday to sundown Saturday. So I'll be hanging out with family then and won't upset them by checking messages until I leave. So excited to see you on Saturday! You know, our official first date. Can you talk around noon today? I'd love to hear your voice before I turn off my phone. Just for official date purposes, of course. Not because I think you're charming or sexy or anything like that. Oh, and I still haven't decided what to wear. Any more ideas? Rebecca*

Sam smiled. It was nice to hear from her this early. A bit like waking up next to her. He texted back.

> *Shabbat shalom! Great to hear from you, and yes, of course that makes perfect sense. I'll call you around noon, if that's good. I'd love to hear your voice too. I'll ask Gauguin what you should wear. Maybe just dress like the painting, and we'll order some Tahitian takeout? Then no one will notice you don't have tan lines. Except me. Just for official date purposes, of course. Catch you around noon! Sam*

Sam looked at the rain beads streaming down the window. It was cooler today, but he felt warm hearing from Rebecca this morning. Like they'd been together all night, in a way. Almost.

Sam walked to the office, picking up his usual breakfast on the way. It would be a busy day, so it was best to have breakfast at his desk, American style. He wasn't planning on doing any work next week, so he could focus on spending time with his mom, Jason, and Steve during the trip to Israel. And Rebecca, of course. What a great start to the year, he thought.

The only thing missing was figuring out the Eden mess on the bribery investigation. If Wechsler were complicit in some bigger scheme with Genesis or whoever was behind this charitable foundation, his client Bacchus could really get burned. It would be important to isolate Bacchus's payment to Wechsler as a one-off having nothing to do with whatever Genesis was doing. Otherwise the conspiracy laws, or just the scandalous media coverage, could pull Bacchus into whatever disaster Genesis had created.

Sam checked his encrypted messages. Nothing from Alexander. Not too surprising, but Sam wanted to see if he'd learned anything new about Genesis through his sources.

> *Hi Alexander, I hope you had a great Epiphany with Amara and the kids. I'm sure the caroling was fun, and hopefully the Christmas goblins are gone now. Just checking to see if you found anything on Fondazione Genesis. I'd like to finish my report soon, and anything you can find would be most helpful. Thanks! Sam*

Sam checked his emails next. A law firm security alert? That's pretty unusual. He was on the firm's Technology and Cybersecurity Committee, and these things were usually covered in the committee meetings before being sent firm-wide. This must have been a bigger deal than they were letting on.

To all firm personnel,

In accordance with firm procedures, we are letting everyone know of a security breach in our data and communications systems. As we have been regularly reporting, external government and nongovernment actors have been increasing their efforts to gain illicit access to the internal records and systems of global law firms, and we are no exception.

We will be following up with the department chairs and office managing partners to ensure that appropriate steps are taken. Our main focus is determining whether any hostile actor obtained records of sensitive outside legal or investigative expenditures that might compromise any of our work.

Thank you for your exceptional work on behalf of our clients as we move forward and resolve this sensitive issue. As always, please refer any press inquiries to the firm's Executive Committee. Thank you.

Regards,

Richard Delacourt
Managing Partner
Faust & Price
Citigroup Center
601 Lexington Ave., 48th Floor
New York, NY 10022
+1 212 963 4000
rdelacourt@faustprice.com

Sam exhaled. Records of sensitive outside legal or investigative expenditures? Like the firm's retainer to Alexander for the Wechsler investigation? This was not good. Sam knew that tracing hackers was next to impossible. The firm's policy was to assume the worst—that hackers were connected to an adversary wanting to learn what the firm was doing for its clients.

Alexander was a smart investigator—the best in the business. Still, he needed to know that an adversary could have learned that he had been hired to trace all the payments that Wechsler had received last year.

Sam dialed Alexander's number. The call went straight to voice mail. Sam hung up and began to worry. But there was nothing he could do for now. He would have to wait for Alexander to call back.

Sam spent the rest of the morning working on the Bacchus report and several other matters he was handling. It looked like everything was going well to be off next week.

Around 11:30 a.m., Sam stopped by Carmella's workstation to say goodbye for the week. He promised to bring her back one of those Dead Sea gift boxes or some cardamom coffee. Maybe some halva candy for the office too.

Sam opened up his umbrella as he headed out into the rain. It was often gray here in January but not usually this stormy. The dark clouds made it seem more like dusk than midday.

Sam got a salad and lemonade at a casual trattoria near the office before calling Rebecca.

"Hi, Sam?" she answered.

"Hi, Rebecca, how's your day going?" Sam asked.

"Pretty hectic," she said. "But I'm glad to hear your voice."

"Me too," Sam said. "So, do you have a few minutes to tell me about your family and this nice tradition of quality time?"

She laughed. "Well, if you consider a phone, email, and text blackout to be quality time, I guess it's pretty awesome."

"It's brilliant," Sam said. "Everyone else in the world is desperate for a day away from work calls and emails, and here's this three-thousand-year-old tradition that solves the whole problem," he said with a laugh.

"Nice thought," Rebecca replied, "but, really, the no-texting rule is pretty much ignored most of the time. Like a lot of people, I'm just keeping my parents happy this weekend."

"Well, at least it gives you some quiet time to decide what you're wearing on Saturday night," Sam said. "Not that you need to. I've pretty much got this figured out for you."

"You do?" Rebecca teased. "That's impressive. What did you decide I'm wearing?"

"At first, I was thinking about Gauguin," Sam teased back. "You know, that casual Tahitian look. But then I remembered that this is our first official date."

"Let me guess, the slinky black dress?" Rebecca laughed.

"You're *good*," Sam teased. "There's a whole wall of books with rules for what to wear on dates and Valentine's Day."

"*Valentine's Day*?" Rebecca shot back. "Sam, we haven't even had our first date. Aren't you getting ahead of yourself?"

"Of course," Sam replied. "Isn't that the first rule in the investigative field? Plan ahead?"

"But we don't even live in the same country," she protested. "How would we possibly manage Valentine's Day?"

"You didn't notice when that Geneva human rights conference is?" Sam laughed. "I guess I snuck that one in on you."

"Yes, pretty sneaky," Rebecca playfully scolded him. "So, what are we doing on Valentine's Day?"

"Definitely a fancy dinner and cocktails," Sam responded.

"That might be hard to resist," Rebecca flirted. "Any particular cocktail?"

"Well, really, it's not just one cocktail. Actually, I think you'll be pretty thirsty," he teased.

"Really?" Rebecca teased. "You know this already?"

"Yes, it gets pretty warm in Geneva in February," Sam explained.

"I hadn't heard that," Rebecca said with a laugh.

"Just weird Swiss weather," Sam went on. "So, you'll want to start with a french kiss. Then a cloud nine, of course."

"Isn't that a lot to drink at that altitude?" she asked.

"Maybe," Sam replied. "We could strip it down a bit and go straight to the morning mule."

"I'm a little indecisive," Rebecca said. "I think I'll just start with a french kiss and decide how I feel."

"Isn't that a little old fashioned?" Sam asked.

"Not at all," Rebecca replied. "I like to enjoy cocktails slowly. Everything tastes more delicious that way. So where are we staying?" she asked. "I mean, where are you staying, and where am I staying? Since you seem to be making all the arrangements."

"The Romantik Hotel, of course," Sam replied. "It's a Geneva classic."

"Sam," Rebecca teased, "it sounds like your interest in this conference isn't just about human rights."

"Well, I signed us up for that Alternative Diplomacy seminar," Sam replied. "It sounds a little touchy feely, but I hear it really works."

"Sounds intriguing," Rebecca said with a sigh. "But I do have to go now. All this bar talk is making me feel tipsy. Maybe we should save something for Saturday."

"That's what I was thinking," Sam said. "See you at Between the Arches at 7:00 p.m. tomorrow. You got the confirming email, right?"

"Yes, Between the Arches," Rebecca replied. "Sounds delicious."

"It will be," Sam said. "I promise."

"See you then," Rebecca said softly.

"See you there," Sam said as they ended the call.

Sam felt a little tipsy too. He took another sip of his lemonade. He closed his eyes. It tasted just like a french kiss.

Sam grabbed his umbrella and walked out of the trattoria. He headed back to his apartment, walking through the steady rain. The wind had picked up, and the raindrops stung on his face. He started mapping out in his head how to handle the meeting with Roy. No more than an hour, he thought. But he did want to see those antiquities Roy had been talking about.

Back at his apartment, Sam mostly finished packing for the Israel trip. Pretty much the same wardrobe as Rome. Maybe just a little more formal. He added a nice red tie for Saturday night. He thought Rebecca would like that.

At 1:45 p.m., Sam walked downstairs and began the short walk to Roy's villa. Sam had looked up the address, and to his surprise, it was only about a ten-minute walk from the Piazza Navona. As he neared the villa, Sam could see the towering dome of St. Peter's Basilica not far away, across the Tiber River.

Sam walked up to the rusty-brown brick façade of a three-story building situated right on the Via Guilia one block from the Tiber. As Sam looked for a doorbell, he admired the marble portal around the massive doorway. Before he could find a doorbell, he heard a voice coming from a speaker.

"*Buon pomeriggio,* Signor Romero," the voice greeted Sam. "*Prego entra.*" Good afternoon, please enter.

Sam pushed on the heavy door when he heard the buzzer. A trim man in his sixties with salt-and-pepper hair bowed slightly and greeted Sam when he entered the foyer. It was the butler, Sam could see on the nametag: *Il Maggiordomo*, Dante Barone.

"Welcome to Palazzo Sacchetti," said Dante the butler. "Mr. Griffin is expecting you. Please come this way."

Sam followed Dante down a wide hallway with an ancient relief sculpture on the wall. Dante showed Sam into an enormous room dominated by two massive antique globes standing almost five feet tall.

He turned his head when he heard a loud voice behind him. "Sam!" Roy called out as he bounded into the room. "Good for you. You're early."

Sam turned around and saw an overindulgent seventy-year-old CEO in the room. He looked a little more slimy in person, with an oily bald head peppered with rows of failed hair plugs and overfed cheeks drooping down over his soft neck.

Roy did have a good tailor, Sam had to admit. His double-breasted charcoal suit looked straight from Savile Row, but the brown Italian-style shoes were a mystery that not even Patricia Cornwell could solve.

"Hi, Roy," Sam said, extending his hand.

"Great to see you, Sam," Roy said, pulling Sam's arm into a man-hug against Roy's plump, doughy body. "You're going to love it here."

Dante bowed at Sam and Roy and left the room.

"It's very impressive." Sam nodded as he scanned the room. "Sixteenth century?"

"How could you tell?" Roy asked.

"The plaque by the door," Sam said with a shrug. "An important work of Mannerism. It says it's been owned by the Sacchetti family since the seventeenth century. You're a Sacchetti?"

"I won it in a card game," Roy joked. "Urbano is terrible at briscola. I had warned him that a king always beats a knight."

"I'm sure he has a few villas and palazzos to spare," Sam said with a grin.

"Don't we all?" Roy laughed with bits of spittle flying out of his mouth. "Actually, I made him an offer he couldn't refuse. Who needs fifteen bedrooms anyway?"

"You must have a lot of grandchildren," Sam said, smiling.

"Never married," Roy growled. "This will all go to my accountants and lawyers one day," he said, waving his arm at the frescoed walls in the hall around them. "Damn parasites," he said with a laugh.

"Let's kill all the lawyers, right?" Sam grinned, setting Roy up for one of Sam's favorite traps.

"Right, kill them all." Roy laughed. "You know your Shakespeare, son."

"Yes, I do," Sam replied. "It's right there in Shakespeare's play *Henry the Sixth*. First, you kill all the lawyers, right?"

"That's exactly right," Roy said, laughing louder and flinging more spittle into the palazzo's stale air.

"Precisely," Sam went on, "that's exactly what one of the traitors said in *Henry the Sixth*. Once all the lawyers are dead, you've got anarchy and civil war. Just the right thing if you're planning a coup or some other treason against the rightful rulers."

Sam felt a chill as Roy looked at him with a cold stare. He imagined seeing his breath in the deathly chill.

"Nothing wrong with a little anarchy," Roy snarled finally. "To the victors go the spoils." Roy's murderous stare softened a bit. "You haven't said anything about my trophies," he said, pointing at the frescoes on the walls around them.

"Very nice," Sam said. "Sixteenth century as well?"

"Lucky guess," Roy said, nodding. "Francesco de' Rossi. His greatest works were for the Medici family. Greatest bankers in history. Heads I win, tails you lose," he said with a smile. "His frescoes here are known as the Life of David. A little too sentimental for me. I applied for a permit to make some improvements, but the Ministry of Heritage hasn't responded yet. Things move slowly here," Roy said, rolling his eyes before pointing to one of the walls. "Come look at the frescoes. Here's a happy family." Roy grinned. "King Saul offered his daughter to his rival David for the price of one hundred dead enemy warriors. David was a musician, so naturally everyone had low expectations for him. Saul figured that David would be killed right away. Big mistake," Roy said, stabbing the air with his index finger. "That David was actually pretty good in battle. David killed the hundred enemy warriors and not only took Saul's daughter but the kingdom as well. Plus another seven or eight wives. I guess they liked his music." Roy laughed, rearing his oily head back.

"Here's another one," Roy said, leading Sam to the next wall. "Eight or nine wives wasn't enough for old David," he said with a laugh. "He saw

Bathsheba bathing in the moonlight and sent for her. One of the perks of being a king, right?"

Roy led Sam to the next frescoed wall. "I don't really care for this one," Roy said, frowning. "King David had something like forty children with all those wives. But, for some reason, his favorite was that pretty boy, Absalom. You know, the most handsome prince in the kingdom and all that. King David should have been tough like his father-in-law Saul," Roy went on. "But, no, he was soft on that young stud Absalom. Even when Absalom led a revolt, kicked David out of the capital, and started sleeping with his mistresses, David told his generals to show mercy and not to kill Absalom. Can you imagine that?" Roy said, shaking his head. "Mercy?" Roy held up his palms. "Nothing but weakness."

"So, what's on the fourth wall?" Sam asked, pointing at the last set of frescoes.

"Ah," Roy said, rubbing his hands, "that's my pride and joy. After Saul's death, David became a great conqueror and captured Jerusalem from one of his enemies. He knew that it was destined to become a great city, so he made it his capital. Now the king of all Israel, David moved the Ark of the Covenant from the old capital to Jerusalem in a big procession. David led the procession, playing the lyre, singing songs, and dancing. David declared that he would build a great Temple in Jerusalem to house the Ark. But this musician's luck finally ran out. The priests said that the Temple would be a place of prayer and peace, and David had spilled too much blood. He would not be allowed to build the Temple.

"See what mercy gets you?" Roy said, scornfully bumping the fresco with his fist. "That First Temple went down in history as Solomon's Temple, named after David's son with that pretty Bathsheba. If David had been tougher, we would know it today as David's Temple. What a shame," Roy said, shaking his head. "But it's still a wonderful fresco." Roy smiled. "Just look at that Ark. So powerful and dangerous. They say that when the Ark was being moved to Jerusalem, one of the priests who was carrying it on his shoulders accidentally touched it. Bam, he was struck dead by the power of the Ark. Arrivederci, priest.

"The Ark is the greatest treasure of the ancient world, without any doubt," Roy continued. "It's the greatest weapon of war ever known to man. It knocked down the walls of Jericho, and every man, woman, and child in the city was slaughtered. Even the oxen, sheep, and donkeys were cut down. At another battle, fifty thousand enemy warriors were struck dead just for looking at the Ark. In another war, a different enemy was foolish enough to capture the Ark and bring it back to their capital. Soon enough, their whole kingdom was suffering a plague of disease and pestilence. After a few months, they had to beg the Israelites to take the Ark back, even offering gold to sweeten the deal.

"As I said, it's the most powerful weapon ever in world history," Roy said, smiling. "Imagine what a real leader could have done with it. Instead of those weak leaders talking about mercy, singing songs, and writing poetry. They called themselves kings, but they only managed to conquer a country eighty miles wide and three hundred miles long. With the Ark, a real king would have conquered Egypt, Babylon, and Greece."

Sam looked at Roy and noticed a shiny streak of drool descending from the corner of Roy's mouth. A little unbalanced, Sam thought.

"It's an impressive fresco," Sam agreed. "But I don't really understand how the Ark would have killed all those people. Don't some people say that it's a metaphor for the power of the divine and also a symbol of peace and unity?"

"Peace?" Roy thundered as he walked over to one of the seventeenth-century globes standing in the center of the room. "You sound like that musician David or the poet Solomon. Only a weak leader talks about peace. When you have power, you use it. You don't have to ask," Roy sputtered, spinning the globe impatiently.

Sam noticed the drool on Roy's chin again. "I hope you have insurance for that globe," he said, starting to be worried. "You've got the world spinning a little out of control."

Roy pounded the globe with his fist, causing the spinning to stop abruptly. Then he looked at Sam. "Don't worry," he said, "we've got the world covered. It's all in the plan."

"Really?" Sam looked at Roy. "What's your plan? And who is 'we'?"

Sam noticed that Roy ignored his question but seemed nervous. Roy's head seemed to tremble a bit, causing the loose skin on his neck to ripple slightly, like a flag in a light wind.

"Come on, I'll show you the plan," Roy replied, waving Sam out of the room and down the hall.

Sam followed behind Roy as they walked down the hall and stopped at a shiny new elevator.

"I got this installed as part of some improvements around here," Roy said, putting his hand on Sam's shoulder as they waited for the elevator to open. "I think you'll like them," he said, leaning close enough to Sam that he could smell Roy's garlicky lunch on his breath.

The elevator opened, and the two men got inside. "Just don't tell the Ministry of Heritage about my little improvements," Roy said with a laugh, filling the air in the elevator with the bitter smell of partially digested garlic.

Sam felt that the elevator was descending much too slowly. Roy must have strong-armed a contractor into a big discount. That's the way these CEO types worked. They bullied and took credit for everything. But, really, they never accomplished much. As the wise economist Adam Smith pointed out two centuries ago, the corporate model was a perfect system for enriching the corporate managers at the expense of everyone else. As managers of other people's money, they somehow ended up with a big share of it in their pockets.

Sam's professor in economics class had persuaded him that the overall benefits of corporations might nevertheless be worth the cost of management corruption and neglect. He had learned to tolerate that. What had always seemed intolerable was the arrogance of those corporate managers. They got the combination to the bank vault and then congratulated themselves for their brilliance in "managing" the money they were looting.

"You'll love this." Roy salivated and wet his lips as the elevator opened. There laid out before them was an ornate underground chamber glowing with the shining hues of gold and bronze.

Sam couldn't believe what he saw. An exact replica of a scene from a coloring book at his summer camp in fifth grade. Right, *Solomon's Temple for Preteens.* Sam's mother had sent him to the Adirondacks for six weeks—for his religious education, she said. The camp was run by the Unitarian Universalist Church, which Sam had heard believed in everything, including Jesus and the Buddha. He was curious how to learn how they celebrated religious holidays like the Super Bowl and Halloween, but he really didn't stay long enough to find out. Their only holiday over the summer was the solstice, which Sam thought was pretty pointless. You never actually saw the sun in New York, and it would have made more sense to celebrate the clouds and the mosquitoes.

Only nine years old at the time, Sam had been terrified to go to this Unitarian camp back east. His friends in LA had told him it was full of wasps, and it was only later that he found out they were talking about White Anglo Saxon Protestants. He found out when he was older that there were a few of those in LA too. But they mainly lived in suburbs with dead presidents' libraries, where no one ever went.

It was a miserable summer, but Sam ended up learning a lot. He won first place for his colorings of Solomon's Temple in that book. He was a little disappointed in the prize, though—a serving of red Jell-O with canned fruit and blue marshmallows. At least in LA, the bad comfort food would have been vegan instead of made from animal bones and skin.

As Roy toured him through this life-size reconstruction of Solomon's Temple, Sam recognized all of the details from the tenth century BC version. The Temple had marble stairs leading up to a porch with massive bronze doors and a bronze pillar on each side. Behind the bronze doors, there was a sanctuary that was thirty feet wide, sixty feet deep, and forty-five feet high.

The sanctuary was ornately decorated in gold, including the walls and ceiling. Inside the sanctuary was a golden incense altar, a golden menorah lamp, and a golden table for sacred bread standing inside. At the back of the sanctuary was another set of stairs, leading up to the smaller, inner sanctuary known as the "holy of holies," with the gold-covered Ark of the Covenant at the center.

Sam looked at Roy. It was actually a little impressive. Roy must have used a better contractor for this underground temple than for the lame elevator.

Sam looked at Roy again. "Is this yours?" he asked, gesturing at the grand space.

"The one and only," Roy replied. "You like it?"

"I'm not quite sure," Sam said. "I don't really know if I'm supposed to be here."

"Come on, you've got to see this," Roy said, gesturing toward the stairs at the back of the sanctuary.

Sam followed Roy up the stairs, curious but wary of going too far.

Reaching the top of the stairs, Roy pushed the golden doors open, revealing a brightly lit inner room of pure, shining gold.

"Wait," Sam said, holding up his arms in the gesture to stop. "A few questions first."

"What do you want?" Roy asked.

"I don't know if this is kosher," Sam said. "First, are you even Jewish?"

"Fine, have it your way," Roy replied. "I consider myself spiritual but not religious, if you must know."

"Spiritual?" Sam asked. "Like what?"

"Well, I drink kombucha, I saw *Hamilton*, and I went to Davos last year. Is that enough?"

Sam rolled his eyes. Personally, he liked kombucha and the *Hamilton* musical. But the Davos conference was a nauseating, incestuous celebration of corporate nihilism by corporate nihilists. Superficially enlightened with bold public announcements that corporate leaders support world peace, healthy families, and cute puppies, the Davos conference had turned into a display of elite onanism, with the attendees congratulating themselves for their "diversity" efforts in allowing female and non-White multibillionaires to attend.

A passport-carrying member of the global cognoscenti himself, Sam wasn't actually that hostile to the global capitalist system upon which prosperity seemed to depend but which had caused great inequality and environmental devastation. He hoped that the system could be reformed and held accountable for economic and environmental justice. What bothered him most was the hypocrisy and lunacy of pretending that expressions of good intentions would produce anything of value. To the contrary, this pretense struck him as intended to numb and neutralize the global actors who *actually* ran the world and could achieve real reforms if they only chose to act.

Sam looked at Roy. "You're a Davos man, huh? I don't think there's anything in the Torah about that. I suppose the kombucha and *Hamilton* make you enlightened, but you lose a few points for Davos. Anyway, you're seriously not allowed to do this. Haven't you heard of the 'Temple warning'? There was a sign in the Jerusalem Temple saying that Gentiles weren't allowed and would probably drop dead if they ignored the sign. Granted, this sign was posted in the Second Temple during the first century, and we don't know if Solomon's Temple had something similar. But you want to be careful about these Temple curses. Second, even if you were Jewish, only the chief high priest was allowed in the holy of holies. I don't think even a Fortune 500 CEO gets a free pass on the high priest requirement. Third, even if you were the chief high priest, you would only be allowed into the holy of holies on the Day of Atonement once a year. You know, Yom Kippur. So, this is completely nuts. I can think of at least four or five different curses that apply to this situation. I'm surprised we haven't been attacked already by mummies or some of those aliens from that *Empty Skull* movie."

"I don't see a problem," Roy said, starting to get annoyed. "It's not even real yet. Until we get the Ark, it's really just a demo."

"The Ark?" Sam said with increasing exasperation. "That creates its own set of problems. Have you learned *nothing* from those movies?"

"Don't worry," Roy said, "we've got all of this figured out. My temple will be so powerful with the Ark and all of that gold from Solomon's Temple. I just need someone's help with finding my treasures," he said with a wink. "Check this out," Roy went on, climbing up to the last stair and pointing inside the holy of holies chamber. "You'll be hooked after seeing this."

Sam shook his head. He would go to the top of the stairs and no further. Even if there wasn't a curse—or five or six—this just wouldn't be right. Temples were for worship and respect for the divine. This was just a facsimile—a graven image.

"See, I told you," Roy said proudly, pointing inside the gold-glowing innermost chamber. "There's no curse."

Sam put his hand on his forehead. "That's what the person who's about to die always says in the movies. Where have you been?"

"The C suite, of course," Roy shot back, using the C-word instead of the word *corporate* as a display of his supposed *suavité* that conveyed precisely the opposite. "When you run a Fortune 500 company—or three of them—that makes you one of the masters of the universe. What do you think?" Roy asked, pointing to the back of the innermost chamber.

Sam squinted. His eyes had to adjust to the glare from the pure golden room. But he began to see something towering inside the room. About thirty feet tall. Shining gold, of course. A statue.

Sam blinked. A statue of Roy. Inside the holy of holies—which, if it were real, would be the most sacred place to one of the world's great religions. Who did he think he was—a Roman emperor?

Sam looked at Roy again. He decided to change strategies. The direct approach wasn't working. Back to Corporate Law 101.

"Nice job, Roy," Sam said. "That statue is really awesome. It's impressive and must be thirty feet tall. And did you see those long fingers?"

"You noticed, huh?" Roy grinned and blushed a bit. "It's really my finest masterpiece."

"What will they think of next? Golden toilets?" Sam asked rhetorically.

"Oh, I've got that covered too," Roy said, laughing. "But that's back upstairs. I didn't want to put one in the temple. I'm a man of taste, remember?"

Sam looked again at the thirty-foot golden statue of Roy. "You definitely have a shitload of taste," Sam agreed. "Who would think of a golden toilet?"

"You know, maybe I had you wrong, son," Roy complimented Sam. "I was beginning to think you were a little dumb, but you're sounding pretty smart to me now."

"Funny how that works," Sam replied. "I'll bet I could sell you some expensive invisible clothes too."

"Really? That sounds pretty interesting," Roy said. "Maybe you learned something at one of those overpriced universities after all. Maybe I'll give you some more work. Or you could even hop a ride in my private jet. It's pretty cool. Air Icarus, I call it."

"How about we go upstairs and you show me one of those golden toilets?" Sam suggested. "That second lemonade was a bit much."

"All right, since you asked nicely," Roy agreed. "I might even give you a souvenir. I got in a shipment of Sankara Stones the other day. They're supposed to work even better than Viagra."

"I'd be honored," Sam said, smiling. "I'm sure you've been an expert on those for a really, really long time. Chasing the ladies, right?"

Roy shrugged. "Well, honestly, they haven't done anything for me. Maybe it's the kombucha, huh?"

"I've heard that." Sam nodded as they boarded the elevator to go back upstairs. "Fermented tea can be rough on the libido. Good thing you've got those long fingers."

"That's really just the statue," Roy confessed as they exited the elevator onto the main floor. "I've been told I'm just average. But I told her it was just the swimming pool."

Disgusted, Sam tried *not* to think of Roy in a swimming pool. Too late. He felt a little queasy. "Okay," he said, "where's the golden toilet?"

"Down the hall, just past my bedroom," Roy said, pointing Sam in the right direction.

Eager to leave but needing relief first, Sam walked down the hall, past Roy's bedroom. As he passed, Sam glanced inside. He noticed a red toga spread out on the bed, with a golden wreath laying on top.

So that's how Roy spends his evenings, Sam thought. A little Nero impersonation. Just hope he doesn't have any matches. Rome can't burn down again, can it?

A few minutes later, Sam emerged from the bathroom and joined Roy back in the main hall.

"So, how about that golden toilet?" Roy beamed.

"It changes the whole experience," Sam replied. "I'll have to get my own now."

"Right? You can't go back to porcelain after that," Roy said with a smile.

"The scroll toilet paper's a nice touch too," Sam said. "Just there because of the lemonade, so I didn't use any, but it's pretty classy."

"That's right." Roy nodded. "I'll bet you've never seen anything that classy before, huh?"

"It's almost as nice as that thirty-foot statue downstairs." Sam said with a smirk. "Now, I should really be going."

"Wait, I have something special for you," Roy said, pulling on Sam's arm. "It will just take a minute. Dante's already on his way."

Wanting to leave but deciding it was better to humor the old man, Sam took a seat near one of the seventeenth-century globes. He glanced at the antique version of the western hemisphere. Strange, the cartographer had somehow left LA off the globe. It should be right there, next to the *Mare Pacificvm*, he thought. Sure, it was a new city, but it wasn't *that* new, was it?

Sam stood up when Dante entered the room with a silver tray with two silver wine goblets. Sam sat back down as Dante handed the goblets to him and Roy.

"It's a special vintage," Roy announced, raising his glass, "to honor the new temple down there in the basement. I call it the Temple of New Jupiter. Original, right?"

"Very clever and almost unprecedented." Sam nodded, raising his glass. "I'm sure Caligula's copyright claim has expired by now."

Sam watched as Roy drained his goblet, small rivulets of red juice tracing down the sides of his chin.

Sam set his goblet down on a table next to his chair, looking back at Dante.

Dante stood motionless, his eyes darting back and forth between Sam and Roy, as if ready to flee the palazzo at any moment.

"You're not drinking, Sam?" Roy looked disappointed.

"I'm still filled up with lemonade," Sam said, shrugging. "Save it for next time," he said. "I may be back here for the exorcism when the authorities find out about your basement."

"Well, don't forget your Sankara Stone," Roy said, motioning Dante to bring the package to Sam.

Sam got up and bowed slightly to Dante as he accepted the package.

"Be sure to tell me if that Sankara Stone works," Roy went on. "Your lady friends will love it."

"I'll be sure to test it out," Sam said. "You know how women are. One-track minds. Nothing but sex, right?"

Roy looked puzzled. "Oh, right. Yeah, I get that all the time too," he said with a smile.

As Sam walked out to the street, Roy called out, "I'll call you tomorrow, Sam. We have a lot of work to do."

"Wait, no," Sam replied. "It's Saturday, I won't even pick up."

"Great," Roy said, closing the door. "I'll call you then."

Sam rolled his eyes and headed back toward the Piazza Navona, relieved to finally escape Roy's palazzo. He looked down at the box with the Sankara Stone under his arm. Some love potion, he thought. If Rebecca saw him with this thing, he'd be stuck at pink negronis for at least another four or five dates.

What a waste, Sam thought. He was glad that he had kept Roy under control, but how long would that last? He was after the Ark of the Covenant—not exactly a sign of good mental health. Well, unless you're an archaeologist with a whip. Because that makes perfect sense. Maybe if the Ark turns up, Sam would try that too.

As he walked the damp streets of Rome, Sam started to feel more worried. Roy was a cipher, but there was still something wrong. Something more ominous. Roy's games and the toga—what if someone more cunning was involved? Someone whose mind hadn't been dulled by decades of corporate double-talk and yes-men?

Roy wasn't *smart* enough to pull off that fake temple. No, there was something bigger, and Sam needed to know what it was.

Back at the apartment, Sam left the package with the Sankara Stone on the coffee table and went directly to the bathroom to shower. He felt an urgent need for cleansing after spending an hour at Roy's palazzo.

After showering, Sam looked at his phone. Still no message back from Alexander. It was late afternoon, and he was worried that something might have happened to him.

Sam called Eric Armstrong, one of his investigators back in LA, and left a message. He figured Eric would call back once the workday had started in California. Eric would find out what had happened. But it was hardly reassuring to need an investigator to check on another investigator who was missing.

Something was definitely wrong.

After a few hours of work at his apartment, Sam went out for an early dinner. It was his last night in Rome until he got back from Israel. He had wanted to celebrate finishing up a good week in Rome. But he wasn't in the mood now.

Sam hadn't heard back from Alexander, and with the sun long gone for the day, he couldn't talk to Rebecca. It had become the highlight of his day, and he missed hearing her voice.

But tomorrow night he'd see her in person. In a slinky black dress. Maybe she'd spill wine on it and need to rub it vigorously with some soap and water. Her curves shaking slightly but firmly again.

At his hotel—or her apartment. With the Gauguin. In the garden with a fruit tree.

Sam's phone rang right after his glass of Primitivo arrived. It was Eric. After exchanging hellos and updates, Sam told him he needed to check on Alexander. Eric was far away, of course, but knew how to track calls, electronic communications, and movements. It was truly a global village these days.

Sam let Eric know he was concerned and wanted to help Alexander if there was trouble. Eric respected that and understood the urgency. He would handle this as a rush and call Sam back on Saturday morning, Rome time.

Sam ordered a pizza *quattro formaggi* and a side of sautéed *spinaci*. Less is more in Italy, he thought. Nothing wrong with Chicago-style pizza, of course. Especially delicious at one of those weird sports bars in LA where everyone's from Chicago or someplace else where people die shoveling snow. In September.

Sam had the *tartufo* for dessert—chocolate truffle gelato in a hard chocolate shell, with a cherry surprise in the center. The restaurant Tre Scalini—around the corner from Sam's apartment—had been tempting him since he got here. It was even better than he remembered from earlier trips, and it made him want to come back soon.

As he took a last bite of chocolate tartufo, Sam glanced at the man in the bar who was pretending to be engrossed with his phone. Maybe the glass of Primitivo was playing tricks on him, but it seemed like the man at the bar was watching him. Feeling a little uneasy, Sam got up and walked past the bar toward the men's restroom. Without looking back, he sensed that he was being watched.

Walking back into the restaurant, Sam looked at the bar where the man had been sitting and saw only an empty stool. His suspicions rising, he noticed that the man had left his receipt copy on the bar. Sam picked it up as he passed and glanced down at the name: Leonardo Salvaggi.

Sam knew he needed to run this down. He would normally have sent the name to Alexander and gotten a report the next day. But Alexander still seemed to be missing, so he would have to send it to Eric Armstrong. He would let him know it might be urgent. It wasn't normal to be followed and watched like this. Something was definitely wrong. The main thing was to know why. Was it the Bacchus investigation, the Wechsler scandal, or something else? Maybe whoever was behind the Genesis Foundation?

Back at his apartment, Sam read more about the first-century history he would need to finish solving the mysteries of the bronze scroll. Then he went back and read more about the Dead Sea cave where the scroll was found. Why did the researchers think that the fourteen papyrus scrolls were unrelated to the bronze scroll anyway?

A few hours later, Sam looked at the time. It was 9:05 p.m. He wondered what Rebecca was doing. It was definitely too quiet here. It was 10:05 p.m. in Israel, and he hoped that Rebecca was having a nice time with her family. Doing Samaritan things, of course. With lots of hugs and homemade matzo, he thought.

Sam wondered whether he might meet them at some point. Maybe they could even meet on that magic mountain. What was its name? Mount Gerizim? Funny, that was one of the treasure locations on the bronze scroll. Maybe it's just a coincidence, Sam thought. Why would the Jerusalem Temple hide treasure from the Romans on a Samaritan mountain?

Or maybe it was just a bad translation, like that Kohlit-Kohelet confusion. Anyway, it was time for bed now.

Sam would see Rebecca in person tomorrow night. She was the real treasure, he knew.

11

PARTING THE WATERS

Sam heard his alarm ring. He tapped *snooze* and looked at the time. It was 5:00 a.m. on Saturday. His flight was scheduled to leave Rome at 9:10 a.m. He needed to get ready and head out soon.

Sam turned off the alarm and got in the shower. He practiced a few phrases he had learned in Hebrew, thinking the shower echo might help.

Boker tov, erev tov, ma nishma? Good morning, good evening, how are you?

Yesh lecha krembos? Do you sell Krembos?

At yefeifiya! You look beautiful!

Sam got dressed and finished packing. He was out the door by 6:00 a.m. and was at the gate in the Rome airport by 7:30 a.m. He exhaled and started to relax a bit.

He was wearing jeans and a light blue long-sleeved shirt with a dark blue sports coat. It felt good to be dressed more casually for the weekend. It felt even better to think that he'd be seeing Rebecca tonight. It had been almost two months since he met her at the conference in November. He remembered every detail of her appearance—there was that video call, after all. He knew that he'd remember everything about tonight too.

A little over an hour later, Sam was on board and had settled in. His preferred seat: 3A in first class. He opened his laptop and started organizing a few projects for during the flight.

After the boarding process was done, Sam looked around the flight behind him. It wasn't a crowded flight, and seat 3B next to him was empty. Funny, Sam thought. Maybe if he took a nap, that poet Solomon would stop by for a visit again. He had more questions for him.

After the flight was airborne and Sam had opened his laptop again, he realized he was sleepy after all. He had gotten out of the habit of waking up this early, and he felt it. He closed his eyes for a moment but decided he should wait until later to nap. He wanted to get some things done first.

He heard a young woman's voice. "Here's your espresso, sir. Can you put your tray table down?"

He opened his eyes and looked up at the pretty flight attendant holding a tray with a cup of coffee and sweetener packages.

"Sorry, sir," the flight attendant said. "We got a little behind in the galley after you ordered this. I figured you weren't sleeping yet."

"No problem." Sam smiled, looking at the flight attendant's name tag: Giovanna. "The coffee was to wake me up anyway."

As Giovanna was handing him the coffee, Sam noticed that seat 3B wasn't empty anymore. He turned his head and looked at the stranger sitting next to him. It wasn't Solomon. Better luck next time, Sam thought. He had started writing a poem for Rebecca, and it wasn't going well. He thought Solomon would have some ideas. There really just weren't any words that rhymed with Krembo. At least, nothing that he could think of that rhymed with a sexy chocolate-marshmallow treat that might tempt Rebecca into a campfire outing under the desert stars.

Sam closed his eyes again. He would catch up with Solomon another time. He wondered who this new stranger was. He was younger than Solomon but just as distinguished. He was wearing a white linen tunic with a loose long-sleeved cloak over that. He had a long curly brown beard and a sort of turban on his head.

The new stranger seemed pretty busy. He was looking at some rolled-up papers, and it seemed like he was trying to memorize some of what he was reading. He didn't seem interested in Sam. Solomon would already have woken him up, Sam was certain of that. This new stranger seemed quite focused. To get his attention, Sam might have to say something first.

Sam opened his eyes again and turned to his right. Sure enough, the stranger was reading something and silently mouthing the words. He was even making some hand gestures. Like practicing for a speech.

"Sir, sorry to interrupt," Sam began, "but I couldn't help noticing that you're working on a speech. It sure seems important."

The turbaned stranger closed his eyes as if to remember his place before Sam's interruption. Then he opened them and continued looking at his papers.

"Good morning," he said without looking at Sam. "Yes, I'm working on something. It's a bit of a rush, really."

Intrigued but not wanting to bother the stranger, Sam leaned his head back and angled his head a bit to look discreetly at the man's papers. They looked like strips of papyrus or leather cut out of scrolls. With Hebrew lettering, like in that bronze scroll.

Strange, Sam thought. There were those same Hebrew characters again. He had studied them again last night, trying to decode the bronze scroll. Translated to English: K-H-L-T. Most scholars thought this referred to a lost ancient village known as Kohlit. But, of course, those same initials referred to Solomon's most famous poem, Kohelet. The title that means the Teacher.

Sam coughed a bit, trying to catch the stranger's attention. That didn't work at all. The stranger kept on working. Sam looked down at his papers and saw it again. K-H-L-T. He knew he had to ask.

"Let me guess," Sam said in his most cheerful, friendly voice, "your speech is in Kohlit."

The stranger turned and looked at him, baffled at Sam's interruption. "Never heard of it," he said and turned back to his work.

Sam tried again. "Of course, it could also be Kohelet. Perhaps you've heard of the poem?"

The stranger looked at Sam again. "Everyone knows Kohelet. Even Romans like you." He turned back to his papers.

"Oh, I'm not from Rome," Sam said. "I'm from LA."

Sam saw the stranger's eyes looking around the first-class cabin for an available seat. There were none.

"I really need to do this," the stranger said. "So, if you don't mind."

"I understand, and I'm sorry for being so curious," Sam said. "Can you just tell me why you're putting Kohelet in your speech? Just so I can go back to sleep. That word's been bothering me."

The stranger sighed and sat back. "Kohelet was The Teacher," he said. "He knew that life is more important than gold and silver. Life is so short that, in one sense, nothing we do here matters. But somehow the warmth of the afternoon sun or the soft touch of a woman's hand connects us to the eternal and makes life worth living. That's Kohelet," he said with a smile.

"Beautiful," Sam said, "and thank you for explaining that. I won't bother you again. Solomon said that the pursuit of gold and silver was vanity, like chasing the wind." He closed his eyes, not wanting to disturb the stranger again.

"How did you say that?" the stranger asked. "Chasing the wind? I was going to add that and just forgot. Thanks for reminding me. As I said, this came up as a rush. It's a little hard to do this all by myself."

"No problem." Sam smiled. "Anytime's a good time for poetry. It seems to solve just about every problem in the world. I have a printout of the full Kohelet text, if that helps. I was using it to work on a poem for this woman I'm dating. Well, we're not really dating yet. That's where Kohelet comes in, right?"

"It worked for me," the stranger said with a wink. "Especially if you throw in some of Solomon's poetry from the Song of Songs. We got married a month later," he said, smiling.

"Great, thanks," Sam said. "I didn't know about that one. I've been meaning to get more of his poems and just hadn't gotten around to it."

"Yes, of course," the stranger said. "My name's Ananias, by the way. Most people call me by my official title. But since you're a Roman—I mean, from wherever you said—I won't expect that much from you. Ananias will be fine."

Sam pulled the Kohelet printout from his bag and started scanning through for his favorite parts. "Did you use the part about the rivers running into the sea and yet the sea is not full? To me, that means that we can't force destiny. We have to accept that some things are bigger than us and all we can do is our best."

"Not bad." Ananias nodded. "I'll add that in," he said, looking at Sam. "You know, for a Roman or whatever, you seem to understand this a bit. Maybe it wouldn't hurt if we worked on this together for a while. I could probably help you with that poem for your lady friend. People say I'm pretty good with romantic advice. Hannah says I've always been a romantic at heart."

"Count me in," Sam agreed. "Where do we start?"

"Here's what I have so far," Ananias said, pointing to the curled-up papers on his tray table.

"What does it say?" Sam asked.

"I'll be speaking tomorrow night at the Temple," Ananias said. "This will be in front of the Bronze Gate, which is a good symbol for what I have to say. Bronze represents the sacrifices and atonement needed to access and worship the divine. It's a man-made alloy that was used to make the sacrificial implements in the Temple, in contrast to the gold implements that represent the divine itself."

"That sounds powerful," Sam said, nodding.

"I will tell the audience that a new instrument of bronze has been made. Like the older bronze implements, it represents the sacrifices and offerings of the people," Ananias continued. "This should get their attention. Then I will read from a few texts that I think are important for the purpose of the meeting."

"What's the purpose of the meeting?" Sam asked.

"The new Roman governor stole gold and silver from the Temple, and the city is in revolt," Ananias replied. "The younger people are especially outraged and are arguing for a violent response. They want a war. The problem is the Romans are too strong to defeat in a war. The people are acting in haste and aren't thinking ahead. Because Judea is under the direct rule of the emperors, there are very few Roman soldiers stationed here. The senate is not involved in governing Judea and has no interest in paying for a large, permanent garrison. So, since the people have not seen any large Roman presence here for decades, they seem to have forgotten about Rome's power and ability to send large forces that can destroy a nation. The young people especially seem to think that a war against Rome would be winnable," Ananias said with a sigh. "It's not. The best we can do is to contain the revolt and negotiate with Roman leaders with whom we have good relationships—for example, the Syrian governor and some of the senior leaders in Rome who understand the east. But if the militants won't listen to reason and insist on a war, then it won't be the war they want. No, it will be a civil war. Judean against Judean. Father against son. Brother against brother. I won't be subtle about that. If war is what they want, they will have it."

"That's tragic," Sam said, looking at the papers on Ananias's tray table. "Do you think there's a chance of persuading the militants to back down?"

"It doesn't look good," Ananias said, shrugging. "The king is giving a speech tonight in the Upper City. I consider him a friend, but really he's not much of a speaker. His speech will basically say that the Romans are invincible and have never been defeated, even by nations much stronger than ours. The king will even say that the Lord is on the Romans' side."

"Really?" Sam was surprised. "Not the usual 'God's on our side' pitch?"

"Right," Ananias continued, "the king will say that because our side follows a set of principles—mercy, justice, honoring the sabbath, and so forth—the Lord is putting us at a disadvantage. He will remind the audience that these principles were the reason the Romans were able to conquer Judea so easily in the first place. Their generals often chose the sabbath as the day to launch their attacks, and we were defenseless."

"Interesting," Sam said, nodding. "Maybe he would do better with the Lincoln quote. You know, 'My concern is not whether God is on our side; my greatest concern is to be on God's side.' That could be a better way of inspiring an audience to reflect on moral principles at a time of war."

"That does sound inspiring," Ananias agreed, "but the king is dead set on giving the speech as is. I don't think it will help much."

"So, you said you'll be reading some texts," Sam said, looking at the high priest. "What do they say?"

"They're pretty blunt," Ananias replied. "I'll start with something from a book called Jubilees, condemning an 'evil generation' that spreads lies and makes false accusations against their fathers and elders. It goes on to say that the Lord will give them over to the sword and captivity, to be plundered and devoured by the foreigners."

"Wow," Sam with a whistle. "That is tough. I'm sure you'll get their attention. Do you think that telling a part of your audience that they're 'evil' will be persuasive to them?"

"It probably won't work," Ananias replied. "But I mostly need to reach the remaining moderates who might be persuaded to turn against radicalism. In a revolt, people tend to get extreme fairly quickly, and our best hope is to get the ear of people who might still listen to reason."

"Like your son Eleazar?" Sam asked.

"You know about that, huh?" Ananias asked, leaning back in his seat and closing his eyes. "It's the worst kind of pain. I think it's evil to falsely accuse your father of corruption and treason. He doesn't understand that real leadership means making tough decisions that aren't always popular. It's easy to play to the passions of the street, like Nero does. Often, doing the right thing means you'll be misunderstood. Like learning to live with the Romans. They're not going away, and we have to make the best of it. We've actually done pretty well, keeping the Temple pure and preventing Caligula from desecrating it with that idol of himself. The Romans mostly leave us alone, and this new governor is just a storm that will pass."

"So, what other texts do you have?" Sam asked, looking at Ananias's papers.

"I'll also read from a book called Ezekiel," Ananias replied. "This says we're all to blame for not respecting the divine and our traditions enough. This text says that Jerusalem was unfaithful to the Lord, murdered her children, and gave gifts to her foreign lovers. It's a way of saying that war is not the answer; a renewed moral commitment is."

"That's pretty rough too," Sam said. "What else do you have?"

"I'll also read from the books of Isaiah and Psalms," Ananias said. "Judea turned its back on the divine and forgot to seek justice and to defend the oppressed. But the Lord laughs and scoffs at the foreigners and will restore the rulers like we had in the days of old. This means that even though the situation looks dark now, the answer lies with recommitting to our beliefs, not with war."

"Can I ask you something?" Sam looked at the high priest.

"I suppose," Ananias said with a shrug. "I'm guessing you'll do that anyway."

"Why all the comparisons to Jerusalem being an unfaithful wife?" Sam asked. "From what I understand, that section in Ezekiel is a little graphic. Something about well-endowed Egyptians, right?"

"What's your point?" Ananias scowled at Sam.

Sam sighed. "With all due respect, it sometimes seems like most religions are just a little tough on women. You know, the double standard. Whatever a man does is just normal lust. When a woman does the same thing, it's somehow shameful. We all understand that a woman can get pregnant, so naturally her role's a little different. But why should a woman be ashamed of having the same natural feelings that a man has?"

"That sounds judgmental and a little arrogant," Ananias replied. "Tell me about where you live. LA, you said? How do you treat your women?"

"Well, in Los Angeles," Sam began.

"*Angels?*" Ananias scoffed. "Really? You live in a city of Pharisees or followers of the Way? People who believe in angels?"

Sam shrugged. "I'm not sure about that, but we are known as the City of Angels."

"It figures," Ananias said, frowning. "So this is some kind of paradise for women? No rape, abuse, violence, or disrespect?"

"I didn't say it was paradise, with or without angels," Sam conceded. "But I think we're making progress toward the idea that women are equal and that it's good for everyone when women are allowed to express their sensuality. Isn't there some spark of the divine in a woman's body and the pleasures she shares with a man? Why is there such a history of attacking that?"

"It's all about promises," Ananias insisted. "We all know that a woman's body is sacred and that physical pleasures are a wonderful gift from the divine. But that's all empty without promises between a man and a woman. Pleasure is easy, promises are hard. It's important to remind people how important promises can be. Otherwise life can end up being impersonal and anonymous. Just strangers alone in the world."

"I partially agree with that," Sam said, leaning toward the high priest. "But that sounds like the old idea that sex is only for marriage and, even then, just for having children. Those old teachings that you're not supposed to enjoy sex."

"Well, that's presumptuous," Ananias said, raising an eyebrow. "No wonder you believe in angels. In Judea, we believe in marriage, and it's part of our law. We believe that sexual pleasure is a sacred bond that deserves promises of care, loyalty, and trust. Like the sacred bond between the divine and mankind, these promises are symbolized by the wedding tent and the tent of the divine, which we call the Tabernacle. But taking promises seriously doesn't mean that sexual pleasure is unimportant. It's really the contrary. It's such an important, sacred part of life that it deserves its own set of promises. Now, what those promises look like in the City of Angels is your business, I suppose. I don't know that I care about the types of promises between men and women there. Or other types of relationships too. I don't know that that's any of my business."

"So a promise could just be respect and caring?" Sam asked. "Not necessarily committing to a future lifetime with all the uncertainties no one can predict?"

"Like I said," Ananias went on, "that's for you and your angels to decide. You could have ten wives for all I care. Or no sex on the sabbath, like in Samaria."

"What?" Sam felt a little dazed. "What about Samaria? What do you mean?"

"Well, the Samaritans are a little more traditional about these things," Ananias explained. "One of those traditions is to not have sex on the sabbath. So, on Friday nights, everyone gets busy with other things."

"That sounds a little harsh," Sam said, frowning. "Don't Samaritans want to have sex on Friday nights?"

"Of course they do," Ananias replied. "That's the whole point. It's a way of disciplining the mind and keeping the soul in charge. Then, of course, on Saturday night, the lights go out all over Samaria."

"Really?" Sam asked, becoming even more curious.

"I'm a high priest," Ananias went on, "so I won't repeat those jokes about Samaria on Saturday nights. But let's just say that the markets sell a lot of flower bouquets on Saturday evenings."

"Charming," Sam said with a nod. "I'll have to remember that."

"Anyway," Ananias went on, "I don't think it's right to say that religion devalues women or is against enjoying sexual pleasure. Maybe there are exceptions, but I don't think that you can say that about religions in general. Maybe the bigger point that we're trying to make is not to become a slave to your passions or even your mind. It's your soul that matters. If you can align your soul with your passions and maybe sprinkle in a few promises, then I have no problem with that. At least in the City of Angels," he said with a wink.

"Fair enough," Sam agreed. He looked down at Ananias's papers on the tray table again. "Now tell me about that bronze scroll," he said, smiling.

Ananias looked at Sam, surprised. "Who told you about that?"

"My dad told me," Sam said with a grin. "At least in a dream."

"You really *do* believe in angels, don't you?" Ananias frowned. "It's really a state secret, so I don't think we should be talking about this."

"But I have questions about it," Sam insisted. "You know, the sixty treasure locations."

"I don't know what you're talking about," Ananias said firmly.

"So who am I *supposed* to ask, the Roman governor?" Sam persisted.

Ananias glared at Sam. "The bronze scroll is sacred. It represents things you won't understand."

"Try me," Sam continued. "I just want to understand this better."

"Well, I certainly won't tell you anything about any treasures—if there were any." Ananias glared at Sam. "But I suppose there's no harm in educating you a bit about some important metaphors."

"I already know about all the treasures anyway," Sam said, waving his hand dismissively. "Like the stolen gold and silver at treasure site number one, the gold and silver tithes in treasure site number fifty-eight, and the bronze sacrificial altar in treasure site fifty-nine. Not to mention all the Essenes' silver at eighteen of the sites."

Sam looked at the surprise on Ananias's face and smiled. Sam would be as responsible with this information as he could, but it really wasn't that hard to figure out. Maybe others had already figured it out and gotten the treasures already. If not, it was only a matter of time. What was more important to Sam was understanding the *meaning* of the bronze scroll. Some of the treasure descriptions sounded almost poetic. He wanted to know about that.

"It sounds like you've already figured this out," Ananias said, frowning. "Maybe you should be telling me about the meaning of the Valley of Achor, Absalom's Monument, the House of Tamar, Job's Well, and Kohelet?"

"*Kohelet?*" Sam slapped his forehead. "I thought it was Kohlit. No wonder. I'll have to tell Solomon about this. So, that's what it means," Sam went on. "K-H-L-T means Kohelet. The poem. Or really, a book in the Tanakh."

"Of course," Ananias said. "Chasing gold and silver—or fighting over it—is like—"

"Chasing the wind," Sam finished his sentence. "All vanity. 'He that loveth silver shall not be satisfied with silver.' It's a dead end."

"Exactly," Ananias said, nodding. "That's what Kohelet means. I'll explain to some of our key leaders that the bronze scroll is a symbol of the Temple's real treasures. Not gold or silver, but the purpose of life. Solomon taught us to enjoy the warmth of the sun and all the days of our lives. He said to follow the law and be in harmony with the divine. This is what our nation needs to hear to find our way out of this crisis. If we fight over gold—or among ourselves—the revolt is lost and Jerusalem will be destroyed once again. That is the lesson we learned when the First Temple was destroyed. It's belief that matters, not who has the gold."

"I understand," Sam said, nodding. "That makes perfect sense. And I already figured out the Valley of Achor."

"That wasn't too hard, was it?" Ananias smiled.

"Right," Sam said, grinning. "Seventeen talents of gold and silver in a chest at a ruin in the Valley of Achor. Sounds like the seventeen talents of gold and silver that Governor Florus stole from the Temple, right? Your Valley of Achor reference is pretty good," Sam said with a smile. "You know, the place where a thief named Achan was stoned to death for stealing gold and silver that belonged to the Temple? Not too subtle."

"The whole point is to be understood," Ananias agreed. "You don't want people running around looking for seventeen talents of gold and silver in a valley somewhere," he said with a laugh.

"I hear you," Sam replied, nodding. "Absalom's Monument was pretty simple too. Young Absalom wasn't very nice to his father. Leading a revolt and sleeping with his mistresses, right?"

"Well, he wasn't sleeping with David's mistresses," Ananias corrected. "He set up a tent outdoors and was—"

"Okay, okay," Sam interrupted. "Too much detail. Some of these religious texts can get pretty personal. But I gather your intent was to compare your son Eleazar to Absalom."

"It's not flattering, of course," Ananias agreed, "but it needed to be said. I don't agree with Eleazar leading a revolt against his own father, and I want to be clear with my words. Hate the sin, love the sinner."

"Love the sinner?" Sam shot back.

"Yes, the meaning of these texts can be subtle and complex," Ananias explained. "People hear the story of Absalom and think it's all about his treachery and what he did in that tent. That's part of it. But the bigger part is how his father, King David, handled the situation."

"What do you mean?" Sam asked.

"David rebuked his son Absalom and made it absolutely clear that his actions were wrong. The worst kind of misdeeds. Betraying your own father. But David *forgave* Absalom and told his generals to spare his life," Ananias said, leaning toward Sam. "He said that he still loved Absalom and would give him a chance to atone for his crimes. It wouldn't be easy for Absalom to make amends, of course. But his father gave him that choice. He could choose redemption and be forgiven. There's always that chance, no matter how bad the crime."

"Even Eleazar?" Sam asked quietly.

Ananias exhaled and looked down, letting his shoulders fall. "Even Eleazar," he said. "I still love him, and redemption is always possible. No matter how hard."

Sam looked at Ananias. He could only imagine the pain of watching as a civil war destroyed your homeland and your own family. Ananias couldn't know that, almost two millennia later, his beloved Temple would still be a symbol of division and unhealed wounds. But Ananias somehow seemed to understand that what you *believed* was more important than what *happened* in the world. There was no true victory or defeat in life; maybe the only *real* experience in this life was the connection between the soul and the divine, Sam was starting to think.

"And the House of Tamar?" Sam asked.

Ananias looked at Sam. "I'll leave that one to your imagination," he replied. "My job's not to make this easy for you. You're supposed to think about these meanings, right? You could decide that it's the Tamar who was Absalom's sister. She was raped by a half brother, whom Absalom killed for revenge. Definitely a tragic story about justice, mercy, and taking the law into your own hands. Or you could decide that this is the Tamar who was an ancestor of King David. It was very important in those days to have children, of course, and Tamar was no exception. When her husband died, her father-in-law, Judah, arranged for her to have sex with her dead husband's younger brother Onan. He was selfish and knew that if Tamar bore him a son, the child would inherit all of Judah's wealth and Onan would inherit nothing. Perhaps you've heard the term 'onanism'?" Ananias looked at Sam.

"Wait, maybe this is one of those stories that's better not—" Sam interrupted.

"Onan pleasured himself with Tamar's body," Ananias went on, "but cast his seed on the ground to prevent her from having a child."

"Okay, I get it," Sam said, raising his hands up to stop. "So that's what onanism is, then? Sort of leaving Tamar unsatisfied, right?"

"Exactly," Ananias emphasized. "A man's supposed to satisfy—"

"Okay, I get it, no need to go on," Sam protested. "I think I get it. There's never something for nothing, right?"

Ananias nodded. "That's right, unless, of course, you believe in angels."

"I suppose that's true," Sam replied, "but, really, I don't know why you think I believe in angels. As I said, I live in LA, which is supposedly the City of Angels. But I've never seen any. At least until I started meeting ancient dignitaries in first-class cabins."

"I don't know what you mean," Ananias said with a smile. "I'm hardly ancient. Hannah says I'm much better now than in our wedding tent all those years ago."

"Right," Sam said, "you do have spirit, and maybe that's what it's all about. With or without angels, you seem to have that spark. I'm sure that makes her happy."

"Yes," Ananias replied, "actually, last Friday night—you know, the sabbath, when we don't light fires or even candles after dark—Hannah said that—"

"All right," Sam interrupted again, "I got it. It's probably best if we stop here. You know, angels can be sensitive about these personal details."

"We're not Samaritans, you know," Ananias said with a wink.

"Got it," Sam said, nodding. "Not like those people who *never* have intimate relations on Friday night. No warmth or body heat. Apparently not even a fire or candle to keep them warm," he said with a sigh.

Ananias put his hand on Sam's shoulder. "It sounds like you're courting a Samaritan woman. Am I right?"

Sam looked at Ananias. "I'm not sure about the courting part. But yes, I'm interested in a woman who's from that tradition."

Ananias leaned closer. "Well, here's my advice. Listen closely. The connection is everything. The details don't matter. Follow your heart, and maybe she'll even become a Judean. You know, body heat on Friday nights. Either way, it's really not important. It's all about promises and sacred moments."

"That sounds wise," Sam said, nodding. "Live each day like it's the last one. Because one day it will be."

Ananias nodded and smiled at Sam. "For a man who believes in angels," he said, "you almost seem smart."

"Thanks," Sam said, smiling. "I felt that way myself when I figured out those mysterious Greek letters."

"Hmm, maybe they weren't mysterious enough," Ananias said, raising his eyebrow."

"No, they were pretty tough," Sam replied, showing Ananias the list of translated Greek abbreviations in a document on his laptop.

ΔΙ for the legal system (ΔΙΚΗ or *dike*)

ΤΡ for banking (ΤΡΑΠΕΖΑ or *trapeza*)

ΘΕ for clergy (ΘΕΟΣ or *theos*)

ΗΝ for the military (specifically described as "chariots") (ΗΝΙΟΧΟΣ or *iniochos*)

ΧΑΓ for Jewish pilgrimages (ΧΑΓ or *chag* in Hebrew)

ΣΚ for the Essenes's treasury (*isiyim korbanas* in Hebrew)

"Pretty good for someone who believes in angels," Ananias said, nodding. "Next time, I'll have to use Egyptian or some other language that's tougher than Greek."

Sam looked at Ananias, reflecting on what he had told him about the revolt and what would happen if the militants didn't stand down.

"Ananias," Sam said, putting his hand on the older man's arm, "what if your speech doesn't work out? You know, if things spiral out of control and the Romans send their legions to do their worst? Are you afraid to die?"

Ananias lowered his head and turned to look at Sam. "No, I'm not. That's a part of life. The important thing is to use your life—and even your death—to express your beliefs. No one wants to die early, of course, but what an honor it would be to die for a cause. I'm really a simple man, and I have no interest in claiming any glory or legacy. I don't need to be right or even understood by those who would judge me. These things belong to the divine, and I am at peace with that."

Sam nodded. "I understand, and that seems wise. Maybe one day your courage will inspire others to stand up for their beliefs too. I get that you're not interested in any fame or glory. But maybe the world needs to know more about you."

Ananias smiled at Sam. "You're very kind," he said. "But that's not important. When in the future people think about these difficult times, I would rather they gain some wisdom from our hardships and sacrifices. Above all, I would want people to understand the need for unity—especially with those with whom we disagree. It's easy to fight over our differences. How to handle the Romans, where our temples should be, what love means on Friday nights—but unity is more important. After all, how can we connect with the divine if we can't even connect with each other? But right now," Ananias said, gesturing toward his papers, "I've got to connect with my audience through that speech I'm working on."

"Right," Sam replied, "that's really important." He closed his eyes and sighed, knowing he would never see Ananias again. These dreams were precious but could be heartbreaking too. Ananias had deserved a better life. But perhaps it was merciful that he had died before the Jerusalem that he loved was put to the torch. Sam thought of Hannah being enslaved in a Roman kitchen or worse. What courage it takes to stand up for your beliefs, he thought. Would he be as brave as Ananias? he wondered.

Sam closed his eyes, and the dream ended.

Giovanna touched Sam's shoulder. "Sir, we'll be landing in twenty minutes. You need to fasten your seat belt."

Sam opened his eyes and looked at Giovanna while buckling his seat belt. "Time for a glass of wine, maybe?" he asked, smiling. "White for me, and red for my friend over here," he said, winking at Ananias's empty seat.

Giovanna looked at Sam. "Your friend?" she asked, looking at the empty seat.

Sam smiled. "He's gone now but not forgotten. A man for the seasons, really. You know, a time for peace."

Sam closed his eyes as Giovanna went to get the wine.

L'Chaim, he thought. To life. An extraordinary one.

12

AN ANGEL BEFORE THEE

The white taxi pulled up at the front doors to the American Colony Hotel in Jerusalem. Sam admired the taxi as he got out to greet the porters gathering his bags. Airports could seem homogenous, but at least the taxis were different around the world. Yellow cabs in New York, black hackneys in London, and red Nissans in Mexico City. And, apparently, white sedans in Israel.

Sam checked in and was upstairs in his hotel room by 4:00 p.m. He would be meeting Rebecca at the restaurant at 7:00 p.m., so he had enough time to check messages and maybe get a little exercise before dinner. Sam had chosen the Between the Arches restaurant near the Western Wall, which seemed sufficiently romantic and elegant for the occasion.

Sam sat down in a chair by the window to check his messages. Everything was going well, he thought. His mom, Jason, and Steve were all on schedule. So far the trip was surprisingly smooth; just the usual friendly bickering in the group text with Jason and Steve. It was still the Samaritan sabbath, so he wouldn't hear from Rebecca before sunset.

> *Hi Sam, I hope you had a good flight from Rome and that you're settled into the hotel now. I'll be arriving late tonight and was hoping to meet you for breakfast tomorrow. Say 9 am in the courtyard? Just a reminder that Jason and Steve arrive on Monday afternoon. I've arranged some touring for the two of us on Sunday, Tuesday, and Thursday. I figured you'd like to spend time with Jason and Steve on the other days, and maybe we could all meet up a few times too. I have some photo ops and a screening here this week for Mata Hari. You and Jason and Steve all have VIP passes, and Ava Stern will be there. I hear she's bringing her veil-dancing costume, so it should be a pretty good show! See you tomorrow! Love, Mom*

> *Shalom Sam! Just checking in before Jason and I fly out tomorrow. We leave LA on Sunday and land at Ben Gurion on Monday afternoon. Looking forward to seeing you and your mom too. Not to mention Ava*

Stern at the photo op. Just saw the trailer for Mata Hari, and she's really hot! Remember, you and Jason already have girlfriends, so she's all mine, right? Steve

Hey Sam, can't wait to see you and Steve out there in Israel. Hope things are going well with your reporter friend. This definitely disqualifies you from dating Ava Stern. But, Steve, I broke up with Irina last fall. So Ava's fair game. May the best man win! Jason

Sam smiled, enjoying Jason and Steve's friendly rivalry. But what if Ava liked *him* best? His mom had told him all about her, and he'd even read the Mata Hari script. A beautiful Dutch woman who had learned the arts of exotic dance was certainly alluring and tempting. Especially if she was as brilliant and deeply spiritual as everyone said. But Sam wanted to avoid any competition between him and his friends. Maybe he should skip the photo op on Monday, he thought. Rebecca had said she might be free during the week, right? He hoped to find out tonight.

Sam texted back to his mom.

Hi Mom, the flight from Rome was good, and I'm already loving it here in Jerusalem. I'm meeting Rebecca (the pretty reporter) for dinner at 7 pm and will get to see a little of the town when we go out. Breakfast downstairs at 9 am sounds great. Have a great flight too, and I'll see you tomorrow! Sam

Then he texted back to his friends too.

Hey guys, great to hear from you, and so glad you're making the trip out here. I just got in this afternoon, and I'm at the hotel in Jerusalem now. It's a bit like LA would be if it were ancient, lush, beautiful, cultural, and deeply spiritual. But other than that, pretty much the same. Looking forward to seeing you guys on Monday. I heard a rumor that those hot scenes in the trailer were just Ava's body double. Maybe I could get you an introduction? See you soon! Sam

Sam looked through the hotel brochure to get more familiar with the hotel and its setting. The hotel alone had a pretty interesting history. Did everything in Jerusalem have a unique backstory? More than a century ago, about one hundred Swedish Americans and just regular Swedes showed up in Jerusalem, looking for a more peaceful life modeled along the lines of the early Christians. Adopting a lifestyle of communal living, shared property, and acts of service to local residents, this so-called "American Colony" soon bought a large home that had originally been built as a palace for a pasha and his four wives.

This community evolved over the decades into a charming hotel for travelers and pilgrims looking for a peaceful oasis seen as neutral by the different peoples of Jerusalem. It had proudly survived several wars and remained popular with diplomats, journalists, and others seeking a tranquil, cosmopolitan island near the Old City.

Needing to burn off some energy after the flight, Sam decided to go for a run before dark. He changed into his running gear, went downstairs, and walked out onto the street. Sam started off at a strong pace, feeling energized after not having run for several days. He took a shortcut up toward the ridge lying to the east, known as Mount Scopus. Climbing rapidly up toward the ridge, Sam could see the sun beginning to set in the west.

What a beautiful city, Sam thought. There was so much history here, but it was also somehow a bit timeless. The green hills seemed to promise an endless change of seasons no matter what happened in the city below. Maybe that was part of what made this place special. A bit like LA, really. The coast was less than thirty miles to the west and the desert less than ten miles to the east. In between lay a thin strip of fertile land—an abundance of sun-soaked nature that seemed like a miracle.

Returning to the hotel, Sam went upstairs to shower and change. He pulled off his sweaty shirt and tossed it into the laundry bag. Walking past the mirror toward the shower, he noticed that his morning yoga sessions had started to make a difference. He had always been athletic, but this was something new. He looked more sculpted and toned. But mostly it made him *feel* better—alert, calm, and focused. He was mostly taking a break from yoga during this trip, but he was really looking forward to starting his daily sessions again soon.

After showering, Sam wrapped a towel around his waist and walked back into the living area of his suite, where he had laid out some of his clothes. He looked over some of the possible combinations. A black jacket and white shirt. Charcoal gray with coral. Dark blue with light blue.

He wasn't quite sure what he wanted. A white shirt might seem a little tame. The coral was a little bold. The light blue was just right. It would go well with the dark blue jacket. He had never acted this way before. What was it about Rebecca?

Around 6:15 p.m., Sam heard a ping on his phone. He picked it up, thinking it might be Rebecca. She had probably left home by now, since she was driving from Tel Aviv to Jerusalem, about forty-five minutes away.

Sam looked at the text message. It was Roy.

> *Hi Sam, Roy here. I left you a voice mail earlier and haven't heard back yet. I need to talk to you about some urgent projects. Anytime 24-7 is good, and it really can't wait. I'll be waiting for your call. Roy*

Even for a CEO, Roy was beyond obnoxious, Sam thought. He had no intention of returning this message before Monday. Maybe not even then. It was Saturday night, and the last thing he wanted to think about was Roy's decaying mind and body. He had better things to do.

Sam finished dressing and looked around the room. He wanted to make sure that everything was in order. He noticed that all the curtains were drawn open. He liked it that way; the sunshine in the daytime was nice, but the moonlight streaming in at night might be even nicer.

Around 6:45 p.m., Sam got a taxi and headed over to the Between the Arches restaurant. He arrived a little before 7:00 p.m. and got a table. He looked around the restaurant. The walls of ancient stone created an almost cave-like experience that was romantic and intimate. Just perfect for their first real date, he thought.

Then he saw her. Gorgeous from head to toe, covered in a short black winter coat with her soft auburn hair spilling over her shoulders. She smiled at the hostess in the reception area and scanned the room. She did a graceful pirouette as the hostess helped to remove her coat. She slipped out of it, exposing her bare back and her long legs accented by sexy black high heels. Her derriere was exquisitely wrapped in a tight black party dress with a hemline just above her knees.

Sam blinked, feeling like this was a dream. Rebecca turned slowly back toward the hostess, pivoting her round hips slightly as though she were starting a long, slow striptease. As he got up from his chair, Sam felt a sensation of heat coursing through his body. He raised his right arm and waved a bit to greet her from across the room.

Flashing a bright smile when she saw him, Rebecca tapped the hostess on the shoulder and pointed at Sam. The waitress smiled and began walking her toward Sam.

Sam stepped forward as they approached. "Rebecca, so wonderful to finally see you again!" he said with a smile, reaching out to her with both arms.

"Hi, Sam, I'm so happy to see you!" she said as he gave her a warm hug. He held on tight for an extra moment or two, not quite ready to let go. She felt so good.

Sam pulled out a chair to seat her at the table. As Rebecca unwrapped her shawl, he admired the sheer soft pink silk pieces knotted together, creating a shimmering effect over the black party dress, almost like the petals of a soft flower. Placing her shawl carefully over the back of one of the empty chairs, she sat down gracefully with the perfect balance of a dancer.

As Sam took his seat again, he couldn't stop looking at her. Her soft hazel eyes seemed to sparkle brightly in the darkened room, as though magically lit by the force of her warmth and charm. Her auburn hair flowed in long slightly curled locks over her shoulders. Her firm, round breasts were bound tightly inside her low-cut party dress, gently pressed upward as a delicious temptation that Sam could barely turn his eyes from.

Sam leaned forward, looking into her eyes. "You look wonderful. I just love your dress. Good choice, right?" he said with a smile.

"I had help." she said, smiling back. "Someone with good taste, I think."

"That sounds right," Sam agreed. "Good taste is really just about knowing what you want. And making it happen."

"I like the sound of that," Rebecca said, looking down a bit shyly. "It's all about how you feel."

"Feelings are everything," Sam said with a nod, looking down at the drink menu. "What kind of cocktail are you feeling like? They seem to have some good ones here. The twisted negroni looks interesting."

"Mmm, strawberry and rosemary," Rebecca said, "that does sound twisted. An intense pairing, but just perfect for a Saturday night, right?"

Sam looked up from the menu. "Endless love looks good too. Maraschino cherry liqueur with a splash of cranberry. But maybe that's better for Sunday morning?"

"I can't think that far ahead." Rebecca smiled. "After that meditation school in India, I pretty much live in the moment. Which right now is Saturday night."

"Interesting," Sam said, leaning forward. "You went to a meditation school in India?"

"Of course," Rebecca said with a smile. "It's important to learn things firsthand. Meditation in India, investigative journalism in New York, a pizza class in Naples. There's nothing like hands-on experience."

"I couldn't agree more," Sam said, nodding. "It sounds like the meditation school was great. You said you learned to live in the moment?"

"Definitely," Rebecca said. "I told you that I'm a Samaritan, and I love that tradition. It's a big part of who I am. But it's nice to go beyond that and to explore other things. Understanding more seems to make all of your beliefs deeper. I've been doing yoga almost every day since then," she went on. "The word *yoga* means to 'yoke' the mind to the soul. I think that's really important. The mind's a wonderful tool, but it should serve the soul, not the other way around. Sometimes the mind just needs to go quiet. Feelings and experiences are more important."

"I know what you mean," Sam agreed. "I went running today, and it really quieted my mind. It's been a busy week, but somehow that cleared it up. Everything made sense, or else it didn't matter, once I got that focus back."

Arriving with their cocktails, the waitress placed the drinks down on the table. "A twisted negroni for the lady and a dirty martini for the gentleman," the waitress said.

Rebecca smiled. "I see you took charge on this one and decided which drink I would like," she said, raising her glass as a toast.

"Cheers." Sam smiled, raising his glass in return.

"Better watch out. Soon it will be my turn," she said, taking a sip of her cocktail. "But before we go any further, I think I'll have a taste of your martini."

"I thought you would say that," Sam said with a smile as he slid his glass across the table to Rebecca. "Sometimes it's fun to get a little dirty."

"Deliciously dirty," Rebecca said, taking a sip and licking the rim ever so slightly to savor the taste. "You seem to know what I like."

Sam smiled. "Maybe a few things you haven't thought of too," he teased.

"It sounds like you've been reading my blog," Rebecca said, a bit shyly. "I mean—that blog I told you about. By the anonymous writer. You know, Veils of Desire."

"I haven't had a chance to read it yet," he lied. "I don't know anything at all about that blog writer's passion for exotic dance. How she enjoys expressing herself through the poetry of her body and sensual movement.

The way it inflames her desires to have her man watching while she slowly unzips and unsnaps, layer by layer."

"That's too bad," Rebecca said, taking another sip of her cocktail. "When you do read it," she teased, twisting a long lock of her hair, "you'll see that what she really desires is the freedom to express herself through whatever movement feels best at the moment. And that sometimes she just wants her man to take charge and give her exactly what she wants. She wants a man who knows what she's feeling and how to make her feel good."

"It sounds like I really need to check that out," Sam said, smiling.

"I think that's a good idea," Rebecca said. "Knowing a woman's mind is just as important as knowing her body, I think. So, tell me about your week," Rebecca said, taking another graceful sip of her cocktail. "I'm so glad you're here so I get to hear about it firsthand."

"Well, there's the usual work chaos," Sam began. "You know, a deranged CEO who worships golden toilets, a missing investigator who's really a friend of mine that I'm worried about, and my father who seems to be in over his head about something. But, really, life is just perfect," he said, smiling. "It's Saturday night with the most beautiful woman and a dirty martini. And maybe endless love after that."

"I think you're just stuck on those maraschino cherries," Rebecca teased. "You know, the sweet, juicy ones that make your tongue tingle. So, I've heard a bit about your work week. What did you do for fun this week?"

"Oh, that's easy." Sam smiled. "I decoded it."

"You decoded it?" Rebecca tilted her head, puzzled. "Decoded what?"

"It's a bronze scroll," Sam replied. "Ninety-nine percent copper and one percent tin. Which tells you that the tin was just added for symbolic purposes. The man who commissioned this wanted the scroll to be made of bronze, not copper. In his homeland—Judea, which the Romans had merged with your ancestors' land, Samaria—bronze represented man's access to the divine through atonement. This man wanted the Judeans and Samaritans to know that their treasures would only be safe through the traditional practices for forgiveness. Apparently, during the revolt, it was getting hard to find tin—most of which was imported from Britain or Spain—so only a small amount was added to the alloy."

"Treasures?" Rebecca asked. "What kind of treasures?"

"Eighteen tons of gold and silver," Sam replied. "The entire treasury of the Jerusalem Temple. Plus, some of the sacred treasures of the Temple—the bronze sacrificial altar, high priest robes, and things like that."

"Oh, you mean the Copper Scroll," Rebecca said, leaning back in her chair. "I did an article about that a few years ago. It's a treasure map with clues that make no sense. Everyone agrees it will never be solved. It's just impossible."

"Unless you decode it, right?" Sam leaned forward. "Did you write about the last treasure site—location number sixty?"

"Of course," Rebecca replied, "treasure site sixty—the decoder scroll. It's an explanation of everything, all you need to know. But it's hidden in some unknown village that no one's ever heard of."

"Kohlit?" Sam smiled.

"Yes, that sounds right." Rebecca nodded.

"Which could also be Kohelet, right?" Sam asked.

"Yes, I suppose," she replied. "The ancient Hebrew script didn't write out the vowels. So the script on the scroll would have been K-H-L-T. That could be Kohlit, Kohelet, or something else."

"It's Kohelet." Sam smiled. "The Teacher. Solomon's poem."

Rebecca looked puzzled. "You're saying the explanation for all these treasures of the ancient world is a poem?"

"Exactly," Sam said, nodding. "It's a bit like yoga or meditation, maybe. The mind serving the soul, not the other way around," he said, smiling.

Rebecca paused and reflected. "So what does the poem say?"

"It says a lust for gold and silver can never be satisfied," Sam replied. "Material things bring no joy. But a man's love for a woman can be meaningful and deep. Take time to live slowly. Enjoy a woman's touch and the warmth of the afternoon sun."

"Sounds like one of the teachers at my meditation school in India." Rebecca smiled.

"I think you're onto something." Sam grinned. "The mind serves the soul, not the other way around, right? Chasing gold and silver is pointless. You can't take it with you. But love is eternal."

Rebecca looked down at her cocktail menu and smiled. "Maybe I'll have one of those endless love cocktails after all. Your poems can be pretty persuasive."

Sam blushed and had to pause for a moment. "Did I tell you about treasure site sixty-one?"

"I thought there were only sixty," Rebecca said, leaning forward. "You know, excluding the sites that have multiple treasures."

"You have to look at the fine print," Sam said with a smile. "Remember, I'm a lawyer, and we notice these things."

"What does it say?" Rebecca teased.

"It's kind of poetic too," Sam replied. "It says to follow your heart and seize the moment. Go for the endless love and feel your passion."

"All that's on the bronze scroll?" Rebecca smiled.

"Like I say, on the back, in the disclaimer section," Sam said, grinning.

"But we haven't even had our main course yet. And what about dessert?" Rebecca sighed.

"That's part of the poem too." Sam smiled. "Penne rosa with the sea kabob, of course. And the hot chocolate soufflé to go. Soufflés are always better in a hotel room, you know."

"I'm not sure about that," Rebecca flirted. "I'll have to decide how I feel when I'm in that moment. Plus, I parked my car in an overnight garage and wouldn't be able to get it back until morning if we stay out late."

"Perfect," Sam said, smiling. "That's the safest place for a car. And they have these adorable white taxis here. I guess there was a shortage of yellow paint at the taxi factory."

As Rebecca reflected on the menu, the waitress arrived and took their orders. An endless love cocktail for Rebecca, a forbidden fruit cocktail for Sam, penne rosa and sea kabob for Rebecca, and fettucine with cream sauce and red tuna medallions for Sam. Plus a hot chocolate soufflé to go.

A few minutes later, as Rebecca sipped on her endless love and Sam on his forbidden fruit, Sam felt his eyes wandering down to the luscious maraschino cherries hidden inside Rebecca's low-cut party dress. Her breasts were so tightly wrapped against her chest that he could imagine them bouncing free a bit if her strapless bra came off.

"You seem distracted by my dress." Rebecca smiled. "Maybe you should try meditation."

"It's not the dress." Sam grinned. "It's you, and I wouldn't call it a distraction. More like a focus. I did one of those meditation classes in India too. Have you heard of red tantra?"

"You mean that type of meditation based on intense physical pleasure?" she asked. "Quieting the mind through the slow, steady flame of attraction and desire until it burns like the sun? I think I did hear about that. And you?"

"I heard all the rumors, of course," Sam replied. "They call it the chocolate soufflé of the yoga world. It's only *one path* to serenity and deeper understanding. And we were taught that it's so powerful that it should only be used after you've mastered meditation and the less intense form of ancient practices known as white tantra. That way you're grounded and can handle the intense experience and transformative powers of red tantra."

"I heard all that too." Rebecca smiled shyly. "Except the chocolate soufflé part. That might be a slight exaggeration. But I definitely agree that this red tantra should only be used in moderation—like maybe on a Saturday night. And only by someone who knows how to control attraction and desire. Like a master chef who knows how to keep a chocolate soufflé going all night."

As Rebecca began enjoying her penne and Sam his fettucine, they continued talking about their experiences with meditation. Sam admitted that he found calming the mind through mantras to be challenging. His mind was so active that it could be hard to calm it through chanting or breathing. Red tantra could be such a powerful connection between two souls—at least, hypothetically, if he would ever explore that in the future, he said, clearing his throat—that the repetition of "om" to quiet the mind sometimes seemed a little weaker by comparison. But he understood that practice was important. The whole point was to master the mind so that it served the soul and not the other way around.

Rebecca agreed—at least, hypothetically, if she ever had the experience—that an intimate connection was one of the most powerful experiences a soul could have. The union of two souls was like the union with the divine, she thought, and nothing could be sweeter. Of course, the endless love cocktail was pretty good too, she admitted.

As Rebecca was served her seafood kabob and Sam his tuna medallions, they agreed that "om" mantras were still the best way to discipline the mind and "yoke" it to the soul. It was a bit like any other form of workout, they agreed. You had to get the basics right before moving onto the advanced practices.

Finally, their box of delicious chocolate-soufflé-to-go arrived. Sam settled the tab—this time, without any protest from Rebecca. He was a man, after all, and it felt good to take care of his woman this way. Well, who knows about tomorrow, but she was his woman tonight, and he was her knight in shining armor. Whatever she wanted, needed, or desired would happen. Any color of tantra she could imagine, he would give her.

Sam held her hand in the taxi from the restaurant to his hotel. As they got closer to the hotel, he gently put her hand down on the seat and put his hand on her thigh. He leaned closer and inhaled the perfumed fragrance of her neck, with her soft hair teasing his cheek and enticing him closer. The same ginger-rose scent he remembered from November. Timeless elegance and beauty that he couldn't resist.

When they got to the hotel, Sam and Rebecca rode the elevator upstairs and walked into his darkened suite. He couldn't resist any longer. He leaned down and kissed her lips. Their first kiss since New York. Her soft lips opened and surrendered to his passion. Their tongues flitted and danced—like a soft, wet ballet that seemed timeless and endless.

As they kissed by the window in the moonlight, Sam glided his hands around Rebecca's naked back and slid them down onto her firm backside. He squeezed her with both hands as he felt his lust and desire begin to explode. He wanted to push her onto the bed and tear off her dress, entering her roughly and making her feel his passion.

But Rebecca had other ideas. She told Sam to wait, and she disappeared into the bathroom. She emerged a few minutes later wearing her flowing pink shawl over gold lingerie. Picking up her phone, she turned on some soft music and set it back down on the nightstand.

Mesmerized by her beauty, Sam watched as her body moved slowly beneath the sheer pink veils of her shawl, concealed like a delicate flower ready to bloom. As she danced, her rose petals blushed pink and began to open slightly as she untied and surrendered each veil to the night. When at last all her veils were gone, her flower lay open to Sam's warm embrace.

Rebecca tensed and shuddered as Sam took her unveiled flower, her petals spreading apart softly and gently to his touch. Embracing her rosy fragrance as he held her close, he tasted her sweet nectar as she slipped into bliss.

Entering her garden, he took her luscious fruit as his own. She surrendered everything to him—her body, her heart, and her mind. Her pleasures were theirs now, no secrets held back. Her desires set free, she was now captive only to him.

Finally, they lay still together, their bodies entwined, with the sensations of pleasure still echoing between them. Their minds calm and still, they rested gently and silently, their arms and hearts bound together under the soft glow of the moon.

Sam held Rebecca tightly in his arms after their passions had left them. He watched her breathing, with the soft motion of her chest rising and falling. He put his hand over her heart, feeling its warm pulsing. He could feel her joyous life energy, as if a stream of light were beaming from her heart. He flattened his palm to feel more of her power flowing through him, and he closed his eyes, imagining the light pouring out of her kind, beautiful heart.

As Rebecca still rested quietly, Sam lay back down beside her. He rolled over a bit toward the nightstand and set his phone alarm for 7:00 a.m., remembering that Rebecca had a workday and would need to get her car and that he had plans for the day as well. He wanted to give Rebecca a nice start to the day. Maybe with another taste of some endless love.

Sam rolled back next to Rebecca and pulled the bed coverings over most of her body. She was asleep now, and he saw no reason to cover up her luscious breasts. He turned off the light on the nightstand and looked at her breasts rising and falling slightly in the moonlight as she rested.

Sam gazed at her face. She was so beautiful and perfect. Maybe this was a little like that story about Solomon's father. David, right? With a woman like this, one look at her in the moonlight would be enough. Rebecca had captivated his heart, and there was nothing to do now but enjoy it.

Sam put his hand against her arm and closed his eyes. Feeling her warmth, he let go of his thoughts and returned to the unseen light.

She was *his* tonight. A pure angel.

13

THIS IS THE LAND

Sam woke up the next morning with his right arm draped around Rebecca and his body snuggled up against hers. It was Sunday, a little before 7:00 a.m., and his alarm hadn't gone off yet. He pulled away from Rebecca a bit to turn it off.

Then he rolled back to snuggle against Rebecca. He pulled his head up a bit and looked down at her beautiful face as she peacefully slept. Her red lips were so enticing, and her long eyelashes expressed an elegant beauty that he couldn't resist. Her auburn hair was a bit messed up now, of course, which made her even more seductive.

Sam could still smell her fragrance. He moved his face closer to hers to quietly inhale her alluring scent. Ginger-rose perfume, mingled a bit with a sweeter scent from her flowing hair. Just delicious.

He moved closer to her hair to enjoy more of her aroma. Rosemary-mint, perhaps? No wonder she was tempted by that strawberry-rosemary cocktail last night. But he was glad that she chose the endless love cocktail. Maraschino cherries suited her perfectly.

Glancing at the nightstand, Sam noticed that they had forgotten about the chocolate soufflé last night. Smiling a bit, he blamed it on the red tantra. And her seven-veils costume. Who needs chocolate when you're busy with transcendent physical bliss and connection?

He tried to remember what the yogi had said about red tantra during that class in Rishikesh. The yogi had warned against overdoing such a powerful way of connecting and achieving complete serenity of the mind and soul. He told the class to practice meditation every day and to go easy on the red tantra.

So two days of red tantra in a row might be too much, right? Of course, under the local calendar, a day starts at sunset and runs until the next sunset. So this really requires a creative approach, he thought.

He would see her again on Monday morning, right? So if they practiced a little red tantra on Monday morning and then again on Monday evening, it wouldn't really be the same day at all. The yogi's warning wouldn't apply, and they wouldn't be overdoing it.

Rebecca stirred a bit and sighed. Last night, she had told him about an appointment she had today at 10:00 a.m. She liked to wake up slowly, she said. No need to rush anything; living in the moment was always better.

Sam sighed. There was just no way to resist this woman. Her name said it all. Rebecca. It means "captivating beauty," or "to tie," to "bind," he remembered from when he had looked it up. It sure felt that way, he thought.

Sam decided to relax and to stop thinking about red tantra. That was really the whole point, after all. This seemed to be Rebecca's secret. Just enjoying life and living in the moment. Surrendering his thoughts to his feelings, he held her closely and let the morning unfold.

A blissful hour and a few shared bites of chocolate soufflé later, Rebecca gave Sam another long, slow kiss and got out of bed to take a shower. Sam offered to help, but she said that *that* kind of help could be distracting. He could watch and talk to her while she showered, she said, but another round of delicious lovemaking would have to wait.

Sam leaned against the side of the bathtub as he watched her shower. He had wrapped a white towel around his waist, and his muscular arms rested against the rim of the tub behind his back. Sam glanced at a full-length mirror with both of their images close to each other. They looked good together, he thought. Her exquisite curves and his muscular frame.

But it was really her beauty inside that made their budding relationship so serene and wonderful. He had never met anyone so kind, loving, and strong. And their connection was so powerful. He knew he would feel her presence now no matter where she was.

As Rebecca finished showering, they talked about when to get together next. Definitely really soon, Sam thought. Tonight, tomorrow, Tuesday, he wished. Pretty much any day of the week.

As they went downstairs in the elevator, Rebecca promised to let Sam know by that afternoon if she could free up tomorrow. She thought it would work and said that she was excited to spend more time with him. Sam thought about that kiss in the elevator the night before and what had seemed an eternity of feelings and emotions since then. He was captivated by Rebecca. He couldn't imagine anything better.

It was getting close to 9:00 a.m. as they got out of the elevator and walked into the lobby. Sam saw his mom approaching and then thoughtfully detouring when she saw him getting out of the hotel elevator with a woman.

As Sam walked with Rebecca through the lobby, he noticed that his mom had sat down on a sofa to watch them with a smile. He felt slightly awkward but was really proud to be with this beautiful woman who was so soft, loving, and kind.

Sam opened the door to her taxi and watched her get in. Leaning in, he put his hands on her cheeks and gave her a long, slow kiss.

"Have a great day," he said softly.

"You too," she said with a sigh. "I'll be thinking about you."

He watched as the taxi drove off and could still hear the sound of her voice as she disappeared for the day. He wished that they had more time together, but he was excited that they might get to spend the whole day together on Monday.

Sam walked back into the hotel lobby. "So how about breakfast?" he said to his mom.

"It depends," Dawn replied with a laugh. "Do I get to hear all about her?" She smiled.

Sam smiled. "She's Rebecca, the beautiful reporter."

"I had guessed that much." She smiled back. "She's just gorgeous," Dawn said, looking a little wistful. "The grandchildren would be adorable."

"How many do you have in mind?" Sam laughed.

"I was thinking two or three." Dawn smiled. "But if you keep looking at her that way, maybe I'll end up with four or five."

"They'd be awfully cute," Sam agreed.

"Let's talk about it over breakfast," his mother said, taking hold of his arm as they walked into the courtyard restaurant. "It's never too early to start planning for grandchildren, you know."

"Four or five, huh?" Sam joked, putting his hand on her shoulder as they walked to their table. "Are you sure your villa will have space for all of us?"

"I have my eye on a bigger villa up the hill," she said, smiling. "Not like those Roman emperors, of course. Something modest with just eight or nine bedrooms."

Sam and his mom sat down to a nice breakfast in the hotel courtyard. Hearing a ping, though, Sam just had to check his phone in case it was Rebecca. Which it was.

> *Good morning again, Sam. What a wonderful night together! And such a delightful surprise this morning too. You're a true angel. I was able to move things around, so I'm free tomorrow now. How about a day trip to the north? I'd love to show you around some of my favorite places. Maybe share some of my secret passions too? Last night was really just a taste of what I'm thinking. And feeling. Want to come with me? Rebecca*

Sam smiled at his mom and explained that he'd need to reply to this. He walked to a quiet, sunny spot in the courtyard and typed a reply.

> *Good morning back, sweet Rebecca. Such an amazing night! It seems like only moments ago I had you in my arms. Yes for tomorrow and anything else your heart desires. Your favorite places up north will be wonderful. I have a few favorite places now too. Maybe we could find a romantic hotel on the beach or some other magical place where we can explore your secret passions? I'm hungry for more and want to know everything about you. Until then, Sam*

Sam exhaled and returned to finish breakfast with his mom. They planned out the day, and he let her know about his new plans to spend Monday with Rebecca. He was fine with missing the photo op and media event with Ava Stern. Dawn said that Ava had forgotten her seven-veils costume back in LA anyway. The event wouldn't be the same in yoga pants, of course.

Sam gave his mom a quick hug after breakfast as they agreed to meet in the lobby again at 10:30 a.m. to start their history tour in Jerusalem. Sam was happy for the distraction and had been wanting to do this tour anyway. His mom had always somehow managed to make history and spirituality interesting, and he was starting to understand that there was more to all this than he had imagined. It wasn't just the amazing sex, he thought. It was the connection. Some unfamiliar feeling like that painting of two hands touching on the ceiling of the Sistine Chapel.

Sam arrived back in the hotel lobby a few minutes before 10:30 a.m. He looked around for his mother and saw her walking out of the elevator. They walked outside and were greeted by the tour guide.

"Good morning, Dawn," said the older gentleman with a white beard as he approached them. "And this must be Sam," he said, holding out his hand to Sam. Sam admired his neatly pressed white linen suit.

"Great to see you, Melchior." Sam's mom bowed slightly. "*Hâlet cheto-re*?" she said in Farsi. "How are you?"

"Nice to meet you." Sam stepped forward, smiling and shaking the tour guide's outstretched hand.

"Are you ready for your tour?" Melchior asked.

"Yes, of course, I've been looking forward to this," Dawn said, smiling.

"Me too," Sam chimed in. "Where are we going?"

"Come this way." Melchior waved them toward the white van with the black lettering "Three Kings Tour Agency." "I'll explain the itinerary once we get going. We have a lot to see."

Melchior opened the side door to the van's comfortable back seats, and Dawn and Sam hopped inside. Melchior climbed into the driver's seat, and the tour began.

"We're going first to the Tower of David," Melchior explained. "I'll start telling you about it on the way. After that, I'll give you a private tour of the Israel Museum. It's one of the most magnificent museums in the world and, of course, has a special wing for the famous Dead Sea Scrolls."

"That sounds exciting," Sam said. "I'm working on a project about one of those scrolls. So that's exactly what I'd love to see."

Dawn looked at Sam, surprised. "You're working on something about the Dead Sea Scrolls? That sounds interesting."

"It sure is," Sam said, nodding. "Jason and Steve took me to a traveling exhibit at the Getty about this bronze scroll. It's usually referred to as the Copper Scroll because that's what the scientists thought it was made of when it was discovered in the 1950s. When it was finally tested, it turned out to be ninety-nine percent copper and one percent tin. So it's a man-made alloy but with only a trivial amount of tin. Normally, bronze is ten or twenty percent tin, which makes this alloy stronger and more resilient than pure copper. But since this scroll was only one percent tin, that means that the tin was added only for symbolic purposes."

"Really? Like what?" Dawn asked.

"Like giving an antiwar speech in front of the Bronze Gate to the Jerusalem Temple, after the Jewish revolt of the year 66 broke out," Sam replied. "The speaker wanted a powerful metaphor made of bronze to remind his audience of the spiritual meaning of the bronze that was used at the Jerusalem Temple at that time."

"Right," Melchior jumped in, "metals have often been seen as powerful spiritual metaphors. This is really quite interesting, Sam."

"What do you mean?" Sam asked, a little flattered by Melchior's interest and intrigued by his comment.

"Well, most ancient cultures viewed gold as a symbol of divinity," Melchior replied. "It's seen as eternal because it doesn't tarnish or rust. Which makes sense because, really, all the gold on earth came from a massive supernova explosion somewhere in our part of the universe billions of years ago. It's truly a special element. Do you remember the story about the Wise Men at the Nativity?"

"Of course," Sam replied, "they brought gifts of gold, frankincense, and myrrh."

"Good answer." Melchior nodded, looking at Sam through the rearview mirror. "Gaspar brought gold from India, Balthasar brought myrrh from Babylon, and yours truly brought frankincense from Persia."

"Yours truly?" Sam looked at Melchior, puzzled.

Dawn put her hand on Sam's arm. "Melchior's just joking, Sam. It goes with the Three Kings theme at his touring business. He's not saying that he *personally* brought the frankincense almost two thousand years ago. Right, Melchior?" she said, leaning over to give him a knowing look in the rearview mirror.

"Right," Sam said, "I assumed—"

"Your mom's right," Melchior interrupted. "I can't remember back that far anyway. At my age, I'm lucky if I remember where I parked this van," he said with a laugh. "The year 4 BC was a really long time ago."

"But that makes it sound like—" Sam began. "Oh, never mind," he said, realizing that Melchior couldn't be *that* old.

Dawn put her hand on Sam's arm again. "You shouldn't be asking people's ages, dear. A reporter once asked me if I was the same age as Cleopatra in one of my movies, and I got him banned from the studio."

"So, anyway," Melchior continued, "gold is a symbol of the divine, and silver is a symbol of purity. The ancient people viewed these metals as powerful symbols of spirituality."

"That makes sense," Sam agreed, "and the bronze that was used at the Jerusalem Temple was seen as a symbol of atonement—something man made and thus a bit separated from the divine. Bronze was used in the main gate to the sanctuary at the Temple and in the sacrificial altar and washing basin that the priests used. So, it was seen as something for man to use to access the divine but that, being man made, wasn't itself divine."

"Interesting." Melchior nodded. "Tell us more about this bronze scroll, Sam."

"Well, it's a treasure map that was found in a Dead Sea cave in the 1950s," Sam replied. "The professionals who've studied it—archaeologists, linguists, historians, and theologists—have all concluded that the treasure clues can't be solved through their disciplines. It would take something more to understanding its meaning and purpose. Like an understanding of the story of *why* it was made."

"So what do *you* think, Sam?" Dawn asked. "You said you've been studying it. For a case at work, I guess?"

"No, I'm just doing this for fun," Sam replied. "Jason and Steve took me to the Getty exhibit as a birthday present, and I just got interested in it. I can't resist an unsolvable mystery, I guess."

"That sounds like you," Dawn said, nodding. "So did you solve it?"

"Not yet," Sam said, "but I've made progress, and I'm still working on it. Jason and Steve are helping too. We divided up the different projects and are working on it together. Just for fun, of course."

"So you mentioned treasures," Dawn said. "What kind of treasures would those be?"

"The Temple treasury, basically," Sam replied. "All the gold and silver that had been hidden that the Romans couldn't find after they destroyed the Temple and most of Jerusalem. Plus all the sacred artifacts of the Temple that hadn't been looted and carried off to Rome."

"Like the Ark of the Covenant and the stone tablets with the Ten Commandments?" his mother asked.

Sam smiled. "Well, I haven't run across those, at least not yet, I suppose. It's mostly just gold and silver coins and artifacts. Lots of it. Eighteen tons, in fact."

"Wow, how much is that worth?" Melchior asked.

"It depends on how much of the treasure is gold and how much is silver," Sam replied. "But, as a wild guess, based on what I've figured out so far, I'd say about a half a billion dollars. But here's the thing. That's not the important part."

"What's that?" Dawn asked.

"It's the poetry," he said. "The high priest who commissioned the bronze scroll wanted to stop the war. A group of militants—led by his son, of all people—had seized the Temple and were doing their best to start a war with the Romans. The high priest included all sorts of biblical references—poetry, really—in the scroll to emphasize the points in his speech."

"That does sound important." Dawn nodded. "What do the poems say?"

"Some of the treasure locations include metaphorical descriptions based on biblical texts, which he used in a poetic sort of way," Sam said. "One of them was called the Teacher and teaches how to live a good life, for instance by not chasing gold and silver. The reason we're here is to love and care for each other and to enjoy warm sunshine and all of the beauty of the world created by the divine."

"That's a beautiful thought," his mother said, smiling.

"The other metaphors involve stories of betrayal and forgiveness—which I think had to do with the high priest's son, who was actively working against his own father's peace efforts," Sam went on. "And stories about Jerusalem itself. Like a bride of the divine who might have forgotten some of her vows. That was one of the metaphors he used, anyway."

"So what happened?" Melchior asked. "Did the high priest persuade his audience to stop the revolt?"

"Sadly, no," Sam said. "The conservatives led by the high priest and the militants led by his son ended up in a civil war. The high priests and most of the other leaders were killed in battles between the different Judean camps long before the Roman legions arrived and began their siege of Jerusalem. Ever since, and in different ways, Jerusalem has been a symbol of conflict and division. You know, the name Jerusalem means the 'city of peace.'" But its history hardly lives up to that. Maybe the high priest was right."

"What do you mean?" Dawn asked.

"Well, in some ways, Jerusalem—and the people who have fought over it, which means *all* of us—might be like a bride of the divine who has forgotten some of her vows," Sam responded. "Like the rules against murder, theft, and envy. Really, these rules are about putting spirituality and the divine first in your life. Loving your neighbor and helping others in need—instead of dehumanizing them and spreading ideas of hate and war. It's hard to believe, but here we are two thousand years later, and we see pictures of people throwing stones at other people and burning their homes and shops. With their faces twisted in hate and anger. Innocent children are dying because we haven't figured out how to actually live by the golden rule. It's *everyone's* fault, and we're *all* in this together. I think that's what the high priest was saying. How much injustice and suffering do we have to endure before we finally figure out how to live up to these words? Can't we do better?"

"That sounds wise," Dawn said, putting her hand on Sam's arm again. "This is exactly what most people in the world believe. The question is how to create a world where people believe it *enough* to put it into practice. We all have work to do, it seems."

"That's an amazing story, Sam," Melchior said, looking at him in the rearview mirror again. "I think you'll see some of these ideas expressed in the history at our touring destinations today," he said as they pulled up to a parking area close to the Tower of David.

As he led Dawn and Sam up to the towering stone walls of the ancient citadel, topped with toothlike ramparts at the top of its walls, Melchior began telling them the history of this place.

"This fortification is known as a citadel," Melchior explained, "and it's been here in one version or another for more than two thousand years. These walls and most of what we see here were built between the fourteenth and sixteenth centuries. But something similar was built more than a thousand years earlier by the Judean king known as Herod the Great. Herod was a monumental builder, and some of the stones from his construction can still be seen here, near the base of some of the current walls. His version of this fortress had three large stone towers—one of whom he named Mariamne—whom he was mourning after he had her strangled to death."

"That's terrible," Dawn exclaimed.

"Yes, he was a great builder and maybe a strong leader in some ways," Melchior said. "But some of his story is pretty complicated and highlights some of the troubling beliefs that many of the rulers had in those days. Most historians believe that Herod was ethnically an Arab whose family had converted to Judaism at an earlier time. His father had been governor of Galilee and had become a close ally of Julius Caesar. Before the age of thirty, Herod had been appointed as the general in charge of Roman forces in neighboring Samaria. He was an ambitious man.

"After Julius Caesar was murdered," Melchor continued, "Herod and his family became close with Mark Antony, who was a rising star at that time. During one of the frequent civil wars between rivals to the succession of the Judean throne, Herod banished his first wife to marry his second wife, Mariamne, who was the daughter of one of the rivals to the throne. After a few more battles, Herod ended up as being crowned king of Judea, which was then a client state of Rome.

"As I said, Herod was very good at raising taxes and spending vast amounts on monumental building programs. He began the expansion and rebuilding of the Jerusalem Temple, which was completed after his death. He founded a new port city named Caesarea Maritima and built massive fortresses at Masada and Herodium in the Judean desert. He built impressive new aqueducts to supply water to Jerusalem. But he had a turbulent personal life and was accused of murder and other crimes multiple times over his life. He married ten different wives and claimed that he loved his second wife, Mariamne, so much that he gave standing orders for her to be killed upon his death. He couldn't stand the thought of Mariamne being with another man. Not surprisingly, Mariamne had a different opinion on this subject. She felt that if Herod really loved her, he would want her to have a long, happy life, even after his own lifetime. Eventually, she was tried for treason for opposing Herod's wishes, and he ordered her strangled to death. Afterward, he felt so sad about this that he named one of his citadel towers in her honor."

"Herod sounds almost as bad as Octavian," Dawn said, frowning. "He said he loved her? I don't think so. The world would have been better off ruled by queens is all I can say."

"You may have a point," Sam agreed. "Treating women as property might have been a part of the problem. There were an awful lot of violent and sadistic ideas in ancient times—then as now, I suppose—and it's easy to imagine a dynasty of queens doing better."

"That sounds right," Melchior said as he escorted Dawn and Sam into the museum. He walked them through the exhibits about Jerusalem's history and the majestic inner courtyards and grounds of the citadel. Jerusalem, as one of the oldest cities in the world, had history as a city that went back more than five thousand years, and he walked them through many of the exhibits interpreting this history.

Sam and Dawn especially loved the vaulted stone ceilings next to the interior courtyards. The exhibits were impressive, but the massive stone building itself was a visual display of the ancient city's history. They both felt it gave them a sense of what it might have been like to live here two thousand years ago. Incredible beauty, timelessness, and spiritual power. It really hasn't changed much, they both thought.

After the tour of the Tower of David, Melchior brought Dawn and Sam back to the van. He recommended a lunch break at Chakra in the city center, near the Israel Museum. He explained that it was one of Jerusalem's most cosmopolitan restaurants, reflecting both the city's history and the cultures of its different communities. He particularly recommended the strawberry-basil cocktail and the beef tortellini with asparagus.

Rebecca would love this place, Sam thought as they arrived and surveyed the menu. Strawberries and herbs were one of her favorite flavor combinations, and he knew that she would like the chocolate "Nemesis" dessert, preferably in bed at his hotel room. He remembered from his ancient Greek legends class in college that Nemesis was a goddess who took revenge against those who disrespected the gods with arrogance. Just the right solution for some of these kings and emperors, Sam thought.

As they were finishing their lunch, Sam excused himself for a few minutes so that he could send a message to Rebecca. He had been thinking about her and was wondering if she was having a good day.

> *Good afternoon, sweet Rebecca. I hope you're having a great day! Last night with you was so amazing, and I'm really looking forward to our day together tomorrow! I'm having a nice time with sightseeing today, but I'll admit to being a little distracted. We went to the Tower of David, and for some reason, all I could think about was chocolate soufflé. Thinking about you! Sam*

As he drove them to the Israel Museum after lunch, Melchior pointed out that Judea had been cosmopolitan and diverse almost from the beginning. As a crossroads of empires, traders, and spiritual seekers, this land had always embraced different ideas and traditions from across the ancient world. They would see this at the Israel Museum, Melchior promised. The region's diversity had always been one of the things that made it such a fertile source of new cultural and spiritual ideas.

Sam nodded and asked Melchior about his own journey. He had grown up in Persia, right?

"Yes," Melchior replied. "The name Persia actually comes from a Greek word. It's what people in this region have always called us. The local name that we use at home is Iran. But it does highlight how diverse and cosmopolitan this part of the world is. There were Persians, Greeks, and Jews and lots of other groups living side-by-side. Mostly peacefully, but sadly with more than a few wars too. Did you know that there was a

Persian town in ancient Israel for centuries? It was called Scythopolis, after one of the ancient names used for the Persian empire. A large group of Persians settled there around the third century BC, and it's believed that their Persian culture and spiritual beliefs had an influence in this region, particularly around neighboring Galilee. The Persian religion at that time was very similar to the Indian tradition, so it's believed that spiritual ideas about enlightenment and rebirth had an influence on early Christianity and some of the more mystical Jewish traditions."

"That's interesting," Sam said. "I studied in India for a while when I was younger, and it would be fascinating to know how those ideas may have gotten into some of the western traditions."

When they arrived at the Israel Museum, Melchior walked Sam and Dawn through the archaeology wing first, showing them some of the prehistoric artifacts found in this region—pottery, spiritual figurines, textiles, and the giant horns of a wild bull. Then they walked through displays about the rise of agriculture and city states, during which time many of the legends and stories about this land began to be told.

As he guided them through the biblical galleries, Melchior told Sam and Dawn that the early Israelites lived in what is now Samaria and Galilee and only later began settling in the more southern area known as Judah. The idea of Samaria and Galilee being this people's ancestral home might have influenced some of their stories, Melchior suggested.

In another one of the galleries, Melchior told Sam and Dawn one of the stories about a Jewish revolt in the second century BC. After the rebels had led a successful rebellion against a Syrian king, the high poured oil into and lit the golden menorah lamp in order to purify and rededicate the Temple. However, only one jar of oil could be found at the Temple, and it would take another eight days for the pressing and production of new olive oil. Despite this, the menorah lamp burned for the full eight days, which has been celebrated since then as the holiday of Hanukkah, in honor of Jerusalem's freedom and the rededicated Temple.

As they were finishing their tour of the archaeology galleries, Sam heard a ping on his phone. He instantly felt it was from Rebecca.

> *So happy to hear from you, Sam! I'm glad you're having fun touring the city. Last night with you was beyond wonderful, but really I'm not distracted at all today. Well, I did put my salad in the freezer, put way too much sweetener in my coffee, and forgot where my car was parked. I'll*

have to meditate extra tonight so I'm focused tomorrow. You know, that kind of focus where you express yourself and show what you're feeling? Kisses! Rebecca

Sam exhaled and sighed. He might need to do some meditation too. He was pretty distracted at the moment.

After completing their tour of the archaeology galleries, Melchior led Sam and Dawn to the Shrine of the Book wing housing the Dead Sea Scrolls. He told them that the first of these ancient scrolls was believed to have been discovered in late 1946 or early 1947 by three Bedouin shepherds in a cave near the ancient ruins at Qumran on the Dead Sea. Consisting mostly of fragments from more than nine hundred different scrolls, plus a few mostly intact scrolls and other artifacts, the Dead Sea Scrolls have been of great interest to scholars and the public for the insights they afford into biblical writings and beliefs in the ancient world.

What makes the Dead Sea Scrolls so important, Melchior explained, is that they are a direct source of ancient religious, spiritual, and other writings, whereas most scholarly understanding of the ancient world is based on indirect copies, quotations, and references to the writings of antiquity in more recent sources. The unique conditions at the Qumran caves helped to preserve this largest set of ancient writings ever found.

As Sam and Dawn inspected the ancient scrolls on display, Melchior told them that the Qumran buildings were believed to have comprised a library and scribal center for a group of ascetics known as the Essenes. There were about four thousand Essenes living in Judea in the first century, and a small group of them lived in the small communal center at Qumran, where they worked as scribes. He explained that there were probably two libraries in Jerusalem—one at the Temple and one run by the Essenes in their part of the city known as the Essene Quarter.

Melchior said that the Dead Sea Scrolls, consisting of more than six hundred separate scrolls, were probably placed in the eleven caves in and around Qumran during the time of the revolt that began in the year AD 66. The Dead Sea Scrolls probably came from the Essenes' library in Jerusalem, as well as the smaller collection of scrolls that had been kept in Qumran. It doesn't look like any of the scrolls from the Jerusalem Temple library were moved to the Qumran caves, he said.

The Dead Sea Scrolls include some of the oldest surviving examples of biblical writings included in the Hebrew Bible, Melchior explained, along with interpretive writings highlighting some of the beliefs of the different communities in ancient Judea. Some of the scrolls describe, using precise measurements, an enormous New Jerusalem to replace the old one, which can be taken either literally as a planned future location in the physical world or as a religious concept for the end of days. Known as the New Jerusalem and Temple Scrolls, these writings may help to explain some of the mystical Jewish and Christian traditions involving prophesies and revelations about the end of the world.

Another one of the Dead Sea Scrolls, known as the Book of Giants, tells a story of a race of giant immortal angels who were sent to teach proper rituals and ethics to humanity but who became tempted by and lusted after the beautiful women of the earth. Breaking the commands of the divine, these giant angels mated with mortal women, spawning a generation of half-breed demons. Until the flood of Noah restored divine order, these demons corrupted the earth with murder, rape, and cannibalism on a massive scale.

As Melchior explained, scholars today believe that the Book of Giants may represent a biblical creation story that predates the Genesis story about the Garden of Eden. It depicts the "fall of man" as the fault of evil angels rather than the serpent's temptation of Eve.

Melchior also told Sam and Dawn about the so-called War Scroll, which describes a prophesy about a war between the Sons of Light and the Sons of Darkness. Believed by scholars to probably describe a prophesied war against the Romans, the War Scroll contains apocalyptic visions of angels fighting alongside the Sons of Light. In the end, the forces of darkness are destroyed, and the world will have eternal peace.

Melchior pointed out that some scholars believe that another scroll, known as the War of the Messiah, is believed to be a companion of the War Scroll, telling the story of the end of the war. According to this scroll, a messiah—which in Hebrew means the "anointed one"—who is a descendant of King David will come to judge and restore the kingdom.

"Not what you'd expect to find in a cave," Dawn said a bit solemnly. "What was the purpose of these prophesies?"

"We're not sure," Melchior replied. "The scribes who wrote them could have believed in these prophesies. Or maybe they were intended as metaphors that were used to interpret events that were already happening. The evidence suggests that the scribes who wrote these scrolls were highly educated. They may have intended the more dramatic stories to be viewed as myths or symbols rather than taken literally."

Sam smiled. "Well, if we see any of those giant angels or someone who's been anointed, I suppose we could ask them. What does 'anointed' mean anyway?"

"Well, a sacred scented oil was used in the Jerusalem Temple to sanctify a priest or a king and to consecrate the Ark of the Covenant once a year on Yom Kippur," Melchior replied. "It was made with olive oil and scented with myrrh, cinnamon, and other aromatics. That would be a specific type of anointing used to honor the divine. So at the Jerusalem Temple, a priest or a king who had been anointed with the sacred oil could probably have been referred to as a messiah. By the first century, though, there were prophesies about a 'king messiah' who was descended of King David and who would lead the world to an era of universal peace."

"Right, that sounds familiar." Sam nodded. "In the Jewish tradition, that hasn't happened yet or, according to some, is meant more as a religious metaphor. In the Christian tradition, that would, of course, be Jesus. Whose real name, as I understand, was Yeshua of Nazareth."

"So you can see why so many people are interested in the Dead Sea Scrolls," Melchior said. "They touch on just about every religious or spiritual belief you can imagine. How the world was created, where evil came from, what the future holds, and who are great leaders are or will be. The scholars say to expect many more interesting discoveries to be made, which will probably just cause more debate about what these scrolls mean."

"Tell me about it," Sam agreed. "You know, that bronze scroll touches on some of this as well. How to live a good life, what love means, how to know when it's a time for war or peace. Maybe it's got some wise things to tell us that we haven't figured out yet."

"So you're still working on it, then?" Dawn asked.

"Yes, definitely," Sam replied. "Jason, Steve, and I are planning to get together sometime this week to compare notes and see what we can figure out. We think we're getting close to solving at least some of the clues."

"Well, it sounds like you're making progress." Dawn smiled with a bit of hesitation. "I know how you love mysteries. But what would you do if you actually figured out where some of these treasures are?"

Sam nodded. "I do love mysteries, but I think I'd have to notify the government if I found any treasures. I've read that there are some legal issues about ownership of the Dead Sea Scrolls. Israel has most of them, but the bronze scroll's in a museum in Jordan—at least, when it's not on tour. Israel, Jordan, and the Palestinians have all made claims of having legal rights to the Dead Sea Scrolls in one form or another. If anyone ever finds some of the hidden Temple treasure, you can expect an even bigger fight about who owns it. Nothing seems easy in this part of the world."

Melchior smiled. "Well, unless a new messiah or some giant angels come along, it looks like humanity will just have to figure this out. Following our sacred religious traditions, of course. Maybe we have all the answers already. Prophets and visionaries have been writing down the words of the divine for centuries or millennia, depending on your tradition. Perhaps the answers are already there and we just need to live up to them. You know, start loving our neighbors and helping people in need."

"You're truly a wise man," Sam said, putting his hand on Melchior's shoulder. "You've been such a great tour guide, and I wish that everyone could learn these words of wisdom."

"You're very kind to an old man." Melchior said, smiling. "This reminds me of something Balthasar said so many years ago—"

"Melchior," Dawn interrupted. "Aren't you going to show us that adorable model of first-century Jerusalem? I think it's somewhere near the Shrine of the Book."

"Right, thanks for remining me," Melchior replied. "Let's go this way," he said, escorting them toward the Second Temple Jerusalem model, adjacent to the Shrine of the Book.

"This beautiful model was the inspiration of a hotel owner who wanted to honor the memory of his son, who had been killed in the 1948 war when modern Israel was created," Melchior said. "It was moved here some years ago so that it could be preserved and enjoyed by this museum's visitors."

As they walked around the model and leaned over the metal railings to look more closely at its features, Sam and Dawn talked excitedly about how realistic the model seemed to be. "It's really amazing," Melchior agreed. "It's the best possible re-creation of Jerusalem before the revolt started in the year AD 66 that anyone could imagine. Just look at the monumental size of the Temple and its courtyards, towering over the city."

Jerusalem then must have been truly magnificent, Sam thought as they circled around the model of this walled city. It was just hard to believe that ancient peoples could build something so exquisite—without electricity, phones, the internet, or even written vowels, he thought. Mankind has such creative powers but also terrible powers of destruction, he knew. So sad that all of this was destroyed by the Romans.

After the tour, Sam and Dawn thanked Melchior, and he drove them back to their hotel. As they parted company in the hotel driveway, Dawn bowed slightly, and Sam shook Melchior's hand. It had been a wonderful day of touring that they would remember fondly, they all agreed.

It was getting late, and Sam and Dawn enjoyed a light dinner at the hotel's brasserie. After dinner, Sam and Dawn headed upstairs to call it a night.

"Say hi to Rebecca," Dawn said with a wink as they rode up in the elevator.

"Oh, right, I guess you figured out I'll be calling her," Sam said, grinning.

"I'd say so," Dawn said with a smile. "Enjoy your day tomorrow, and let's catch up when you're back."

As the elevator opened and Dawn was getting on the second floor, Sam leaned over to give her a hug. "Have a good night. Say hi to Jason and Steve tomorrow."

Sam walked into his empty hotel suite, instantly recognizing Rebecca's fragrance from last night. As he savored her rose-ginger fragrance, he got comfortable and sat down on the sofa with his phone.

> *Just got back to the hotel, and still thinking about you! I'll do some meditation in a little bit so I'll be focused tomorrow too. Sorry to hear about your distractions today. I promise there won't be a frozen salad, oversweetened coffee, or missing car tomorrow. Just a man who knows what you're feeling and how to make you feel good. Are you good for a call in a bit? I'd love to hear your voice. Sam*

Then Sam started looking on his tablet for a few ideas for his day with Rebecca tomorrow. It was exciting that Rebecca was deciding where they went and what they did. This was her homeland, after all, and he was really curious to experience some of her favorite places. He just wanted to make sure they had a romantic place to stay that night if she was open to that.

Finding a nice one on the beach in Netanya, Sam made a tentative reservation as a placeholder and then began to look for good restaurants in that area.

Sam heard a ping and knew it was from Rebecca.

I'd love a call! Are you free now?

He picked up his phone again and tapped on her name.

"Hi, Sam," she answered. "Great to hear from you."

"Me too, happy to hear your voice," Sam said. "Other than a few distractions, how was your day?"

"Oh, it was really busy," Rebecca replied, "and I learned a few more things about Wechsler. But we can talk about that tomorrow. I'm still a little obsessed with chocolate soufflé and some of those secrets you showed me last night. And I want to hear about your day. How was the sightseeing?"

"Secrets? You mean like slow dancing in the moonlight?" Sam teased. "Or the world's most beautiful woman washing her hair in the shower? You know, the sightseeing today was great, but the Seven Wonders of the Ancient World really don't hold up compared to a night with this certain reporter."

"Flattery will get you everywhere." Rebecca sighed. "Especially if there's a chocolate soufflé involved or some of those things you did."

"Well, I feel like I'm learning a lot on this trip," Sam said. "We went to the Israel Museum and learned some things about some giants, some olive oil that makes the world end, and some things about the Samaritans too. Did you know that they like strawberry-basil cocktails?"

"I hadn't heard that," she said, laughing. "I always thought that being Samaritan was just about the charming, red hats, and having fresh lamb for Passover."

"Well, it sounds like I have a lot to learn about Samaritan traditions," Sam teased. "Maybe I should focus on that and learn everything I can—you know, firsthand. That's the best way, right?"

"That's what I was thinking too," Rebecca agreed. "I was hoping to show you some of my favorite places tomorrow. The north is so beautiful—even in winter. Lots of green hills and valleys and a cold spring that's one of my favorite places to picnic. Want to go?"

"I'd love to," Sam replied. "Where do you want to meet, and when do we start? It's probably easier for you if I rent a car here and pick you up. Say nine in the morning? It will save you some driving, and maybe that way we can get an earlier start. I'm good anytime."

"Hmm, that's thoughtful," she said. "Nine in the morning is good. You seem to know what I want even before I do."

"It seems that way," he agreed. "I can tell you more tomorrow about the things that I know you want," he jokingly teased.

"Somehow I have a feeling you will." Rebecca laughed. "And I'm guessing it will involve strawberries and basil. Since you know how to read my mind."

"Exactly," Sam replied, "and I'm thinking you like the beach too. Maybe a romantic hotel on the Mediterranean with sea-view rooms and a nice place for breakfast the next morning?"

"You planned this already, huh?" Rebecca teased. "You reserved a hotel room before I even said yes?"

"Only because I already knew what you want," Sam teased back. "Besides, it was just a tentative reservation. A woman always gets to decide these things. I'm just here to help her *feel* what she really wants."

"Hmm, it sounds like it will probably work, then. I'll let you know later tonight," she said. "What about your mom and your friends? Are they okay with changing the schedule for tomorrow? Didn't you say you had plans with them?"

"Yes, and that's all good," Sam said. "My mom is doing a screening and photo op for a new movie, and she got my friends Jason and Steve VIP passes. You know that actress Ava Stern? The one who's playing Mata Hari and everyone says is so hot? She'll be there too, but it turns out she forgot her seven-veils dancing costume. So it sounds like there won't be any dancing. But they'll be fine and will have fun."

"That's too bad about Ava's costume," Rebecca said. "A girl's wardrobe isn't really complete without a seven-veils costume, right?"

"That's what I think," Sam agreed. "It's really either a seven-veils costume or nothing at all. I was thinking maybe you should wear that again tomorrow night. Or even in the morning too, of course."

"I don't know," Rebecca teased, "being in that costume really awakens some of my most intimate desires. You might learn more of my secrets, and I might not be ready for that yet."

"Take your time," Sam replied. "There's no rush. I'm learning better how to live in the moment, and that's really the most important thing."

"I like how that sounds," she said, sighing. "Maybe I'll wear it after all. We'll just have to see how I'm feeling. I should say good night now so I can work on my schedule for Tuesday morning and you can do your meditation. Maybe an extra session too. I really like it when you're focused."

"Me too," Sam agreed. "There's nothing like the calm serenity of letting your thoughts go. Just feeling and being what's in your heart."

"So good night, then," Rebecca whispered. "Sweet dreams."

"Sweet dreams to you too," Sam said back softly. "See you tomorrow."

Sam set down his phone and felt relaxed and happy. Rebecca just made him feel so *good.* He knew that tomorrow with her would be wonderful, and he would see her in just a few more hours.

After doing more planning for tomorrow on his tablet and checking some emails, Sam sat down in the living area to meditate. He hadn't practiced this in a while and was a little rusty. But somehow Rebecca's magic made it easy. His mind calmed and relaxed, and his thoughts left him. He went toward the light. Timeless and perfect.

After his thoughts returned, Sam got up and got ready for bed. As he put his phone on the nightstand, he heard a ping.

> *All good for Tuesday! So yes to that romantic hotel you already booked for us, lol! No need to rush back home on Monday night. I do love the seaside and hearing the waves crash all night. Sweet dreams! Rebecca*

Sam smiled and texted her back.

> *A night with you and the waves will be magic! Just finished meditating, and I'm really focused now and not distracted at all. Well, maybe a little. I'll be dreaming about you all night. I'll be there at 9 am and will bring a few treats. Sleep tight! Sam*

Sam exhaled. She would be in his arms again tomorrow night. A pure angel. Timeless and perfect.

14

BETTER THAN WINE

Sam's alarm rang. He picked up his phone. It was 6:00 a.m. and time to get started. Turning off the alarm, he crawled out of bed. It was Monday, and he would be picking up Rebecca in a few hours.

Sam needed the extra time to get a rental car so he could do the driving on their trip. He felt that he had always respected women as equals—which, really, didn't account for their magic—but he still enjoyed taking charge on things like this. Rebecca seemed to like it too. If not, he knew she would let him know. Women are always in charge of the important things. The dance is more about knowing what they want and making it happen without having to ask, he thought.

After taking a shower, Sam went through his clothes to find the right combination. Blue jeans and a black V-neck sweater. Just perfect for a day with Rebecca in the countryside.

After getting dressed, Sam checked himself in the mirror. Brushing his fingers through his hair, he noticed it was getting a little longer than usual. Rebecca had seemed to like running her fingers through it, though. It was fine this way, he thought.

Sam headed down to the gift shop next to the hotel lobby. The clerk had kindly arranged to order some Krembos and Lieber's Honey Grahams for him so he could bring them with him today. Rebecca really seemed to like these treats, and it wasn't practical to bring flowers on their trip. Hopefully, a little chocolate-marshmallow bliss would do the trick.

After grabbing a take-out coffee from the restaurant, Sam took a taxi to the car rental location and was soon back on the road in a red Opel Corsa decorated with Israel's golden license plates.

Exiting the Ayalon Highway toward Neve Tzedek, Sam felt an Angeleno's sense of pride in navigating the Tel Aviv freeways. He was following his GPS, of course, but it still felt good being able to drive in a foreign country where it was notoriously difficult to drive. He had heard that the drivers here were really aggressive, and good luck finding a place to park.

As the GPS told him that he was approaching Rebecca's apartment, Sam realized that he had gotten here a little early. He pulled into a parking space about a block away. It was just past 8:30 a.m., and he knew she wouldn't be ready. He texted her, just in case.

> *Boker tov! Good morning and happy Monday! Traffic's not like LA here, so I got to your street a little early. I'll just hang tight out here with my box of Krembos until it's time, unless you're somehow ready ahead of time. So excited to see you! Sam*

He waited for a few minutes and looked at his phone again when he heard a ping.

> *Boker tov to you too! So glad you're here early! You'd be a dear if you came upstairs and helped me with my bags. I won't be ready for a bit, but it would be wonderful to have your company while I'm getting ready. Just so you know, I've already showered, so I won't need any help this morning with soaping up. But tomorrow morning's another story. Kisses! Rebecca*

Sam smiled and was happy to help, even if she didn't need any help soaping up. He went upstairs and rang her bell.

Rebecca answered the door with a white towel wrapped tightly around her hair. She looked heavenly. Hazel eyes and pink lipstick. Wearing nothing but a white robe fitting tightly around her curves. What a wonderful start to the day, Sam thought.

"Hi, Sam." Rebecca smiled as she opened the door to let him in.

Stepping into her apartment, Sam leaned forward to give her a kiss. Her lips were soft and warm. Their lips still together, he put his hands on her arms, not wanting the kiss to end.

Rebecca took a half step back as their lips separated. "Good morning," she said warmly, pulling the two sides of her robe a little closer together after their kiss. "You're just an angel to help me. I'm feeling a little overwhelmed getting ready and packing. My apartment's such a mess, it's a little embarrassing."

Sam smiled, enjoying the lingering taste of her lips from their kiss. He glanced around her apartment, remembering that video call. The first time he had seen her curves that way. "Well, I've already seen your bedroom," he reminded her.

"My bedroom?" she said, a little surprised. "Oh, right, we did that video call last week."

"Yes, I remember it really well," he said with a smile. "Don't worry about the apartment. Everything I saw on that video was just perfect."

"Well, we all like to make a good impression," she said, a little puzzled. "I can't believe I spilled wine on my sweater. I hope you didn't mind having to wait for me."

"It was no trouble at all," he replied with a grin. "I kind of enjoyed the show."

Rebecca looked confused for a moment. "Oh, the Gauguin," she said, suddenly remembering. "I suppose you like nudes." She smiled, pulling at her robe again to make sure it was closed.

"I sure did last Thursday," he said, smiling. "Great art can be so inspiring."

"Would you like some coffee?" Rebecca asked, a little puzzled why Sam would be so inspired by her painting.

"My pleasure." Sam grinned. "Do you have Turkish, American, or upside down?" he asked, showing off what he'd learned about coffee in Israel since arriving on Saturday.

Rebecca smiled. "You're a fast learner. But I guess I already knew that from Saturday night. I can make Turkish or American. I just haven't figured out how to make upside-down coffee at home yet. I've been wanting to learn all those homey things. Maybe I just haven't had a reason to do that yet." She smiled.

"Turkish coffee sounds delicious." Sam smiled back. "I've only been here for a few days, and I'm already hooked. It's that perfect mix of sweet and bittersweet flavors. You know, like on Saturday night with our chocolate soufflé."

"Chocolate soufflé?" she teased. "I don't think I got any of that. I seem to have gotten distracted."

"Well, I tasted it for you," he teased back. "Silky and luscious. Moist and passionate. I'd go back for that anytime."

"Well, maybe we can have some more tonight," Rebecca said with a smile. "But right now, I've got to finish packing. And you have a way of distracting me that could make us lose our day in the north."

"Yes, it's better to focus," he said. "You should go finish your packing. If you need any help deciding what to wear, or not wear, just let me know. I have an eye for lady's fashion, you know."

"I think it's more the lady you're interested in," she said, winking. "But she does like a helping hand now and then."

As Rebecca disappeared to her bedroom, Sam began looking around her living area. Just what he had expected from a brilliant, sensuous woman with a thousand different interests and talents.

He wandered over to the bookshelves in her living area. This looks about right, he thought, scanning through the book titles.

Astrophysics for People in a Hurry.
Flavors of India.
Abraham: One God, Three Wives, Five Religions.
The Notebook.
NYC Ballet Workout.
Italian Without Words.
The Essential Kabbalah.
Pride and Prejudice.
Practicing Mindfulness.
Red Hot Tantra.

Sam hadn't read any of these books but was now pretty interested. He wanted to learn whatever would explain how amazing she was. That book on kabbalah seemed fascinating. He knew that kabbalah was a form of Jewish mysticism. Rebecca was a Samaritan, of course, but maybe there's something about the mix of religious ideas that would help explain that sense of spirit he felt in her presence. Maybe growing up in this part of the world could inspire you to become more spiritual?

And *Red Hot Tantra*? This could be good. He pulled it from the shelf to check out the chapter titles. Looking over the titles gave him the impression it was the real thing. Make Love Blindfolded? Fire Woman? Tantric Role-Playing? This could keep a couple busy for quite a while, he thought.

Noticing that Rebecca was back in the kitchen and had started to make some coffee, Sam put the book back on the shelf. Then he noticed an old-school LP record player in the cabinet next to her bookshelves. He pulled out some of the LPs that were lined up next to the player to see what kind of music she liked.

Lana Del Rey, *Paradise.*
Sofi Tsedaka, *Sofi and the Baladis.*
Jessy Lanza, *Pull My Hair Back.*

Taylor Swift, *Folklore.*
Din Din Aviv, *Sodotai.*
Empire of the Sun, *Walking on a Dream.*
Beatles, *Abbey Road.*
Andrea Bocelli, *Amore.*

Looking around Rebecca's living room, Sam noticed a guitar and a cello against the wall near the sofa. He could picture her on a Friday night practicing the cello while she studied astrophysics. Maybe that helped to explain how accomplished she was. She had extra time on Friday nights, right?

"With our without sugar?" Rebecca called out from the kitchen.

"With please," Sam called back. "Medium sugar will be perfect," he said, having learned to ask for that happy balance between nuclear black and insanely sweet. He really liked the Turkish coffee here, but it could be really potent with too little or too much sugar, he thought.

Still in her robe, Rebecca walked into the living area with a small white coffee cup with the letters "I♥NY" on the side. "Here you go," she said with a smile.

"Cute, did you get these on your trip?" he asked, taking a sip of her perfectly sweetened spiced coffee.

"I sure did," she answered. "Aren't they adorable? It's fun to have souvenirs from the places you've been. And, you know, I lived in New York when I was in school there."

"Yes, I remember we talked about that." Sam nodded. "Investigative journalism at Columbia, right?"

"That's right," she said. "The best part was living in New York. I had a tiny apartment with a roommate, and it seemed like it rained every day. But there's so much energy there, and the people are amazing."

As Rebecca disappeared to her bedroom to dress and finish packing, Sam pulled the *Practicing Mindfulness* book from the shelf and sat down on the sofa. He looked at the list of chapters and flipped through the book to see if there was some secret here that would explain how awesome she was. The chapter on Stilling the Mind looked good. And Driving with Mindfulness? From what he had seen on the Ayalon Highway this morning, this should be required reading in Israel.

Sam noticed there were a few sticky notes in her *Mindfulness* book. Cute little pink ones, actually. With some handwritten notes in Rebecca's adorable feminine handwriting. Here's one: Chapter 13, Unhooking from Thoughts—*So important!* Another one: Chapter 46, Stealth Kindness—*Smile! It can brighten someone's day*. Maybe this was part of her magic, he thought.

Sam heard Rebecca's voice from the bedroom and looked up. She walked into the living room and was just dazzling. Her long auburn hair was pulled back in a ponytail. She was wearing formfitting blue jeans and a tight dark blue sweater. Low cut, of course, and it was hard to resist looking there. But they had a relaxing day in the countryside ahead, and there would be plenty of time later for *that*, he hoped.

Sam brought his empty coffee mug to the kitchen and put it by the sink next to her empty mug. He squeezed a little dish soap onto the mugs and began washing them in her kitchen sink.

"You didn't have to do that," she said with a smile, walking into the kitchen. "But it's very thoughtful. I always wash my coffee mugs right away so they won't get stained and will stay white. I just love these and want to keep them nice. Plus, the New York ones are my favorite, and I don't want it to get stained."

After finishing in the kitchen, Sam picked up her bags and a coat she had selected in case it turned colder. She protested a bit that he was carrying all of her things while she was empty handed, but they both enjoyed this, really. He felt like her knight in shining armor and sensed that she might be feeling that too. When they got to the rented Opel, she asked about the bag with the Krembos inside, and he told her that there was a little chocolate-marshmallow surprise inside. She didn't seem to mind that either.

After loading the car, Sam held Rebecca's door for her and then got in the driver's seat. As he navigated the Opel out of the parking space and down the street toward the highway, he moved his hand to Rebecca's knee and slid his hand up a bit, stopping on her thigh just above her knee. He kept his hand there, feeling her warmth and their powerful connection.

Minutes later, they were cruising on the Ayalon Highway toward the countryside in northern Israel. Sam looked at Rebecca as she set her GPS for their first destination. "So, where are we off to?" he asked, glancing at the curves under her tight sweater as she moved around in the seat, angling her legs toward Sam in the driver's seat. He still felt the warmth of her thigh on his hand as he noticed that the weight of his hand had pulled her a bit toward him so that her legs were slightly spread apart.

"The wine country up toward the Carmel Mountains," Rebecca said. "There's a little winery up there called Tishbi. It's one of my favorite places. It's between the Mediterranean coast and the Samarian Hills. The wine region is called Shomron, which translates to Samaria. The wines are delicious, and I think you'll like the green country up there."

"So is the wine country in Samaria?" he asked.

"Yes and no, it gets complicated," she replied. "Most people would say that Samaria's inside the West Bank. We won't go there today because much of it's off limits to rental cars, and the travel routes can get complicated. But basically, the countryside that you'll see is much like Samaria. And we'll be in Galilee later too, which has the same natural beauty."

"Sounds wonderful," Sam said, glancing at Rebecca's pretty smile and reddish-brown hair pulled back in the ponytail, with a few loose silky strands falling down past her ears. She looked amazing, he thought, looking down at the curves under her dark blue sweater. "It seems like Israel has more than its share of beauty," he said, smiling.

"I know what you mean," Rebecca said, blushing slightly and looking back at Sam. "It's really a little like LA," she said. "You can be in the desert in the morning and the beach in the afternoon."

"Yes, but I'm a little envious about these green hills," he said. "In LA, our hills are mostly brown with oil wells on them. And you have to drive pretty far to get to any wineries. But I do know a few neighborhoods in LA that I've heard are off limits to rental cars."

"Well, you wouldn't be the first person to visit here and never leave." Rebecca said, smiling. "It's a nice place. Have you heard of Jerusalem syndrome?"

"No, what's that?" Sam asked.

"Sometimes, visitors go a little crazy here," she said. "It might be a combination of all those religious shrines, the ancient history, and the sunny Mediterranean climate. Some of them don't want to leave."

"I can relate to that," he said with a smile. "It was nice being in Rome, but this place feels pretty homey. Maybe it's the company," he said, winking.

"Just so long as you're not going crazy," she said, smiling back. "They might not let you have any wine."

About an hour later, they drove up to the Tishbi Winery near the small town of Binyamina. As they parked, Sam admired the rolling green hills surrounding the winery. While he moved their items around so that the

Krembos wouldn't be melting in the warm January sun, Rebecca pulled two empty glass bottles out of one of her bags.

"Getting refills, of course," she said with a smile, noticing his puzzled look. "Don't you do this in LA?"

"We don't really have wineries in LA," Sam said, laughing. "Well, not like this, anyway. And no, we definitely don't come back for refills. It makes it sound like you're old friends or something. All this perfection might give me that syndrome, you know. I might have to stay here," he said, half-joking.

"It does feel like visiting old friends," she said with a sigh. "I wouldn't mind living here either."

"I'm starting to love it," Sam agreed as they walked through the front door of the winery. "Now, if we can just get the drivers here to start practicing mindfulness, it would truly be perfect."

"It sounds like you've been looking at my books." Rebecca smiled as Sam escorted her to the wine-tasting counter.

"Just the ones on astrophysics and mindfulness," Sam said with a grin. "I didn't even see that one about red tantra," he joked.

"Right, I haven't seen that one either." She laughed as they got to the counter. "I don't know anything about the lotus touch or those supernovas."

Sam grinned. "I know, that's just in your astrophysics book. Red tantra isn't anything like that at all."

"Precisely, the big bang and universal bliss are purely astronomical terms. You wouldn't want anything like that happening in your bedroom, would you?" she teased.

Sam laughed, making a mental note to order that *Red Hot Tantra* book right away. He wondered if they had Prime Now in Israel.

"I'll have to get back to you on that," he said, smiling as the server poured each of them some reserve chardonnay. "But I'm also curious about the guitar and cello in your apartment. Do you play those?"

"Not every day," Rebecca said. "I learned how to play them in school and got really involved with them when I was writing that musical in college."

Sam's eyebrows raised. "You wrote a musical in college?"

"Well, I had to write *something* for my composition class," she said. "I based it on James Joyce's *Ulysses*, and it really wasn't that hard."

Sam shook his head. "I'm assuming you got an A for that, right?"

"Well, the professor liked it so much that he signed me up for his musical theater class," Rebecca replied. "We did some performances that summer in English and Hebrew. Ooh, I really like this brut," she said, savoring the white sparkling wine. "Dry and fruity," she said, wrinkling her nose.

"Let's get a couple of bottles to go," Sam said. "You know, if you're free on Saturday night." He winked.

"I'll have to look into that," she teased, grabbing his arm. "Can you get us some of that dessert wine too? It might pair nicely with chocolate soufflé," she teased. "In case you get hungry tonight."

He smiled. "I'll get two bottles, and I'm already hungry."

"We'll stop at Tishbi's bakery on the way out," she said. "We'll get some sandwiches and fruit for our picnic at my favorite cold spring in Galilee. I wouldn't want you to be hungry all day. I know how distracting that can be."

"Yes, it's better to be mindful," he agreed. "Especially while driving on that Highway Four we were on. People drive fast here."

"We'll be changing highways again," Rebecca said, laughing. "But yes, please do stay mindful. Being calm and centered is just perfect for our picnic spot. It's really a special place. It's called Gideon's Spring, and the cold water is so fresh, you'd think that the cave it pours out from has some kind of magic."

"A magic cave?" Sam lit up. "I can't wait to see this. Maybe we should get some more wine," he joked while Rebecca had her empty bottles filled with fresh olive oil and sauvignon blanc.

About an hour later, they pulled into the parking area at Gideon's Spring. It was actually a large green park with a sprawling natural pool in the middle, which was fed by a small stream. Sam got the picnic basket and blanket that Rebecca had brought along and grabbed a bottle of the chilled chardonnay he had gotten at the winery.

Sam spread the red-and-white-checkered blanket on the grass, and they sat down underneath one of the large eucalyptus trees near the stream. It was heavenly here, he thought. As they each enjoyed a sandwich and a glass of wine, Rebecca told him that one of her favorite ancient stories was about this place.

"Gideon was the smartest and strongest man in the land," she began. "In other words, he was really good at soaping your back."

"I can see why this is one of your favorite stories," Sam said with a grin. "Was there a beautiful woman in his life with an amazing smile who dazzles you with a thousand different interests and talents?"

"It's not really a love story," Rebecca said softly. "This one's about courage and wisdom. You know, the important things you want to get right before you get to those love stories."

"Our hero was a little short on courage and wisdom?" Sam asked.

"He was like every one of us," Rebecca replied. "Learning courage and wisdom takes a lifetime. It's all about *how* you do it."

Sam glanced at Rebecca as she was taking in the leafy scenery around them. He could tell that she really loved this place and seemed at home here. She seemed so calm and serene, and they both savored a few minutes of quiet as they enjoyed their sandwiches and wine.

"This Gideon story sounds really interesting," Sam said, leaning closer to Rebecca. "How did he learn to be brave and wise? You know, so he could move on to those love stories?"

"The nation was in great danger," Rebecca said. "Its leaders went from crisis to crisis, making decisions based on the people's fears and passions of the moment. There was no plan for peace, and so there was war. Putting power above principle, the leaders made excuses about having to cut corners to make the system work. Politics is all about conflict, they said, and giving the people what they want.

"One day," Rebecca went on, "an angel appeared before Gideon. The angel told him that he would be the great leader the nation needed, if he only learned courage and wisdom. Gideon laughed and said he was a simple man. He knew he was smarter and craftier than most, but what did he know about courage and wisdom? The angel told him that the divine had chosen him to lead and would be on his side. Gideon scoffed and told the angel that if the divine were truly on his side, the nation wouldn't be at war and afflicted with one problem after the other.

"This next part is important," Rebecca said, taking a last bite of her sandwich and washing it down with another sip of chardonnay. "The angel told Gideon that the divine doesn't work that way. The spirit works *through* people and not by waving a magic wand to solve all our problems. To the extent miracles happen, they're just there to remind us of our own limitless powers when we align ourselves with the divine."

"That does sound important," Sam said, nodding. "It's almost like people are the *hands* of the divine. We have to take charge of our lives and solve our own problems. The spirit is really there to inspire and guide us so the things that we do will have meaning, right?"

"That's what the angel said," Rebecca said with a smile as she lay down on her side across from Sam, folding one arm to prop up her head. "Gideon was starting to catch on."

"So did the angel teach him how to be brave and wise?" Sam asked, enjoying the view of Rebecca as she reclined on her side, facing him.

"He sure did." Rebecca agreed. "And Gideon didn't like this part at all. Learning courage can be really hard. The angel told him to go cut down the pole of the mother goddess that had stood in the center of his village for centuries."

"That does sound a little risky." Sam grimaced as he finished his own sandwich. "Some of those ancient people were pretty fond of their goddesses. They were symbols of fertility, wisdom, and sexual pleasure. Not things you really like to do without. Except for Friday nights around here, I guess," he teased.

Rebecca laughed, picking up a red apple. "You heard about that, huh?"

He smiled. "A few things, but not too much. Just that the mother goddess might not show up on Friday nights around here," he joked.

"But you know what that means, right?" Rebecca said with a mischievous smile, holding the apple in her hand. "It just makes things more delicious on Saturday nights. You know, that feeling of satisfying your most forbidden desires," she said, taking a bite of the apple.

Sam became quiet as he looked at Rebecca biting the apple, her pink lips pressed against the red skin of the apple. He could almost taste those forbidden desires wanting release on a Saturday night. He thought about the flight schedules. He could fly here every Saturday morning and then back to Rome on Sunday nights. It really wouldn't be that hard at all.

"So, let me guess," Sam said as his head cleared, "the people in the village were a little annoyed when Gideon chopped down their goddess pole. No fertility, wisdom, or sexual pleasure for them. Even on Saturday nights?"

"Yes, they were pretty frustrated," Rebecca said. "Gideon had cut down the pole in the middle of the night. But that didn't fool anyone. They knew it was him. A mob gathered outside Gideon's house the next morning. They were ready to tear him to pieces. He was terrified and realized his mistake."

"What was that?" Sam asked.

"Never hide from conflict. Always show your true colors," she said. "The mob smelled weakness and lack of resolve. He should have cut down the pole in broad daylight and shown that this particular goddess had lost her power."

"That does sound courageous," Sam said, nodding. "It's not enough to *do* the right thing. You have to show that you *believe* it to be right."

"Exactly," she agreed. "So now that he had learned about courage, Gideon came out of his house and stared down the mob. He told them that he had been right to chop down that worthless goddess pole to prove that she was powerless. As he laughed and mocked her, the people began to laugh along with him, cheering that the powerless goddess was gone.

"Quite pleased with himself," Rebecca continued as she finished her apple, "Gideon sent word throughout the land that he was assembling an army to defeat the enemy and bring peace. Soon after, he had an army of thirty thousand soldiers under his command. But, as he prepared to lead them into battle, the angel appeared before him again. Now bursting with courage and confidence, Gideon rebuked the angel, telling him to leave. He had all the courage and wisdom anyone could want, and he didn't need the angel's help.

"The angel became angry," Rebecca said, "and told Gideon that he still lacked wisdom. Leading an army of thirty thousand men was beyond foolish. The enemy would surely be defeated. But then what would happen? All these soldiers would think that they had won the war through their *brute strength* rather than by the justice of their cause. True leaders govern through purpose and meaning, not power, the angel said. Power has no master and serves only itself. A truly wise man knows that he must lead by example and do the right thing."

"That does sound wise," Sam agreed. "So what did Gideon do next?"

"He sent orders to the thirty thousand soldiers to assemble by this pool here," Rebecca said. "Then he told them to drink to prepare for battle. Naturally, this turned into another mob scene as the men pushed and shoved and jumped into the water, lapping it up like savage dogs."

"So I'm guessing he figured out a wise solution to this mess," Sam said. "Maybe get some advice from that angel?"

Rebecca smiled. "Exactly, and this is often the hardest part. Wisdom doesn't mean always having the answers yourself. What it really means is trusting the divine and the people around you enough to ask for help. We're all in this together, and no one can do it alone."

"So what did the angel tell him to do?" Sam asked.

"The angel pointed out that there were a few soldiers—three hundred, to be exact—who had ignored the mob and behaved in a civilized way," she said. "After all the shoving and pushing had died down, these men calmly and quietly walked to the stream, bent down, and cupped water in their hands, scooping it up to drink with dignity and restraint."

"Then he led those three hundred men to victory?" Sam asked.

"You nailed it." Rebecca smiled, sitting up and moving closer to Sam, sliding her arm around his and leaning in to rest her head on his muscular shoulder. "Gideon became one of the greatest rulers ever. He was smart, courageous, and wise. And he knew enough to ask the divine and those around him for advice and guidance. It was a time of great peace and prosperity."

"That's wonderful," Sam said, feeling her warmth on his shoulder. "So he lived happily ever after?"

"You mean did he find love?" Rebecca said quietly, holding on to Sam's arm. "Well, he had a few dozen wives and about a hundred and fifty children. So I suppose so."

"Wow," Sam said with a whistle. "All that for learning how to ask for advice? Have I ever told you how much I value your opinion? I could really use your advice on lots of things, you know."

"I don't think you really want one hundred and fifty children," she said, snuggling against his shoulder a bit. "That wasn't even your question. You were asking about 'happily ever after,' remember?"

"You're right," he agreed, "I did say that. But you promised me a love story, remember?"

"I didn't promise you a love story," she said, her head still on his shoulder. "I said it *might* happen if our hero proved his courage and wisdom."

"And he asked for advice now and then too?" Sam asked, looking down at her pretty face.

"That's right," she said, turning her head to look up at Sam.

Sam gazed into her hazel eyes. "Do you think we should go find that magic cave? I could use your advice on that. Maybe we'll find a love story on a scroll in there."

"Sam, I don't think there's anything in that cave," she said, gazing back into his eyes. "I think you're just excited about that bronze treasure map and have started thinking there's treasure everywhere."

"Well, I know treasure when I see it," he said softly as he pulled his arm from her grip and slid it around her shoulders to pull her in closer.

"I like the sound of that," Rebecca said with a sigh. "Maybe I'll remember one of those love stories after all."

His mind calm and still, Sam sat holding her for what seemed like endless minutes, watching as the breeze softly stirred the branches over their heads, the sun dancing across the green grass around them.

He remembered that poem he had looked up last night before bed. One of Solomon's, the old man on the flight to Rome. Something about a song.

Kiss me tenderly
Your love is better than wine,
and you smell so sweet,
Everyone adores you,
the very mention of your name
is like a beautiful perfume.

As they sat on the picnic blanket in silence, Sam leaned over to kiss Rebecca's soft cheek. He moved to her ear and breathed softly against her skin. He could feel her body tensing with pleasure as he moved back across her cheek to her lips. She turned toward him, opening her lips to his.

She was soft and warm and ripe with desire. His arm held her shoulder closely as their kiss lingered. She pulled back a bit and then came back harder, drawn into his embrace.

Finally, it was time to go. Sam squeezed Rebecca tightly and nuzzled against her. "Let's go see that magic cave you were talking about," he whispered in her ear.

"Still looking for a love story on a scroll?" She looked up at him.

"I just have a feeling about it," he said. "Maybe there's some kind of angel there who'll give me some advice, like that Gideon."

"All right, lead the way," Rebecca said with a sigh as they got up and stretched their legs. Rebecca began picking up but then smiled as Sam took the basket and winked, letting her know he had this too. He could tell that she was used to taking care of herself but that she enjoyed being treated like a princess now. After putting the empty wine bottle and what was left of their lunch into the picnic basket, he took her by the arm and began walking with her back to the parking area.

After Sam had put everything back in the rented Opel, they walked along the stream to its source at the cave. He looked at the iron fence that had been installed across the cave opening and the No Trespassing sign next to the fence.

"That fence does make you wonder, huh?" he said.

"Do you think there's something in there?" she asked.

"I don't know," Sam replied, taking hold of her hand as they stood in front of the cave. "Maybe I'm learning to accept I don't have all the answers."

Sam turned to Rebecca and slid his arm around the small of her back. He leaned down and kissed her, softly at first and then more firmly. Her lips parted, and her tongue brushed his lips lightly and slowly.

"I think we found that love story," he whispered in her ear.

"On a scroll?" she whispered back.

"I think so," he said softly, "with secret desires. You know how I like to solve mysteries. Uncovering layer after layer until you get to the naked truth."

"What do you think you'll find?" she said softly.

"Secret treasures in a magic cave," he whispered. "Something precious and hidden for me to discover."

Driving back in the red Opel, Sam placed his hand on Rebecca's leg again. This time on the inside of her thigh, close to the forbidden desires she longed to set free.

They drove quietly for about a half hour, and then Sam remembered that they had wanted to compare notes a bit on the Wechsler investigation. Sam didn't want to ruin the moment but realized that he wouldn't see her again until Wednesday night, and they had promised not to get distracted and forget to cover this.

"So, now that we're relaxed from the countryside"—he smiled at her—"do you want to take a minute to cover a few things on that Wechsler case?"

Rebecca smiled back at him, enjoying the green scenery passing outside. "Sure, what have we got to lose? Who goes first?"

"Well, I haven't really learned much of anything new lately," Sam said. "I still don't know who's behind the Genesis Foundation and responsible for that million-euros bribe. So why don't you go first?"

"I think I can help you with that," she said, smiling. "It's pretty confidential, but I think the rules allow me to tell who it is, just for background."

"Let me guess, it's some Roman emperor or general," he joked. "Who else would be digging around at the Jerusalem city walls?"

"Good guess," she said. "He's a rich CEO of a multinational corporation, but the rumor is that he likes to dress up in a toga and pretend he's Nero late at night."

"Uh-oh," Sam groaned, "that sounds like trouble. I think I know this guy."

"Roy Griffin?" Rebecca was stunned. "You know Roy Griffin? The CEO of Eden Holdings? How do you know him?"

"He popped up last week," Sam said. "I'd never even heard of him before then. He's one of my dad's clients and had an issue that he needed help with, so my dad referred him to me. Not really a favor at this point, I think."

"Well, I hope you turned down the work," she said. "But I guess you had no idea he was involved in the Wechsler case, right? So how would you know there was a conflict?"

"It's a huge conflict," he said, "but you're right. I had no idea that he had anything to do with Wechsler, and he certainly didn't volunteer this during the conflicts check. What a disaster. I took the assignment, and now I may need to tell my contacts at Bacchus that I'm representing someone else who's involved in the Wechsler case. Even if the assignment has nothing to do with it. We still have to disclose these things."

"I know you'll do the right thing," Rebecca said, "but there's really another part of this that's important."

"What do you mean?" Sam asked.

"It's the journalism rules of ethics," she said. "Remember my presentation at the conference in New York? A reporter's supposed to be careful about personal relationships with sources. And now it turns out that you're an attorney for Roy Griffin, who I'm investigating. That's a little messy."

"I see what you mean," Sam said, exhaling. "I'll get rid of him, and it was just a small project that's already done anyway. But I do understand that appearances matter with these ethics rules. I'm sorry that this happened, and it seems like just one of those unfortunate coincidences."

"We'll figure it out," Rebecca promised. "But in the meantime, we might want to be careful with what we do next. These last few days have been so special, and I want us to keep dating. But seriously, you might have to report this to your firm, and I might have to let my editors know about it too. We might have to call things off for a while until we can clean this up."

Sam sighed. The day had been so perfect. Roy did have the Midas touch, after all. Everything he touched turned into a mess.

"I understand," he said, "and good thing our hotel room's a suite. I can sleep on the sofa, and we can tell everyone who needs to know that we haven't had a romantic relationship since we found out about this."

"I'm afraid that's a good idea," she said, "but maybe you should take me back to my place instead. It sounds like a bad idea for us to be in a hotel room together. As of tonight, you're Roy's attorney, and he's now the main suspect in a police investigation that I'm reporting on."

"I hear you," he said, "but you know that we're the only ones who know about this. We're not telling anyone about this until tomorrow, and we just found out about it ourselves. Besides, I'm not *Roy's* attorney. I was doing some work for Eden, but I'm all done with it now anyway. Maybe we don't have to change our plans, and I'll just sleep on the sofa."

"Well, *we* know about it," Rebecca said, "and you know how important it is to do the right thing. Can we really trust ourselves to be just friends tonight?"

"Sure, I brought a box of those Krembos, remember?" he joked. "We can melt them over a firepit on the beach and enjoy ourselves another way."

Rebecca laughed. "This isn't California, and we don't have firepits on the beaches here. But I like your idea. It will be a test for us. Can we resist forbidden love?"

Sam gulped. "Good thing I've started meditation again. I'll practice a few mantras before going to bed."

"There's just one other problem," she said before agreeing to the plan. "I didn't bring a nightgown or anything plain like that. I just have some skimpy black lingerie. This won't distract you too much?"

"No, not at all," Sam said, coughing. "I did that yoga course in India, remember? I'll just stay focused on calm serenity. I won't notice your lingerie or heavenly curves, and I won't even think about your warm, sensuous body while I'm trying to go to sleep."

"Good, it's a deal, then," she agreed. "We'll clear things up in a few days, and maybe we can get together this weekend? Just not on Friday night, remember? I'll be with my parents again, and you know that Samaritan tradition about Friday nights."

"Yes, of course, Saturday will be amazing." Sam nodded. "Only five days away. Not really an eternity at all."

When they arrived at the Mediterranean shore in Netanya, Sam gave the keys to the Opel to the valet at the Vert Lagoon Hotel. As they walked into the hotel lobby, Sam took Rebecca's hand as they walked to the elevator and went upstairs with their bags.

"Remember, we're just friends tonight," Rebecca said as they rode upstairs in the elevator.

Sam nodded as they walked out of the elevator and toward their room. As he opened the room and walked in after Rebecca, he saw the silver bucket of ice with a champagne bottle and suddenly remembered that he'd reserved the Honeymoon Special. There would be candles and a bowl with rose petals by the bathtub, with more candles on the nightstands and a special "lovers' breakfast" delivered to the room in the morning. Maybe this was a little riskier than he had thought.

"Sam?" Rebecca said, a little exasperated. "What's all this romantic stuff? We're not supposed to do this tonight, remember?"

"I'll be a perfect gentleman," he assured her. "I ordered all this before I knew about our little conflict of interest. Which is only temporary until I fix things tomorrow."

"This isn't going to work," she said, sighing. "Maybe I should go home. I'm not sure I'll be able to resist temptation."

"I think I can help with that. You just need to relax and get your mind off romance," Sam replied. "I'll be back in a minute."

He went into the bathroom, began to draw the bath, and tossed in the rose petals from the bowl. Then he noticed Rebecca standing at the bathroom door. "Rose petals? How are they going to help keep my mind off romance?" she asked with a frustrated smile.

"I guess they're a little romantic," he responded, "but it would be a shame to waste them. You really deserve a long soaking bath, and at least it will be relaxing."

"I know, that does sound nice," she said. "A warm bath will be really good. But it's probably better if you don't watch me this time," she said with a wink.

"I promise," he replied. "Go relax now. The bathtub's all yours."

Rebecca disappeared into the bathroom and closed the door. After a while, she turned off the running water and relaxed in the warm bath with a garland of red rose petals floating on top. Sam got busy putting his things away and checking for messages.

A few minutes later, Sam heard her voice from the bathtub. "Sam?" she called out. "Can you help me?"

He opened the bathroom door a bit and called back, "Do you need something?"

"I forgot the soap bar," she said softly. "It's on the counter. Could you bring it to me? I'm all warm now and just starting to relax."

Sam blushed and felt warm too. "I'm not sure that's a good idea. We're supposed to be focusing on those journalism rules, right?"

"Well, I'm pretty hidden with these rose petals floating on the water," she said. "I don't really think we're breaking any rules."

"All right, then," he said, opening the door and walking into the bathroom. He unwrapped the soap bar and sat down on the flat rim of the tub. He could see her gorgeous curves under the water, only partially hidden by the red rose petals floating on top.

Rebecca sat up and looked at Sam, covering her chest with her arms and gazing at him with her soft hazel eyes. "Would you mind soaping my back?" she asked softly. "It's so hard for me to reach, and you're really good at this. You just have to promise not to touch me anywhere else. That would really be against the rules."

Sam wasn't sure where this was going, but it was awfully hard to say no to this woman. Plus, he was pretty good at soaping her back, he thought. She liked the slow, circular motions and the soft gliding of his fingers against her skin.

"Sure, that's fine," he said. "I don't think that will be breaking the rules. Lean forward and just relax," he said, dipping the soap bar into the warm water and sliding it around her back, moving slowly in circular motions as she sighed and enjoyed the sensations.

"This is just heavenly," she said softly. "I could do this all night."

"Close your eyes," he said, "and focus on pure relaxation. Take a deep breath and then slowly exhale. Tonight is just for relaxing," he went on as she started inhaling and exhaling slowly. "We can save the romance for Saturday night, right? Maybe something sexy with jasmine-scented candles, a four-poster bed, and red silk sashes?"

Rebecca turned to Sam, looking surprised. "How did you know? I mean, I didn't—oh, the blog. You're reading Veils of Desire now? By that anonymous writer?"

"Well, now you know *my* secret." Sam smiled. "Yes, I'm reading that blog you told me about. By the anonymous writer. All I can say is, if she's dating someone, he sure is a lucky guy."

Rebecca blushed. "I think you're right. But maybe he's even more lucky than he knows. She's pretty imaginative, and he might find out that her secret desires are really powerful. Are you sure he's ready for that?"

Sam smiled. "I'm sure he understands that she's beyond amazing. Who knew that red silk sashes could be used that way? He knows he's lucky to have her and really just wants more."

After a few more minutes of gliding and rinsing her back, Sam felt that she was probably pretty clean by now. "How's that?" he asked.

"Well, I think I missed a few other spots too," she said with a sigh, looking up at him. "Would you mind staying a little longer and being a little more thorough?"

"Of course," he replied, "being thorough is really my passion in life. I just don't want to cross any lines that I shouldn't. I might not be able to resist temptation," he said as his soapy hands slid down to her thighs.

Rebecca sighed. "Well, now that you've told me your secret, maybe I can tell you mine." She closed her eyes again, enjoying the sensations of his hands on her thighs. "I've always dreamed of a passionate, forbidden affair," she said quietly as his hands moved down to wash her smooth, silky calves. "With every sensation on my skin feeling naughty and indulgent. We both know we're breaking all the rules, but you touch me everywhere, and I can't restrain my desires. I just want more."

Rebecca went on with her story, telling Sam each delicious detail of her deepest secret passion she had always wanted to share. This was her greatest fantasy, she said, and she had dreamed for so long about making it come true.

Finally, after the room went quiet, Sam helped her out of the bath, wrapping her in thick white towels before showing her back to the bedroom, with the curtains drawn open to the moon and the dark blue Mediterranean Sea below.

After removing the towels gently as she stood by the bed, Sam laid her down on her back in the center of the bed. Now, stroking his fingers lightly across her skin, he cleared her mind with his forbidden touch. Trying madly to restrain her desires, she let him touch her everywhere, her body surrendering to his in the soft moonlight and the sound of the sea below.

Rebecca whispered softly in his ear, "This is wrong, we shouldn't do this," while she lay still on her back. Then pulling him closer, her body rose and fell like the sea as she began moaning. "We can't do this, we're breaking all the rules," she cried out. Then, as she closed her eyes, his touch guided her slowly toward the waves they could both feel approaching.

When at last he felt that she could no longer resist her passions, he dove into her crashing waves like a powerful incoming tide. "Don't stop, don't stop," she cried. "It's so wrong, but I want you." He plunged ever deeper as her body rocked and heaved like the waves on the sea. He closed his eyes and could feel a storm of their inflamed passions about to break. Then, at last, enormous waves of pleasure enveloped them as their bodies rocked and convulsed with the full fury of their forbidden desires.

After the sea had calmed, Sam and Rebecca lay silently in the bed, their bodies still feeling as one. Their thoughts and cares gone for the night, they rested gently and silently, their arms and hearts bound together under the soft glow of the moon over the dark blue sea below.

Her name like a beautiful perfume. The scent of love.

15

THE WATERS OF JORDAN

Sam woke up not long after dawn, with Rebecca still in his arms. Her head was resting gently on one side of his chest, with his arms wrapped tightly around her as she slept.

He turned his head slightly to look out the window at the blue Mediterranean Sea below. The morning clouds had started to break, and beams of warm winter sun cast golden rays on the sparkling sea.

After they were both awake, they agreed to keep seeing each other and to just take it day by day on whether they should be sleeping together. Rebecca said she knew it would be better if they played by the rules, but somehow, she said with a smile, the thought of their romance being off limits made it even more irresistible.

Sam promised to follow the rules as strictly as he could and to clean things up with Roy as best he could. He knew that wouldn't be easy. He had noticed a few messages from him with the word *urgent* in the first sentence, but he hadn't been interested enough to read them.

Kissing him softly on the ear, Rebecca whispered that she understood and would be all his on Saturday night, even if they would be breaking the rules. It might even be sweeter that way, she admitted with a blush. Plus, she had a few more secrets to tell him.

Sam smiled and promised to make it a special night on Saturday. Whatever color of tantra she wanted, he would bring it for her. He had a few secrets of his own too, he said. Maybe some other forbidden desires that she had dreamed about too?

After enjoying a relaxing morning with a traditional Israeli breakfast in their room—fried eggs, bread, hummus, and salad—Sam and Rebecca finished packing and started planning their next date the following day. Or a "platonic evening" or whatever they decided it would be.

Rebecca wanted to make him a home-cooked dinner—some of her favorite dishes like quinoa tabbouleh, white bean soup, and beef kebabs with pomegranate glaze—so they agreed that Sam would get to her place around 7:00 p.m.

As they drove down the Coastal Highway for the short drive back to Rebecca's apartment, Sam placed his hand on Rebecca's inner thigh to feel her warmth again. She felt so good, and that feeling of connection between them felt even better.

When they got to her apartment, Sam walked Rebecca upstairs, carrying her bags without further protest. With a last kiss at her doorway, they hugged and said their goodbyes, hoping to be back in each other's arms the next evening.

Hearing pings on his phone as he began looking forward to the rest of his day, Sam drove back to the rental car place to return the Opel. Then he took a taxi back to the American Colony Hotel in East Jerusalem.

As he got into the back of the taxi, he started looking at the messages on his phone. He saw one from Rebecca and had to click into it first.

> *Hi Sam, just wanted to say thank you for the wonderful day and evening and to let you know I'm thinking of you. Being with you is like a dream come true, even if we're breaking a few rules along the way. You know that's not my style, but I trust you and feel it will all work out. Kisses! Rebecca*

He smiled and tapped out a reply.

> *Sweet Rebecca, so happy to see your message! Yesterday and last night with you were amazing, and waking up to your sweetness was pure magic! I know what you mean about the rules. It's important to do the right thing, but somehow being with you can never be wrong. Can't wait to see you tomorrow night! Even if you don't need your back soaped up and we're just melting a few Krembos. Yours, Sam*

Then Sam sent a message to Roy. He would put a stop to all of his chaos and nonsense.

> *Roy, I see you've been leaving me quite a few messages. I finished the Copper Scroll project and, after updating our conflicts information, can't do any more work for your company. I'll be happy to explain, but as of now, I'm not Eden's attorney, and we'll have to go our own ways. Have a good day. Sam*

Sam hoped that would end it but suspected that Roy would make things difficult. Eden was up to no good with those construction permits in Israel, and things just didn't add up. There had to be something bigger behind all this, and maybe Roy wasn't even the main player. He was a weak man, after all, and would probably be whiny about Sam walking away.

Sam needed to start thinking about the rest of the day anyway. Jason and Steve should be here in Israel now, and the plan was for them to meet up with him and his mom for sightseeing at the Dead Sea this afternoon. He would enjoy this and wouldn't let Roy spoil it.

Walking into the hotel lobby, he heard his name. "Sam!" Turning to the voice, he saw Steve striding toward him.

"Hey, Sam!" It was Jason's voice, right behind Steve.

"Hey, guys!" Sam shouted out. "Awesome to see you!" A round of man-hugs followed as the friends were back together, joking about how long it had been since that Cabo trip in early December.

After catching up on his friends' arrival the day before and their plans to join his mom for some sightseeing, Sam reminded Jason and Steve that they would all be meeting in the lobby in about fifteen minutes.

After dropping his bags upstairs and changing into a short-sleeve white linen shirt for the warm Dead Sea climate, Sam headed back downstairs. Jason and Steve were already there, and his mother arrived a few minutes later.

Sam smiled and gave his mother a big hug. "Hi, Mom," he said. "So glad to see you. It's so wonderful that you did all this. You're an angel."

"Sam, dear," Dawn said, smiling. "It's just lovely to see you, and I'm so happy it's working out. We all have our angels, and Mirabella's mine. You remember, she's my assistant. She took care of everything, and I'm sure we'll all have a great visit."

Sam smiled at his mother. "Do we get to have another tour with Melchior today? He really knows his history. Almost like he was there."

"No, he has some volunteer work today—something about delivering some gifts," she replied. "So one of his partners will do the tour instead. I think I see him, actually. Let's get started."

Dawn smiled and waved across the hotel lobby as a man about Sam's age with a dark neatly trimmed beard strode toward them.

"Balthasar, so good to see you!" she called out as he approached.

"Hi, Dawn, wonderful to see you again," Balthasar said, bowing slightly and smiling at her.

"Hi, nice to meet you," Sam greeted, stepping forward to shake Balthasar's hand. "These are my friends Jason and Steve," he said, waving his arm toward them as they joined in.

"Hi, Balthasar," Jason greeted him, shaking his hand.

"Nice to meet you," Steve said, joining the group and shaking Balthasar's hand.

"Let's get going," Balthasar said, leading the group to the white van with Three Kings Tour Agency written in black on the side. After seating Dawn in the front passenger seat and the rest of the group in the back, he got into the driver's seat and started the tour. Before leaving, Balthasar handed everyone a bottle of Ein Gedi mineral water for the trip.

"This water is a symbol of our journey," Balthasar told them with a flair of drama. "We'll be leaving Jerusalem for the desert, a voyage that had great power and meaning in ancient times. For the ancient Judeans, Jerusalem was the home of the divine and a destination for hundreds of thousands of religious pilgrims each year. It was a beautiful city and almost like a garden. It was watered by the winter rains each year and by aqueducts that had been built over the centuries. But for some of the people, Jerusalem's beauty and abundance were seen as a distraction from spiritual devotion. Like in many other cultures around the world, there were groups of people who saw abundance and pleasure as dangerous for the soul. Such people are often referred to as ascetics, and some of them have served the world's religions as monks, nuns, swamis, or something similar.

"Here in Jerusalem, there was a group of ascetics known as the Essenes," Balthasar explained. "There were about four thousand of these Essenes living in Judea, mostly in Jerusalem. It's believed that they had a library and scribal center at a place called Qumran that's now an archaeological park. It may have also served as a retreat from the city. With their focus on purity, water was a central part of their beliefs," he added while driving the van onto Highway One, heading east toward the Dead Sea, about twenty-five miles away.

"Why do you say 'it's believed'?" Sam asked. "The historians aren't sure who lived at Qumran?"

"Right," Balthasar said, "there's a lot of debate about who lived there. Part of that has to do with all the silver and bronze coins that archaeologists have found there. Some historians say that there was just too much wealth there to have been the ascetic Essenes. These historians have some kind of formula based on cash flow. They use this to tell them how wealthy an excavated ancient settlement was based on how many coins were found by the archaeologists. According to these historians, all the coins found at Qumran must have belonged to some other group."

"How many coins are we talking about?" Sam asked.

"I can help with that," Steve jumped in. "I've been working on the history of Qumran for our project. According to my calculations, the fifteen treasure sites at Qumran with silver coins add up to about a hundred pounds of coins, which would be around four thousand shekels, which was one of the most common coins you would find in a treasury like this. The archaeology reports for Qumran can be pretty confusing, but apparently 561 silver coins were found in three earthen jars there. So it sounds like there were fewer coins left at Qumran when the war ended than when it started."

"Nice work, Steve," Sam said, smiling. "I think those historians' cash-flow analysis was all wrong. The Essenes certainly weren't wealthy, but they didn't spend too much either. So it sounds about right for the bronze scroll to say they had about four thousand coins in their treasury at the start of the war. And it makes sense for them to have had only about five hundred silver coins left at the end of the war. The war lasted almost seven years, and Qumran wasn't destroyed by the Romans until the end, in the year 73. So you'd expect that they would have spent some of their treasury on food and necessities during the war. But I don't think we have to look too closely at the quantities of coins at Qumran to know they belonged to the Essenes."

"Why not?" Jason asked.

"Because the bronze scroll specifically says that the fifteen locations in Qumran where these four thousand coins were hidden belonged to the Essenes," Sam replied.

"What do you mean?" Steve asked.

"It's one of those sets of Greek letters," Sam replied. "This one translates to S-K in ancient Hebrew, which clearly refers to *Isiyim korbanas*, which means the Essenes' treasury in English. It's really a slam dunk."

"It sounds like the mystery's solved, then," Balthasar said, smiling at Sam through the rearview mirror. "It makes more sense to me anyway."

"What do you mean?" Sam asked.

"You'll see when we get to Qumran," Balthasar replied. "It's the perfect place for the Essenes to put a library and scribal center, which they could also use as a getaway from the city. Really, for the same reasons that people like to visit the Dead Sea today. It's an escape—a retreat from the busy urban world, where you can swim in the Dead Sea or a pool with fresh water from one of the nearby streams and to enjoy the pristine nature there. It's so hot most of the year that there's really not much else to do except go swimming or maybe do some pottery or scroll writing. If you want to get away from it all, Qumran's the place. It's at the lowest land point on earth—more than 1,400 feet below sea level—and there's almost no rainfall at all. You certainly wouldn't be herding sheep or growing crops. Maybe we're all a little bit Essene." Balthasar smiled. "Some of the best days and nights of my life have been spent camping out by the shore of the Dead Sea, with my camels and—"

"What he means is that some of the resorts here are just amazing," Dawn interrupted. "Right, Balthasar? A perfect place for tanning, without those annoying UVB rays that cause sunburns?"

"Exactly, Dawn, that's what I meant," Balthasar said with a grin. "You're right about the unusual tanning conditions at the Dead Sea. At such a low elevation, the level of those burning UVB rays is about fifteen percent lower than at sea level during the summer months. But you'll still need that sunblock," he said, winking. "The elevation's not low enough for the atmosphere to block all of those rays."

When they arrived at Qumran National Park, Balthasar parked the van, and the group got out for their tour. "So, Balthasar," Sam asked, taking a drink from his water bottle as they walked toward the visitor center, "you said that water was a powerful symbol for these Essenes. Can you tell us more about that?"

"Of course," Balthasar said, nodding as he held the front door open for the group. "The Essenes saw the world as divided between the pure and the impure and as a battle between the Sons of Light and the Sons of Darkness. They had pools of water built into their communal housing, which they used for ritual cleansing throughout the day. Ritual cleansing pools had been a part of the Jewish tradition for centuries, but the Essenes took it to a new level. In fact, some archaeologists believe that they used the pools so much, and without an adequate fresh water supply, that the water may have actually created some sanitation issues out here in the desert."

"So were they on the side of light or darkness?" Jason asked, half-jokingly.

"They saw themselves as the Sons of Light, for sure," Balthasar replied. "They believed that messiahs and prophets would lead the people toward a more spiritual focus and would restore Jerusalem and its Temple to what they believed was a pure form of living."

"Who were the Sons of Darkness?" Steve asked.

"Probably the Romans," Balthasar replied. "It's pretty clear that the Essenes felt that Greek and Roman influences had corrupted Judean culture and made it impure. But you could also look at this more metaphorically. We have to rely on their writings, since we can't talk to them, of course. Sometimes modern people make the mistake of reading ancient writings too literally."

As the group gathered around a display about the Dead Sea Scrolls, Balthasar explained that the historians were still debating who had written them. But he said that a consensus was emerging that the Essenes had libraries both in Jerusalem and in Qumran and that the scrolls that were found in the caves were probably from both locations. He said that this probably happened when the Judean revolt began in the year AD 66 or perhaps later when the Essenes began to prepare for an expected attack by the Romans in the year AD 68.

"That's interesting," Sam said with his hand on his chin. "So if a scroll was kept at the Essenes' library in Jerusalem—maybe kept there because the militants had captured the Temple and its library with it—then it would have been moved to the Dead Sea caves along with the rest of the Essenes' library in Jerusalem?"

"Yes, that's what the scholars think," Balthasar said, nodding. "They believe that the Essenes' library in Jerusalem was more than just the esoteric writings and would have included scrolls with more general interest, like maybe something that the Essenes were holding for the high priests after the Temple had been captured by the militants. Anyway, it's interesting to consider whether the Essene scribes who wrote the more esoteric, mystical scrolls viewed them as literal prophesies, or maybe they thought of them more metaphorically."

"What do you mean?" Dawn asked.

"Well, since most of us have never spoken directly with the ancient people," Balthasar replied, "there's a tendency to view them with awe and reverence. That's fine and actually kind of appreciated." He winked at Dawn.

Sam looked at Balthasar, puzzled. "*Most* of us?"

"Sam, don't interrupt him, please," Dawn broke in. "We really shouldn't interrupt his private tour."

"That's fine," Balthasar said, smiling. "I really don't mind. But what I was saying is that sometimes the awe and reverence for our ancestors means we might misunderstand them. There's a tendency to take their writings literally, in ways that we normally wouldn't do with writings from our own era. After all, people throughout history have loved stories. It's the most important way we communicate. It's perfectly natural for those stories to be embellished or exaggerated in certain ways for dramatic effect or to make a point."

"Like Noah living nine hundred years?" Jason said.

"Or Moses leading the Israelites for forty years in the desert?" Steve added.

"Everyone has to decide these things for themselves," Balthasar replied. "Some people believe these things to be literally true, and other people see them as metaphors for a more important meaning. Maybe when these texts were written down, the authors simply wanted to make the point that living virtuously—as those first patriarchs in the biblical texts did—was its own reward. Or the authors wanted to say that it was important to accept the price for your mistakes, maybe by wandering in the desert for a long time. Perhaps everyone's right in this debate."

"What do you mean?" Dawn asked.

Balthasar smiled. "What if these biblical texts were literally the words of the divine *and* intended metaphorically? Maybe the divine understand metaphors better than we do. After all, didn't the divine say, 'Let us make mankind in our image'? Why *wouldn't* they use metaphors the way we do?"

"You mean 'in *His* image,' right?" Jason asked.

"No, it actually doesn't say that," Balthasar replied. "It says 'our' and 'we' throughout the biblical creation story. Just something else to think about." He winked.

"Maybe what this means is we're supposed to *think*," Sam jumped in.

"Exactly," Balthasar agreed. "All that awe and reverence for the ancient people is understandable. But it's not good if it stops you from thinking."

"So, Balthasar," Dawn interrupted, "what's in those ancient ruins outside? It's such a nice day, maybe we should go out there and look around?"

Balthasar led the group outside and began his tour of the ruins that had been excavated several decades earlier.

"So, Sam, any chance there are still some treasures buried here?" Steve asked as they walked toward the ruins.

"Other than those Essene coins, I don't think there ever was any gold or silver out here," Sam replied. "The bronze scroll seems pretty clear that the silver and bronze coins that were here belonged to the Essenes, and apparently there were only about four thousand coins in their treasury out here. All of the other treasure sites were in or around Jerusalem, Jericho, Samaria, Galilee, and the Decapolis. That's where most of the gold and silver was—mostly in coins, it seems. I think, when I added it up, it was something like five million shekels. After all, each pilgrim was supposed to donate a half shekel during a visit to the Temple. There were hundreds of thousands of pilgrims for each of the three festivals each year, so it wouldn't take long to accumulate a pretty healthy treasury."

"What was that place you mentioned? The Decapolis?" Jason asked.

"It was a league of mostly Greek cities that the Romans had given semiofficial autonomy," Sam replied. "The bronze scroll seems to say there's some treasure hidden at one of the cities."

"What's that about?" Steve asked.

"I'm really not sure about that one," Sam responded.

"What's the treasure?" Steve asked.

"It just says 'hidden donations,'" Sam replied. "Some of the locations on this treasure map seem to go out of their way to be vague. My favorite one is treasure number thirty-three."

"What does it say?" Jason asked.

"It says there are 'donations and scrolls,'" Sam replied. "Then it gives a warning: 'Do not break them open!' It's pretty mysterious when a treasure map tells you not to break open one of the treasures. Why would it say that?"

"Interesting," Steve said, rubbing his chin, "I'll bet it means something. Maybe the container was more important than what's inside? Like something was written on the container?"

"That's quite possible." Sam nodded. "I've really learned to take everything that's written on this bronze scroll seriously. Especially the metaphors. I think Balthasar is right about the importance of those."

"Well, it sounds like you guys have figured a lot of this out," Dawn broke in. "So no treasures here, then? Aside from some pottery you're not supposed to break?"

"I don't think so," Sam replied, "and it wouldn't have made sense for the Temple to move any of its treasury reserves here. Until the revolt started, Jerusalem had always been seen as the safest place to store the Judean treasury reserves. It was well defended with high walls. Even when the Romans came with their legions, it took a seven-month siege to conquer the city. But when the revolt started and descended into a civil war between the Jewish factions, Jerusalem was suddenly not so safe. But by then, it would have been too late to move any large amounts of gold or silver. The militants would have noticed and gone after them."

"Didn't you say there were treasures in Samaria and Galilee too?" Dawn asked. "And that other place?"

"Yes, the Decapolis," Sam clarified. "I've been wondering about that too. It really looks like the Jerusalem Temple administrators were in charge of the treasury not just in Judea but in Samaria, Galilee, and the Jewish communities in the Decapolis as well. Either way, the high priests clearly wanted to make the point that we're all in this together. United we stand, divided we fall. That's why all those otherwise-insignificant Essene holdings of silver were included in such detail. The high priests went out of their way to say that the nation needed to be united—and that even the Essenes were throwing their treasury into the common pool."

"So maybe the Essenes had forgiven the high priests in Jerusalem for being too cozy with the 'Sons of Darkness'—you know, the Romans?" Jason suggested.

Sam nodded. "It sounds like it, at least for one shining moment of unity before the civil war really got going. Or maybe the Essenes, or whoever wrote those stories, intended them as metaphorical to some degree. We really don't know, but we should be careful about reading these things too literally."

Balthasar continued the tour of Qumran and showed the group the different parts of the ruins, with the excavated rooms and walls. As they walked through the site, he pointed out some of the caves in the distance, where some of the scrolls were found. He explained that cave three, where the bronze scroll had been hidden, was farther away—probably signifying its importance and the Essenes' interest in protecting it.

After the tour of Qumran, Balthasar drove the group to Kalia Beach for lunch, just a few miles away. Piling into the open-air restaurant for pitas, falafels, fried eggplant, and Goldstar beer on tap, the group enjoyed a quick lunch by the Dead Sea. Jason and Steve went off for a while to wade in the water, returning with streaks of the famous black mud on their hands and feet.

After lunch, Balthasar drove them south on the Dead Sea Highway. He told them their next destination was the ancient fortress of Masada, about forty minutes away. As they drove along the seaside, the group admired the magnificent views of the blue water and the golden-hued hills on both sides of the sea.

"Why is it called the Dead Sea?" Steve asked.

"That's a translation from the Arabic name for this lake," Balthasar replied.

"A lake?" Jason asked. "I thought it was a sea."

"It's salty like the ocean," Balthasar explained, "but scientists call it a lake because it's fed by fresh water—mostly the Jordan River—and it's not connected to an ocean. In fact, it's one of the saltiest bodies of water in the world. It's almost ten times as salty as the ocean—more than thirty percent salt. That's why the Arabs called it 'dead.' It's too salty for fish or plants, and the only life in it are a few tiny microbes. We won't have time for a swim today, but I do recommend that you come back and spend at least half a day at one of the beaches here. Because of the salt, the water's so buoyant that it's a little hard to swim in. Basically, the only thing you can do is float."

"That sounds like fun, Balthasar," Dawn said. "And, of course, the mud is good for the skin, right?"

"Yes, Dawn," he replied, "the mud is very good for the skin. You put some mud on your skin, leave it for ten minutes, and then wash it off. Your skin will feel amazing—tightened and toned, with fewer wrinkles and blemishes. Just don't shave before going into the water. You'll really notice the sting from the salt."

"Sounds great," Dawn said, smiling. "I feel younger already. That Dead Sea mud is supposed to have wonderful healing properties."

"That's very true," Balthasar agreed. "It's a lot like that myrrh that I give to people. Myrrh's a wonderful cure—all mixed into wine or vinegar. It's been used as medicine or incense for thousands of years, and it's kept me young. And, of course, it's a symbol of the powers of the divine."

Dawn looked at Balthasar. "Maybe we should focus on the Dead Sea right now. Aren't those resorts supposed to be wonderful? Maybe I should check into one of them for a while. Anyone want to join me?"

"Count me in," Jason chimed in.

"Same here." Steve said, nodding. "Dawn, especially if you can bring your friend Ava Stern along again. Her dancing was just incredible last night. It turns out she didn't really even need that seven-veils outfit. Sam, how about you? How about another week in Israel?"

"Um, I'm open to spending more time in Israel," Sam replied. "But maybe closer to, say, Tel Aviv?"

Jason groaned. "It sounds like someone had a nice date last night. Want to tell us about it?"

"Well, let's just say I'm not heartbroken over missing Ava Stern," Sam said, smiling. "Rebecca's pretty amazing."

"Sam, I'm sure Rebecca's wonderful," Steve jumped in, "but really, there's nothing like Ava Stern's dancing. They call her the 'flower of the Orient' in that new movie. Watching her dance is just really hypnotic."

"I'm sorry I missed it." Sam said with a mischievous smile. "I guess I really missed out on the dancing and flowers and all."

"So, Balthasar," Dawn asked, sensing she needed to change the subject, "tell us about where we're going. You've got a few stories about Masada, I'm sure."

"Yes," he said with a nod. "Masada was a great fortress built by Herod the Great on top of a cliff 1,300 feet above the Dead Sea. The views from the top are spectacular. I'll tell you about the history along the way. King Herod began building a palace at the top of the Masada cliff not long after he took the throne. His marriage to the beautiful Princess Mariamne that same year had helped him become king due to her family connections. But he really loved her, and—"

"Wait, isn't he the one who had his wife strangled to death?" Dawn interrupted.

"Um, yes, Dawn," Balthasar agreed. "That was his second wife, Mariamne, the one who was responsible for him being king."

Dawn frowned. "This is the king who was jealous that if he died, she might love some other man, so he gave standing orders for her to be killed as soon as he died, right?"

"Yes, that's right," Balthasar said, nodding. "Not a really nice man."

"He was despicable." Dawn scowled. "Worse than Octavian. I'm sure Cleopatra would have had nothing to do with him."

"Well, actually, Dawn," Balthasar said, treading gingerly, "I was about to get to that."

"No, don't tell me." Dawn sank into her seat, cupping her head in her hands. "If he was one of her lovers, I don't even want to know."

Balthasar smiled. "Not at all. They were bitter enemies."

"I knew it!" Dawn said, sitting up. "Her instincts about men were quite good. Except for that fling with Octavian."

"It was mostly about Mark Antony," Balthasar explained. "Herod knew he wouldn't have become king of Judea without Mark Antony's support—and from having married into Mariamne's family, of course. He became jealous of Cleopatra's close relationship with Antony, and they started feuding. It got so bad that Cleopatra demanded that Antony dismiss Herod and turn Judea over to her rule. After all, Cleopatra was the heir to a dynasty that still claimed the right to rule Judea, and she never gave up that claim. Antony decided to let Herod keep the throne, but he did take away Herod's profitable date plantations in Jericho and balsam plantations here at Ein Gedi on the Dead Sea and gave them to Cleopatra."

"What's balsam?" Steve asked.

"It's a plant that grows on the Dead Sea shore that produces an essential oil used in perfumes," Balthasar replied. "In those days, balsam resin was worth twice its weight in gold. That gives you an idea about the priorities of the ancient people. The scent of love is more important than gold, right?"

"That sounds about right," Sam agreed.

Enjoying the spectacular scenery around them, the group listened as Balthasar continued telling them about the history of Masada and the Dead Sea. He told them about the magnificent palaces that Herod had built on top of the cliff above the sea.

The first palace that Herod built at Masada was on the western side, facing away from the sea. It had a grand throne room, a swimming pool, and an elaborate mosaic room. The mosaic room had steps leading to a second floor with separate bedrooms for Herod and Mariamne.

Dawn wasn't surprised. Who would want to sleep in the same room with a husband who wanted you dead? A husband who actually had you strangled to death for complaining about it?

The next palace built was on the northern side, with an amazing view of the Dead Sea below. It had a bathhouse, lavish rooms, and terraces for banquets and parties.

Dawn wasn't having it. "Mariamne should have thrown Herod off the balcony," she said.

Balthasar sighed. "Well, by then, the first Mariamne had been executed at Herod's orders."

"The *first* Mariamne?" Dawn said, rolling her eyes. "There was a second one?"

"Yes, Mariamne the Second," he replied. "She was Herod's third wife."

"So let me guess, it was a true love story?" Dawn asked sarcastically.

"Not really," Balthasar responded. "It sounds like she was forced into the marriage by her father. Herod promised to appoint the father as chief high priest if he could have his daughter as his wife."

"I hope she had her own bedroom," Dawn said, frowning.

"Well, at least she wasn't strangled to death," Balthasar said, trying to look on the bright side.

"They lived happily ever after?" Dawn asked.

"No, not at all," Balthasar replied. "Eventually, she started plotting to have him killed. He was King Herod, after all. Nobody could stand him. When Herod found out, he divorced Mariamne the Second and had her father dismissed from the Temple. It wasn't a good deal for her father in the end. No one ever came out ahead making deals with Herod."

Fortunately, the group arrived at Masada before Balthasar had time to tell the stories of Herod's other seven wives or about Herod's sons that he had tried for treason and executed. These stories of injustice could be so maddening. The group rode up to the top on the cable car, with spectacular views of the Dead Sea and its surrounding hills along the way.

As he led the group on a private tour of the fortress, Balthasar told them the story of the last battle of the revolt, with the Romans laying siege to Masada for several months in the year AD 73. According to the historian Josephus, the remaining militant defenders committed suicide rather than surrender to the Romans. Modern historians are less certain about what actually happened, but either way the war ended as violently as it had begun.

After touring the clifftop, the group looked at the sun sinking lower in the western sky, casting golden shadows over the blue sea onto the rust-colored hills of Jordan beyond. Nature's beauty here was truly inspiring, and it was easy to understand why this land had been contested for thousands of years.

On the way back, Balthasar talked about some of the current struggles over who had rights to this land. He talked about the mines that had been placed near the Dead Sea and the difficult relationships among the Israelis,

Jordanians, and Palestinians over this magic place. He expressed the hope that by finding ways to cooperate, these great peoples would be able to prevent the Dead Sea from drying up more and to protect this sacred land for the future.

Returning to their hotel, the group thanked Balthasar for the wonderful tour. Then they headed off to dinner at Turquoise at the St. George Landmark Hotel, a few blocks from their own hotel, which Balthasar had recommended as a great place for Lebanese food in Jerusalem. He told them that Lebanese cuisine was generally viewed as the most delicious and sophisticated in the Middle East and that they were lucky to have this place near their hotel.

The waiter at Turquoise suggested they start with a round of a drink called arak and some small plates known as *mezze*. The waiter explained that arak, an anise-flavored distilled wine, was quite strong, both in alcohol and flavor, and was usually enjoyed along with some food. The group ordered some fresh almonds, briny olives, lemony hummus, and stuffed grape leaves as cold mezze and began studying the menus for ideas on which hot mezze to order after that.

When the waiter returned with the first cold mezze and a tray with Lebanese arak and an assortment of carafes and small glasses, some with spring water and some with ice, he brought along a pamphlet showing how arak was made and served. The ice was always added last, he showed them, so the clear liquor turned a proper cloudy white instead of a dense oil floating on top of the drink. The best arak, like this one, he explained, was aged in clay amphoras like the ones shown on the pamphlet, which had been used since ancient times.

As the group was deciding on their hot mezze choices, Sam heard a ping on his phone. Sam looked down and noticed the message from Eric Armstrong. It was good to hear from Eric, whom he had asked to check on what had happened to Alexander Lambros, the investigator who seemed to have disappeared after helping Sam with the Wechsler case. But Sam was really concerned that almost a week had passed without any word from Alexander, and he wasn't sure that this would be good news.

It was the worst possible news. Sam gasped as he read Eric's message.

Hi Sam, I can send you a full report by email, but I wanted to get you an update here on encrypted chat. I'm afraid I have bad news about your friend Alexander. I know you've worked with him a long time, and I can

> *jump on a call if you'd like. It's morning here in LA now, so anytime is good. I spoke with the Cyprus police, and there was a car bombing outside Alexander's home last Thursday. It was some kind of holiday there, and apparently he was going out that morning to pick up something for the children. The police are still investigating the details, so I don't have much to report. There was a memorial service for him yesterday. I'll stay on this until I find out more. I know you guys were close, so if there's anything I can do, just let me know. Eric*

Sam had to leave the table to compose himself, walking out of the dining room and down the hall by the restrooms. He had been working with Alexander for years and had gotten to know him pretty well. They had met a few times at investigative conferences that Sam had attended in Europe. Alexander was one of the best, and Sam felt lucky to know him. What about his wife and children? Sam couldn't even imagine what they were going through. But he didn't know if he could help. It might be even more painful if he tried to contact them.

Who could have done this? Cyprus was a pretty political place, but Sam didn't think Alexander would have been involved in anything like that. Could it be the Wechsler investigation? A million-euros bribe meant there was enough at stake to get someone killed. But why? Could Roy Griffin actually be that crazy? Sam had met some difficult CEOs over the years. But none of them had been a *murderer.*

Sam looked at his phone again, checking his unread messages. There were a few emails from the office, but he knew that none of them were urgent. They would have called or texted him about anything important. Then there were those texts from Roy—the ones that had been obnoxiously sent over the weekend and that Sam had ignored. It was beyond intrusive for Roy to even be texting him—Sam hadn't given him his mobile number, after all.

What was *wrong* with Roy? His behavior made him look like a brutal savage. Or a murderous Roman emperor. Hadn't he seen a toga laying on his bed, Sam recalled, when he walked by to find the bathroom? The one with that golden toilet? None of those things were signs of good mental health, he thought.

Sam scrolled through the new messages from Roy.

Hi Sam, Roy again. I've been trying to reach you about some urgent projects. I know you're busy, but this is more important. Call me as soon as you get this. I'll be waiting. Roy

Sent: Saturday, January 9 at 9:25 p.m.

Sam, we really need to talk. Things are moving fast now, and you're at the center of this. I hired you to help with that Copper Scroll, and some things have come up that need your attention. It really can't wait. Roy

Sent: Sunday, January 10 at 7:14 a.m.

Sam, call me. That Copper Scroll's been stolen. I sure hope that contract you did is solid. You're in the middle of this mess, and I need you on this right away. Roy

Sent: Monday, January 11 at 1:22 p.m.

Sam exhaled. This *was* a mess, and he needed help. He had already told Roy that he wouldn't be doing any more work for Eden, but he suspected that wasn't going to end it. But there was no point in ruining the evening for his mom, Jason, and Steve. He often thought the most valuable lesson he'd learned in his career so far was not to act in the heat of the moment. Your first reaction is usually not the smartest one. What had that angel said? In Rebecca's favorite story from Gideon's Spring up north? Life was about intelligence, courage, and wisdom. We need all three. But maybe Sam needed an angel too, he thought. After all, Gideon hadn't become a hero all by himself.

Sam breathed deeply and walked back to the dining room, taking a seat at the table. He tried to look like everything was fine.

"Is everything okay, Sam?" Dawn asked, looking concerned. "Is there something going on at work? You were gone for a while."

"Some things have come up that I'll have to take care of," he replied. "But there's nothing I can do tonight. No reason to walk out on a nice dinner. With the best company," he said, raising his glass.

Jason and Steve offered to help with anything he needed, and Sam said he might take them up on that. Just a bit later. He said he needed to think some things over, but he was sure that he could use their advice.

Sam made the most of the dinner and was glad to be with his mother and his friends. He wanted to talk to Rebecca too but didn't want to bother

her with his bad news right away. But what if she was in danger too? The *Jerusalem Post* had published some articles about the Wechsler scandal under her byline. If whoever did this—and it might have been Roy—thought that Rebecca was getting too close to something, they might hurt her too. He knew he would need to call her, but he needed to calm down a bit first.

Sam sent a message to Rebecca before leaving the restaurant and heading back to the hotel.

> *Sweet Rebecca, I hope you're having a wonderful evening. I'm excited to see you tomorrow, but can we talk tonight? I got some news that may be related to the Wechsler investigation, and it's really tough. It's not directly related to your reporting and certainly not to the little project I did for Roy before learning about his activities there, so we can talk about it. I know you'll be strong and everything will be fine. But we'll need to figure this out. I'm at a restaurant with my mom and friends now but will be back at the hotel soon. I'll try to reach you when I get there, if that works. Yours, Sam*

After saying good night to his mom and his friends, Sam went up to his hotel room. As he walked into the room, he got a message back from Rebecca.

> *Hi Sam, everything's good here, and I had a nice day at work and went out with some friends tonight. I'm still tingly from such a wonderful time with you, and I can't wait to see you tomorrow! Yes, I'd love to chat. Can you talk now? Kisses! Rebecca*

Sam called her right away. "Hi, Sam?" she answered, sounding a little worried.

"Hi, Rebecca," he said, "I hope my message didn't worry you, and I don't want to be alarming."

"No, it's fine," she said. "What's going on?"

"I got a message during dinner," he told her. "A friend of mine—the investigator I was using for the Wechsler investigation—who found out about the million-euros payment to Wechsler, he was killed by a car bomb last week."

The call went silent for a while. "I'm so sorry," Rebecca finally said, stunned. "A car bomb? Are you sure? How did you find out?"

"After the investigator—my friend Alexander—went strangely silent last week and stopped responding to calls and messages," Sam explained,

"I asked another investigator to find out what had happened. When something's urgent, hiring the right person to run something down is always the best way. Even if it's bad news that you don't really want to know." He sighed.

"So what does this mean?" she asked.

"I don't know yet," he replied. "But we should assume the worst."

"What's that?" she asked.

"Someone doesn't want the authorities to know that Wechsler was bribed to issue land development permits all around the country," he replied. "And they're ready to kill to silence anyone who gets too close to the truth."

Rebecca was silent again. "You mean like you and me?"

"We should assume the worst," Sam said again. "That means we're both in danger. Whoever did this to Alexander will do whatever it takes to protect their secrets."

"I understand," she said quietly. "So what do we do?"

"We need a plan," he replied. "Some of that courage and wisdom, for sure. Until then, we should sit tight while we figure this out. Where are you?"

"I'm at home," she said. "Safe and sound, I think."

"Please stay there while we figure this out," he said. "I'd call the police if I thought that would help. But we just don't have anything they could use. It's all speculation at this point. Private security will be better."

"You mean like a bodyguard?" she asked.

"Yes, definitely," he said. "I'll start making some calls."

"Are you okay?" Rebecca asked.

Sam paused. No, he thought. But what was the point of that? "Yes, of course," he answered. "Everything will be fine." Maybe he even believed it. Courage and wisdom? Were they enough? Or did that story mean that you really needed an angel?

"Good, we'll focus on that," she said. "Now tell me more about Alexander."

They went over everything that Sam had learned from Alexander. Sam told Rebecca the full story about his meeting with Roy. It wasn't part of his legal work for Eden, after all, and Roy hadn't even been his client. An attorney represents the corporation, not the CEO, and maybe Roy had forgotten that.

Then she told him everything she had learned about Wechsler, right down to the murder weapon. A Jericho 941 pistol. The police were working to track down the serial number.

They agreed to talk again first thing in the morning. A good night's sleep would help with their planning. But they knew that this changed everything. They would need to get ahead of this.

"Good night, Rebecca," Sam said as they ended the call.

"Night, Sam," she replied. "Talk to you in the morning."

Sam sat down on the edge of the bed and exhaled. He felt better after talking to Rebecca. He was glad they had shared everything. They would handle this together, and this gave him a feeling of strength and peace.

Sam got up and walked over to the desk in his hotel room. He sat down and started working on a plan. He typed up some bullet points in his laptop and sketched out some diagrams on a legal pad.

Several hours later, Sam felt better. This plan would work, he thought. He was sure that Rebecca would have a few ideas too, and they would cover everything in the morning.

There was just one last thing he needed to do before getting some rest. He picked up his phone and typed a message to Roy.

> *Roy, I'll call you tomorrow. I've seen your messages, which are frankly unacceptable. As I've already told you, I'm not your attorney, and I've already finished that little project for Eden. There's really nothing to discuss, unless you're willing to answer some questions about what you've been doing. But let me be clear. I'm not your attorney, and nothing you tell me will be private or privileged. Sam*

Sam got ready for bed and put his phone on the nightstand. As he was getting into bed, he heard a ping. It must be Roy, he thought.

> *Sam, we'll talk tomorrow. I hope you enjoyed your olives and grape leaves. Good thing they weren't poisoned. But you should really be more careful. Bad things happen when I get angry. Roy*

Sam felt a chill down his spine. He knew Roy was serious, but none of this made sense. What was Roy up to? This was getting dangerous. Sam knew that he needed to figure this out.

Sam tossed and turned for much of the night. Roy was disturbing, but somehow Sam felt something darker and more powerful behind him.

The troubling images that came to him while falling asleep weren't of Roy. No, it was a beautiful woman. Alluring like Rebecca, but in a different way. Insatiable lust and passion. Dark and predatory, but with an incredible feeling of power and strength.

Behind that raging fire, though, sadness and fear. Like a frightened child, all alone, with such anger toward the divine. Determined to learn so much power that she would never feel that way again.

Sam had never felt anything like this before. Knowing he needed to sleep, he cleared his head and let these feelings go for now. He thought of his father in those dreams from long ago. Stories about travels and adventure. The more recent dreams too. It was usually his father. Not Donovan, but the other one. Calm and serene. He could sleep now.

16

THOU SHALT NOT KILL

Sam woke up to the sound of his alarm. He grabbed his phone and turned it off. It was 5:00 a.m. on Wednesday, and he needed to get going. He sat up in bed and sent a message to Rebecca.

> *Good morning! Sorry about the disturbing news last night. I have a few more ideas now, and we should talk whenever you're ready. We'll need to get ahead of this. Yours, Sam*

Sam took a shower and looked out the window of his hotel room. It was still dark, with no hint of the morning approaching on the eastern horizon. Turning to look to the north, he saw low dark clouds moving over the Judean Hills. It looked like it would rain soon.

He got dressed in blue jeans and a casual maroon sweater. It would be a chilly, rainy day, and he wanted to stay warm.

Sam sat down in a large comfortable chair and started working on his outline again. He had typed up some ideas about handling Roy and wanted to think this through more carefully. He had often found that organizing his thoughts helped him to think more critically and creatively.

After a couple of hours working on his outline, Sam decided that the plan was pretty good. He knew what Roy wanted and could use this against him. Obsessive, driven people like Roy were usually quite predictable. Like a bullfighter with a red cape, Sam would let Roy's impulses and cravings defeat him. He was a weak man with virtually no self-control at all. Everything still had to go right, but at least the basic strategies were lined up well, Sam thought.

Sam looked at the clock on the nightstand. It was just past 7:00 a.m., and it was time to check in with his mom and his friends. He needed to update them on what was happening and then put his plan into motion.

He sent a group message to Jason and Steve.

Hey guys, hope you got plenty of rest and you're ready for a busy day. I got some news last night, and there's a change of plans on my end. I'll explain everything at breakfast. Can you meet me in the courtyard around 7:30 a.m.?

Then he sent a message to his mom.

Good morning! Hope you slept well and are ready for some adventure. I got some news that changes the script a bit and was wondering if you could help with a leading role. It's not exactly Cleopatra, but there's definitely a snake and some poison. Can you meet me and the guys in the courtyard around 7:30 a.m.?

Sam heard a ping. It was a message from Rebecca.

Hi Sam, good morning! Yes, of course, I can do a call anytime. How about in five minutes? Kisses, Rebecca

After more pings, Sam confirmed the breakfast plans with his mom, Jason, and Steve in a half hour. Then he called Rebecca.

"Hi, Sam," she answered. "I've been so worried about you. How are you doing?"

Sam frowned. He didn't want her to worry. "Good morning. I'm holding up fine. Better than that, actually. I have a few ideas about how to handle this. Roy's messing with the wrong people."

"I'm sure you're right," she said, sounding a bit relieved. "Roy's definitely dangerous, but a part of that is that he's reckless. We can use that against him, don't you think?"

"Nice work," Sam said, "you read my mind. The problem always presents its own solutions."

As they talked, Sam told Rebecca more of what he had learned at Roy's villa in Rome. He told her about the basement with Roy's golden statue of himself and his obsession with finding the lost Ark of the Covenant and the other sacred treasures of the Hebrew Bible and the Christian Old Testament. It seemed like some of Eden's construction projects were aimed at creating controversies and protests to make it easier for Roy to focus primarily on the Temple Mount. But perhaps Roy actually thought that some of the treasures were at these other sites as well. Maybe Roy had someone working on deciphering the Copper Scroll. How else would he know about these sites?

Rebecca agreed, explaining that it would be very difficult for Eden to work underneath the Temple Mount without first creating distractions at these other sites. But some of the sites were unusual and suggested that Roy believed there was treasure there as well. The Silwan tombs were in a Palestinian neighborhood in East Jerusalem, and Eden's visible presence there would be sure to cause a disturbance. Likewise, Hezekiah's Tunnel was a historic underground waterway associated with an ancient Jewish king, such that a construction project there without advance community input would likely lead to media attention and controversy.

In the West Bank, Eden had gotten a permit for construction at the summit of Mount Gerizim, well beyond the Land Authority's jurisdiction. Likewise, it had obtained permits for construction at Gideon's Spring—that nice park where they had picnicked earlier in the week—and at the ruins of Megiddo in northern Israel.

That last site, Megiddo, was better known as Armageddon, Rebecca pointed out. Exactly the kind of place Eden would be digging around if it wanted to cause trouble. Most of the major religions viewed Armageddon as a spiritual metaphor, but some religious groups interpreted the texts more literally as predictions about the end of the world. Whatever Eden was doing in these places wasn't good, Rebecca thought.

Both a bit pressed for time, they agreed to check back with each other later in the day. He promised to call her in the afternoon and to let her know if anything important happened before then. He asked her to promise to call him if she needed anything and to be extra careful. Roy was becoming extreme, and Sam wasn't sure how far he would go to get what he wanted. Sam was making arrangements for several bodyguards to be assigned to Rebecca, working in shifts around the clock. Rebecca said that wasn't necessary, and Sam reluctantly agreed to revisit this later in the day.

"Take care and be safe," Rebecca said.

"You too," Sam replied. "See you soon."

Sam sat back in the chair and exhaled. He took a few long, deep breaths and felt calm. He needed to call Roy and wasn't sure how this would go.

"Hello, stranger," Roy said sarcastically as he answered the phone. "It's about time you showed up. You've really got a mess on your hands."

"It's really just a courtesy call," Sam replied. "You can clean up your own messes, and I've already finished that project for Eden. There's nothing else I need to do."

"You just don't get it, do you?" Roy snarled. "You're my lawyer, bought and paid for. There are some things I need you to do, and you don't really have a choice. This will get ugly otherwise."

"You've already made this ugly," Sam responded. "My project for Eden is done, and I was never your lawyer anyway. I was working for Eden, not you, and I don't owe you anything."

"You owe me big time," Roy replied. "You messed up my deal on the Copper Scroll, and the insurance company sent a letter saying they might not pay for it being stolen. Something about intentional conduct or words to that effect. You're responsible for this, and I'm holding you to it."

Sam laughed. "Intentional conduct? What, do they think *you* stole the Copper Scroll? Why would they say that?"

"Well, since you're my lawyer, I'll tell you," Roy said. "I did steal it. You didn't get the right coverage, and now you have to help me."

"I'm not your lawyer," Sam said, raising his voice. "And stop talking to me as if I were. I'm *not* your attorney, and I can report you to the police."

"A lawyer can't do that," Roy said with a laugh. "You're right in the middle of all this and have to keep your mouth shut. Besides, I have something you want. Just a little treasure map I happened across. You know, the one you wanted."

"That *I* wanted?" Sam shot back. "You're crazy, I never said I wanted you to steal the Copper Scroll."

"It's called a conspiracy, Sam, and you said you'd be able to solve it if you could look at some of the sections up close," Roy replied. "You even told me which sections you wanted. It's too late for you to back out now. You're in this up to your neck, and the only way out is to help me solve this thing."

"Conspiracy? You must be joking," Sam said. "I didn't say anything about stealing the Copper Scroll, and I can definitely report you to the police. I'm not your lawyer, and there's nothing private about this conversation."

"I thought you were smarter than this," Roy said, sneering. "You can't say a word to anyone, and I own you. I don't need all of the sixty treasure sites. I really just need your help on a few of them. I'll send you what you need to make this work. But just be careful if you go outside," Roy went on. "I hear there's a contract out on you. A little something that happened when you weren't returning calls."

Sam couldn't believe what he was hearing. Was Roy really crazy enough to threaten him? To send contract killers after him?

"You're not *that* stupid," Sam said, breaking the silence. "Who would put a contract on someone and then confess to doing that?"

"It's not a confession at all. Just a private discussion with my attorney," Roy responded. "You're my attorney, and you can't say a word to anyone about this. Besides, I'm a CEO of a Fortune 500 company—actually, three of them—and that means I can do whatever I want."

"Look, I'm going to hang up now because I'm done talking to you," Sam said firmly. "But before I do, I'll just say this. If you're actually stupid enough to put a contract out to hurt me, then you need to cancel it right now. Otherwise I'll have you arrested today and you'll be facing some serious felony charges."

Roy laughed. "I know attorneys, so I know you won't do that. And if I hired someone like that, it wouldn't be to just hurt you. I don't do half measures. If someone makes me angry, they pay the full price."

"This is ridiculous," Sam said, "and this call is over. I don't believe a word you're saying, but I'm reporting all of this to the police anyway. Expect a visit from them."

Sam ended the call and whistled quietly. What could possibly make Roy act this way? Did he actually think the Copper Scroll listed a treasure like the lost Ark? Even if it did, why would Roy think that he could solve it? Maybe Donovan had told him he was a great lawyer, but a treasure hunter too? One who could magically find the lost Ark from an ancient scroll?

He stood up and got ready to head downstairs. Just then he heard a knock at the door. Opening the door, he saw a bellman with a large rectangular cardboard box.

"Good morning, sir," the bellman said with a smile. "This just came in for you. Please sign here," he said, handing him a receipt.

Sam signed the receipt and asked the bellman to put the box on the coffee table in the living area. Then the bellman excused himself and left the room.

Standing at the door, Sam looked at the large box. He'd have time for this later, he thought. He hadn't ordered anything, but maybe the office had forwarded him something. Law books and case files can be surprisingly large, he knew. Maybe it was just some evidence he needed to review. Whatever it was, it could wait. He left to go downstairs without opening the box. At this point, he really didn't need another surprise.

Sam walked up to the table in the leafy courtyard. "Hey guys. Hi, Mom," he called out. Jason and Steve stood up, and Dawn got up to give him a hug.

After an exchange of greetings, Sam sat down and began to tell the group a little of what was going on. But as he started to explain, the whole story started coming out. He told them the news about his friend Alexander being killed in a car bombing, along with a general description of his conversation with Roy. He said he thought that they were all in danger and that they might all need bodyguards. Like Rebecca, they all felt that might be awkward and only a short-term solution anyway. Everyone agreed that it made the most sense to push back on Roy and find some way of stopping him.

What about the police? Dawn felt that Roy had gone so far that he should be reported to law enforcement. Sam shrugged and said he didn't think the police would do much. It was Sam's word against Roy's, even if some of Roy's text messages were a little threatening. The police might assign a detective to interview Roy, but it probably wouldn't go much farther than that. Besides, Sam knew that Roy could cause trouble with his law firm and his attorney license. It may sound innocuous, but the bar association tightly regulates attorney activities. Like most bureaucrats, the bar officials would probably split the difference rather than do the work necessary to figure out what had actually happened. That was the easy path that public officials often followed, making these kinds of things inherently damaging for everyone involved.

Sam suggested that he had a better plan. He still wanted everyone to consider having a bodyguard, but he agreed that having an organized plan to deal with Roy was even more important. Sam told the group that he had made progress toward solving some of the Copper Scroll treasure locations and that he could use some of what he knew against Roy. He would use Roy's greed and insatiable lust for treasure against him. These were weaknesses, after all, and he intended to fully exploit them. He told them some of the specifics of what he was planning, and they nodded that this might work.

As Dawn's phone rang and she picked up the call and excused herself from the table, Sam asked Jason and Steve if they could spend part of the morning and afternoon working on their Copper Scroll project together. They readily agreed and said that they had been wanting to do this anyway.

Jason and Steve each said that they had made progress too and had been wanting to compare notes.

Sam laughed. Maybe they would get those eighteen tons of gold and silver after all. That's how these things often go, he thought. You encounter a problem and have to get creative to solve it. At the end of the day, you end up in a better place than if there had been no problem. Unless, of course, one of Roy's assassins gets to you first. Sam knew he would just have to stay a few steps ahead of Roy.

While Dawn was away, Sam told Jason and Steve a little more about his plan. He was a bit relieved that his mother wasn't at the table to hear this because some of the plan frankly sounded a little dangerous. Jason and Steve thought that some of it was *really* dangerous. Going after Roy on his home turf in Rome would be risky, they thought.

Returning to their table, Dawn told the group that she was being called away on a work emergency. This didn't sound good, Sam thought. He didn't think there were any genuine emergencies in making movies, so she might have toned this down not to worry the group. But she assured them that it wasn't about Roy and was something quite different.

After hugs all around, Dawn headed out directly without packing her things upstairs. Sam thought that meant it was something local. If she were flying somewhere, she would have needed to pack. He was a little worried but knew that his mother could take care of herself. She had disappeared like this quite a few times before, and Sam could even remember her leaving on unexpected emergencies a few times when he was a child. He had never really understood what those events were, and she had always been vague about it.

Around 8:30 a.m., Sam, Jason, and Steve went upstairs. They all went to Sam's room to begin comparing notes about some of their work on the Copper Scroll. Walking into the room, Steve asked about the large box that the porter had left in the living area. Sam said he didn't know what it was and suggested that Steve go ahead and open it.

Removing the packing tape from the top of the box, Steve opened up the box and whistled. There, partially hidden under clear Bubble Wrap, were two long, curved sections of the legendary Copper Scroll.

"What the hell?" Steve said, stunned.

Joining him and looking into the box, Sam and Jason shook their heads in disbelief. The sender was listed as Eden Construction at an address in Caesarea, Israel.

"Roy sent this?" Sam said incredulously. "He really thinks I can find the lost Ark with this?"

As Jason and Steve gave him puzzled looks, Sam explained that Roy's obsession was finding the lost Ark and putting it in the fake temple he had built in the basement of his Roman villa. Sam had made clear that he hadn't found anything like an Ark on the Copper Scroll but that Roy seemed to think that his help was somehow needed in finding this lost artifact.

"So he's not looking for gold and silver after all?" Jason asked.

"Oh, I think he wants to fill up his fake temple with gold and silver too," Sam replied. "Especially if it came from the Jerusalem Temple. But he seems to be mostly interested in searching for the lost Ark. Maybe these other locations are partially intended to create distractions so it will be a little easier for Roy to operate under the Temple Mount without as much attention."

"So what's the plan for this morning?" Steve asked. "Should we go looking around at some of these sites?"

"You read my mind." Sam nodded. "I think that's exactly what we should do. Seeing things in person can really help, and we might even see something that helps explain what Roy's up to."

Before leaving, Sam phoned a tour guide at one of the locations he thought might be important. He had been reading about some of the legends of the treasures from Solomon's Temple being hidden near the Ophel Hill, south of the Temple Mount. With so many legends having similar stories about this place, maybe there's some truth in these stories, he thought.

Around 9:00 a.m., Sam and Steve went downstairs and walked outside to where Jason had pulled up in a blue Mazda crossover. Sam had brought the Copper Scroll pieces with him, still wrapped securely in the shipping box. He knew they would be safer with him than left at the hotel. They got into the Mazda, and Jason drove off toward the Temple Mount to the south. After passing below the Eastern Wall of the Temple—the oldest part of the walls, believed to date to the earlier Solomon's Temple—Jason drove them past the Southern Wall and the Ophel Hill, where King David's palace had stood three thousand years ago.

After turning left to drive to the eastern side of the Ophel Hill, Jason pulled into a parking spot near the Gihon Spring. They all got out of the Mazda and walked up to the entrance.

"You must be Sam." A tour guide with a red checkered kaffiyeh stepped forward. "I'm Hadi Habib, and we spoke on the phone a few minutes ago. Are you ready for the tour?"

"Yes, of course," Sam said as Jason and Steve said hello to Hadi. "We're not exactly tourists today. It's really an amateur archaeology project, so we mainly want to focus on a few details. We'll come back another time to see this place as visitors more properly."

"Let's go, then." Hadi smiled. "I'll give you the amateur archaeology tour. I think you said you're interested in the legends about where Solomon's gold was hidden. Some people even say the lost Ark was hidden here too. This place has quite a history."

As they walked into the narrow opening of a rock-carved tunnel, Hadi told them that this channel, known as Hezekiah's Tunnel, had been built around the eighth century BC to draw water from the Gihon Spring. The city's leaders had thought carefully about how to defend it from imperial invaders. As one of the few reliable sources of underground water in the area, the Gihon Spring would be an essential resource for both the invaders and defenders in a siege. Large walls had already been built to enclose the spring itself, but the city's planners wanted an artificial channel to direct the outflow from the spring into the city rather than into the Kidron Valley, which couldn't be defended in a siege and would provide a water source for the invading army.

Hadi told the group that Hezekiah's Tunnel was over 1,700 feet, or 500 meters, long, about the length of five American football fields. Hand carved from the rock to carry water from the spring, the tunnel itself wouldn't be a good hiding place for treasure. But maybe there's a secret chamber or similar type of hiding place around here, he suggested with a wink.

Steve reminded Hadi that they weren't really treasure hunters and were just working on an amateur archaeology project. But, Steve added, they were curious about what had happened to the treasures of Solomon's Temple. Was it really possible for them to be hidden here?

More than possible, Hadi replied. As he continued leading them through the long ancient tunnel, he explained that the limestone was a relatively soft rock that was easier than most to dig through. It wouldn't have been hard, he said, to carve out a few secret hiding places in this area. There were natural caves too, and maybe one of them was used to hide the treasures of Solomon's Temple before or during the Assyrian invasion in the eighth century BC.

Those stories about the treasures of Solomon's Temple being hidden in the desert made little sense, Hadi went on. The safest place in the land had always been inside Jerusalem's city walls. The tunnels and caves in this area would have been one of the best hiding places in ancient times, so maybe some of those treasures were hidden here.

After about a half hour of walking, the group emerged at the western exit of the tunnel. This area was known as the Pool of Siloam, Hadi told them. Now part of the busy neighborhood of Silwan, this had been a large immersion pool used by most of the pilgrims who visited Jerusalem for one of the three annual festivals. Hadi walked them to an area where archaeologists had partially excavated some of the stone steps surrounding the pool.

Sam looked at the spreadsheet he had saved on his phone. He pulled aside Jason and Steve to speak with them privately. "Look at this," he said. "Treasure site forty-seven, somewhere in the Old City. Three hundred talents of gold, hidden at the pool of the pure valley, hidden on its western side. Past the black stone, go two cubits to the entrance."

"How much is a cubit?" Steve asked.

Jason looked at his phone. "It's a measurement from an average person's elbow to the tips of his longest finger. About eighteen inches or forty-five centimeters."

"So about three feet?" Steve asked.

"That's right, pretty close," Sam replied.

"Are you thinking there might be actual treasure here?" Jason asked.

"It's the most obvious location of the 'pool of the pure valley,'" Sam responded. "The Pool of Siloam was the largest pool used by pilgrims and the first place they arrived upon entering the city gate here. The pool was believed to spiritually purify the pilgrims so they would be allowed to walk up to the Temple and join the festival. I've looked pretty hard, and I can't think of any other place in Jerusalem that matches this description as well."

"What's the treasure again?" Jason asked. "I mean, if there's something hidden here, what would it be?"

"It's three hundred talents of gold," Sam replied. "Which is an unusual description for the Copper Scroll in three ways. First, it's specific about the type of precious metal. Many of the sites on the scroll don't tell you which type of precious metal it is. But this one does. Second, it's a round number, and most of the treasures are more precise numbers like seventeen, twenty-five, forty-two, sixty-two, and so forth. Based on what I've sorted out, I think these large rounded numbers are references to something external to the Copper Scroll. They all match up to something external that's either a metaphor or something real. Everything that was in the actual Temple inventory is a more specific number that isn't rounded."

"What do you mean?" Steve asked.

"Well, treasure sites three, fifty-six, and fifty-eight all match up to the amounts of annual taxes paid to Rome," Sam explained. "The total was 960 talents, of which Judea, Samaria, and Idumea paid 600 talents. It breaks down further by geography, and these amounts match up perfectly with these three treasure sites. I think that the Copper Scroll inventory includes the amounts of taxes paid to Rome each year. These amounts are very clearly spelled out in the historian Josephus's writings. It was important enough for him to put in his historical account, and I think it was important enough to be included in the Temple inventory that was engraved on the Copper Scroll. But treasure site forty-seven is a little different. It's a round number that matches up with Josephus's history of Kings David and Solomon. He said that King David had ordered that 300 talents of gold be set aside for his son Solomon to build the inner sanctuary of the Temple.

"Here, let me read you what Josephus said," Sam said, holding his phone and looking at Jason and Steve. "After describing all the gold, silver, jewels, and timber that had been set aside for building the Temple, Josephus went on to describe what would be used in building the inner sanctuary. He said, and I quote, 'Three hundred other talents of pure gold, for the most holy place, and for the chariot of God, the cherubim, which are to stand over and cover the Ark.'"

"Wow, that's pretty specific," Jason said, rubbing his chin. "So the three hundred talents included the Ark? But wasn't that built under Moses's orders centuries before?"

"That's the story." Sam nodded. "I think the point of the story was that a large quantity of gold went into the inner sanctuary and the Ark, regardless of when and who built these things. In other words, those three hundred talents are like a symbol or code for the 'pure gold' that was used for the inner sanctuary and the Ark."

"So you're saying that treasure site forty-seven could be using that code—the three hundred talents of gold—to mean that the gold from the inner sanctuary, and maybe the Ark too, were hidden here?" Jason asked.

"I think it's quite possible," Sam said. "This also seems consistent with another text known as *The Treatise of the Vessels*. It says that an ancient king named Hezekiah hid the Ark of the Covenant and some of the other treasures of Solomon's Temple in a cave near a spring named Kohel or Kahal. That seems like it might be a reference to *The Book of Kohelet*. As it turns out, the last set of verses in Kohelet, known as the epilogue, seems to refer to the creation of the Ark and the rest of the Exodus story, with references to the almond blooms on Aaron's rod, locusts, silver, and gold. But it also talks about a spring and a cistern, which could be an allusion to the spring and cistern described in *The Treatise of the Vessels*. This text also identifies the Gihon Spring as part of this story, so it seems that there's a pretty strong legend that the Ark and the sacred treasures of Solomon's Temple were hidden in a cave near the Pool of Siloam."

"Wait a minute," Jason said, looking at Sam. "You're saying that someone—maybe this King Hezekiah—wrote a secret code into the Bible to record where the Ark and the sacred treasures of Solomon's Temple were hidden?"

"I guess you could say that," Sam said with a slight grin. "How else would you explain this language in the Kohelet epilogue about almond blooms, locusts, silver, gold, a spring, and a cistern? It sure sounds like the Ark story, except for the spring and the cistern. If the legends described in *The Treatise of the Vessels* can be taken seriously, the spring and the cistern could be a reference to the Gihon Spring and a cistern here that was used as a hiding place."

"But the Bible's not a treasure map," Jason protested.

"Are you sure about that?" Sam asked, raising an eyebrow. "It's a spiritual story about the Jewish people and their covenant with the divine for sure. But there's quite a bit in there about gold, silver, and sacred treasures. It might have seemed natural for an eighth century king to have his scribes add a few verses as a code for where some of those treasures were hidden. We can't know any of this, of course, and it's just a theory."

"What about the Copper Scroll?" Steve asked. "Do you think it's possible that the high priest, or whoever had it made, knew about this legend and this, uh—secret code in the Kohelet epilogue—and *that's* why the name Kohelet is in so many of the treasure site descriptions?"

"I don't know," Sam replied, "but that's a good question. If the Ark and Solomon's gold were actually hidden by an ancient king, it would have been pretty important for each generation to pass on the information about where it was hidden. That could get tricky, of course. You would want to closely control who knew where the hiding place was.

"We won't know if anything's here without digging. But Roy won't know that. He's so obsessed with finding the Ark that he'll believe virtually anything that makes him think he might find it. That makes this place a perfect part of our plan."

As Jason excused himself to go get the rental car, Sam and Steve walked back over to Hadi. He smiled and suggested that they walk around the partially excavated pool area. After walking over, the group looked down into the excavated area, with the stone steps surrounding the former pool area. Sam and Steve looked around and, in particular, at the garden resting on a few dozen feet of earth above the unexcavated western side of the pool.

"The garden's owned by the Greek Orthodox Church," Hadi told them. "I think the archaeologists would really like to dig here. But, of course, that's the story in much of Jerusalem. There's so much hidden history here, but most people prefer that the digging be on someone else's land."

When Jason pulled up in the rental, Sam and Steve thanked Hadi and got into the vehicle. Jason drove a short distance north and then stopped, pointing at a low cliff to their right underneath a collection of flat-topped stone buildings.

"This is Silwan," Jason announced. "Sam, you wanted to stop here. Something about some tombs?"

"Right." Sam nodded. "Do you see those square and rectangular openings in the rock? Those are the ancient Silwan tombs. Treasure site thirty-eight on the Copper Scroll."

"More gold and silver?" Steve smiled, leaning forward from the back seat.

"Not hardly," Sam said. "This is actually the smallest treasure site on the scroll. Just a few silver bars and four Greek coins."

"You call that treasure?" Jason said, squinting. "That's barely worth the copper it's engraved on."

"Very funny," Sam said, shaking his head. "It probably means that this treasure is somehow more important than gold and silver. Some kind of religious or historical treasure."

"Four Greek coins in a tomb, you say?" Steve asked with a smile. "Sounds like Charon's obol."

"What are you talking about?" Jason groaned. "You history majors seem to have your own language."

"It's really simple," Steve replied. "There was a tradition in ancient Greece to put a coin in the mouth of loved ones when they died. It was the price for the ferryman, known as Charon, to take the departed across the River Styx to Hades."

"Very impressive," Jason said, smiling. "This would be really helpful information if we were in Greece."

"Not so fast," Sam interrupted. "There were a lot of Greeks living here in ancient times. Don't you remember our project on Antony and Cleopatra's tomb? Cleopatra was Greek, right? And no one knows where *her* tomb is."

"Don't remind me," Jason said with a sigh. "Do you think their tombs are here in Jerusalem? Our professor would be pretty impressed if we actually solved that mystery."

"I'm pretty sure they're not here," Sam said, laughing. "But you may be right, Steve. The Copper Scroll's pretty specific about there being four Greek coins in one of the tombs here, known as the Dovecote. That's the word for ancient dove houses, and that's what these cliffside tombs look like. Maybe it's referring to the tombs of four Greeks or so-called Hellenized Jews, which is the term used for Judeans who had adopted a Greek-influenced lifestyle."

"That's pretty interesting," Jason agreed. "But I'm guessing it's not something that Roy wants for his temple. Should we move on?"

"Yes, let's get going." Sam said. Then, hearing a ping, he looked down at his phone and saw a message from his mother.

> *Hi Sam, sorry for rushing off this morning. Just had to do some unexpected meetings. Can we all meet for lunch at noon? I'm bringing a friend and was hoping we could meet at a Middle Eastern place called Family Restaurant. My friend recommended this place, and the reservation's under his name (Tariq Abdallah). It's in the Arab market in the Old City, so we can do some shopping and sightseeing too. Tariq will probably arrive early, so just ask for him when you get there. Hope to see you then!*

After confirming these lunch plans with his mother, Sam updated Jason and Steve on the schedule. Looking at the time, Sam suggested that they head to the Arab market, known as the Souk, so they could get some coffee and talk about the plan for dealing with Roy.

Jason nodded. It was a few minutes after 11:00 a.m., and this would give them some extra time to talk about using the Copper Scroll treasure sites in their planning for handling Roy.

Jason turned the Mazda around and drove south for a minute before turning right and heading west up the Hinnon Valley. Circling around the Temple Mount on the western side, he drove the Mazda to a parking area near the Arab Souk, to the west of the Temple Mount.

After getting out of the car, the group began walking toward the Souk, the colorful marketplace in the Old City where merchants sold fragrant spices, candies, antiques, and souvenirs. Its sprawling shops and ancient alleys starting just a few blocks away, this was a good place to take a break from working on their plan.

As they walked toward Family Restaurant, Steve got distracted by some of the Middle Eastern trinket shops along the way. After Jason said he was interested in finding a few souvenirs too, the group agreed to split up for a few minutes and to then meet up at the restaurant. This would give Sam some extra time to work on his planning, based on some of the things they had seen at the treasure sites this morning.

Sam looked at the time. It was already 11:30 a.m. Maybe his mother's friend Tariq would already be at the restaurant. She hadn't said who he was, but good chance he was another professor or some kind of expert on some aspect of their treasure research. She seemed to know an expert in pretty much every field, he thought.

As he walked into the restaurant and admired its arched stone ceiling and stucco walls, Sam looked around. The place was empty except for a man sitting at one of the larger tables, with a spread of Arabic tea and spice jars on the table. He must be Tariq, Sam thought, walking toward his table. Sam noticed that the man seemed muscular and not the usual "professor" physique he had been expecting. Maybe he was an actor or stunt double on one of his mother's films.

"Hi, you must be Tariq." Sam smiled, offering his hand. "I'm Sam Romero, Dawn's son."

The man stood up and smiled at Sam, shaking his hand. "Yes, of course. Nice to meet you. Your mother's a wonderful woman."

"Yes, she's always busy and had some kind of emergency this morning," Sam replied, sitting down in a chair across the table. "I'm just glad we can catch up with her."

"We?" the man asked. "Who's 'we'?"

"Yes," Sam replied, "my mother must have mentioned my friends Jason and Steve. They'll be here any minute."

Sam watched the man shifting in his seat and looking around the dining room, seeming a little anxious.

"Would you like some tea?" the man said with a smile.

"Yes, please," Sam replied, turning over a white porcelain cup as the man leaned toward Sam to pour some tea.

"Help yourself to some cardamom, cinnamon, and sugar," the man said, motioning to the small white porcelain pots next to the Samovar-style silver teapot. "It's Arabic tea and quite good with sugar and spice."

Sam noticed the man's sports coat opening up as he leaned forward, revealing a shoulder holster strapped over his shirt. This didn't seem right, Sam thought, watching the man finish pouring the tea and quickly buttoning his sports coat at the waist.

"It's a fresh pot, so it's quite hot," the man warned. "You should let it cool off before taking a sip. Otherwise you might burn yourself."

"Thanks for the warning." Sam nodded, looking at the outline of the weapon holster on the man's chest. "I think I can handle this," he said, pulling the small pots of sugar and spice closer. "So, *Tariq*, you probably know that my mom's working on a new film project," Sam went on, watching the man shifting more in his seat. "You know, Octavian the Great? He's her favorite Roman emperor, right?"

"Oh yes," the man replied, "she mentioned that. He was the greatest Roman leader of all. Your mother really knows her history and is a big fan."

That was more than enough, Sam thought. This man wasn't Tariq or anyone else that his mother knew. This imposter had apparently not gotten the memo that Dawn Hughes couldn't stand Octavian. She really loved playing Cleopatra in those movies and was Octavian's greatest modern detractor.

"So, how's Roy doing?" Sam asked the man, leaning forward in his chair.

The man smiled at Sam. "I don't know what you mean," he answered finally. "I don't know any Roy."

Sam knew that he had initially mistaken this hit man for his mom's friend. But how had the hit man learned where they would be meeting for lunch? He looked down at his phone, which he had placed on the table. Maybe Roy's thugs know how to hack a phone, he thought. This was getting serious.

"How much is the contract anyway?" Sam asked. "You know, how much is Roy offering for you to kill me?"

The assassin laughed. "You seem to have mistaken me for someone else," he said. "I'm just an archaeologist, and I get paid in ancient coins. I'm working on a new tomb today, and I'll get seventeen talents of gold and silver when the job's finished. That's a half ton. A pretty good payoff for digging a hole in the desert. Would you like to join me?"

"No, thanks," Sam replied. "There's really no treasure left out in the desert. Just bones and broken jars. But it sounds like you haven't heard about the curse on those seventeen talents of stolen coins. You could get hurt if you're not careful."

The assassin's eyes darted back and forth as he scanned the dining room. He scooted his chair back from the table a bit and unbuttoned his sports coat. Sam looked at the table between them and calculated his next moves and countermoves, as in a game of chess.

Then the assassin pulled an Arabic-style silver dagger from his shoulder holster and lunged across the table at Sam, swinging his arm with the dagger wildly from his right to left. Feeling a sharp pain of torn flesh across his chest, Sam knew that the razor-sharp dagger had ripped through his sweater and grazed across his chest. Quickly moving to his left, Sam grabbed the small pot of ground cinnamon and flung it directly at the assassin's face, coating his eyes and nose with the pungent, stinging powder.

Blinded, the assassin lost his balance and fell backward onto his chair as both he and the chair crashed to the floor. Picking up the silver teapot, Sam leaped from his seat to where the man had fallen. With his right foot stomping down hard on the man's arm with the dagger, Sam leaned forward and smashed the teapot against the side of the man's face.

Steaming-hot tea streamed across the assassin's face, scalding and reddening both sides of it as he began screaming in pain. Still holding the metal teapot, Sam smashed it again against the other side of his face, feeling the burning-hot liquid on his hand as it poured all over the man's head and neck and down his shirt.

The assassin howled in agony, letting the dagger fall from his hand. With the man still blinded by the pungent cinnamon and hot tea, Sam knew he had to act fast. Looking around the room and seeing a waiter standing in shock near the back opening to the kitchen, Sam threw the Samovar teapot down hard onto the man's face, watching as blood erupted from his nose and from the wounds and cuts that were now etched into his forehead and cheeks. Then Sam stomped one of his feet down hard on the assassin's right knee, hearing the snap and crunch of some of the small bones inside. The man howled again, doubled over in pain as he writhed on the floor.

Sam looked toward the door to see whether the assassin might have a companion. Seeing no one else in the room except the stunned waiter, Sam picked up the man's dagger from the floor and stood over him, watching him writhe in pain from the blows and burning-hot tea. Then Sam walked briskly back to the restaurant entrance, looking back at the assassin still sprawled on the floor as he walked out onto the street.

Walking quickly down the street in the direction where he had left his friends, Sam saw them walking in his direction.

"Sam, what the hell?" Jason shouted, pointing at Sam's torn, bloody sweater.

Looking down at the ripped sweater with splattered bloodstains, Sam nodded at his friends. "I'm okay," he said as Jason gripped his shoulder and began checking for wounds. "You should see the other guy," Sam said, attempting a grin.

"Okay," Steve said sternly, "this is serious. Roy wants you dead if you won't help him, and whoever did this almost made that happen."

"Let's get out of here," Sam said. "The last thing we need is to spend the afternoon with the police explaining what's going on with Roy. We still have those Copper Scroll pieces in our car too. If the police do a search, we might have some trouble explaining why we have stolen property."

Sam felt the adrenaline in his system starting to wear off as they sprinted through the narrow streets of the Souk, back toward the rental car. He was feeling the pain from the cut across his chest. It wasn't deep, but it was still bleeding. He knew it would need some attention soon, but the most urgent task was to get out of the Souk before anything else could happen.

Finding the parked car, the three friends jumped into it, with Sam and Steve climbing into the back. Sam pulled off his bloody maroon sweater, balled it up, and pressed it against his chest to stop the bleeding, grimacing in pain as he pushed against the wound, as Steve looked for a first-aid kit in the rental car.

Jason drove quickly but cautiously back to the hotel, parking a few blocks away on the tree-shaded side street. They had agreed on a change in plans. Jason would go into the hotel to pick up a few things while Sam called his mother to warn her and let her know what happened. They knew that it was no longer safe to stay there.

On the call with Dawn, Sam reassured her that they would be fine, but she insisted on making arrangements for Sam to stay at a safe house. At least for tonight, he agreed that this would be better than staying in Jerusalem. Sam needed time to think about plan B. Sam appreciated his mother's concern and was more than a little impressed that she had a friend with a safe house. He had always known about her unusual friends, but this was a step beyond that.

Looking at Steve as he fumbled with the first-aid kit he had found in the car, Sam assured Dawn that he was fine and that it was just a small cut. As he hung up the phone, Sam noticed Jason walking down the street toward them carrying an overnight bag over his shoulder. As Jason approached, Sam noticed that his fists were bloody. What had happened *now*?

Jason climbed into the driver's seat, looking calm despite the wounds on both sets of his knuckles. "What happened to you?" Sam asked, taking the overnight bag from Jason.

"You should see the other guy," Jason said with a grin. "He lost this," Jason said, tossing a wallet onto Sam's lap.

Sam pulled an identification card out of the wallet and whistled. "I know this guy," he said. "Leonardo Salvaggi. He was following me in Rome. Must be one of Roy's thugs. What happened?"

"I went into your hotel room," Jason said, wiping blood off his knuckles with a paper tissue that Steve had handed him. "This jerk was waiting there for you. We struggled a bit until I knocked his lights out. There was definitely some redecorating going on."

Sam groaned. "I'll have some explaining to do with the home office. I put that room on the firm card, since this is partially a business trip on one of my cases. I don't even want to ask if you broke anything."

"Right," Jason replied, "it might be easier for you to ask what *didn't* get broken."

"Well, I hope that card has insurance against being attacked in your hotel room," Sam joked, pulling a clean sweater out of the overnight bag and putting it on. "Let's get out of here."

As they drove off, Sam used Jason's phone to call Rebecca so he could warn her to take extra precautions. She didn't pick up, so he left her a voice mail and sent her a text message as well.

A few minutes later, Dawn called the group on Jason's phone as a precaution given that Sam's phone might have been hacked. She put the group in touch with her friend Hakim Faris. He lived in the West Bank and could help Sam with his plan B—going underground in a safe house for at least tonight while he maneuvered the next steps with Roy. Sam agreed that this was the best way, and Jason and Steve both wanted to join him, even if it would have been safer for them just to leave the country. They insisted on staying here until the end. Whatever that would mean.

As Jason drove north toward Jerusalem's northern suburbs, Sam used Jason's phone again to call Rebecca. "Hi, Sam," she answered, "sorry I haven't called you back yet. I saw you left a message, but I've been busy with some interviews at work."

Sam told her what had happened, and the call went silent. "I just want to make sure *you're* okay," Sam told Rebecca. "You could be in danger too. They might be watching all of us, and it makes me nervous that you're involved in this."

"This is awful," Rebecca agreed. "I'm so glad you weren't hurt, and I'm so worried about you. I wish I was there with you."

"I'm fine," Sam reassured her, "and everything will be okay. But we need to get you a bodyguard. Roy's out of control, and who knows what he might do."

"I hear you," she replied, "and I'm open to having a bodyguard, but really I think we should all disappear from sight for a while. A bodyguard is nice, but I think we'd be safer if we just went underground now. You know, that plan B we had talked about."

"Right, I'm on my way to a safe house now," Sam said. "My mother put me in touch with someone who will get there and keep an eye on things too. He seems to have a security background, and she said he's one of the best. So I think we're all in good hands here. The more important thing is to make sure you're safe."

Rebecca assured Sam that she would go to the safe place she had told him about, the home of one of her cousins in Holon, a suburb of Tel Aviv.

The Samaritan community there was closely knit and paid careful attention to outsiders. No one would get near enough to hurt her, she promised. If a bodyguard was needed, she would work with Sam on that the next day, if only so that he wouldn't worry about her so much.

After exchanging promises to stay safe and to talk early the next morning, Sam and Rebecca ended the call. They each told each other they would be thinking about the other, and he was tempted to say more. But he wanted to say those things when they were back together. He felt better after talking to her.

Jason pulled over near the Qalandia checkpoint about twenty minutes north of Jerusalem. Everyone got out and walked toward the checkpoint. After crossing, Sam noticed a tall, slim man standing with a small handwritten sign: Romero.

Sam walked up to Hakim and introduced himself and Jason and Steve. Hakim grasped Sam's arm warmly and smiled as if he had been an old friend of the family for decades. "How's your mother doing?" Hakim asked.

"Great, really," Sam replied. "She seems two steps ahead of everything, as always."

"More like ten steps, I think," Hakim said with a laugh. "Your mom is a legend around here, you know. I'll tell you about that hostage crisis one of these days. She has a way of bringing everyone together, no matter how much they hate each other. A rare talent, and I don't know what we'd do without her."

"Uh, right," Sam said, shrugging and a little confused by the new information about his mother. "Ten steps ahead sound about right. I have a few stories too. Mostly about the things I never got away with as a teenager. I thought it was a curse then, but now it sounds pretty good to have those supernatural maternal powers on your side," he said with a grin.

After crossing the checkpoint, the group got into Hakim's white BMW 330e for the ninety-minute drive up to Mount Gerizim. Along the way, Hakim told them about a few of the adventures he had with Dawn. Nothing confidential, he explained, as he was sworn to secrecy about those things. Just a few close calls on rope bridges in Indian rain forests and in those flaming caves on the southern coast of Turkey.

Sam shook his head. Apparently he had missed a few of these details while growing up. He couldn't picture his mother on rope bridges or in flaming caves, but maybe he had underestimated her.

As the sun was sinking low on the western horizon, Hakim pulled up at a secluded stone house on the Samaritan mountain known as Mount Gerizim. On the drive up, Hakim had explained the difference between the Samaritan religion, which was really a branch of Judaism, and the Samarian people. Nationality and religion were closely related, of course, but he explained that these ideas had mattered greatly over the centuries. How else could a small group of religious dissenters have survived in this crossroads of empires for the last two thousand years?

Sam, Jason, and Steve got out of the BMW and walked over to the stone house. Hakim had the keys and opened the house, showing them around and letting them know it was theirs for the night. He suggested that they stay in for the night and not go out. They were in Kiryat Luza, he explained, a small Samaritan community on Mount Gerizim, where anything they did would be noticed by the elders and others who paid attention to strangers. It was a perfect place to stay safe for the night, but it would be better to stay quiet and to not attract attention.

Sam and his friends readily agreed and were happy to have a safe house for the night. This would give them a chance to work on the Copper Scroll mysteries too, they agreed. After making an early dinner with the supplies left for them in the house, they sat outside, enjoying the mountain scenery and comparing notes on what they had learned.

After dinner, Hakim handed out three new phones to Sam, Jason, and Steve. He explained that these were clean phones that they could use without any risk of having been hacked by Roy's associates. He said he would get up early and get a fourth clean phone to Rebecca so they could all communicate securely. Everyone tested out their phones and thanked Hakim for keeping them safe.

Around 10:00 p.m., the group decided to call it a night. They had made good progress and would start again in the morning. They thought they were done brainstorming and agreed to do this in an organized way. Each of them would explain what they had learned from their assignment—Jason on religion, Steve on history, and Sam on the Copper Scroll story.

Sam wished he could have done a call with Rebecca tonight, but until they had his security person go check their mobile devices, they both thought it was safer to talk in the morning instead. If Roy somehow could trace their phone signals, it would be better if they didn't talk until they were already leaving their safe locations.

Before going to bed, Sam walked out on the patio and looked at the view of the mountain peaks. He recalled from his reading that the lower peak to the north had the ruins of a Roman temple on it, and the higher peak to the south had the ruins of the Samaritan temple. In between was a small gulley. It was beautiful, he thought. No wonder the Samaritans considered it sacred.

Sam turned to look in the western sky, gazing at the half moon starting to slip down toward the horizon. He closed his eyes for a moment and could picture Rebecca getting into bed. She was safe tonight, and that's what mattered most.

17

JUSTICE LIKE A RIVER

Sam woke up before dawn. He grimaced as he rolled over. The assassin's dagger had only grazed across Sam's chest, but it felt even worse this morning as it was beginning to heal. He wanted to send a message to Rebecca, but he knew better. Hakim was getting her a clean phone this morning, and they wouldn't be talking or messaging until they could be sure that they would be secure.

Sam rolled out of bed carefully and looked out the window. It was about a half hour before sunrise, and the sky was moonless and dark. It was Thursday, and he knew it would be a busy day. He wanted to stay on schedule with the plan he had worked up.

Sam washed up and changed into the running clothes that Jason had brought for him. He bandaged his two-inch chest wound tightly and figured it would feel better after a run on the mountain. After checking in with Jason and Steve, who were just getting up, Sam headed out around 6:30 a.m., with the first light of dawn showing behind the clouds to the east.

Already feeling better from the adrenaline and endorphins, Sam ran along the side of the main street of Kiryat Luza, heading east toward the summit of Mount Gerizim. As the sunlight began to cast a warm glow above the rain clouds, the summit seemed to shine a bit in the cold morning light. Sam could imagine why the Samaritans saw this mountain as sacred. He could feel its power, even on a cold, overcast winter morning like this one.

As he approached the peak with the ancient Samaritan temple ruins, Sam stopped running and looked across to the other peak with the Roman temple ruins. He had checked his map earlier this morning and had remembered the history of the mountain. It was unusual for the temples of different religions to share the same mountain, he thought. There must really be something special about this mountain.

Feeling stronger, Sam began running again, circling around the ruins of the Samaritan temple. The wound on his chest still hurt, but he felt a little better. The street boxing classes and personal trainer sessions back in LA must be helping, he thought, pulling up the lower part of his sweater to blot the sweat from his face. At least he had learned how to take a hit and stand strong.

Sam heard the unfamiliar ring of his new phone in the pocket of his running shorts. He pulled out the phone, pressed to answer, and put it up to his ear.

"Hello, Sam," he heard Rebecca's voice.

Sam knew it was Rebecca but was feeling better and decided to tease her a bit. "Who's this?" he asked, looking at the unfamiliar number on his new phone. "Is this the girl with the veils?"

"Sam! That's supposed to be our secret," Rebecca teased back. "But you knew it was me already."

"Right, but we have new phones," Sam joked. "After getting hacked, you can't be too careful."

"Well, it's definitely me," Rebecca said. "Except I'm not wearing veils at the moment. Not really wearing anything at all."

The call went silent.

"Sam? Are you still there?" Rebecca asked, a little concerned by the silence.

"Uh, yes, I'm still here," he teased. "I was just thinking about you naked in your bedroom with that Gauguin. I got a little distracted."

"You'd be even more distracted if you were here now," she flirted. "But how are you feeling? I just wanted to check in before heading out."

"Not bad, really," he answered. "I'm out for a run, actually. It's really helping to keep moving. How are you doing?"

"I'm worried about you," she said. "You had a close call yesterday, and Roy's thugs are still out there. I hope you can stay on the mountain for a while. You're safer there."

"I'll be fine," Sam assured her. "We've got a good plan for dealing with Roy and will be driving back to Jerusalem this morning."

"You're not going back to the hotel, are you?" Rebecca sounded alarmed.

"No, not at all," Sam replied. "We'll be checking into the St. George Hotel. It's a few blocks away, and Hakim has arranged for us to use the personnel entrance and freight elevator. We'll be okay. "I promise to be careful. I'm really more worried about you. I see Hakim dropped off your phone. Did you talk to him about you getting a bodyguard?"

"I really don't need one," Rebecca replied. "I'll be fine too. I'm meeting a source at 8:30 a.m., and then I'll be free after that. Can we meet up somewhere?"

"Yes, I'd really like that," he said. "We'll be at our new hotel by 9:30 a.m. We'll need to work on some things for dealing with Roy, and the St. George will be a good place to do this. I'll have Hakim contact you about getting you in there safely as well."

"That sounds good," Rebecca said. "I'll be there before 10:00 a.m. My meeting's pretty quick."

"Can you skip the meeting and go straight to the hotel?" Sam asked. "I don't like the idea of you being out in the open like this."

"I'll be extra careful," she assured him. "The meeting's at a café across the street from my office. I'll check in with security there, so I don't think there'll be a problem. Well, I should let you go. I need to get ready anyway, and you should finish your run."

"Can I call you before you leave?" Sam asked.

"Yes, of course," Rebecca replied. "I'd like that. You have my number. Actually, I think you're the only one who has my number. I guess you like that, huh?" she teased.

"Now, why didn't I think of this sooner?" he said, laughing. "A few assassins running around can be a great way to keep you to myself."

"Well, just don't get too used to it," she joked. "We'll have our lives back soon enough. Besides, there are other ways to keep a girl around. You've been doing pretty good at it. You know, the red tantra and all that."

"Just promise to stay safe," he replied. "And maybe bring a day or two of clothes with you. We might need to stay together overnight. You know, for security reasons."

"How convenient," she said with a sigh. "Just remember that we're not supposed to be dating now. You know, until we fix that conflict of interest. Anything romantic or physical is really forbidden."

"Just don't bring the veils costume this time," he teased. "You know how I can't resist you in gold."

"Okay, I'll bring my black lingerie instead," she flirted. "That shouldn't distract you at all. Stay safe, and don't think about me in my black bra and panties. We really shouldn't break the rules this time."

The call went silent again.

"Sam, are you still there?" Rebecca asked.

"Yes, I was just thinking," he said, sounding distracted. "Maybe I blacked out," he joked. "You know, thinking about your lingerie. But it's really okay. I'm feeling good."

"All right, talk to you in a bit, then," she said.

"Great, talk to you then," he replied as they ended the call.

After about an hour of running on the mountain summit, Sam returned to the safe house in Kiryat Luza. Jason and Steve had gotten packed and were almost ready to leave. They talked for a few minutes about their planning for the day. Steve mentioned that he had wanted to talk about that treasure site on the mountain summit, number fifty-seven. Especially since they were up here, and maybe Rebecca might have some insights about the site, since it was so close to the ancient Samaritan temple ruins.

After changing and packing up, Sam joined Jason and Steve in the living room, and he called Rebecca and put her on the speaker setting.

"Hi, Sam?" she answered.

"Hi, Rebecca," he said, "I've got you on speaker here with Jason and Steve. Hakim should be back in a few minutes, and we'll head out then. But before we leave, Jason and Steve wanted to join our call to get your thoughts on that treasure site up here on the mountain."

"Yes, of course," she replied. "We talked about Mount Gerizim a bit yesterday. I told you that Eden had gotten a construction permit up there. It makes no sense. They don't have any projects in the West Bank. So you said there's a treasure site there? It's listed on the Copper Scroll?"

"Yes, and it's one of the more mysterious sites," Sam said. "The Copper Scroll doesn't really tell you much about it."

"What's the treasure supposed to be?" Rebecca asked.

"Well, that's just it. It doesn't really tell you. Let's see," he said, looking at the spreadsheet on his laptop. "Here we go. It's a carrying chair with all of its contents. Plus six hundred silver coins. What do you think?"

"A carrying chair?" she said, puzzled. "Like for carrying someone around? With its contents? What's supposed to be in it?"

"It doesn't say," he said. "And remember, the Copper Scroll was the *Jerusalem* Temple's inventory of its treasury. Why would the high priests in Jerusalem hide something valuable on the Samaritan mountain?"

"They definitely wouldn't have," she said. "Judea and Samaria were bitter rivals. They'd been fighting for centuries."

"Yes, I've been reading about that," Sam said. "A Samaritan king named Jehoash had invaded Judea in the eighth century BC. Some people say that this king may have even taken the Ark of the Covenant from the Jerusalem Temple. There were quite a few battles over the Ark."

"Well, to be fair, the Judeans started some of those wars," Rebecca replied. "A Judean king had even destroyed the Samaritan temple in the second century BC, believing that there should be only one sacred Temple in Israel."

"There's quite a history of conflict over whose mountain was sacred," Sam agreed. "It sounds like both sides had agreed there should be only one Temple. They just disagreed over where it should be."

"Right," Rebecca agreed, "and that has to do with the Ark story, of course. In the Samaritan tradition, it was always up on our mountain. No one had to steal it, and it had always been ours. It was just hidden in a time of crisis in a cave near the summit. No one could find the cave after it had been hidden, so it's supposedly still there."

Sam looked at his notes. "A carrying chair, huh? With all of its contents?" He grinned at his friends. "Maybe we should head over to the summit," he said. "I'm a little hungry now."

"What are you talking about?" Steve asked. "We need to go soon. There's really no time for breakfast."

"It's just take-out food," Sam said, smiling. "A pot of manna to go."

"Sam, what are you talking about?" Rebecca asked over the phone. "Are you sure you're feeling okay?"

"I'm feeling great," Sam replied. "We could go hiking too with that ancient walking stick. You know, the one that turned into a snake when thrown at the pharaoh. Or we do some reading with a couple of stone tablets."

"You're talking a little crazy now," Jason said. "What does this have to do with that treasure site?"

"It's the Ark," Sam said with a smile, looking at Jason's and Steve's puzzled expressions. "I mean, we don't know if it's actually there. But I think that's what this treasure site means. It uses the Hebrew word *siddah*, which means carrying chair, instead of the word *aron*, which means Ark. But otherwise it seems pretty clear that this 'carrying chair with all of its contents' is referring to this story about the Ark being there. Maybe it was the high priest's way of making a strategic compromise with the Samaritans. The Judeans would agree that both mountains were sacred, and the

Samaritans could rebuild their temple. But the Judeans weren't agreeing that the Ark was actually on the Samaritan mountain. No, it was just a 'carrying chair,' even though everyone would know what the high priest meant. It's pretty brilliant, actually. This is what diplomats do. They write peace treaties where both sides can declare victory of some sort. Both sides can see something different, but overall there's a peace deal that both sides can live with."

"I think you may be right," Rebecca agreed. "That sounds exactly like something a smart political leader would do. Our side has the Ark, and your side has a carrying chair. Sort of a compromise to make everyone happy. Or at least a little less unhappy."

"So do you think this treasure site is another metaphor?" Jason asked. "A political concession intended to unite Judea and Samaria in negotiating with the Romans?"

"That's what it looks like," Sam replied, looking down at his notes. "But there's just one thing."

"What's that?" Jason asked.

"What about those six hundred silver coins?" Sam wondered. "They don't sound like a metaphor. They sound real."

"Sam, that's pretty intriguing," Rebecca said over the phone. "This treasure site on the mountain has an Ark that's not officially an Ark next to six hundred silver coins? If it's just a metaphorical site intended to placate the Samaritans, what are those six hundred coins doing there?"

"I don't know," Sam said with a shrug. "Maybe a Samaritan high priest went up to the mountain and counted them. And grabbed some of that manna for a snack on the way back down the mountain."

"Sam, you really shouldn't joke about our religious traditions," Rebecca cautioned. "Manna may seem pretty funny now, but to my ancestors, it was part of an important story."

"Well, it sounds like airline food to me," Sam replied, still joking a bit. "No one really knows what it was, which was just like that chicken dish on my last flight."

"You're hopeless," Rebecca teased. "Just don't start making fun of our Ten Commandments. You might get struck by lightning or something."

"Right," Steve joined in, "the Ten Commandments are nothing to joke about. They're like the Bible, the Magna Carta, and the Declaration of Independence all wrapped into one writing. The most important document in western civilization, even if it's written on stone."

"You've got that right," Jason agreed. "Before Moses brought those tablets down from that mountain, religion was mostly about nature. People had worshipped the father god of the sky, the mother goddess of the land, and so forth. The Ten Commandments were something different. Nature can seem cruel and indifferent. Basing a religion on a set of laws meant that there was at least the promise of justice and mercy, no matter how many times that promise might be broken."

Steve nodded. "Some people argue, of course, that the monotheistic religions were the downfall of nature. We banished the mother goddess, sold off her land, and treated it like a commodity. They say that maybe if we treated nature as sacred again, mankind might have a better future."

"Well, I don't think we'll solve any debates about religion today," Sam replied. "Unless you want to go up there to the summit, dig up the Ark, and see what's written on those stone tablets." He winked.

"There's a disagreement about that too," Rebecca said over the phone. "The Judeans and Samaritans could never agree on what the Tenth Commandment was."

"Seriously?" Sam said with a little exasperation. "Can't the different religions agree on *anything*?"

"Well, first, I'm not sure what you mean by 'different religions,'" Rebecca said. "Samaritans and Jews are really part of the same religion. There are a few differences, how to respect the sabbath and so forth. But it's not true that the Samaritans are Gentiles, like some of those Judean kings had claimed. But the disagreement over the Tenth Commandment was whether the sacred mountain was Mount Gerizim in Samaria or Mount Moriah in Judea."

"Shouldn't we just agree that both mountains are sacred?" Sam asked. "And agree that everyone has the right to worship at the place they believe is sacred?"

"Count me in for that," Rebecca agreed. "That would solve quite a few problems. You know, the Samaritans and the Romans managed to share Mount Gerizim for centuries, with each having a temple next to the other, near the summit."

"I read about that too," Sam said. "Maybe that's what treasure site fifty-seven on the Copper Scroll was about. The high priest agreed that the Samaritans could rebuild their temple here and share this place with whoever wanted to honor the divine here."

"So how does this work with treasure site forty-seven?" Jason asked. "It seems like those three hundred talents of gold that were supposedly hidden underground near the Pool of Siloam might be referring to the Ark too. Are we supposed to believe there were two Arks?"

"I have no idea," Sam replied. "But for purposes of today, we just need to persuade Roy that we know where the Ark is—at least one of them—so we can trap him with our plan. Let's just hope that Roy doesn't know about all this complicated history and that he just thinks the Ark was hidden under the Temple Mount. The last thing we need is for him to demand *two* lost Arks."

Just then, Hakim walked in the front door. "Hi, guys," he said, looking at the secure phone in Sam's hand. "Are you talking to Rebecca? Everything good?"

"Sure," Sam replied. "Everyone's ready to head out soon. We're just getting our stories straight about the Copper Scroll treasures. We'll need to be all over this to make Roy think we can find that missing Ark for him. Or both of them, apparently."

Hakim shook his head. "Are you sure you're okay? You had a close call yesterday, and now you're seeing double. Two lost Arks? Maybe you need some more rest."

"It's hard to explain," Sam said, shrugging. "Ancient legends can be pretty mysterious."

"Right, I thought that finding Cleopatra's tomb was the toughest ancient mystery to solve," Jason said. "But this double Ark story goes way beyond that. Maybe we could go looking around Egypt instead? We could solve something a little easier?"

"Look, we've got a good plan," Sam replied. "We don't need to find the Ark. Or both of them, or whatever. We just need to make Roy think we can so we can turn him over to the authorities in Rome for antiquities crimes. We've got a good plan and just need to make it work."

"Sam, I've got to go now," Rebecca said over the speaker on his phone.

"Right, sorry, Rebecca," Sam replied. "We'll be heading out soon too." Then, taking the phone off speaker, he told her to be careful.

"I promise," she said. "See you in a few hours."

"See you then," he said. "Take care."

After hanging up, Sam picked up his bag and walked outside to Hakim's BMW 330e. A few minutes later, Hakim, Jason, and Steve joined him, and they headed back to the Qalandia checkpoint near Jerusalem. Hakim left his car in a parking area there, and after clearing the checkpoint, they all got into Jason's rented Mazda crossover for the last few miles back to Jerusalem.

Following Hakim's directions, Jason drove the Mazda to a back entrance at the St. George Hotel and parked in the employee parking area. Then, after Hakim returned from getting everyone's room keys, they rode up the employees-only freight elevator directly to the hotel room that had been reserved for Sam.

Arriving at Sam's new room around 9:30 a.m., everyone got busy with their arrangements for the rest of the day. Hakim opened a package that had been delivered earlier that morning and pulled out three identical blue hoodie sweaters. Handing two of the sweaters to Jason and Steve, Hakim kept one for himself and smiled.

"Maybe we should steal some art while we're at this," Hakim said with a laugh. "Sam's thugs won't know which of us to follow when we leave the hotel."

"Right, and after we're done stealing some art, we can go pick up those Arks too." Jason said, grinning.

"You're really having fun with those two Arks, huh?" Hakim smiled. "Don't you think this will just confuse people? The Ark's been missing for 2,500 years. And you think you can go find *two* of them all of a sudden?"

"No, we're definitely not saying that," Jason said, picking up his blue hoodie sweater. "We really have no idea if these lost Ark stories are true. I don't think anyone's going to be digging anytime soon. So I guess we'll just keep open minds about it all."

"That makes sense," Hakim replied. "Just remember that the Ark is not of this earth. Man was not meant to disturb it. Or both of them, I guess."

Sam smiled. "You're a wise man, Hakim. But maybe these things aren't surrounded by death after all. If there's more than one sacred mountain, maybe man can start learning to share these places. Like the Roman and Samaritan temples that used to stand close to each other on Mount Gerizim. Not a bad example for what might be possible in Jerusalem."

Hakim nodded in agreement as Sam looked at the time. He was worried that Rebecca hadn't checked in yet. She should have been on her way long ago and should have checked in already.

Realizing that Sam might need some time alone, Hakim motioned Jason and Steve that it was time for them to get some things from their rooms. Then Hakim headed downstairs to the lobby to arrange for their rental cars.

Alone now in his hotel room, Sam called Rebecca from his new phone. No answer. He texted her.

> *Hi Rebecca, I hope your meeting went okay. How's it going? Are you on your way here? Sam*

He waited a few minutes. Still no answer. He got busy adding a few extra clothing changes to his bag. But he knew something was wrong. If she were getting close to the hotel, she would have called him. Maybe something went wrong at her meeting. Or even when she left home.

Sam sat down in a chair and looked out the window at the dark clouds moving across the sky. There was nothing he could do but wait.

Then he heard a knock at the door. Sam looked at the time. Yes, 10:00 a.m. finally. It had to be Rebecca.

Sam jumped to his feet and walked quickly to the door. But somehow this just didn't feel right. He hadn't heard anything at all from Rebecca. Something was wrong.

He turned the handle, and his heart sank.

Donovan? What the hell?

"What are *you* doing here?" Sam said, stunned. "Where's Rebecca?"

Donovan's face was stone cold and ashen. "Your mother said you'd be here. We need to talk."

"I have no time for that," Sam said angrily. "Where's Rebecca?"

"You'll want to hear this," Donovan said gravely. "Can I come in?"

"Where is she?" Sam demanded.

"You need to know what's going on. I can explain," Donovan said, walking into the living area and standing a few feet from Sam.

"I'm really not interested," Sam said angrily. "This is all your fault. You got me involved with Roy. The worst person in the world. What were you thinking?"

"Roy's a nobody," Donovan said with a shrug. "He was just following orders. None of this was supposed to happen."

"None of this what?" Sam demanded, his anger growing. "What are you even talking about? Where's Rebecca?"

"He has her," Donovan said, looking down at the floor with his shoulders sinking.

In the blink of an eye, without even thinking, Sam exploded in rage. "Shut up!" he shouted, hurling himself with full force at Donovan.

Donovan reeled backward as Sam grabbed him violently by the shoulders, pushing him across the room and slamming him hard against the wall with a booming shudder.

As he heard the sound of glass shattering, Sam looked at the smashed wall hanging that had crashed to the floor. Then he looked again at Donovan, still clutched in Sam's clenched hands, gripping his collar tightly. "You idiot!' Sam shouted. "What are you talking about?"

"She's in danger," Donovan cried out, gasping for breath. "He's gone rogue."

"This is all your fault!" Sam yelled, his mind spinning with fury. "Roy's the worst, and you got me involved with him."

"Sam, listen," Donovan said as he caught his breath. "It's not how it looks. Roy's just a foot soldier. There's someone worse. And she's been watching you from the beginning. Waiting for the right time."

Sam released his grip on Donovan and stepped back. "I don't know what you're talking about. I don't have time for this. We have to get Rebecca. Where is she?"

"I don't know," Donovan said, looking at the floor. "I just know that he has her. This wasn't supposed to happen. But she's in danger now."

"What the hell is going on?" Sam snapped even more angrily.

Donovan looked at Sam, quiet for a moment. "Roy's dying," he said finally. "We didn't know. But it changed everything. He stopped following orders and got caught up in some delusion about becoming immortal and divine. He's building some temple somewhere and wants to fill it with the lost gold and silver of the Jerusalem Temple. And the lost Ark, apparently."

"Who's 'we'?" Sam demanded.

"It's complicated," Donovan said, his face growing dark with worry. "It all starts with the dreams. You can't stop them, you know. Good ones and bad ones. You start wanting answers. Then she finds you. She's got these powers—"

"Enough of this," Sam interrupted. "We have to get Rebecca. We don't have time to talk about dreams. Where is she?"

"He has her," Donovan said, looking down. "She can't be far away. He wants the Ark. He'll do anything to get it. We have to move fast."

"Where's Roy?" Sam asked, looking at Donovan in disgust.

"He's here," Donovan replied. "I flew to Rome to meet him, and he told me about his illness. Everything fell apart. We flew here together in his private jet. I knew there would be trouble and wanted to stop him. I just don't know how to yet."

"What do you mean you don't know how to stop him?" Sam sputtered. "He's a fool. There are a hundred ways to stop him. Just report him to the police, for starters."

"I wish it was that simple," Donovan said with a sigh. "She wants the Ark too. That's how this all started. Getting rid of Roy is just the first step. Things will only get worse from there."

"Who are you talking about?" Sam said, frowning. "You make it sound like—"

Just then Sam's old phone rang. Sam looked at the display and saw it was Roy.

"Roy, where are you?" Sam demanded. "You're in deep trouble—"

"Sam, my boy, so nice to hear your voice." Roy cackled. "You picked up my call. I guess I have something you want. Something nice and soft and warm—"

"That's enough," Sam cut him off. "You're not running this show. You need me, and we both know it."

Roy laughed and then started coughing. "It's the golden rule, my boy. He who has the gold makes the rules. You'll do what I say. That is, if you want to see her again."

"Where is she?" Sam demanded.

"Your little treasure is safe," Roy said before starting to cough again.

The call went quiet for a moment, and then Sam heard a hacking spit on the other end. Roy seemed really ill.

Roy got back on the phone. "If you want to know where she is, just keep reading that scroll and solving the clues. But we don't have much time," he said, clearing his throat. "You've got three hours. Let's see. It's ten thirty now. So you've got until one thirty to get me the Ark. Otherwise it's lights out for your princess. Tick tock. You don't want rope burns on her neck, do you? Or maybe an assassin's dagger in that precious heart?"

"Listen, Roy, if anything happens to Rebecca—and I mean anything—you'll wish you were dead," Sam threatened darkly. "You'll get your Ark. But only if she's unharmed. I think you know about my dreams. I know where the Ark is. It's powerful and can save you. It has powers beyond *your* wildest dreams. I know you want it, but you'll only get it if Rebecca stays safe. If anyone even goes near her, you'll never get the Ark."

"Tick tock," Roy replied. "Two hours and fifty-nine minutes left. Tell me where the Ark is, and I'll give you a clue to where Rebecca is. You're wasting time. My assassin's already sharpening his dagger."

Sam's phone fell silent as Roy ended the call. Sam looked at Donovan, whose face was now a pale white.

"Get out of here," Sam demanded. "I need some time to work on this. I'll meet you downstairs in a while. Just stay in the lobby and don't cause any more trouble. Call me right away if you hear anything. Understood?"

"But I want to help," Donovan objected.

"Damn it, just stay in the lobby," Sam replied. "Stay put and don't screw up anything else."

"Got it," Donovan replied. "Sam, I—"

"Don't," Sam interrupted him. "Just keep quiet and stay away from me. I've got this."

Donovan nodded and looked at the floor. He turned to leave just as there was a knock at the door.

Sam went to the door. "Who is it?"

"It's us." Sam heard Jason's voice from the other side.

Sam opened the door to let Jason and Steve in as Donovan went to the door to go.

"Hi, Donovan," Steve said, recognizing him.

"Hey, Donovan," Jason joined in.

Donovan looked like he wanted to say something but after pausing for a moment walked to the door and left.

"What was *that* about?" Jason asked.

"What's he doing here?" Steve wondered.

Sam was livid, his mind reeling with fury and rage. He drew a long breath and knew he needed to calm down. "Donovan had some news," he said finally. "And Roy called. We have three hours to get Rebecca back."

"What?" Steve asked, alarmed. "Where is she?"

"Roy has her," Sam said, not believing his own words. "Or one of his thugs, it seems. Donovan knows Roy and found out somehow. I don't have the whole story, and I'm not sure I want to know. We just need to get her back."

"How do we do that?" Jason asked.

"Roy wants the Ark," Sam replied. "He had Rebecca kidnapped to make sure that we'll help him. I'm not quite sure why, but he thinks that I'm the only one who can get the Ark for him. It's something Donovan told him about. It turns out that Roy's dying and has some supernatural ideas about how to save himself. Roy said we have three hours to locate the Ark. He said we'll get Rebecca back when he gets his prize. Of course, there's no guarantee about that. We'll need to work on our planning. And we'll need more time. Three hours isn't enough."

As Jason and Steve absorbed this news, stunned, Sam sat down and opened his laptop. He started rearranging the timetable on the spreadsheet. The key was getting more time. He would meet Roy in one of the Western Wall tunnels beneath the Temple Mount while Jason and Steve searched for Rebecca.

This was all a game to Roy. Sam thought about where Roy would be keeping her. He was crazy enough to take Rebecca to one of the treasure locations on the scroll. It actually made sense. Roy didn't just want the Ark. He wanted all the other treasures too. Sam knew that if he actually delivered the Ark to Roy, that would just be the beginning. He would keep Rebecca hostage until he got everything important that was listed on the Copper Scroll.

"We'll tell Roy that we know where the Ark is," Sam said after a minute of reflection. "We'll tell him that we deciphered the Copper Scroll and that it says the Ark was hidden in a tunnel underneath the Temple Mount. We just need to spend some time going over some of the treasure site clues. We'll have to make sure that Roy believes us when we tell him we've solved it. Then, when we're ready, you two will go looking for Rebecca. My guess is that she's being held at one of the treasure sites. I hope we can narrow those sites down with a clue from Roy. Hakim and I will work on the plan for what's going to happen underneath the Temple. Whatever it is, it will be shocking and Roy won't know what's coming. We'll just need to play along for now."

There was hope, Sam thought. Roy had crazy motives but was still behaving logically. They just needed to stay ahead of him. The Copper Scroll was the key. They had plenty of work to do.

Around 11:00 a.m., Sam looked up when there was a knock on the door. Hakim had returned from getting the rental cars. Then Sam updated him on Rebecca's kidnapping and the change in plans. He also told him about his surprise visit from Donovan and his unfortunate connection to all of this.

Over the next couple of hours, the group worked on revising the plan. Sam and Hakim worked out the arrangements to get one of the tunnels underneath Temple Mount ready for a visit with Roy. Jason and Steve pored over the scholarly articles about the Copper Scroll and its treasure sites. Working furiously to make sure they could pull off their deception, they would need to know enough about all these Jerusalem treasure sites to make Roy believe that they could find the Ark hidden underneath the Temple Mount, even if none of them believed it was there.

After a while, Jason went to go check on Donovan. Sam stepped into the hall as Jason was leaving and told him not to trust Donovan. He was involved somehow with Roy and apparently with someone else whom Roy reported to. Sam didn't understand any of this, but he asked Jason to be careful.

A few minutes later, Jason returned to the room. He said that Donovan was quietly sitting in the lobby and seemed to be calm. He looked really upset, but otherwise he seemed to be under control for now.

Sam looked at the time. It was 1:30 p.m. now, and Roy would be calling. He nodded at Jason and Steve, who each gave him a thumbs-up. They were ready.

Sam's phone lit up and rang. He answered. "Time's up!" Roy shouted. "Tell me where the Ark is, or your princess is history. You've had enough time."

"Not so fast, Roy," Sam replied. "We need another three hours. You didn't send us the right pieces of the Copper Scroll, and we're having trouble with some of the Hebrew script without being able to see it in person. This is your fault for screwing up which pieces we needed."

Roy sputtered. "That was Leonardo's job, not mine, and he'll pay for that. But right now, I need him to help guard Rebecca. You know how it is. Hired help comes and goes. Life is cheap."

"Three hours, Roy, and you'll get the Ark," Sam promised.

"Tell you what," Roy replied. "I'm a sentimental old man. I'll give you one hour before we drown her." Then he started laughing. "Oh, oops, I guess I gave you another clue. Just don't get too close if you figure out where she is. Water can be dangerous, you know."

"Roy, just make sure she stays safe," Sam threatened. "I'll figure out exactly how to get the Ark, but it will only work if Rebecca's unharmed. This thing's supernatural, and you have to respect its powers."

"Don't worry." Roy laughed. "I won't have her killed for the next fifty-nine minutes. I wouldn't want to jinx your Ark hunting. But after that, she'll be drowned like a rat. Leonardo says he can't wait. She kicked him in the leg, and he's already lost his temper. You'd better get going on that Ark."

Sam knew that Rebecca was at one of the two sites that had water, and Gideon's Spring was one of those sites. Sam turned to Steve and said it was time for him to drive up to Galilee, since it was the farthest site from Jerusalem and the drive would take longer. They knew Steve would be followed by one of Roy's henchmen. Steve just needed to be careful and keep his distance from any of Roy's team. If Rebecca was being held at Gideon's Spring, Steve would need to rescue her. Roy had given them a clue, and there was no reason to think he was lying about it. Rebecca was being held at a treasure site with water, and Gideon's Spring was one of the sites to match that description.

Steve promised to be careful and to bring Rebecca back safely, if she was there. Then he left the room and disappeared down the hall.

A few minutes later, Hakim left the hotel room to go work on the plans for underneath the Temple Mount. Sam still needed Jason to help decipher some of the Jerusalem locations to make sure they could persuade Roy that they knew the Ark's exact location underneath the Temple Mount. They got to work and did as much as they could for the next hour.

At 2:25 p.m., Sam signaled to Jason that it was time to call Roy. They were finally ready.

Sam dialed Roy's number. "My boy," Roy answered, "you're so attentive today. I guess that's the secret to getting your lawyer to call you back. Kidnap his girlfriend, right?" He laughed.

"Stop it, Roy," Sam demanded. "I'd tell you to drop dead, but from what I understand, it's too late for that. I hear you'll be leaving us very soon."

"Not so fast," Roy said with a laugh. "Once I get my hands on that shiny new toy, I might just live forever."

"Well, I'm not sure how that would work, but we do have good news. It's in the tunnel adjoining Warren's Gate under the Temple Mount," Sam told him.

"I knew it! I just knew it!" Roy shouted through the phone. "Those experts I hired were just idiots. They kept talking about other places in Jerusalem and even on a mountain in the West Bank, of all places. But I knew all along that the Ark was under the Temple Mount. It's my spiritual intuition, you might say."

"I hadn't noticed you had a spiritual side," Sam said, shaking his head. "But yes, you guessed right about where the Ark is. It's just in a dangerous spot. We can get in there after dark, but you'll need to follow my directions or else a tunnel could come crashing down on us."

"No need for that," Roy replied. "You just don't understand how spiritual I am. Remember I went to Davos once? That really proves how deep and enlightened I am. Plus, I'll be wearing my toga. I'll be divine like Caligula once I find the Ark."

"Just don't open the lid," Sam said, marveling at Roy's shallowness and naivete. "This thing's powerful, and you don't know what can happen."

Roy began laughing and stopped only when it turned into a hacking cough. "You're funny, my boy. Just get me the Ark, and I'll take care of the rest. I wrote out an ancient prayer in Hebrew, and I'm pretty sure it will do what I tell it to. Remember, I'm a CEO, a master of the universe."

Sam shook his head again. He was glad they wouldn't be going anywhere near the Ark. He wasn't sure that it actually had any supernatural powers. But if it did, this fool would be sure to trigger some death rays or a new plague.

"Sure, Roy," Sam replied. "But I need to talk to Rebecca. I need to hear that she's okay."

"Bollocks!" Roy laughed. "There's no need for that. She'll be fine."

"No, that's our deal," Sam insisted. "No Rebecca, no Ark."

Roy sputtered. "Fine, wait a minute. This damn phone," he muttered as Sam heard him fumbling with the phone.

Sam listened as Roy placed another call and merged them together. "Sam? Are you there?" came Rebecca's voice through the phone.

"Rebecca!" Sam called out. "Are you okay?"

"It's dark in here, and I hear water," she said. "But, yes, I'm fine. Just do what he says. He's pure evil, do you understand?"

"I know what you mean," Sam replied, nodding at Jason. "We'll clean all this up and get you back, pure and simple."

"Just hurry," she said. "I love—"

Sam heard some scuffling as the phone was pulled away from Rebecca. "Are you okay?" he shouted.

"Now it's your turn to shut up," Roy's voice boomed over the phone. "You heard your precious girlfriend. Time's a wasting. Better hurry up."

"Make sure she's all right," Sam demanded, "or you won't get your prize. It's after two thirty now, only a few hours before dark. Meet me at the Western Wall tunnels at five o'clock. You'll get your Ark, but only if you bring Rebecca and prove she's fine."

"Who put you in charge?" Roy laughed. "I'll give you proof of life, but she stays put until I get my little box from heaven. Oh, and be sure to bring those Copper Scroll pieces with you. They're mine, and I want them back now that you're done with them."

The phone fell silent as Roy hung up. Sam looked at Jason. "She's definitely near water. Probably a mikvah, a Jewish immersion bath, since she seemed to be using 'pure' as a code. It could be the Pool of Siloam, where we went yesterday, or another treasure site with purifying water. Let's check the list."

After studying the list of treasure sites and comparing notes on how to handle the next few hours, Sam looked at the time. It was 3:30 p.m., time for Jason to leave. They had decided that he would go to Job's Well first and, if she wasn't there, then to the Pool of Siloam. These two sites were close to each other, so this should be manageable.

"You're good for this?" Sam asked Jason as he gathered his things.

"Of course, why do you ask?" Jason shot back.

"These places can be dangerous," Sam said darkly. "In ancient times, Job's Well was known as the Well of Fire. It's not a place to take lightly. Just be careful."

"You got it." Jason nodded before heading out the door and down the hall.

Sam looked at the time and sighed. It seemed like a good time for a check-in with Hakim. Sam called him and confirmed that all the arrangements had been made. They agreed to meet in Sam's hotel room, along with Donovan.

About fifteen minutes later, Hakim and Donovan arrived at Sam's door. Letting them in, Sam sat down on the sofa and motioned them to sit in the chairs next to him. Donovan seemed to have calmed down but had a hopeless look on his face.

Sam looked at Donovan with disappointment and disgust. He thought about all the things he wanted to say but knew that none of those things would help. He knew he needed to set his emotions aside, to keep things on track.

"So, Donovan, you said earlier that Roy's just a foot soldier. Who does he report to anyway?" Sam asked, looking at Donovan.

"It's better if you're not distracted by the details," Donovan replied. "At least not yet. You've already got a full plate."

Sam shrugged. Have it your way, he thought. Then the three men discussed their plans for meeting Roy at the Western Wall tunnels. The tunnel leading away from Warren's Gate that Sam had described to Roy had been controversial for decades. It had often been speculated that the Ark might be in a chamber connected to it, but Sam doubted it. There were so many aqueducts and water channels underneath the Temple Mount that it wouldn't have made a dry hiding place. For its part, the Copper Scroll seemed to be a pretty complete inventory of the Temple treasury in AD 66, even including two possible hiding places for the Ark—or Arks, if there were more than one—and it said nothing about this artifact being hidden underneath the Temple.

At 4:00 p.m., Sam's new phone rang. It was Steve. "Hey, Sam, it's all quiet up here in Galilee. I don't see anything unusual here. Just some families spending the afternoon in the park."

"Glad to hear it," Sam said. "Come on back, then. I'll be meeting Roy around five o'clock. We'll need you to meet up with Jason. Just stay in touch with him, right?"

"You got it," Steve replied. "I'll start heading back now."

As Sam, Hakim, and Donovan were finishing up their remaining tasks, Sam's phone rang again. It was from Jason's new number. "Sam, I'm here at Job's Well," he said. "It took me a while to look around. There's a mosque built on top of the well, and I walked around discreetly, checking to see if there was anything out of order. I was able to look down in to the well too, and there wasn't anything suspicious. I don't think Rebecca's here."

"Good," Sam replied, "then she must be at the Pool of Siloam. That makes sense, with her clue about purity. I'm glad you checked out Job's Well, but get on over to the Pool of Siloam now. And be careful. It sounds like Leonardo's guarding Rebecca. With maybe another guard or two too."

"I'm on it," Jason said, ending the call.

At 4:30 p.m., Sam knew it was time to leave. As they were getting ready to go, Sam's phone rang again. It was Jason. "Hey, Sam," Jason said in a low voice. "I'm here outside the Pool of Siloam. It's really different than yesterday. There are Eden Construction signs all around, and the place has been shuttered and locked down. I can see at least one guard through one of the gates. Do you want me to go in there and see if I can find her?"

"No, stay put there," Sam said. "I'm sure she's there, so just sit tight and make sure nothing happens while we deal with Roy. If anything does happen, do whatever you think is best. But you'll need help. Steve should be there in about an hour, and I'll get there as soon as we take care of Roy."

"Count on it," Jason said. "I'll keep things quiet here and will call you if I see anything."

"Thanks, Jason," Sam said tensely, ending the call. They were running out of time.

Sam called Steve and told him to meet Jason quietly at the Pool of Siloam and explained that Rebecca was being held there. Sam took a deep breath and exhaled slowly. It was time to go.

"Let's get going," Sam said to Hakim and Donovan as he headed toward the door. "We've got a lot of work to do."

As the three men were walking through the lobby, Donovan pulled Sam aside. "I really don't have time for this," Sam objected. "Whatever it is, make it fast."

"I'm sorry," Donovan said, looking heartbroken. "We'll make this work. We'll keep her safe."

Sam felt his anger rising again. He leaned close to Donovan, looking him in the eye. "If anything happens to Rebecca," he warned darkly, "you're dead to me." Then Sam walked off toward the lobby doors as Donovan stood in the lobby, his shoulders fallen and head hung low.

About fifteen minutes later, the three men pulled up near the Western Wall in a green Land Rover that Hakim had rented for the evening. Sam looked at Donovan angrily as they emerged from the right side of the Land Rover. He still couldn't believe that Donovan had gotten involved with rogue actors like Roy and whomever he reported to. Was it money or a need for excitement? He should have known how this would end up. Playing games with criminals who broke all the rules was always a losing proposition. Donovan should have known better.

Sam watched as Hakim and Donovan carried some equipment from the back of the Land Rover to one of the openings to the Western Wall

Tunnel. The area near the opening had been coned off by Eden Construction signs and traffic cones. It was almost sunset, and the buildings to the west cast long shadows across the Western Wall Plaza.

As the sun disappeared below the city horizon, Sam watched as a black SUV with Eden Builders magnetic signs on the sides pulled into the darkening parking area. The SUV rolled to a stop, and Roy climbed down from the front passenger seat, a little unstable as his chubby legs hit the ground.

Roy waddled toward the men, followed by a security guard in a dark suit and sunglasses. Wearing an unbuttoned dark overcoat and a tall yellow construction helmet, Roy looked ridiculously out of place, even without considering the white toga that could be seen underneath the overcoat as it flapped against his wobbly frame.

Sam stood with his arms folded across his chest, looking at Roy as he came closer. "Proof of life, Roy," he demanded as they stood a few feet apart.

"She's fine," Roy said with a dismissive wave of his hand. "We have more important things to do. Let's get going."

"Not before I hear from Rebecca," Sam insisted.

"Fine, but this makes you weak," Roy said with a sneer. "Look at me," he said proudly as his overcoat caught the breeze and blew open, revealing the white Roman toga beneath. "I'm celebrating a delicious victory, and all you can do is whine about your girlfriend. Tell you what, I'll let you talk to your little girlfriend if you give me those Copper Scroll pieces back. They'll be good for the photos with me and the Ark."

Sam motioned to Donovan to retrieve the box with the Copper Scroll pieces from Hakim's car. Returning with the box, Donovan handed it to Sam and looked at Roy.

"So, Donovan, I guess this was supposed to be your moment," Roy said mockingly. "You were supposed to get her the Ark. She won't be happy when she learns that you failed her and that I got it instead."

Donovan shook his head. "I wouldn't want to be in your shoes, Roy, when she finds out. Or in your toga, I guess," he said, looking at Roy's strange attire.

"Don't worry," Roy said with a laugh. "I can take care of myself. Besides, I have nothing to lose. I'd be dead soon without my little magic box. Proof of life, huh?" Roy smiled as he tapped on his phone and handed it to Sam.

"Sam? Where are you?" Rebecca called out over the phone.

"Rebecca! How are you?" Sam shouted into the phone. "Are you okay?"

"I'm fine, but hurry," she replied. "It's getting dark here, and dumb and dumber here are getting impatient."

"I hear you," Sam said, "and I'll be there as soon as we're done here. Killing two birds with one stone, you know."

"Just hurry," Rebecca said, "the birds are getting anxious. Outside and—"

"That's enough," Roy interrupted, grabbing his phone back and hanging up the call. "You can have Leonardo and his friend Marcello when we're done here. They screwed up, and I don't have any use for them."

"With pleasure," Sam said. "Now, let's go find that tunnel," he said, motioning to Hakim and Donovan to follow him.

Roy waved off his driver and a security guard as Sam, Hakim, and Donovan walked with him across the plaza toward the entrance to the Western Wall Tunnel. Walking past more Eden signs and cones and through the tunnel entrance, the four men each put on one of the headlamps that Hakim had brought.

Sam looked back at Roy, who was following a few steps behind him. He looked even more ridiculous now, with the headlamp strapped onto his forehead below the comically tall construction helmet. He was already struggling with the bulky box holding the Copper Scroll pieces and was starting to breathe heavily in the humid tunnel air.

"You okay, Roy?" Sam called to him. "We've got some walking to do."

"Don't worry about me," Roy said with a cough. "I've been dreaming about this moment, and I wouldn't miss it for anything."

"Just don't check out before we get Rebecca," Sam said sarcastically. "We need you alive to make that phone call."

Roy scoffed. "I won't be dying anytime soon. Once I get that golden box, I'll have the powers of a god. But you're right to be concerned about my health. If I don't call Leonardo and Marcello by six o'clock to tell them I've gotten my prize, they've been ordered to kill Rebecca. We've got less than an hour."

Sam was horrified but not surprised by this news. He had been sure that Roy had made some backup plans in case something went wrong. They just needed to work quickly. And keep Roy from hurting himself.

Looking ahead, Sam saw the construction lights that Hakim and his crew had set up inside the tunnel earlier in the day. "This is the place," Sam told Roy as they approached the lights and the opening that Hakim's crew had made at the previously sealed tunnel connection at the spot known as Warren's Gate.

"Is this the tunnel to the Ark?" Roy asked, his face shiny with sweat and a sliver of drool hanging from the corner of his lower lip. "Let me see, let me see," he said, pushing past Sam.

Sam watched as Roy climbed over the large stones that had been cut and pulled out of the side tunnel entrance and disappeared into the dark side tunnel. "Wait up, Roy," Sam called out. "It's dangerous in here, and I don't want you getting killed before we get Rebecca."

Sam climbed over the same stones and looked into the side tunnel, his headlamp shining into the dark corridor. Roy was about ten feet ahead and turned back to face Sam, his headlamp shining back toward the tunnel entrance.

Sam stepped carefully over the large, thick electrical cables that Hakim's crew had laid on the tunnel floor leading into the dark side tunnel where Roy was now standing. Hakim and Donovan followed after him, with all four men now standing inside the side tunnel leading directly into the heart of the Tunnel Mount.

"Let's go," Roy said impatiently as he removed his overcoat and stood in the corridor wearing his white toga, oddly paired with heavy construction boots. "I really can't wait any longer," he said, starting to gasp in the heavy tunnel air.

Sam shoved Roy out of the way and walked past him, heading down the dark tunnel, with only the light from his headlamp shining dimly ahead. He led the group down the narrow tunnel lined with large square stones, walking carefully around the heavy electrical cables that Hakim's team had installed there as a source of lighting for what lay ahead.

"Me first, me first!" Roy shouted as he followed behind Sam, trying to push past him.

"Stay back," Sam insisted, "it's dangerous in here. These are live electrical cables, and just look at all the water in here," he said, pointing down. "You need to be more careful, at least until you make the call to release Rebecca."

"Don't worry," Roy replied, "nothing can happen to me. I'm the new Moses and will have that magical walking stick in my hands. Plus, some pot of food and those silly tablets. Maybe I'll do some editing while we're down here." He laughed.

Sam shook his head as they got to the end of the tunnel. Terminal illness or not, Roy was pushing his luck. There were at least a dozen ways for this idiot to get killed in here, but Sam wanted to keep him alive long enough to get Rebecca back.

Sam waved Hakim and Donovan toward the small opening in the rock wall facing them at the end of the tunnel. Each man grabbed one of the picks that Hakim's crew had left there and began hacking at the opening to make it large enough for Roy to squeeze his plump belly through.

"Let me see!" Roy cried out when the opening was large enough to crawl through. "What's in there?" he called out, putting his head into the opening.

Sam nodded to Hakim that it was almost time. "Roy," Sam called out, "it's time to get your treasure. You know, the one you bribed Daniel Wechsler for so you could get a construction permit to dig here."

"What are you talking about?" Roy said, still busy pulling a few rocks from the opening to make it large enough for his heavy frame. "Wechsler was a nobody. He just did what I told him. It's too bad he started talking and had to leave us. You can blame Leonardo for the messy ending. He's just so sloppy at everything."

Sam looked at the microphone that Hakim's team had placed on the wall above the rock opening, with a long cord leading up through a small hole in the rock above them. He nodded at Hakim again, signaling that they had what they needed.

Hakim walked over and stood near the microphone. "It's time," he said loudly, aiming his voice at the microphone. "It's time," he said again.

Still digging around in the rock opening, Roy looked back at Sam, Hakim, and Donovan. "What are you talking about?" he asked. "Time for what?"

Hearing a noise coming from back toward the tunnel entrance, Sam turned his head and looked down the long, dark corridor. He heard the shuffle of boots walking briskly toward them and began to see flashlights shining on the tunnel walls and floor.

"Roy," Sam called out, "get back here. We've got something to show you."

"I'm busy and can almost make it through now," Roy shouted back. "Whatever it is will have to wait. Hand me those Copper Scroll pieces and get your cameras ready. I'm almost through."

Eager to get those stolen Copper Scroll pieces back into Roy's hands before the Waqf guards arrived, Sam reached into the box he had set down on the tunnel floor and pulled out the two Copper Scroll pieces that Roy had sent him. He walked over to the tunnel wall where Roy had climbed into the opening into an adjoining chamber. After handing the ancient copper pieces to Roy, he walked back to where Hakim and Donovan were standing, watching Roy still moving some rocks out of the opening.

The Waqf guards were responsible for security on the Temple Mount and had helped Hakim with setting up the electrical cables and microphone so they could catch Roy down here for illegal entry of a protected shrine area and turn him over to the Israeli authorities for suspected murder and bribery too. Through Hakim, Sam had given them more than enough information to keep Roy locked up while the authorities completed their investigation.

Sam looked down the tunnel as the sound of footsteps grew louder. Then he turned to look at Roy, now starting to crawl deeper into the opening in the tunnel wall, desperate to get to his imagined Ark.

"Stop!" the Waqf officer shouted at the group with his pistol drawn as a group of four guards stormed into the area at the end of the tunnel where Sam, Hakim, and Donovan were standing. "Nobody move!"

Sam, Hakim, and Donovan all raised their arms up to their shoulders and nodded their heads toward Roy, alerting the guards that Roy had crawled up in the rock opening.

"Roy Griffin, get down here!" the Waqf officer thundered, pointing his pistol at Roy.

Roy turned his head and saw the officer, his sweaty face turning bright red. "Sam, you can't do this!" he shouted. "Call them off."

"It's over, Roy," Sam shouted back. "The Ark's not here."

Roy sputtered. "You're lying. I can see it in the shadows in the next chamber. I'm almost there. Now, call off those guards or I'll tell Leonardo to ice your lady friend."

"With what?" Sam asked mockingly. "This place is under thirty feet of rock. You won't be making any phone calls from here."

Roy picked the Copper Scroll pieces up again and scrambled down from the opening in the rock, landing with a thud on the tunnel floor. Standing next to the electrical cables by his feet, he shouted for the guards to leave. "Get out of here!" he yelled. "I've got a permit to be here, and you'll all be in trouble soon."

"Get down on the ground!" the officer shouted at Roy, aiming his pistol at Roy's head as he stood in the middle of the tunnel area, about ten feet from Roy.

"I found the Ark," Roy shouted at the officer, "and you don't want to mess with me. You have no idea of my powers."

"Careful, Roy," Sam shouted out, noticing that Roy now had one of his feet on top of an electrical cable near a small pool of standing water on the tunnel floor. "Those are live cables, and there's water on the floor too. Don't step there."

Roy looked down at his feet and then reared back in laughter. "I have the power of the gods," he shouted. "The Ark is mine."

Holding a Copper Scroll piece in each hand, Roy raised his arms over his head and mocked the guards with an improvised victory dance, his now-dirty toga swaying around his thighs.

"Look out, Roy," Sam called out, noticing that Roy now had both of his feet on the electrical cables and that one of the Copper Scroll segments he was holding was getting dangerously close to the microphone with its cable installed on the tunnel wall above his head. "You've got live cables all around you, and there are pools of water on the floor too."

"No, you look out!" Roy shouted. "I've got the power now. I have the power of the gods."

Sam took a few steps back, away from Roy, and motioned to Hakim, Donovan, and the guards to get farther away from Roy. He was out of control, and all they could do now was watch.

As Roy continued his mock victory dance, waving the Copper Scroll pieces in the air above him, it finally happened. One of the copper pieces knocked the microphone loose from its metal anchors so that it dangled from the power cord, with the microphone and connected power cord spinning around just above Roy's head.

"I have the power!" Roy shouted as one of the copper pieces he was holding above his head cut into the electrical cord with a flash of blinding light and a loud boom.

The tunnel disappeared into an explosion of blinding white light, followed by a burst of orange flame as Roy's toga incinerated and a web of interlaced electrical currents burst through his body. The boom turned into a roar as the electricity tore through Roy and roasted him from the inside out. Roy's flesh turned bright red and began smoking as the electrical currents kept tearing through his body until his arms dropped to his sides.

Then, as Roy stood teetering under the now-torn electrical cable above his head, he began to fall forward, his lifeless eyes staring blankly at nothing. Finally, Roy fell forward in a heap, his flaming toga shooting sparks into the cloud of smoke filling the area where Roy had been standing.

Sam gagged as the stench of burned vomit, feces, and flesh began spreading through the tunnel. He grabbed Hakim by the arm and pulled him down the corridor, waiving at Donovan to follow them out to the entrance. The Waqf officer and guards followed immediately behind as the seven men raced to the tunnel's exit and back to the Western Wall Plaza. Emerging from the tunnel onto the plaza, Sam and Hakim quickly thanked the Waqf officer and guards and headed back to the parking area.

As they were leaving, Donovan took Sam by the arm and pulled him aside. "Sam, there's something I need to do," he said. "You're still in danger, but I can help. Go get Rebecca, and hurry."

"Will I see you later?" Sam asked, worried that Donovan was really in over his head now.

"I think so," Donovan replied, brushing aside a tear. "But right now, I've got to try to fix this."

"But we can do it together," Sam said, grabbing Donovan's arm.

"I've got to do this on my own," Donovan replied.

"Be careful," Sam said. "I love you, Dad."

Donovan gripped Sam's forearm tightly, looking grim but relieved. "That means everything," he said. "I love you, son. Now go!" Donovan said loudly, pushing Sam away as he blotted his eyes with the backside of his hand. "Get Rebecca!"

Sam ran off to catch up with Hakim, turning back one last time to glance at Donovan.

Hakim had already started the Land Rover when Sam got there and climbed into the front passenger seat. Sam looked at the time as Hakim gunned the engine and the Land Rover roared out of the parking area and onto the city streets, heading to the Pool of Siloam a few blocks away. It was now 5:50 p.m. They had only ten minutes left to save Rebecca.

"Here, you may need this," Hakim said, handing Sam a large black revolver. Sam looked down at the gun, nodding his head.

As they pulled up to the street curb nearest the Pool of Siloam archaeological site, Sam leaped out of the Land Rover. He sprinted over to the chain-link gate that had been installed with an Eden Construction sign placed on it. As his eyes adjusted to the darkness, he saw a shadow moving about twenty feet away.

"Sam!" he heard a whisper. Looking to his right into the overgrown ground cover, he recognized Jason crouching down behind a large rock.

Sam ducked down and moved closer to Jason. "You alone?" he whispered.

"Yeah, Steve's on his way," Jason whispered back. "He should be here around six."

"That's too late," Sam said softly. "Roy gave orders to Leonardo to kill Rebecca if he doesn't call him by six o'clock. And Roy's dead now. So we'll have to take these guards down. There's two, right?"

"I think so," Jason whispered. "I've been here for an hour and a half, and I've only seen two."

"Good," Sam whispered, motioning to crawl toward the gate, "Rebecca gave me a signal on our call that there were only two. So I think it's safe to assume that. Let's both take care of the first one here, and I'll go right away and take down the second one."

As he and Jason crawled out of the vegetation and toward the chain-link gate, Sam saw that Hakim had slunk over to the gate and quietly opened it. Waving a thumbs-up at Hakim and a hand signal for him to stay here and guard the entrance, Sam moved quickly with Jason to get through the gate and get their bearings inside.

As both men crouched behind a stone outcropping, Sam looked ahead at the silhouette of a man standing guard on a sidewalk about thirty feet ahead. Sam picked up a small rock and threw it high over the guard's silhouette and watched it fall back down about twenty feet behind the guard.

The guard looked startled when the rock crashed onto a stone walkway with a loud crack. Walking about six feet toward the sound, the guard stopped and started looking around him.

Sam threw another rock, this time about twenty feet to the guard's right, as he motioned Jason to follow and began sprinting toward the guard. Sam flung his body full force into the guard, tackling him down violently to the ground. Sam looked down at the man. It was Leonardo.

Sam grabbed a pistol from Leonardo's hand and, with his other hand holding another rock, pummeled his face with the side of the rock. Now bleeding profusely, spitting broken teeth, and choking on the blood filling his mouth, Leonardo gasped for air and shuddered as Jason leaped in to help, landing with his feet on one of his lower legs, shattering his tibia.

His arms flailing, Leonardo tried to call out but was choking on his own blood and could only manage a gurgling coughing sound. Sam finished him off with a crack of the rock against his left temple, knocking him out cold. As Sam got up, Jason rolled Leonardo over and stomped on his back in a not-so-gentle Heimlich maneuver. As blood gushed out of his mouth, the unconscious Leonardo gasped and choked, barely clinging to life.

Sam sprinted past the partially excavated Pool of Siloam and down the steps to the tunnels they had toured the day before. Seeing the Eden signs and coned-off area below, he thought he knew where Rebecca would be. He picked up a few small rocks and quietly descended halfway down the stone steps until he could faintly see the opening of the dark tunnel.

Sam pulled out his phone and looked at the time. It was now 5:55 p.m.—only five minutes left. Blinking and trying to adjust to the nearly pitch-black excavation area leading to Hezekiah's Tunnel, Sam finally saw the faint silhouette of a guard. He looked a bit like the assassin from the restaurant and seemed to be limping and in pain.

Good, at least he'll be distracted, Sam thought. Breaking his knee earlier was pretty cruel, but it would pay off now. It wouldn't be easy to take him down, but the man's shattered knee would make it less difficult.

Sam threw a rock into the arched tunnel entrance, watching the guard spin on his heels at the crashing sound. "Marcello!" Sam shouted out before ducking back behind a stone wall.

"Romero?" the assassin named Marcello called out in Sam's direction. "You there? I've got something you want."

"Marcello," Sam called back, "let her go. Roy's dead, and my friend back near the gate has taken down Leonardo. He's in worse shape now than you are. How's your knee, anyway?"

"You destroyed it," Marcello shouted. "Come here, and I'll show you."

"Where's Rebecca?" Sam shouted. "Throw your gun over here, and we'll get you some medical attention."

"She's in the tunnel," Marcello called out. "I can see her shadow. I could use her for target practice. What time is it?"

"Time to give up, Marcello," Sam yelled to him. "You're cornered, and the police will be here any minute."

Sam looked down at his gun and made sure that the trigger lock was disengaged. He might need this. Then suddenly startled by a hand on his back, Sam swiveled and pointed the gun at whoever was there.

"Jason!" Sam whispered. "You startled me. Be careful. I've got a gun now. I think Hakim's pistol is a forty-five. It'll blow a hole through anything."

"Good to know," Jason whispered. "Is it just the one guard down there?"

"Yeah, and his name's Marcello," Sam whispered. "He's pretty ticked off that I messed up his knee at the restaurant. Let's circle around him and take him out. I'll take his left side, and you take his right."

Sam waved Jason to circle left down to the tunnel below while Sam would take the other side. As he crawled through the overgrown weeds and ground cover, Sam kept the pistol aimed at Marcello.

As he saw Jason get to within twenty feet of the guard in the tunnel below, Sam called out, "Marcello! Drop your gun. It's over."

Then Sam saw a flash of light and heard the crack of Marcello's pistol and the ricochet of a bullet glancing across a stone outcropping near Sam. "Don't shoot!" Sam called out, still pointing his gun at Marcello as he saw Jason approaching behind Marcello out of the corner of his eye.

"Let her go before the police get here," Sam called out. "We'll let you go, and they'll never find you. But you need to leave now."

"Drop your guns," Marcello called back, "I'm taking the girl with me. Just a little security and maybe some fun."

Just then Jason leaped down from an outcropping above Marcello and crashed onto him, with Marcello's gun skittering across the stones and resting five feet away. Sitting on the man's chest, Jason beat his face with a right hook and then a left. Then he stood up and drove his heel onto Marcello's right knee, breaking the remaining bones that Sam hadn't shattered earlier in the day. Marcello bellowed in pain, shrieking and holding his ruined knee.

Sam leaped from the undergrowth and ran down the stone steps to where Jason was standing over Marcello, now holding Marcello's gun and pointing it at his head.

"You got this?" Sam asked.

"Yeah, just get Rebecca," Jason said, nodding. "She must be in there," he said, motioning to the dark tunnel entrance.

Sam sprinted over to the tunnel entrance and called out her name. "Rebecca? Are you here?"

Hearing her muffled cries, Sam raced into the tunnel and finally saw her. She was tied to a chair, sitting blindfolded and gagged. He untied the rope from her hands and picked her up, carrying her out of the tunnel to the stone landing where Jason was guarding Marcello.

As he held Rebecca in his arms and stood next to Jason, Sam looked up and saw that the tunnel and archaeological park had suddenly been illuminated with flashing blue and red lights. The Jerusalem Police had arrived. It was over.

Sam looked down at Rebecca's face as he held her in his arms. She still seemed terrified but managed a bit of a smile. "I knew you'd get here," she said. "Did my clues help?"

"You mean 'dumb and dumber'?" Sam smiled. "Yes, that was really good. That's how we knew that there were two guards here."

"I'm glad it helped." Rebecca sighed. "Let's get out of here."

"You got it," Sam said, leaning down to kiss her. Pure beauty, he thought. And a pure golden heart. No matter what else would happen, he had finally found his treasure.

18

LIKE THE LIGHT OF DAWN

Sam opened his eyes. It was pitch black and felt like the middle of the night. Why was his phone ringing?

Blinking, he looked at the display. It was his mother calling him. At 5:00 a.m. He answered the call and whispered to her, "Hang on."

Sam turned and looked at Rebecca snuggled up next to him in the bed. They had gotten back to the hotel room late last night after having to spend a few hours at the police station explaining the unexplainable. That lieutenant just didn't seem to understand anything about a *siddah* or carrying chair, and he was clueless about the legend of King Jehoash. Didn't they learn *anything* in police school?

Sam walked into the living area and closed the bedroom door so he wouldn't wake up Rebecca. "Hi, Mom, how's it going?" he asked her quietly over the phone.

"Hi, Sam, I'm fine. How are *you* doing?" she asked. "And how's Rebecca? I know this was rough on both of you."

"Yes, definitely," Sam agreed. "But she slept all night. I mean, at least until now. It's pretty early. What's up?"

"I'm sorry to call so early," Dawn apologized. "Normally I would never do this. But there's someone here I want you to meet. He has to catch a flight later today, so there's not much time. I have some other news too. Can you meet us in my room?"

"Sure, just give me five minutes. Room four-ten down the hall?" he asked.

"That's right," Dawn said. "See you then."

After freshening up and throwing on a pair of jeans and a gray T-shirt, Sam knocked on the door to room 410.

"Hi, Sam," his mother greeted him, opening the door and hugging Sam as he walked in.

Sam grimaced a bit, not quite yet healed from the dagger wound inflicted two days before. "Easy, Mom," he said as she hugged him tightly.

"Oh, honey," Dawn said, "that's right. You're still healing. Can I get you anything?"

"No, thanks," Sam replied. "Did you say there's someone you want me to meet?"

"Yes, sit down, dear," his mother said, motioning him to the sofa in the living area as she sat down in a chair next to the sofa. "He'll be right out. How's everyone?"

"Jason and Steve are good," Sam said. "Jason just needed a little medical attention for his knuckles, but it was minor. Steve got there when the police did, so, as usual, he missed all the action. But he's great. Plus, we couldn't have done this without Hakim. He's a knight in shining armor."

"You're catching on," Dawn said with a smile, looking at the bedroom door as it opened. "Now here's another knight I'd like you to meet."

Sam recognized him right away. A tall, muscular man in his midsixties with longish dark brown hair flecked with silver at the temples and a big smile, like the one Sam remembered from his dreams.

"Hi, Sam, so wonderful to see you after all these years," said his father. Sam got up to greet him, choking up and feeling flustered as he wiped the wetness from the corners of his eyes.

"Dad?" Sam could hardly believe his own words. "I mean, your name's Phil, right?"

"Yes, Phil Koenig, how did you know?" his father said as he walked closer to give his son a big hug.

Grasping Sam in a bear hug, Phil gripped him firmly and then slapped him on the back. "You're all grown up," he said, laughing.

"You told me your name in one of those bedtime stories," Sam said with a grin, wiping more wetness from his eyes. "It was some story about King Arthur or Aladdin, and I guess we both decided that you were one of the knights in the story too."

"That sounds right," Phil said, patting Sam's forearm with his hand. "You always liked those knight stories." Phil grinned at Dawn. "Your turn," he said.

"So, Sam," his mother began, "do you remember when I had to leave you with your aunt Liz while I was filming *Cleopatra Returns* in the Sahara?"

"How could I forget?" Sam smiled as he sat back down on the sofa. "She lives in New Mexico, and I nearly died when I put some of that hot chili sauce on her huevos rancheros."

"I'm glad you survived." Dawn said, smiling back. "But I hadn't told you the truth. I didn't go to the Sahara. I've had a few other projects like that too. Plus, a few times when I've met up with your father. I mean Phil, your real father."

"How did you guys meet?" Sam asked. "And what happened?"

"We fell in love, of course." Dawn said, looking up at Phil. "And we never stopped loving each other. But we had to break up before you were born, and I married Donovan. As you know, that didn't last long. There were complications."

"Okay, I appreciate the explanation," Sam said, perplexed. "But none of this makes sense. If you still loved each other, why did you break up?" Then Sam looked up at his father. "Why did you leave us?"

"It's about the knights," his mother said. "It's who we are. Who *you* are," she said, looking at Sam. "You've been around these people your whole life. They've been protecting you even if you didn't even know it."

"You mean, like all those friends of yours? Father Luigi? Balthasar? Hakim? What about Donovan?" Sam asked.

Dawn nodded. "Some of those people are knights, and some are not. Hakim's one of us, and Donovan is not. In fact, Donovan's story is complicated, as you may be figuring out. It's not an easy one, I'm afraid."

"So what is this knighthood about anyway?" Sam asked. "It doesn't sound quite like those King Arthur stories."

"It's pretty simple," Phil jumped in. "From the beginning of time, there have been leaders who believed in peace and spiritual unity. In the early days, this mainly involved an exchange of ideas between cultures and doing our best to identify and protect prophets and spiritual teachers. But as time went on and civilizations got more complicated, the spiritual unity broke down and people began fighting over religious ideas."

"Right, like over whose mountain is sacred," Sam said.

"Exactly," Dawn agreed, "and in their blindness, people have been fighting about these things for thousands of years now."

"So this ancient tradition of interfaith unity began to get organized," Phil explained. "They formed a secret knighthood with blood vows thousands of years ago, with a few members in each part of the world. There are about two hundred, actually, at any given time. Enough to make a difference."

"How?" Sam asked. "Most people agree with these ideas. Peace, love, harmony—nothing wrong with that. The tough part is making it happen."

"You nailed it," Phil said, nodding. "Peace and unity and even civilization are quite fragile. The peacemakers need help. The knights got organized to help key people communicate and work behind the scenes. Mostly by the usual mortal methods."

"Mostly?" Sam asked, intrigued. "Not always?"

"No one knows how or why," Dawn said, "but over the years, the knights started noticing some spiritual powers that would surface when needed."

"Like dreams and visions," Sam said, remembering his conversations with Donovan.

"Yes, exactly like that," Dawn said, a bit surprised. "And even more powerful things. Some of the knights' powers were becoming so strong that the elders decided they needed to be carefully controlled and managed. They founded an academy for training young knights so they learn to use their powers wisely."

"So you haven't answered why you guys split up," Sam noted.

"It's those powers," Phil said, leaning against the armrest of Dawn's chair. "They grew stronger over the centuries, until the knighthood elders decided that there might be something in the blood—what we now call DNA. They made a rule forbidding knights to marry one another or to have children together. The concern was that the powers were getting so strong, and the thought was that the bloodline was getting too concentrated. No one knew how that might end up if it continued, so the elders decided not to take any chances."

"Take any chances?" Sam asked. "So you're saying that someone like me isn't supposed to be born because my spiritual powers might be too strong?"

Phil got up and sat down on the sofa next to Sam. "You weren't supposed to happen," he said. "We knew it was wrong for us to be together, but we were in love. And we still are," Phil said, looking at Dawn. "If the elders had learned about you, they would have banished both Dawn and you from the knighthood, ending Dawn's bloodline. I would have been banished too, but that was a sacrifice I was willing to make to be with you. But I didn't want Dawn to have to leave the knighthood that she loved, so the only thing to do was for me to leave, as painful as that was. We broke up before you were born, and we decided that you would not become a knight, to be on the safe side. If you had become a knight, your powers would probably have given you away as a pure-blooded knight and created problems. No one but Donovan ever knew that I'm your father as far as we know. Until now."

"So what's next?" Sam asked. "Will you disappear again?" He frowned at his father.

"I have to leave today. There's been a change of leadership," Phil replied. "There's actually a lot going on. But I'll be back soon. We have quite a bit to talk about."

"That's right, and I've been appointed to chair the elders," Dawn said. "I only accepted on the condition that they make an exception to the bloodline rule for you. It was a close vote, but it's been approved now."

Sam shifted in his seat, still feeling pain from the dagger gash across his chest. "So what happens next? You said something about an academy?"

"That's right," Dawn said, getting up and walking to the window. "It won't be easy. Normally a young knight starts the academy at age twenty-one. You're thirty-six now, which is a pretty late start. But fortunately, you've kept in shape pretty well, so you'll probably pass the physical part. It's the spiritual and mental trainings that can be more difficult. You'll have to face your fears."

Sam looked at his mother, who was now standing by the window, gazing at the first light of the morning. "Fears of what?" he asked.

"The darkness," Dawn said, turning to look at Sam, her strawberry-blond hair reflecting the golden hues of the early morning light. "In the most ancient times, the knights had a temple where people of all faiths would come and tell their stories and share their spiritual ideas. This was represented by the sacred fire kept at the temple, which was believed to be eternal. But there was some sort of disaster. No one knows what happened, but the temple was destroyed and its location forgotten. The fire was lost. Since then, some of the knights became afraid and turned to the dark ways. There are a few knights today who believe in these things. We don't really know how many."

Phil walked to the window and put his arm around Dawn's shoulders. "Some say that darkness is just the absence of light," he explained. "But there's something different about these dark knights. Some kind of force or energy that is itself dark, as if in opposition to the light."

Dawn looked and nodded. "Her name's Mara," she said, turning to face Sam.

"What do you mean? Who's Mara?" Sam asked.

"She was one of us," his mother replied. "We were close, with her being a bit younger than me, and both of us with busy careers. She had especially strong powers, but she wanted more. It's a dark story for another time."

"Is that who Roy was reporting to?" Sam asked.

Dawn nodded. "That's right. Roy was a fool. He thought he could use her and just throw her away when he got what he wanted. That was never going to work."

"And Donovan?" Sam looked at his mother.

"Somehow he got involved with Mara and her people," Dawn said, looking out the window again. "We knew that would never end well. Your father has to go soon," she went on, turning to look at Phil. "Before he does, we wanted to leave some prayer notes at the Western Wall. So much has happened that it seems like the right thing to do. Can you join us?"

"Yes, of course," Sam replied, looking out the window. The golden streaks of the morning sunrise were just starting to streak above the Judean Hills to the east. It would be a beautiful sunny morning with a bright blue sky above.

"There's nothing like dawn," Sam said, standing close to his parents. "So beautiful."

"You're so right," Phil said with a smile, looking at Dawn. "I've waited a lifetime to be here."

"Let's go," Dawn said, smiling back at Phil. "We've got some things to do."

About an hour later, the entire group gathered in the Western Wall Plaza. Sam had woken up Rebecca and asked if she wanted to join and had called Jason, Steve, and Hakim too. Everyone wanted to join, and soon they had all gathered in the plaza, parts of which were now brightly lit by the warming winter sun.

After everyone had written their prayers on the small prayer sheets that Dawn had brought along, they all walked over to the Western Wall and tucked the notes into crevices between the large stones. Then each of them stood silently for a minute, their eyes closed.

Sam thought of Donovan and wished him peace, no matter where he was or what had happened.

Finally, with everyone's prayers sent, Sam took Rebecca's hand, and everyone began walking back across the plaza.

Jason and Steve would be flying back to California on Sunday, so Sam and Dawn made plans for much-needed relaxation before then.

"Where are you off to after this?" Jason asked Sam. "Mexico? India? Mecca? Peru?"

Still holding Rebecca's hand, Sam looked at Dawn and then back at Jason. "Apparently I'll be starting knight school next week," he said. "Somewhere in Athens, I think."

"Night school?" Jason asked. "What's up with that?"

"You're going for an advanced law degree?" Steve asked, surprised.

"Something like that." Sam said, smiling.

After the group had returned to the St. George Hotel, Sam said goodbye to his father in the hotel driveway as the taxi pulled up. Dawn gave Phil a big hug and kiss, and Sam was already thinking about when they would be together again.

As Phil's taxi drove off, Dawn looked at Sam. "Are you free for dinner for tonight?" she asked. "It would be wonderful if Rebecca, Jason, and Steve could join us. I'll ask Hakim too."

"Dinner would be great," Sam replied. "Rebecca will be with her parents for the sabbath starting tonight. So it'll just be the guys."

Back in his hotel room, Sam looked out the window. He could see the Temple Mount not far away. He closed his eyes and thought of the prayer notes they had left at the Western Wall.

Having gotten up so early that morning, Sam felt a little tired. Rebecca was taking a nap in the bedroom, and he didn't want to wake her. He sat down on the sofa and closed his eyes again. He saw a warm light and thought of the prayer notes tucked into the crevices in the stones.

Sam stirred a bit and opened his eyes. He went to the window and saw that the sky had darkened and that a cold winter wind had arrived, with the trees outside his window swaying back and forth. He imagined the prayer notes blowing across the Western Wall Plaza, scattering everyone's hopes and dreams across the ancient stones.

Sam thought about what life would be like with Rebecca. He felt that they had gotten much closer on this trip, surely closer than he had expected. Of course, living seven thousand miles apart would be a challenge. All the travel and separation could become draining. But he felt their connection was strong enough to make it work.

Then he heard her voice, as if in a dream. "Sam, could you come zip me up?" His face brightened. Rebecca must have woken up. He walked into the bedroom and saw her standing by the bed.

He admired her royal-blue pencil dress, his eyes moving up slowly to her naked back and her hair pulled up from her neck, looking more fiery red than he had remembered.

Slowly zipping up the back of her dress, Sam couldn't resist wrapping his arms around her and kissing her softly on the nape of her neck. "That tickles," she said coyly, wriggling a bit and letting her hair fall down.

As she turned around to face him, Sam felt his chest tighten. It wasn't Rebecca. "Who are—"

"Sam, it's me, Mara," she said as she raised her hands and cupped his face, looking deeply into his eyes. "You've been working too hard. You're so tired and tense."

Then Mara pushed herself up to kiss Sam on the lips. "Mmm, like a delicious young wine," she said, her hands resting on his chest. "But you'll have to let me go now, dear."

Sam looked down and realized that he was still holding this unfamiliar temptress around the waist. As he let go and took a step back, Mara's fingertips lingered on his chest. Then she turned to go, walking with a fierce elegance to the door, grabbing the handle and pulling it open.

As she stood in the doorway, Mara paused for a moment. "Sam, be sure to study hard at your knight school," she said, smiling. "I'll be checking in on you. I want to see your powers growing stronger. And let's keep this visit to ourselves. There's no need to bother anyone with our little secret."

Then, tossing her hair to the side as she turned to leave, Mara smiled again. "Oh, and Sam, honey, don't bother trying to resist me. I have big plans for us."

And so it began.

ABOUT THE AUTHORS

Paul Donsbach is an attorney with thirty years of experience in corporate investigations and complex legal claims in the United States and abroad. His investigations and other legal matters include high-profile whistleblower claims for Fortune 500 companies and other clients in the United States, Europe, Latin America, and the Middle East. His experience includes landmark cases in the United States Supreme Court, international arbitrations, and multijurisdictional practice around the world. After leaving corporate practice seven years ago, he has devoted his practice to helping individuals and families with domestic law, business law, and property law while beginning to write a series of novels and screenplays. Paul has traveled widely and has enjoyed living abroad on extended assignments. He is the proud father of two children working in law enforcement and advanced technology, respectively. A first-time author living in California, he is currently cowriting the next novel in the Knights of the Lost Temple series.

Alia Sina holds a law degree and undergraduate and master's degrees in the arts and sciences. Although she enjoys the legal world, she focused on starting a family with her husband. With a passion for fantasy drama and supernatural stories, Alia has interests that encompass multiple genres, along with multiculturalism and interfaith ideas as well. Raised by first-generation American parents who emigrated from Afghanistan, she draws strength from her cultural and religious traditions and from her parents' stories of their lives in Afghanistan and their successes in a new home.

Alia enjoys traveling with her husband and children and has visited many of the places that inspire her writing. With a busy career of his own, her husband has been incredibly supportive of Alia's interest in writing as a full-time career, as well as providing inspiration for some of the most admirable and dashing characters in her fiction world. In the interest of privacy, Alia publishes pseudonymously under this pen name. As the mother of young children in a small community, she prefers to write pseudonymously for now. She is currently cowriting the next novel in the Knights of the Lost Temple series.

www.ingramcontent.com/pod-product-compliance
Lightning Source LLC
Chambersburg PA
CBHW021623030826
48979CB00036B/1920/J
* 9 7 8 1 7 3 7 3 9 7 8 2 3 *